Hawker's Drift

Book One

The Burden of Souls

Andy Monk

Copyright © 2014 Andy Monk
All rights reserved.
ISBN-13:978-1500360818
ISBN-10:1500360813

The Gunslinger

Only three people trudged behind the coffin-laden wagon.

He assumed the woman in the black dress was the widow. A dark veil covered her face, but her back was straight, and she moved as freely as the cloying mud allowed. A young widow. A small, bookish man peering through rain-smeared spectacles laboured next to her, struggling to hold an umbrella over them both in the wind. Behind came a cadaverous-looking old bird clutching a dog-eared Bible to his chest. A preacher.

Amos pulled his horse to the side of the road, if that wasn't too generous a description for two mud-choked ruts. It meandered towards a town sitting astride a low-slung hill, the only feature on the vast tableland of grass. He took off his hat and let the rain sting his face as the little procession passed. The widow glanced at him before nodding an acknowledgement. From behind the shadows of her veil, he got the impression of an attractive woman with no intention of crying. Sadness, not unexpectedly, was coming from her, but interspersed between those dull grey waves came prickly spikes of fear too.

The preacher also flicked a glance in his direction, but quickly dropped his eyes and scurried by, body bent forward against the driving rain. He looked terribly unhappy with his lot. The preacher was suffering, a physical pain beneath a terrible craving.

The third man, his jacket flapping in the breeze, ignored him, and the gunslinger tried to do the same to the hot, fetid desire rolling off him like a burning fever.

Whoever they were burying had not warranted much in the way of gestures from the rest of the town. What did you have to do to end up with only two mourners and a sour-faced preacher at your funeral?

As the wagon bearing the coffin rattled on towards a cluster of crosses poking above the surrounding long grass, he let the rain wash the scent of their souls from the air before replacing his hat and pushing his weary horse on towards the town.

Out here, where seas of grass washed towards too far away horizons and the earth squatted beneath colossal skies, it amounted to civilization.

He slipped his coat back and made sure his gun was free to draw.

Civilization, he'd found, tended to suck.

*

Small unfussy wooden houses spilt down the lower slope of the hill and onto the surrounding pancake ground of the plains.

HAWKER'S DRIFT, a sign proclaimed as he reached the outlying buildings. Underneath, in smaller writing, *A Peaceable Town*.

The Burden of Souls

The settlement was larger than he'd first thought. The road became a respectable Main Street after it rose up the slope to run along the top of the hill, which was long, flat and broad. Numerous small streets splintered off into clusters of compact wooden buildings before the road reached a square.

The rainstorm seemed to have sluiced the place of its population. The boardwalks rising above the thick mud on either side of the street were deserted, save for a few old-timers watching the world wash by with faded eyes lost behind clouds of pipe smoke.

A large glass-fronted palace, *Jack's Saloon*, took up most of one side of the town square along with a few shops and eateries; the others boasted a church and meeting hall, stables, livery yard, and a gunsmith. An impressive four-storey mansion, sitting behind precisely manicured lawns, filled the entire north side of the square bar one corner, where the Sheriff's Office nestled up against the big house.

The only other thing of note within the square itself was a set of gallows. A sturdy wooden pole, with two beams forming a cross at its top from which four nooses could be hung.

Guess there's not much to do here in the winter...

Amos eased himself from the saddle. He led the horse into the stables and paid a gangling youth with buck teeth and dull, flat eyes enough to shelter his ride for the night.

Carrying his saddlebag over one shoulder and his rifle in his free hand, he stood outside the stables and let the rain pitter-patter on the brim of his hat. His eyes flicked between the saloon and the gunsmith.

He was tired and saddle sore, but he was low on shells.

He headed towards the gunsmith. In his experience, there was no such thing as a peaceable town.

The gunsmith was housed in a simple but well maintained, two-storey wooden building. The whitewashed front bore the sign *John X Smith – Gunsmith*.

Inside, the store was empty save for a wooden counter facing the door, the faint dry smell of gunpowder and grease, and a shaven-headed black man tossing spent cartridges towards a bucket by the door.

"Business is slow..." the man explained, landing a cartridge in the bucket before turning his eyes towards the door.

"It's a peaceable town?"

The gunsmith flashed a smile and straightened up, "So people say; guess that's why they let a black man own so many guns."

"John X Smith?"

"That's me."

"X?"

"Makes for an easy signature."

He placed the saddlebag on the floor and his rifle on the counter, "I need shells."

"How many?"

"Couple of hundred for the rifle, same for this," he tapped the handle of the pistol on his hip.

"You planning on doing a lot of shooting?"

"You never know in my line of work."

John X Smith didn't need to ask what kind of work he did.

"Mind if I take a look?" He nodded towards the pistol.

He hesitated but didn't sense the gunsmith was showing anything than professional interest. He slid the gun across the counter.

John X Smith juggled the weapon in his hand before raising and aiming it along the counter. He half-cocked the weapon as if he were going to start peppering the far wall with slugs. Instead, he lowered his hand and spun the chamber a few times before turning back to face the gunslinger with a little nod.

"This here is a fine piece of work," he stroked the barrel reverentially before reversing the gun and handing it back.

"I know."

Smith took the rifle and swung it around to face the wall, squinting along the barrel, "...this, however, has got a heavy kick and pulls to the left a tad?"

"You know your guns."

"Always on the mark, my friend," he returned the rifle to the counter and winked, "that's why they call me X."

"Do people call you X?"

"People around here call me lots of things, but I generally prefer John X... distinguishes me from all the other Johns..." he held out his hand across the counter. Amos swallowed his reluctance and took it - he got nothing from the man other than his grip was firm while his skin was gnarled and rough. He didn't look much past fifty at most, but his hand felt like it belonged to a far older man while his eyes looked older still.

"John X..."

"You?"

"Amos."

"First name or second?"

"Either works for me."

"You planning to stick around town for a while?"

"Maybe, if there's work, just passing through otherwise."

"We're a long way from anywhere out here, not the kinda place you pass through to get to somewhere else."

"I'll take those shells now."

"Not a man for questions, huh?"

He shrugged his answer.

"No problem with that... best to keep most things to yourself anyways..." he sank down behind the counter like a folding sail. The sound of rummaging joined the patter of rain hitting glass.

"Some weather..." he moved to the window to watch the downpour make the mud dance.

"Oh, we gets all kinda a strange weather out here," John X bobbed up momentarily to drop a box of shells on the counter before diving back for more.

The sky had darkened noticeably since he'd entered the store; the clouds above the grand house opposite bunched like great bruised fists poised to deliver the coup de grace to a bloody, punch-drunk foe.

"That's a fancy house for a town a long way from anywhere?"

"Yeah... the Mayor's place."

"Civic duty pays well here."

The gunsmith picked up the rifle and hoisted it to his shoulder again, "You want me to look at this? Think I can get her firing true."

He glanced back at the Mayor's residence. Small town, small men. None of his business unless someone was paying enough.

"Sure, so long as you don't break it."

John X chuckled, "I only break hearts..."

"How much?"

"Let me take a look. Come back tomorrow; I'll give you a price then."

"And the shells?"

"Pay me when I'm done."

"You're a trusting soul?"

"I'm a good judge of character. Besides, this is worth more than those shells, even if it does kick like a bitch mule in heat."

"Fair enough," he stuffed the shells into his saddlebag, "they do rooms at the saloon?"

"Sure... if you don't mind a bit of noise."

"Bawdy, is it?"

"Oh, it's a long ways from here to the next den of iniquity, so people make the most of it."

"Not a God-fearing town?"

"Not God people fear here..." John X held his eye for a moment, "...but I'm sure the saloon will do you fine, and they got plenty of girls too if you need one to help you sleep. Some of em are even pretty."

"I'll keep it in mind," Amos let himself out after hoisting his bags back over his shoulder.

The sound of an empty shell spinning around a bucket mixed with the thudding patter of the rain as the door closed behind him. He stood under the gunsmith's awning, looking across the square towards the Mayor's Residence.

It was a grand place, especially for a faraway spit of a town like Hawker's Drift. It loomed over the other buildings huddled around the square, the only one built of brick rather than wood, though mock gothic wooden towers adorned each corner and several smaller ones protruded from the roof.

Ignoring the deluge, he sloshed through the mud towards the saloon rather than skirting around and sheltering under the shop awnings. His slicker and hat had kept him dry enough out on the plains.

The saloon's main bar was large, smoky, and generously stocked with both booze and folk who had nothing better to do on a wet afternoon. A couple of card games were in progress, and men who passed their days looking at the world through the bottom of whiskey glasses occupied half the stools along the ring-stained bar. A few saloon girls lounged around a neglected old piano beneath stairs leading up to a shadowy balcony; they looked as tired and limp as the faded feathers in their dishevelled hair.

He hovered in the doorway; so many people in one place. He was used to being alone, going days on end without seeing anyone. He felt their souls scour his skin like sand on a hot desert wind. Part of him wanted to turn tail and run out into the biting rain. To go back out onto the grass, wrap himself in solitude and pretend he was still a man.

He blinked a couple of times, snorted a breath and closed his mind as best he could before crossing the saloon and ordering a beer.

"Whiskey is free," a young bartender with prematurely thinning hair and a lop-sided grin announced.

"Sorry?"

"Whiskey is free!" the bartender repeated, "Well, first shot anyhow."

"I'll take a beer."

"But whiskey is free!"

"Must be rough if you have to give it away."

"No, sir, it's fine stuff!" he assured him, "it's just the law here."

"The law?"

"Compliments of the Mayor! Every man in Hawker's Drift gets his first shot of whiskey a day free."

"Does the Mayor own this place?"

"No, Monty Jack owns the Saloon," he nodded along the bar towards a portly man with too many chins and not enough hair, talking animatedly with a young woman clutching a canvas bag before her.

"Very generous of the Mayor."

"Oh yes, the Mayor is a most generous man, sir!" The bartender announced, grinning from ear to ear. He glanced at the row of barflies on the other side of the counter. They all mumbled agreement into their booze.

"I'll still take a beer."

"But whiskey is free!"

Amos rolled his eyes.

"I'll take that whiskey if you don't want it..." the nearest barfly growled, his voice so deep, raw, and wet it sounded as if his throat were full of blood.

"I'll take a beer *and* a whiskey then."

The bartender's smile faltered, "Think the law says you have to drink it yourself."

He leant forward, "Well, I won't tell the Sheriff if you won't," he glanced towards the barfly, "you gonna snitch on me?"

The barfly grinned and pushed a grubby, unsteady finger against his compressed lips.

The bartender looked at his boss, but Monty was still talking with the young woman, leaning over her to either emphasise a point or get a better view of her breasts, "Ok... guess it will be alright as you ain't from around here. Just this once, mind."

"Thank you."

Once the drinks arrived, he tossed a coin at the bartender before sliding the whiskey to the barfly. He snatched it like a hungry baby at the teat.

"You're welcome," he took his beer and saddlebag along the bar to a stool near Monty and the young woman.

She wore a long coat and a bonnet from which a few blonde strands poked out. He doubted she was much more than twenty. She wore no ring, and her jaw jutted out slightly in stubborn annoyance.

"But there must be *something* I can do?"

Monty sighed, "I told you, I don't need bar staff, kitchen staff or maids. I've only got vacancies for *one* kind of work."

She followed his gaze to the saloon girls in the corner.

"And I told you already. I don't whore."

"You'd make good money... lovely little thing like you."

"I don't whore."

Monty shrugged and held out his hands.

"Anywhere else in this town hiring?"

"This ain't a big town, honey..."

"But there must be something!"

"There is," Monty nodded towards the saloon girls again.

"How many times do I need to tell you? I don't whore. Are you deaf?"

"Well," Monty straightened up, "If you don't mind me saying, you need to brush up on your interview technique, young lady."

"I'm sorry... I've just come a long way, and I don't have any money. I really need a job."

"I wish I could help, but I ain't no charity Miss."

"What about the big house across the square," she asked hopefully, "...they must need maids?"

"Well... um... maybe..."

"Guess I'll try there; thank you for yo-"

"Wait a second!" Monty barked, making her jump as she turned to leave, "Isn't there anything else you can do?"

"I don't wh-"

"Yes, we've established that!"

"I can cook, clean, make beds, serve be-"

"No, Miss, anything else?"

Her eyes flitted around the bar before settling on the saloon girls at the back.

"I can play the piano?"

"We got someone who can play the piano."

"We got someone who can abuse the piano," a well-built young man, who'd been following the conversation while eating at one of the nearby tables, corrected to a smattering of laughter.

"I can sing too."

"You can?"

"Real good!" She nodded and dropped her bag onto the floor, "You wanna hear?"

"Monty, you sure ain't got anyone who can actually sing," the young man chipped in again, mopping up a bowl with a chunk of bread, "less you count Maurie, of course, but that's more like wailing than singing."

"I guess not," Monty Jack scratched his balding pate.

"Let me sing, just one song. If you don't like it, I won't bother you no more."

"Can't do no harm," the young man pushed his bowl away before wiping a sleeve across his mouth.

The woman nodded and smiled brightly back and forth between Monty and her supporter.

"Ok, ok... *one* song."

"Great," she picked up her bag and shoved it into Monty's arms, "hold this for me!"

"Sure... why not... what's your name anyhow?"

"Cecilia Jones, people generally call me Cece, though."

Monty shook his head and looked directly at Amos, noticing him for the first time as Cece negotiated her way towards the piano.

"You're new in town too, aren't you?"

He nodded, "Just arrived."

"You're not going to ask me for a job as well, are you?"

"Nope," he replied, "I don't whore either."

Monty forced a smile and placed Cece's bag on the bar. It looked too clean for a bag that must have travelled a long way to get to a town so far from anywhere.

The saloon girls watched Cece with a mixture of amusement and disdain; none of them seemed interested in moving out of the way for her until Monty clapped his hands loudly and demanded to know why they weren't working.

One by one, they slunk away from the piano as Cece took off her coat. She wore a simple white blouse and long grey skirt, unfussy and conservatively cut. A lost little creature amongst the gaudy colours of the reluctantly dispersing saloon girls.

She carefully folded up her coat and hung it over the back of a newly vacated chair before taking off her bonnet and shaking out blonde hair that tumbled to her shoulders.

One barfly whistled, "Monty, you sure you can't get her to whore?"

Monty Jack pulled a face. *What more could he do?* The girl clearly didn't know a good thing when offered it.

The young man who'd been eating at the table glanced at the barfly in irritation. He looked like he wanted to say something but thought better of it and shuffled his chair round to face Cece instead.

He was tall and strong, with mousy fair hair and the sun-darkened skin of a man who spent a lot of time outdoors. A farmer or rancher. He'd noticed the young man hadn't been able to drag his eyes from Cece. Amos noticed lots of things. It was what he did best. That and killing.

To be honest, most of the men in the bar still sober enough to notice their surroundings were staring at Cece, but their expressions and souls were hungrier and easier to read. The young man was the only one who didn't look disappointed she'd refused to whore.

Cece settled herself behind the piano; she played a few notes and wrinkled her nose, "This thing's not tuned, right?"

"Don't worry, honey, ain't anyone here likely to notice," Monty shot back.

She took a deep breath and shook her head. She liked things just so and was used to having them that way. Not spoilt, but used to everything being right. She really must be a long way from home.

"Very well," she shrugged, accepting she was just going to have to make do with the battered old piano, "this is an old song my mother used to sing when I was little. It's not exactly a cheerful tune when you listen to the words properly, but I always like to sing it when things aren't going too well." She looked directly at Monty Jack and gave him a smile halfway between sweet and patronising.

Although *Jack's* customers had noticed Cece well enough, they hadn't considered interrupting the serious business of drinking, gambling, chatting, and flirting with the saloon girls for her, but as soon as she'd sung the first line of her song, a complete hush descended on the bar.

Even Amos, who struggled to find anything in life to smile about, felt the ghost of a grin haunt his face.

Cece had been right; it wasn't a particularly happy song. A ballad about returning troubles and lost love, but she sang it so sweetly he couldn't help but find his spirits lifted.

She was facing the wall rather than looking towards her audience, but her voice was so strong and clear it still filled the whole saloon, like morning sunlight streaming into a room once the curtains were pulled apart; her voice chased all the shadows away.

The room was transfixed. Even the saloon girls, who he guessed knew a thing or two, were smiling gentle little smiles as if reminded of long-forgotten loves from the days before they'd come to sell themselves in the rooms above Monty Jack's saloon. A couple of them seemed to be on the verge of tears.

When Cece finished, and the last note from the old piano had faded into the smoke and whiskey fumes, the hush lingered around the bar as if everybody had quite forgotten what they were supposed to be doing.

Monty wiped a hand over the few long greasy strands of hair sticking to his shining scalp and exclaimed, "Well fuck me five ways to next Sunday!"

Which was the cue for a round of thunderous and rather astonished applause.

Cece blinked and blushed in the face of the saloon's enthusiasm, which slowly abated until only the young farmer remained, wildly clapping and stomping his feet. When he eventually realised everybody else had stopped, it was his turn to blink and blush, followed by a sheepish grin as he found his seat again.

"Well?" Cece asked Monty once she'd returned to the bar.

"That was beautiful," Monty replied. He pronounced the word "beautiful" as if it was one he was so unfamiliar with he wasn't entirely sure he'd got it right.

"Thank you," Cece beamed, "do I have a job?"

"If he doesn't want you," the barfly next to Amos interrupted, "you can come an sing at my house any day of the week... and Mrs Crane can just pack her bags if she don't like it!"

"If it meant you were home more, she'd be out the door before sunset," his neighbour at the bar cracked, slapping him on the back.

"Well, it's against my better judgement, but it'll sure make a change from listening to all these drunks bellyaching about my whiskey all night long," Monty sighed.

"Your whiskey is shit," someone slurred.

"One month trial; bed, three meals a day, and you keep half your tips."

"What about pay?"

Monty looked at her blankly, "Bed, three meals a day, and you keep half your tips."

"No pay?"

He nodded towards a couple of the saloon girls who were trying to hustle up some business at one of the card tables, "If you want to earn more…"

"Ok, ok… bed, three meals and… three-quarters of my tips."

"Young lady…"

"I'll make a lot of tips," she smiled sweetly.

"Fuck, I'm getting soft," Monty shook his head before spitting in his palm and holding out his hand, "Deal."

Cece looked at him like he was holding out a turd but gingerly accepted his hand anyway.

"We've established you don't whore, but it's only fair to warn you this place can get rough, especially on payday. I hope you don't mind getting pawed on a regular basis?"

"Not if you don't mind your customers getting slapped in the face on a regular basis?"

The barfly laughed, "Hell, gonna be more fun with her here; think I'll have to come by more often from now on."

"Stan, you could only spend any more time here if I let you sleep on the bar," Monty replied.

Stan threw his hands out towards the saloon owner, "You only gotta ask nicely..."

Monty waved one of the saloon girls over; she had a hard careworn face and soft green eyes, "Josie, Cece's gonna be staying with us for a while; settle her into Mary's old room for me, will you?"

"Sure, boss," Josie grinned, "Welcome aboard, hun."

"What happened to Mary?" Cece asked as Josie took her by the arm.

"Oh, don't fret about that, sweetie," Josie smiled, "the rug cleaned up real nice..."

As the two women turned towards the stairs, the young farmer stood up, clutching a beaten old hat before him, "Miss?"

"Yes?"

"Can I ask what that song's called, it was very pretty, but I don't think I ever heard it before? I sing a bit too, not as good as you, but I'd love to learn it."

"I'd be happy to teach it to you..." she stuck out a hand which he stared at for a full five seconds before enveloping it in one of his own.

"Sye Hallows," he smiled.

"Cece Jones... a pleasure to meet you."

"Me too," he beamed, "when will you be singing again?"

"Tonight, I guess."

"Great, I'll come back later."

"Not like you to be here at night, Sye? Your Ma don't like you riding out after dark," Monty grinned as he retreated behind the bar.

"Well, once in a while is alright... for special occasions," a mixture of annoyance and embarrassment flowed over his features, momentarily making him look both younger and uglier.

"I'll see you later then," Cece turned to follow Josie.

"The song, Miss?"

"Oh, sorry," Cece called back over her shoulder, "it's called *Yesterday*..."

Amos swivelled back to face Monty, who'd started wiping down the bar with a cloth dirtier than the floor.

"Was there a stagecoach today?"

"No stage till next week... if it even turns up. It ain't what you call a reliable service. Why?"

"No reason," he slid his empty glass across the counter for a refill. As the barman poured, he wondered how a girl who had just arrived in town during a rainstorm, had a hat and coat that were bone dry...

The Widow

Molly McCrea's first thought when she saw the stranger riding towards them through the rain was the Mayor had sent a man to finish the job. She found herself leaning towards Mr Furnedge. He reeked of orange blossom and old paint today.

Furnedge, mistaking her fear, pulled the umbrella down over them. Given the wind was driving the rain in sheets, the umbrella was about as much use as he was, but she suspected he was enjoying being this close to her.

She relaxed as the rider pulled his horse from the road and doffed his dripping hat. He had a hard, weathered face, but not a cruel one. He lowered his head and showed more respect than the whole town had managed since her husband's death.

Since her husband had been murdered, she corrected herself.

She nodded her thanks as they trudged past the rider in the wake of the wagon. He let them pass before replacing his hat and continuing towards the town.

Keep riding, she wanted to shout back at him, keep riding into the rain!

Instead, the coffin carrying her husband's body pulled her

eyes back; the wind tugged at her veil, trying to unmask her as the fraud she was.

You never loved him anyway...

Tom McCrea had been a hard man to love, quick to temper and slow to forgive, but he'd offered her security and occasional comfort. Until he'd been fool enough to come out here in search of his fortune, or whatever it was he'd been looking for. Now she was alone again...

She lowered her eyes and stared at the mud clinging to her skirts. She wasn't overly concerned; she'd already decided she was going to burn everything she wore to the funeral.

Her clothes were sodden, splattered with mud and no doubt infused with the stink of Mr Furnedge's overpowering cologne. However, she wouldn't need them once she got home; Molly McCrea had no intention of being a widow for long.

*

The funeral of Molly McCrea's husband was as brief and sparsely attended as their wedding had been six years earlier. It had rained then, too, bitter winter rain, spat into their faces by a furious north wind as soon as they'd stepped out of the church, accompanied by only the preacher who had married them and two witnesses, whom they'd persuaded to leave a nearby bar in return for free beer.

The rain was warmer for his funeral, it was summer after all, and the view was better out here. Long swaying grass and vast turbulent skies surrounded her here, rather than the abattoir facing the church in the dirty little cattle town, the name of which she had quite forgotten, where she'd married Tom McCrea.

She no more listened to Preacher Stone's words over Tom's grave than she had to those of the man who'd married them. At least she had the excuse of being drunk then. She could recall he'd had a kind face and a soft voice, whereas Preacher Stone had neither and looked mighty inconvenienced Tom McCrea required a burial at all.

She wished she was drunk now.

Perhaps she would march into *Jack's Saloon* in her sodden, mud-splattered mourning dress, throw away her veil and drink whiskey at the bar till she cared about nothing at all anymore. Maybe after that, it wouldn't hurt so much when they got around to killing her too.

At least it might give her the courage to tell the inhabitants of this creepy godforsaken town what she thought of them all.

She shut her eyes as the town's gravedigger and his apprentice lowered Tom's coffin into its muddy socket. They took as much care as a couple of labourers dropping a sack of rotten potatoes off the back of a wagon.

Preacher Stone was droning on about dust and ashes, but she wasn't really listening. Perhaps they wouldn't kill her; who was she anyway? She didn't know anything; she wasn't going to make a fuss. All she wanted to do was sell everything she and Tom owned that wouldn't fit into a suitcase and get out of town.

Maybe she'd go back east, if anything was left of it, or move on west. Any point of the compass would do, so long as it took her away from Hawker's Drift – a town seemingly dumped slap bang in the middle of this endless plain, as far away from anybody else as it was possible to be, for no obvious purpose.

The land here was good, as evidenced by the lush grass that would soon be waist high, but it was so far away from anywhere else it cost a fortune to transport grain or cattle back to what passed for civilization these days.

She realised Preacher Stone had finished. The only sound now was the rain falling on the hollow wood of Tom's coffin. They were all looking at her; Preacher Stone, Mr Furnedge, the gravedigger and his apprentice, even the horse tethered to the coffin wagon. They expected her to do something.

She bent down and scooped a handful of mud from the pile next to the open grave; rivulets of rainwater washed down the sides of the mound as if nature objected to the little manmade hill out here where everything was supposed to be flat. She should have taken her gloves off, they were soft black leather and expensive, but as they were going to burn too, she didn't care.

She should say something. *Goodbye. I love you. Rest in Peace*, but nothing would come. Her mouth was as dry as her eyes. Tom McCrea had never been a bad man; feckless maybe, a dreamer for sure, too fond of his drink probably and cursed with a foul temper certainly. But he'd been good to her, in his own way. Even when he got so angry with her, his eyes bulged, and the veins in his neck stood out so much she feared his head might explode, he'd never laid a finger on her. Not the once. Plenty of other people he'd laid out for no good reason, which had meant they'd had to stuff their bags and get out of a town as quick as you like, but no, he'd never laid a finger on her.

But was that enough? Enough to follow a man for mile after thankless mile, following wherever his latest foolhardy dream led him?

It had been more, of course. He'd made her laugh now and then; they'd sat and drank whiskey till neither of them could stand. He'd never let anyone bad mouth her, he'd always carried her bag and opened the door for her. He'd been a real gent like that. He made her feel safe. Made her feel like she wasn't alone. He made her feel, for the only time in her life, that someone gave a damn about her.

But no, it hadn't been enough, nowhere near enough, to bring her out here to a place as wrong as Hawker's Drift.

As the wet earth thumped on the coffin lid, she turned her back and walked away without a second glance.

*

The rain stopped before dark, and she burned her funeral clothes in a large metal bucket she'd first filled with coal. For a while, she'd toyed with keeping them as Mr Furnedge wanted her to come by his office the next day to settle Tom's affairs, but no, she couldn't face wearing that dress again.

It stank too much of mud and death and cheap cologne.

Everything went into the fire; dress, shoes, shawl, veil, hat, stockings, underwear, gloves, even the pointless inadequate umbrella Furnedge had tried to shield her with.

She fed them into the fire one by one and stood watching till nought but embers, and the blackened metal frame of the umbrella remained. By then, it was night, and the moon was high and bright. She wondered if the neighbours were watching her. Mad woman, they'd whisper to each other out of the sides of their mouths. They'd probably whispered it long before Tom died too.

Before Tom was murdered, she corrected herself again.

She should let it go. There was nothing to be done here. There would be no justice, no recompense. No one would hang from the town square gallows. Better to let it go. Move on. Start again.

Alone...

She doused the embers and returned to the house. It was empty. She'd given the maid the day off. The girl had wanted to come to the funeral, but Molly had shaken her head. "No need to catch your death," she'd said, not sure if she was talking about the rain or not.

She sat in the big chair by the fireplace. Her hair was a mess, long and knotted; she should have combed it when it was still wet, but what was the point?

Tom had always loved her hair. He used to run his fingers through it whenever he could. He loved both its length and colour, like rust in the sunset he'd called it once, in possibly the only poetic moment of his entire life. They had been in bed, her head resting on his chest, listening to his heart when he'd whispered it to her, twisting the long strands around his fingers.

That was the closest she'd ever come to loving him. But he was gone now, so why bother to comb it, or wash it, or do anything at all with it? Maybe she'd chop it off, cut it short, wear britches and pretend to be a man. Maybe life would be better as a man.

She poured herself a whiskey and then another when the first didn't touch the sides. Sitting back, she stared into the dark, cold fireplace.

They'd done well here. They'd arrived with little two years earlier, and now they had a decent house and a part-time maid. She had a wardrobe of fine dresses, some of them even silk, they had a big coal fire, a pantry well stocked with food, a large feather bed and heavy curtains to keep out the dark and the chill.

Oh, and Tom had a wet, muddy hole in the ground.

She'd never asked. Not once. It was such an obvious thing, but she'd never uttered the words. *Where is the money coming from, Tom?* She told herself it was because Tom was a proud man; he wanted to impress her, be successful for her. To make something for them and the child she'd never been able to give him. If she'd asked, it would have been questioning him; questioning the choices he'd made for them, suggesting something wasn't right.

And of course, something *wasn't* right, but she'd said nothing, not because of Tom's pride, but because she hadn't cared. Life was suddenly good, comfortable; there was no more running from town to town, often in the middle of the night, because of Tom's temper or Tom's hair-brained schemes or Tom's debts.

Did it actually matter where the money was coming from? He was close to the Mayor, so he couldn't be doing anything wrong. Could he?

Except... except there shouldn't be so much money in Hawker's Drift. There was nothing here. A few farms, a few ranches, but their produce went to feed the town. There were no mines, no industry, no manufacturing. Few travellers passed through Hawker's Drift as the road leading here didn't go anywhere else. Nothing to bring in money. Yet the shops were always fully stocked, not just with essentials, but fancy stuff too, like the silk dresses and the silly underwear Tom had liked her to wear for him.

The saloon and restaurants were always full, and the shops were always busy. Nobody seemed to go without; even the people in the shacks down on the Flats got by easily enough, and the town's few vagrants and vagabonds never starved. There were no church soup kitchens, no crowds of desperate rough-handed men forming when someone was hiring, no threadbare children begging for scraps, no real crime as far as she knew. Nothing like the other places she and Tom had drifted through.

There were more young people and children here, too, not that it was devoid of old-timers, but it wasn't a walking cemetery like some of the places she'd been to either.

Hawker's Drift was a prosperous town, but she'd never figured out why it was so different to most other towns.

Tom had become strange and distant in the weeks before his death, the way he usually did when things were starting to go wrong. He wouldn't tell her, of course; he never did. But she'd started to worry more and more about the money they had. Was the Mayor really paying him *that* much? Had he been stealing it? The thought had crossed her mind continually, but she'd never asked, and Tom just became more distant, more withdrawn. And then he died.

Ever since Sheriff Shenan had come to tell her about

Tom's "accident", people had been uncomfortable around her. Staring at her. Whispering. Falling silent when she came near. She'd the feeling she was being watched too. Just her imagination, perhaps, but she didn't think so.

Tom was dead, and she felt like she was a loose end someone wanted to put a knot in.

She downed another whiskey and tried to convince herself she was being stupid. Was it likely anyone would want her dead?

Who was she anyway?

Molly McCrea. Thirty-two years old. Red hair. Green eyes. Long nose. Full lips. Big mouth. Widow.

"Molly McCrea..." she stared all the way down into the bottom of the glass.

Perhaps she should go back to her maiden name, though she'd always hated it. The opportunity to be rid of it was one of the reasons she'd agreed to marry Tom in the first place. She'd liked his name. It wasn't a great reason to marry a man, but she hadn't been able to think of many, and it had seemed as good as anything else she could come up with at the time.

"Molly Herbert..."

No. She still hated it. The name reminded her of her father, who, like Tom, had been a short-tempered drunk but, unlike Tom, had laid a hand upon her at every possible opportunity. Albert Herbert, an evil son of a bitch who'd made the first eighteen years of her life a misery. Bert-Bert they'd called him in the saloons where he'd spent most of his life and nearly all their money. A big man with a big mouth and a big gut, who was always happy to spend money buying strangers a drink but resented every dime it cost him to put food on his family's table.

No, she didn't want to carry his name again.

She'd run away in the end, believing life on the road would be better than staying at home to be abused. Instead, she'd followed a string of men who, more or less, had been little better than Bert-Bert.

She was tall, with striking red hair and intense green eyes. Men noticed her. She could drink most of them under the table. She'd a loud, dirty laugh and a brash mouth that could be both quick and foul if she let it run away with her. Which she usually did.

She'd followed one useless waster after the next, never knowing what she saw in them, especially when they screwed other women, blew all their money on cards or whiskey and slapped her face if she made too much of a fuss about anything.

Tom had been different. In fact, he'd seemed like a knight in shining armour in comparison; for all his faults, he'd been a better man than any other she'd ever lain with. It was just a shame she'd never been able to love him.

Now he was gone, and if she ever got out of this town alive, she'd eventually end up with another piece of trash like Bert-Bert Herbert, no matter how many times she told herself she wouldn't.

Molly hauled herself to her feet and went upstairs to the silent bedroom. She opened the top drawer of the dresser and pulled out a fearsomely heavy revolver wrapped in a cloth beneath Tom's shirts.

He'd tried to teach her how to use it once. Lining up old

bottles on a fence, he'd shown her how to load and fire the weapon. She hadn't managed to hit anything with it, though she had scared the hell out of the wildlife.

Tom had grinned and told her if she ever needed to hit something more threatening than an old beer bottle, she should try to look like she knew what she was doing, cuss as much as possible and hope she'd frighten them off without needing to pull the trigger as he doubted she'd ever trouble a barn door from more than five paces away.

She loaded the pistol and returned downstairs to her chair; placing the gun in her lap she poured herself another large whiskey. She doubted the booze would help her aim much, but it usually did wonders for her cussing.

*

She awoke with a fuzzy head from too much whiskey and a sore neck from sleeping in a chair. Bright sunlight was creeping around the corners of the room's heavy drapes.

Tom's old pistol still lay on her lap. She hadn't needed it after all, and, as an added bonus, she'd avoided shooting herself in her sleep to boot.

After carefully placing the gun next to the half-empty whiskey bottle, she pulled open the curtains and winced as the morning light rushed in.

Perhaps they weren't interested in her after all.

She rubbed her watery eyes with her palms. The window faced due east and the morning sun was blindingly bright. The sky was dark blue and cloudless. Trust Tom to get himself buried on such a foul day; she didn't know whether to laugh or cry. Tom's timing had always been lousy. She had used to tease him about it, how he'd always choose the worst possible moment to do anything. Sometimes it annoyed him; sometimes, a big slow smile would spread over his face.

She missed him.

Strange, she never thought she would. She'd always known they wouldn't be together forever. One day either he'd get bored with her and find himself another woman, or his temper or tomfoolery would get him killed. She'd been wrong about a lot of things in her life, but she'd been right about that one. Pity it hadn't been a woman; she'd rather him in another's bed than a muddy hole.

A woman who actually loved him.

Had he known she'd never loved him? He'd told her regularly that he loved her. It had taken a long time for her to believe him; it just seemed so unlikely any man would, and she'd just put his words down to the fact he wanted to keep her sweet and in his bed.

Eventually, long after they'd been married, it dawned on her he genuinely *did* love her. As far as she knew, he'd never been with another woman from the day they had met, on a dusty stagecoach trundling between somewhere and nowhere.

Sometimes she would catch him staring at her, and he'd have the strangest little smile on his big round face. Like a man might have if he opened his door one day and found a whopping pile of gold coins sitting there for no obvious reason. He looked like he couldn't really believe his luck.

She'd often wondered what that must be like and why she

couldn't return the feeling. Perhaps her father had burnt it out of her; perhaps she'd been born with a little bit of her soul missing. She'd never figured it out.

She was about to head to the pantry to make breakfast when she noticed two figures across the road, leaning on Mrs Claybourne's rough little fence. Their hats were pulled down low; it was hard to make them out against the glare of the harsh morning sun, but she knew who they were, alright.

One of the men put two fingers against the brim of his hat in greeting.

She stepped away from the window. Someone seemed to be interested in her after all.

*

Mr Furnedge, as he usually did, stank of cologne. He seemed to believe pouring copious amounts of perfume over himself negated the need for a regular bath. He must have quite a collection at home as he never seemed to smell quite the same from one day to the next. This morning he'd masked his body odour with the delicate aroma of aniseed and embalming fluid, or so it seemed to Molly.

She tried hard not to wrinkle her nose. She really did.

"Are you unwell, Mrs McCrea?"

"Just a little nauseous. I'm sure it will pass quickly."

"Good, good..." He eased himself back into his chair and indicated the one on the opposite side of his desk.

"I hope you managed to sleep well after yesterday's... ordeal?"

"As well as can be expected," she patted down her skirt,

clutched her bag on her lap and hoped he couldn't smell the whiskey over his own fumes.

"Of course, such a tragedy... our thoughts are all with you, my dear." He gave her what he no doubt considered his most sincere smile, though personally, she wouldn't have trusted the man to sell her a bucket without a hole in it.

"You wanted to see me?"

She glanced behind Furnedge, but she couldn't see if the two men who had followed her less than discreetly from her home to his office were outside, thanks to the frosted glass.

"Yes, yes... I am so sorry to intrude in your time of mourning." If he noticed she no longer dressed head to toe in black, he didn't comment.

"Life goes on."

"Yes," he said more brightly, "indeed it does!"

She opened her bag and produced a sheaf of papers which she slid across the desk. "My husband's last will and testament, naming me as his sole beneficiary. I'm sure you will find everything in order, particularly as you drew the papers up in this very office."

Furnedge made no move to pick up the will. "They are perfectly in order. All legal and proper. All most *tickety*. Mr McCrea was particular about the details. A prudent man. Most prudent."

This was news to Molly, who had always found Tom to be exceedingly imprudent about pretty much everything.

It'd taken her aback when Tom announced he'd drawn up a will; two weeks to the day after he'd signed it, he was dead. It'd been just one of a series of things Tom had done during the last weeks of his life that should have told her something was very, very wrong.

"I will be leaving town once our things are sold. They don't amount to much, so I don't envisage the matter taking long."

"Leaving us?" Furnedge frowned.

"There is nothing here for me. I have relatives... back east."

Other than a couple of half-witted second cousins she hadn't seen in nearly twenty years, she had nobody in the world, but she didn't want the little lawyer to know how alone she was.

"Well, I'm sure, but we all hoped you would be staying with us. You're a valued member of our little family here in Hawker's Drift."

So valued nobody bothered to come to my husband's funeral...

"There are too many memories here."

"Of course, but it is so soon. To leave all this behind... to act rashly can be a mistake."

"I have made up my mind."

"Well, I can only wish you the best, Mrs McCrea. Wherever you end up."

Furnedge had always vaguely given her the creeps; she hadn't worried about it much in the past because Tom was prone to try and rip the head off any man who even looked at her the wrong way, a habit that had gotten them into trouble several times. Molly had found it more than a little irritating; she'd learned to look after herself where men were concerned a long time before she'd met Tom. A barbed put down was usually enough to keep unwanted advances at bay, generally with far less blood and recrimination too. Now she was alone again and felt terribly vulnerable, even in the company of the town's puny and overly fragrant lawyer, who, at a push, she fancied she could beat to a bloody pulp with her handbag.

There was something about Furnedge's eyes she didn't like; narrow, sly, scheming little slits, distorted by the thick rimless glasses he wore. In truth, the list of things she didn't like about the lawyer made a long read, but his eyes were the worst. They lingered on her, hungry and devious, like a snake eyeing a mouse and calculating just what it had to do to gobble up dinner.

"So, if the will is in order..." she began to rise to her feet.

"There is no issue with the will... however, there is one *complication*." Furnedge seemed almost to smack his thick lips together as he finished the sentence as if he found the taste of it to his liking.

She sank back into her chair, "Complication?"

"Oh, I'm sure it's nothing too serious, my dear, easily rectified, easily made *tickety*," Furnedge pulled out a paper folder which he placed directly in front of him, resting his hands upon it as if to prevent her snatching it away.

"As well as your late husband's estate, you also inherit his debts."

"What debts?" she demanded, though her heart sank. Tom had always been adept at running up debts. And running away from them too.

"Well..." Furnedge opened the folder and started laying out bills, "...it appears Mr McCrea bought considerable provisions shortly before his death. All on credit."

"Such as?"

"A horse... two pack mules... a tent... various tools... a

The Burden of Souls

rifle... binoculars... dry provisions for several months... a pickaxe... a-"

"What on earth would my husband want with all that?"

"Well, I assumed you knew. Didn't he mention it?"

"It seems to have slipped his mind."

"It would appear to be prospecting equipment."

"Prospecting for what?"

"Gold, presumably."

"There's no gold here! There's nothing here but fucking grass!"

Furnedge stared at her before clearing his throat with a scratchy little cough.

If he complains about my language, I'm going to slap him...

"There is equipment here for gold panning..." Furnedge continued, "...not to mention a fairly substantial amount of dynamite."

Her mouth was hanging open. "*Dynamite?* Why would he want dynamite? Where would he even *get* dynamite in this town?"

"Oh, Mrs McCrea. You can get most anything in Hawker's Drift. If you know who to ask." Furnedge's eyes had narrowed even further than usual.

Molly thought she'd read somewhere a snake couldn't bite with its eyes open.

"How much?" she demanded, "How much does my husband owe?"

"Your husband owes nothing, Mrs McCrea, on account of being dead. You, however, owe this..."

He pushed a piece of paper across the desk with a number on it. An exceedingly large number.

"I haven't got this! Everything I own doesn't come to a fraction of this!"

"Do not fret Mrs McCrea; I have taken the liberty of speaking to your creditor on your behalf. There is great sympathy, given the circumstances. You have three months to clear your debt or return the purchases in satisfactory condition."

Furnedge pushed the invoices across the desk.

"I've never seen any of these things!"

"Well, this isn't a large town, Mrs McCrea; I'm sure you'll be able to find and return them in short order. Unless you have a use for pack mules and dynamite, of course?"

"I don't."

"Well then, you just need to return them, and the matter will be closed. No harm done. Everything *tickety*."

"I see," she flicked through the various invoices, all dated in the weeks before Tom's death. What damn fool nonsense had he gotten himself involved in this time?

She felt like telling Furnedge exactly where he could shove his paperwork, but she bit down on the impulse. Her fast mouth had gotten them into trouble almost as often as Tom's temper and foolhardy schemes in the past, the only difference being she had eventually learned to control her tongue. Mostly.

"I will set about returning these items at once," she forced a grudging smile onto her face, "who exactly are my creditors, Mr Furnedge?"

"Just one creditor, Mrs McCrea; it seems your husband wasn't one for shopping around."

"And he would be?"

"The Mayor."

"I see," she tried to sound calm, "if we're quite finished, I should get to work."

"Of course, there is one small condition you should be aware of."

"Yes?"

"If you leave the town limits before the debt is discharged, then payment will become immediately due."

"And if I can't pay?"

"The Mayor will have to be recompensed for his loss in other ways…"

Furnedge smiled, and she swore his big fat tongue almost slithered out of his mouth in excitement..

The Gunslinger

He arrived at the stables just in time for a woman, who wore her wild red hair in a loose ponytail and her face in a crumpled scowl, to mow him down.

"Asshole," she spat at him after he'd bounced off the stable door.

He watched her stomp across the square towards the saloon before turning to one of the stable hands, "What's her problem?"

"Her husband mislaid a couple of mules... and some dynamite."

Amos stared at him blankly.

The young man shrugged, "It's that kinda town..."

Once satisfied the stables were looking after his horse properly, he arranged another week's keep for the animal.

"You are sticking around, huh?" The stable lad made a note in a dog-eared pocketbook.

"For a while."

"Folks usually find it hard to leave here." He flashed a goofy smile before wandering off to shovel more horse dung.

The day was bright and the sky mostly cloudless; the sun had yet to dry out the thick mud still being churned by horses and wagons into a cloying rancid glue. The better weather had encouraged more locals out onto the town square, and while it could hardly be described as crowded, Hawker's Drift didn't feel like the half-abandoned ghost town it had when he'd arrived during the previous day's rainstorm.

He sauntered back to the saloon where he'd taken a room, it'd been as noisy as the gunsmith had warned, but the bed was passable and vastly more comfortable than a blanket on the ground. He'd managed to fall asleep despite the rhythmic creaking from the room above.

He recognised several of the barflies, mostly slumped on the same stools as the day before, as well as the foul-tempered redhead from the stables. She already had an empty whiskey glass in front of her.

He stared at her long red hair and tried hard not to remember. He usually avoided women if he could, but he found his feet took him to stand next to her despite himself. He knew why and hated himself for it. As if the world wasn't torture enough.

"I'll have a beer," he said to the bartender, at least managing to keep his eyes away from her.

"But whiskey is-"

"Yes, yes, I get it! I'll take a whiskey too."

Once the drinks were poured, he slid the whiskey in front of the woman next to him, "You look like you need this more than me."

She looked sideways at him. "Hope you're not looking to get laid..." she downed the whiskey in one "...I'm in mourning."

He cocked his head, recognising the woman. "I saw you yesterday, didn't I?"

"Yeah. Guess I look a bit different without the veil and the big wooden box."

"I'm sorry for your loss."

"Thanks... you must be new here?"

"Just arrived."

"Take my advice, saddle up and get out. Quickly."

He raised an eyebrow, "Doesn't seem too bad a town."

She snorted and tapped her empty glass on the counter for a refill, "Yeah, it'd be a great place if it wasn't for the collection of screwed up, inbred lunatics who live here."

She swivelled on her stool and raised her latest drink in the direction of two men in long coats sitting nearby before downing it in one.

Neither man had a drink before him, and they were openly staring at the redhead; both wore metal stars pinned to their lapels. The younger of the two men looked mildly discomforted for a moment. His companion was a little older, and his face was quite expressionless as he watched them intently with cold, muddy eyes.

He's dangerous.

"Friends of yours?"

"Not exactly. They're just making sure I don't skip town. I think..." the words drifted off with a shrug.

"Why?"

"You don't want to get involved."

"Why?" He knew she was right but couldn't stop himself.

She sighed, "Tom, my fool of a husband, got himself into something stupid. Again. Then he died, fell off his horse, they said... but..." she hunched back over the bar.

"You don't think it was an accident?"

"You drink real slow."

"I was planning on still being conscious for dinner," he sipped his beer, "Why don't you think it was an accident?"

"I'm a natural pessimist. Just a glass half empty kinda gal, or, in this case, *completely* empty..."

The bartender jumped in with another shot.

"Why don't you just leave the bottle?" Amos said to the bartender.

"Whiskey ain't free," he replied, looking slightly confused.

"Leave it, Sonny; I'll make it easy for you to keep track of what I've had. I'll finish the bottle."

Sonny the bartender thought about it for a second, rolled his thin shoulders and placed the bottle in front of her, "Your funeral."

"Not the best choice of words," she helped herself as Sonny wandered off to attend to the other barflies.

"I'm Amos, by the way."

She looked at him squarely; her eyes were a vivid, sparkling green. They were only slightly bloodshot. "Molly," she eventually replied, "or the Widow McCrea if you prefer."

"Molly has a better ring."

"I told you I'm still in mourning, didn't I?"

"I'm not trying to get laid."

"Weirdo."

"Pardon?"

"Why not? I'm emotionally vulnerable and getting drunker by the minute. Most men would."

"I'm not most men."

"Sure..."

She was scared and lonely, which he supposed wasn't entirely unusual for someone recently widowed, and even more so if the town's deputies were following her around. She was trying hard to hide it behind a quick mouth and quicker drinking. Not entirely successfully, though few people could hide much from him.

"Hey, you haven't seen a big crate of dynamite lying around town, have you?"

"No..."

"Pity, I need to give it back to the asshole who sold it to my idiot husband."

"Why'd he need a crate of dynamite?"

"Some damn fool get rich quick scheme, I guess. Tom was always brilliant at thinking up get rich quick schemes. Shame they were all so fucking useless... now he's left me with another god-awful mess. I really shouldn't be surprised." She flashed a small, pained smile at him and shook her head before sliding off her stool, "You staying here, in the saloon?"

He nodded.

"Guess I'll be seeing you again then. I intend to be spending every cent I have left in this place over the next three months." She spread a row of coins on the bar before scooping up the whiskey bottle and turning for the door, "I wasn't joking about getting out of here while you still can..."

She crossed the bar in a dead straight line. The door hadn't swung shut before the two deputies rose and followed her out...

*

"Well, I'll be..."

He lowered the rifle and stared at the spot where the old can had sat a moment before.

"Dead bang on, eh?" John X Smith grinned and looked pleased with himself, "even after you've been drinking."

"One beer."

"Devil's brew."

"You abstain?"

"Damn right, that stuff will rot your guts and your brains," the gunsmith warned, before pulling a hip flask from his jacket and offering a slug, "I stick to brandy myself."

He didn't usually drink spirits but took a swig in the hope of masking the smell of corruption hanging in the air. The hip flask was old and dented. The brandy was smooth and expensive.

"I am a man of some refinement," John grinned as he nodded appreciatively, "just don't tell anyone. I got my reputation to think of."

They stood on the edge of a large refuse tip, about a mile downwind of town. For a small place, it sure produced a lot of shit. Smith had explained firing guns in Hawker's Drift tended to make the local law enforcement twitchy, so he came out here to test his weapons. The stench of rotting food and excrement ensured he was left in peace.

"Kicks less too, huh?"

He nodded; he was impressed.

"Got better rifles back at the shop, but I know a man can get attached to his gun despite its faults, much the same as with his woman in that respect."

"Do you fix women too?"

John laughed, "What would be the point? Faults are what makes em interesting in the first place. A perfect gun is a thing of beauty. A perfect woman... well, that would just be downright dull."

"You married?"

"I got too much love for just one woman, my friend," he grinned.

"That must be interesting in a small town?"

"Oh, you'd be surprised just how many faults there are here to enjoy."

A rat scurried out of a pile of rotting vegetables, but he ignored it. As a rule, he only bothered killing the two-legged variety.

"How'd you end up here?"

"Much the same as most of the others; I got washed up and found myself marooned."

"You make it sound like you're trapped?"

"Trapped? No, Hawker's Drift is just a hard place to leave."

"So people keep telling me."

"Like?"

"You know Molly McCrea?"

"Not as well as I'd like; fine looking woman."

"Recently widowed too."

John X nodded, "Husband was a fool. Not a bad man underneath, but a fool with a hot head all the same."

"He bought a load of dynamite before he died, apparently."

"Like I said."

"Anything worth blowing up around here?"

"Can think of a few people who'd benefit from a stick of the stuff up their behind... but otherwise, no."

"She thinks a couple of the deputies are following her."

"She's got a vivid imagination."

"Is she..."

"Mad? No... grief can do things to your mind, though."

"I suppose."

"You ever known grief?"

Amos looked off towards the sun, which was slipping behind a sheath of cloud hugging the western horizon.

"Yeah..."

"Then you know what it can do."

He thought of all the years he'd spent in the saddle following a thin rider upon a grey stallion, searching for a man he'd never find.

"It can consume you..."

"Best to let it go. Move on. Start again."

"Probably is," he agreed, without asking what you did when you'd nothing else.

The two men began to walk back towards the town, the sun slipping behind the clouds as dusk fell early.

"Why did nobody go to the funeral?" Amos asked after a while.

"Did you see the weather?"

"Apart from that?"

"Tom McCrea had a short temper, upset a lot of folk, not an easy man to like sometimes."

"Must have been a helluva temper?"

Smith looked at his boots and skirted a large muddy puddle on the road, "Word has it he'd crossed the Mayor, which ain't a smart thing to do. People like to keep on his good side here"

"Is that why his widow is afraid?"

"You'd need to ask her... but if you want my advice, it's best not to get involved."

Amos looked at him enquiringly.

John glanced around; the road heading towards the town on the slopes of the hill ahead of them was deserted. Nothing moved bar grass, swaying on the breath of a warm and gentle evening breeze.

"Life can be good here, but... it's best to know who is in charge and keep to your own business. I don't know what Tom McCrea did, and I don't want to know, but he did something to piss off the Mayor, which was a dumb thing to do."

"And then he died?"

"And then he died," John agreed, avoiding his eye.

"How?"

"Riding accident, horse threw him, out here on the grass, cracked his head open on a rock and spilt whatever passed for his brains over the dirt. Horse got spooked by a snake or some other critter, most likely."

"A two-legged critter maybe?"

"Nobody is saying that, save maybe Mrs McCrea," John looked across at him before adding, "hope you ain't one of them heroic types who gets all het up when they think there's a damsel in distress?"

"Nope... I've been called plenty of things, but never heroic."

"Good," the gunsmith replied firmly, "this ain't a place for heroes."

The two men walked on in silence, the town of Hawker's Drift looming over them in the twilight.

*

He'd offered to buy the gunsmith a drink when they got back to town, but he'd just said he had plans and gave him a theatrical wink before sauntering off back to his shop.

He'd been in Hawker's Drift for a day, and although John X Smith was the only black man he'd seen in the town, he'd already spotted two women out and about with children with coffee-coloured skin and tight wiry hair.

He had a fair idea what the man's plans might involve.

He returned to his room above the saloon and, after laying his rifle by his bags and kicking off his boots, he laid back on the bed with his hands behind his head, enjoying the rare comfort of a ceiling to stare at and not having to keep one eye open for men who might want to kill him. For the moment at least.

He hadn't looked for work yet, and he didn't seriously need to. He still had most of the money he'd earned for killing two men out beyond the grass plain in what had once been a mining town but was now little more than a nest of outlaws and degenerates.

The money on offer had been good, and it was the kind of desperate hole Severn might have ended up in. He hadn't been there, of course, and nobody had heard of him, so he killed the two men, which had been easy as they were both stupid and drunk, and got out of town, which hadn't been, as they'd been popular, and their friends came after him.

It had taken days to shake them, but his horse was strong and young. He'd collected his money and headed out onto the plains to continue his pursuit of a man who was likely years dead without appreciating how vast and empty this place was.

He'd never heard of Hawker's Drift and hadn't planned to end up here, much the same as John X. He'd been adrift for years before he'd ever ventured on to these plains. The town was just a tiny rock people clung to, like all the other little broken pockets of humanity he came across on his endless journey. He would rest a little, replenish supplies and sleep on a feather mattress until, one day, he realised his butt missed the hard leather of his saddle, and the possibility Severn might be just beyond the horizon became too insistent to ignore, even if out here that horizon seemed impossibly far away.

He dozed a little, but the buzz of voices from the saloon below, interspersed with the occasional guttural cries from the rooms above, ensured he never fully succumbed to sleep.

Hunger began to gnaw after a while. It was fully dark now, and the night had crept into the room. He felt half inclined to roll over and go to sleep. Hunger wasn't an unfamiliar feeling, but it was unnecessary with food available in the saloon below. It'd been a long time since he'd stopped taking his next meal for granted and learnt to eat whenever food was available. He'd had to flee more than one town at short notice without provisions, and the prairie offered few easy meals.

As he left his room, a half-naked man with long unkempt white hair and an overgrown face ricocheted past him, rapidly followed by a shoe, which whistled past the man's head to dislodge a faded brown painting of a vase of flowers from the wall.

"I don't care how much you're willing to pay," a woman screeched, "don't ever try to do *that* again!"

The white-haired man grabbed his shoe and added it to the bundle of clothes he was clutching to the soiled grey vest hanging over his scrawny chest.

"Don't ya just love em fiery?" he cackled before ducking out of the way of his second shoe and scurrying down the staircase to get out of missile range.

Amos glanced up the stairs; a dark-haired young woman dressed only in a red and black striped corset and stockings was standing with her hands on her hips and a scowl on her face.

"*Men!*" She shouted in exasperation before noticing him and adding in a softer voice, "Hi, honey, wanna come up?"

Part of him wanted to go up to her, wanted to know how she felt beneath her tight-fitting corset, wanted to know what she smelt like and tasted like, but that would be a torture too terrible for even him to endure, so he shook his head and mumbled an apology before hurrying down the stairs.

"Suit yourself," he heard her say but didn't trust himself to look back.

The Preacher

A woman's laughter cut across Pioneer Square, raucous and drunk. It was a warm night, and the upstairs windows in *Jack's* were mostly open; the girls didn't seem to care who heard their work. They probably considered it advertising.

William Eustace Stone, simply Preacher Stone to the vast majority of Hawker's Drift's inhabitants, stood on the steps of his white clapperboard church and stared across the square towards *Jack's Saloon*.

Jack's Saloon, Casino and Whorehouse would be a more accurate title, though the cost of the extra signage would discourage a more honest description of the place from an old skinflint like Monty Jack.

Right across from his church, a veritable den of wanton drunkenness, gambling and fornication enjoyed by most of the men of the town and the surrounding farms, ranches and homesteads, even the ones who dutifully plodded through the door of his church every Sunday, some of them still smelling of whiskey and perfume.

"Lucky bastards..." Preacher Stone whispered, eyes following the ghostly diffused shadows moving back and forth behind the saloon's towering, frosted windows.

The Burden of Souls

A long time ago, he would have held nothing but contempt for the saloon and its patrons; sinners and wasters one and all, but it had been a long time since he'd enjoyed a young man's convictions. Now he was old, his guts hurt most of the time, and his congregation thought he was a mean-spirited old goat with little time for anybody but himself and God, which wasn't entirely fair. He didn't actually have much time for himself anymore either. He knew he wasn't popular in the town, but he was too old to care.

He'd become a preacher all those decades ago because he thought he could make the world a better place; he'd wanted to turn guns into plough shears and get the lions to lay down with the lambs. He'd been young and idealistic, proud and vain, too, if he was going to be honest.

Thirty years of preaching to all those upturned faces who had, by and large, ignored everything he'd told them and got on with the business of sinning as soon as their front doors closed had slowly ground him down.

Then he'd found himself in Hawker's Drift, which, in its own peculiar way, was about as Godless a place as one could hope to find.

Did he even believe in God anymore? He supposed he did, but it didn't stop part of him wanting to toss his Bible aside, cross the square, throw as much whiskey and beer down his throat as he could manage and awake the next morning in a strange bed with two young whores wrapped around him.

Why shouldn't he? Everybody else in this damn town seemed to.

He winced as pain flared up from his stomach, which suddenly seemed to hold a roasting stone where his dinner should have been. He grasped the handrail of the little flight of steps rising to the doorway. His head swam, and his mouth filled with sick-sweet corruption. He feared he was going to tumble down onto the little patch of half-hearted brown grass his parishioners shuffled their feet reluctantly over every Sunday, where he'd lay till someone who hadn't quite drunk all his wits away in *Jack's* noticed him.

Just when the pain became so bad hot little tears squeezed out from behind his eyelids, it passed. Not completely, but almost, leaving only a dull, distant ache as an unwanted reminder.

He spat at the ground and wiped the back of his hand across his mouth. It was getting worse. The pain was coming more often and more intensely. It'd been a long time since he'd quit telling himself it was just indigestion, but not so long since he'd admitted to himself he was dying.

He'd gone to Doc Rudi a few times, but not anymore; the quack had given him pills and powders. All expensive. All useless. Nothing worked, nothing save one thing, and maybe the pain was better than that.

So, after all these years, this was how it was going to end. His guts rotting away inside him, dying in a town where nobody liked him, a town he didn't much like himself, but one he knew he could never leave.

He turned his back on the square and returned to the comforts of his church. It was a simple, straightforward, unfussy affair. Wooden benches, a pulpit, an unassuming altar and a cross; what more did a church need? He'd heard about the big fancy churches and cathedrals they'd had back east and in the old countries. All covered with gold, stained glass and ornate sculptures. Nothing but vanity. No wonder that world had fallen to pieces.

A few candles burned around the pulpit where he'd been scribbling down the next sermon his parishioners would ignore. He didn't much care for lanterns, they were too harsh and bright, so shadow blanketed most of the room. Which was why the preacher didn't see the man sitting in the first row until he spoke.

"Been taking the night airs, Preacher?"

He gave out a startled little cry, which he tried, unsuccessfully, to mask with a cough.

"Mr Mayor... you... startled me."

He hovered, caught between the pews and his pulpit, squirming under the attention of the Mayor's restless eye. When the Mayor remained seated and silent, arm draped along the back of the pew he was lounging upon, he retreated behind the pulpit; sadly, he'd nothing more substantial to put between them.

"Working late, Preacher?" the Mayor asked eventually.

"Finishing off my sermon for tomorrow. It's Sunday, in case you'd forgotten."

"Of course, something profound and moving, I trust?"

He looked down at his scribbled notes. Between the crossings out, underlining and circled words, there was a sermon. Of sorts.

"It's about neighbourliness."

"It will be riveting, I'm sure..." the Mayor yawned, "...however, personally, I find a little fire and brimstone never goes amiss."

"I make my point... for those with ears to listen."

"A preacher needs to move souls. Trust me! Fire and brimstone. And obedience. Make sure the congregation know they're going to burn in hell if they don't behave. It's what keeps the masses in line after all."

"I do God's work. Civil order is your responsibility."

The Mayor cracked a grin, "Of course, but you need to keep your congregation enthralled, Billy; otherwise, they'll all end up listening to Wizzle instead."

He snorted, "Really? That sad old clown. You think people would rather listen to him than receive the word of God from me?"

"Who can say who is more touched by God's grace, eh Preacher?"

He tried to glare at the Mayor from his pulpit, but as soon as that damn roving eye settled upon him, the Preacher found his gaze wavered.

"How did the McCrea funeral go?" the Mayor finally punctured the silence.

"Quietly, no one attended other than the widow and Mr Furnedge," he replied carefully before adding, "as you wished."

The Mayor's eyebrow, the one above his good eye, shot up a notch, "I don't believe I asked for any such thing."

"It was put out she and her husband had crossed you?"

"I never put anything *out*; there is a small financial matter, which I can't discuss obviously, but nothing more."

"Tom McCrea crossed you and promptly fell off his horse; that's what people are whispering."

"Small town gossips," the Mayor's eye rolled upwards, "Tom McCrea's death was a tragic accident, and I have no grudge against his widow."

He wrapped his hands around the edge of the pulpit, his stomach spasming again, "Of course."

The Mayor rose, "Excellent! I'm glad you understand. Just make sure you mention it to your parishioners once they've enjoyed your uplifting little sermon. I do know how much you like to have a chat with them afterwards."

"I tend to their needs," he replied, swallowing hard. The pain was starting to boil his guts again.

"Are you quite alright?"

The Mayor was standing directly below the pulpit; he hadn't even noticed him move from the pews. He must have screwed his eyes shut against the pain for a moment.

"My stomach... playing up a little."

"Again? Oh dear, such a shame. Now we can't have you laid low, can we? Not with that flock of yours to care for, all those souls to fleece..."

"Just a bit of indigestion."

"Now, now Billy, you know you can't lie to me," the Mayor reached up and placed a small black bottle upon the Preacher's scribbled notes, "this will help."

"I told you..."

"Tsk, tsk, don't be such a stick in the mud. You know how much better it makes you feel..."

"It... is... wrong..."

"Wrong? It's just a little something to put you on your feet and to keep you there."

"I don't want any more."

The Mayor's eye stopped moving. He suddenly felt impaled upon its stare, "Take it, Billy, you know what it can do for you. It will make all your pain go away. And your cares too. It's what you desire…"

The Preacher looked down and found his hand had curled around the little bottle; he knew well enough what was inside it. Or at least what it did. His whole body ached for it as if something had awoken inside and noticed what was before him. Something he wanted, something he needed, something that would make everything more bearable; what did it matter what happened after? It took his pain away. Nothing else did.

When he looked up, the Mayor was already at the door looking back at him, his eye once more flicking hither and thither, "Remember though, Preacher. Not too much, a little of a morning, a little of a night and none in between. It's strong, sweet candy, Billy."

The Mayor tipped his hat and slipped out, his final words hanging in the air after him, "Just don't forget to keep telling everybody what a wonderful chap I am…"

Preacher Stone pulled out the little cork and took a hurried swig before he could hurl the bottle against the wall.

Soon after, his pain went away…

The Lawyer

Miss Dewsnap placed his coffee and two of her home-baked cookies on the desk, just as she did promptly at ten-thirty every Monday, Wednesday and Friday.

"Chocolate chip?" Guy Furnedge looked up from the papers spread before him.

"Your favourite," she nodded, hovering, eyes expectantly fixed upon him.

"Well, I don't know about that," he picked up one of the cookies, "I'm very partial to your almond and peanut too."

"Yes, of course, but I think you prefer these more..." Miss Dewsnap insisted. As with most matters, she tolerated little dissent.

"They are quite delicious," he agreed, taking a bite. He knew she wouldn't retreat until she'd seen him eat.

"Why thank you, Mr Furnedge," she gave him one of her small, twitchy smiles, "will there be anything else?"

"Not for now." When she remained, he added, "I'll call when I need you."

"Of course you will," she beamed. It wasn't quite a fulsome smile as she always kept her lips firmly clamped together; he'd never been able to fathom why, given her teeth were no more unattractive than the rest of her. She turned on her heels and closed the door behind her.

Once he was certain she was no longer lurking on the other side of the frosted glass, he opened the bottom drawer of his desk and threw the cookies into the paper bag he kept solely for disposing of Miss Dewsnap's infernal baking.

His wife, for reasons best known to herself, had decided to keep pigs at the bottom of their garden, and, in addition to fresh bacon and ham, they had the benefit of being able to eat almost anything. Even Miss Dewsnap's cookies.

He kicked the drawer shut and washed the dry cookie ash out of his mouth with the coffee, which was at least drinkable.

If it weren't for the lack of suitable part-time help in the town, he would have disposed of Miss Dewsnap's services years ago, but Hawker's Drift had yet to produce anyone capable of filing, typing, note taking, and general dog's bodying of a higher standard than Miss Dewsnap. At least not one who was in the slightest bit attractive anyway.

He would enjoy having some cute young thing running around for him, but his wife would not stand for such perks, which was a shame as he would prove to be an exceptionally generous employer for the right girl.

A quivering smile spread across his face; it was only what he deserved, after all. Almost singlehandedly, he kept the town running smoothly; land deeds, property sales, wills, birth, marriage and death certificates, divorces (admittedly not many of them), disputes, he arranged the collection of the town's taxes and made sure everyone was up to date with what they owed, not a cent more, not a cent less. He kept the town accounts, he minuted town meetings. Heck, he did everything required to keep the whole town *tickety*. And just what did he get as his reward? A drunk, half-mad wife and a slightly deranged old prune of a secretary.

It just wasn't right!

He carried his coffee to the window and looked down the street through the clear upper pane. The sun was shining, the town was out and about on its business, and everything looked as it should.

Mrs Godbold was ambling along the boardwalk with her youngest daughter Ruth. She was a fine-looking woman to admire on a sunny day, pretty as a picture with her wide-brimmed summer hat, cream dress and pert titties. Oh, the things he'd like to do to her. She was definitely on his to do list.

He just had to be patient and wait for his moment. And his moment was coming alright. He was going to get more of the things he deserved. Soon he was going to be free, soon he was going to have the thing he'd spent the last two years craving above all other. Soon he was going to get the keys to the kingdom.

And then every goddamn thing was just gonna be *real tickety...*

The Farmer

"You look... *spruced*."

"Do I?" Sye tried to sound nonchalant.

Cynthia Hallows looked up from her darning and fixed a steady eye upon her son. It made him feel guilty in one effortless movement. It was a trick she'd been using on him for as long as he could remember, and it still made him feel like she'd caught him with jam smeared over his face when he'd been supposed to have been doing his chores.

"Sunday best, I'd say."

"It's Saturday."

"Yes, precisely, and you're off into town. Again. Looking *spruced...*"

He glanced down at the better of his two pairs of shoes and tried not to shuffle them.

"If you've got something on your shoe, go clean it off in the yard, not on my only good rug."

"Sorry, Ma."

His mother's face softened, "I know you're young and want to have some fun, but I don't like that saloon... it's no more than a fancy shop window for fallen women."

"I only eat there, Ma," he replied truthfully.

"Your father wouldn't approve at all."

The Burden of Souls

He stood in awkward silence as he often did when his mother invoked the memory of Tobias Hallows; God rest his soul.

"I don't do anything that would shame Pa," he said eventually, though his Father was entitled to cut him a bit of slack; after all, he'd been doing most of the work on the farm since his old man's heart had given out and he'd gone down face first into the muddy furrows of the North Field one frosty February morning eight years ago.

His mother returned to her darning, "You seeing that Burgess girl tonight?"

He went back to inspecting his shoes. Ma had been trying to get him hitched for years; unfortunately, their respective lists for "desirable qualities in a wife" were so disparate that the only thing they really agreed on was the prospective candidate should be a girl.

Mrs Hallows wanted a solid, reliable young woman, from a good family, well versed in homely skills, with a strong constitution and not averse to rolling her sleeves up to help birth a calf or sow a field. Her son was more interested in a cute smile, plunging cleavage, sparkling eyes, the ability to make him laugh and kissable lips.

Particularly the kissable lips.

Life out here was hard, even more so on a small homestead than in Hawker's Drift itself; from burning summers to freezing winters and the back-breaking work required to keep a farm ticking over during both. A cute smile was a virtue that would not last forever, unlike, say, being able to birth a calf. But he wasn't interested in forever, or even next year. He was interested in now, and he'd let tomorrow look after itself; after all, who knew if they would even be around to see tomorrow anyway? Maybe tomorrow he'd be face first in the mud like Pa.

No, he knew what he wanted, and he wasn't going to compromise, no matter how much his Ma might complain. He wanted a wife who was beautiful and funny and smart and who would make him ridiculously happy.

And if she just so happened to sing like an angel too...

"No, I'm not seeing Estelle."

"Why ever not?"

He considered mentioning the fact most of their dairy cows had smaller backsides and better table manners than Estelle Burgess but doubted his Ma would quite see the problem, "She's been stepping out with Albie Huggins."

Mrs Hallows rolled her eyes and sighed expansively, "Well, that's another good un you've let slip through your fingers, my boy – it's not like there are herds of eligible girls around here, you know?"

On that point, at least, they could agree.

"So, what's your plan now? The Hortez girl, she's just turned sixteen, bit waifish for my liking, but she might fill out a bit in time. Actually, I did hear from Mrs Coburg that..."

He drifted off. It was a very well-trodden path. Ma would take a good long while to rattle through all the unattached young women in Hawker's Drift and the surrounding area. He also knew better than to interrupt, as she'd just think he wasn't taking the matter seriously. Then she'd inevitably conclude he'd been spending his time cavorting with whores at *Jack's* and generally blackening the family name when he should have been tracking down prospective brides.

Although he *was* interested in a particular girl, he knew it wouldn't appease his Ma any given she worked at *Jack's*. Regardless of any other qualities, that alone would be enough for his Ma to disapprove of her thoroughly.

Cece Jones...

Even her name excited him. She was beautiful, smart, talented, and, unlike most of the girls he'd met before, he could actually talk to her! This was, in Sye Hallows opinion, a significant bonus.

For the most part, he turned into a fumbling, tongue-tied buffoon around girls, or at least the ones featuring on Hawker's Drift's Young and Eligible list anyway. But Cece was different; she seemed so confident and assured, not to mention exotic and exciting. Wherever she was from, it was nowhere near Hawker's Drift.

The thought of the two of them disappearing over the horizon had crossed his mind more than once since he'd met her. He had his guitar, she had her incredible voice. They could travel forever, singing for food and rent, seeing the world. No cares other than which fork in the road to take. No more rising before dawn, no more shovelling cow dung, no more mud. No more grass. No more farm.

Even more than his disinterest in the childbearing potential of a girl's hips, the stoutness of her shoulders or the quality of her bread making, it was the thing he could never mention to his Ma. He didn't want to marry a girl suited to life on the farm because he didn't want that life for himself.

He wanted to roam, and explore, and love, and laugh and live! Which, by and large, were all things his Ma neither cared for nor understood. All that mattered was the farm, their small homestead out on the grass, which the Hallows had been working for generations. She wanted someone to take over from her, someone who could be trusted to look after him, someone who would produce the next generation to be tethered to this small patch of flat grass-covered land.

And it would break her heart to know her only child wanted nothing more than to run away from it.

The Widow

Molly stared at the figure on the sheet of paper before her. She cursed. Again. She'd always considered herself quite inventive when it came to cussing, but no matter however colourful the abuse she threw at the figure, it remained the same, as stubborn and ugly as a mule; a small, flea-bitten, and wholly inadequate mule at that.

Was that all her life was worth? *Really?* Every last thing she owned didn't come to a fraction of the sum her fool of a dead husband owed the Mayor. They'd made good money since coming to Hawker's Drift, but saving had never been one of Tom's strong points.

She screwed the list up and threw it across the room. Which wasn't at all satisfying. She needed something that would break, preferably loudly and spectacularly, while she screamed the foulest words she could think of. Sadly, the only suitable thing to hand was a bottle of whiskey, and she wasn't quite desperate enough to waste hard liquor yet.

Outside the window, her new friends were still loitering across the street. They looked bored. She guessed they'd look even more bored in three months' time.

Was the Mayor really so worried she'd skip town? Admittedly, she would if she could, but the only way out of the town was the supposedly twice-weekly stagecoach, and the stage office, like virtually everything else in the town, was owned, directly or indirectly, by the Mayor. She'd never be able to buy a fare without it getting back to her new chaperones, and even if she did, they'd ride her down.

Maybe she could get a horse. No doubt the livery had been briefed not to sell her one without reporting it. She could just steal one and ride off into the night. Of course, if they caught her, she'd be hung as a horse thief, strung up high in the town square for her neighbours to gawp at. Unlike poor Tom, she'd get a bumper crowd to see her off. A good hanging was as much about public entertainment as law and order in Hawker's Drift.

How far could she walk? They were a long way from anywhere here. Save for a ring of farms and ranches, nothing but grass circled the town for an awful lot of miles. They'd just catch her and bring her back. And when her three months were up? She didn't know what the Mayor had in mind for her, but she suspected it was something she wouldn't like.

Her only hope was to find the provisions Tom had bought, but she'd run out of places to look. For a fool, he'd turned out to have a remarkable talent for hiding stuff.

If there *was* anything to hide, of course.

She poured herself another slug of whiskey. It had crossed her mind all the bills might be false, that, for reasons unknown, the Mayor just wanted her to stay in town. That was just nonsense. Why would the Mayor want to keep her in town? It made no sense; if they thought she knew something she wasn't supposed to, why didn't they just kill her? If they thought she knew nothing, then why not let her leave?

Her eyes moved over the stack of bills. If they weren't real, most of the town was in on the game. Mr Murphy in the livery had confirmed he'd sold Tom a horse and two mules, and no, he didn't know what he'd done with them. Mrs Pickering had sold him dried foodstuff, Mr Smith had sold him a rifle and ammunition, Mr Jacobson had sold him a tent and a shovel, Mr Calhoun had sold him dynamite (which she'd thought was a bit odd for a baker).

They'd all confirmed he'd come into their shops, and all had no idea what he'd done with the goods he'd bought. Apparently, Tom had just mumbled something about having "plans" when he'd been asked.

That, at least, sounded like Tom; shifty and uncommunicative.

Accepting her husband had been breezing around town buying provisions, all on the Mayor's credit, was one thing, but she didn't have a clue what he'd done with them or why he'd bought them.

She didn't know what else she could do to find the stuff. The only conclusion she could come to was that he'd stashed them away from Hawker's Drift, the town whose limits she was now precluded from leaving.

However, she figured one person in town might have an idea why Tom had bought so much prospecting equipment.

*

"I've come to see the Mayor," she announced the moment the door swung open.

A tall, wiry twist of a man with a long, wide nose and a small, narrow mouth peered down at her. She felt beads of sweat forming on her neck, partly due to nerves and partly from the sun beating fiercely down on the front door of the Mayor's Residence. The heat didn't seem to concern the man who'd opened the door, however; he wore a long black coat, a woollen vest and sharply starched collars.

She didn't recognise him; it seemed even a small town harboured a few strangers.

She'd half expected to be shooed away; instead, the man stepped back and cracked what might have been either a thin smile or a thinner grimace and ushered her inside.

"The Mayor's expecting you," he said as she crossed the threshold into the bright hallway.

"He is?"

"The Mayor is sensitive to the needs of his constituents," the man closed the door, which was heavy and studded with iron, "almost precognitive, in fact."

"Shame he didn't know my husband was gonna fall off his horse... that would have been useful." she met the man's gaze and held it.

The Mayor knew damn well Tom was going to fall off his horse, and it had squat to do with precognition, but either the man really was in the dark about her husband's death, or he didn't find redheads with a big mouth particularly intimidating. His long face remained utterly impassive.

Of course, she might just be plain wrong, and the Mayor was entirely innocent. But being wrong was something she usually considered the unlikeliest scenario in any given situation.

"Please, come this way, Mrs McCrea..." he said, after a further moment of not being intimidated.

"I don't believe we've been introduced?"

He rested one hand lightly on her elbow and indicated which way she should walk with the flattened palm of the other, "No, we haven't."

"Then how do you know my name?"

The man smiled his tight-lipped little smile again; it looked like the smile of a man to whom such things didn't come naturally, "Your reputation precedes you..."

Reputation?

Despite her better judgement, she let that little remark pass and moved into a hallway dominated by an imposing staircase rising from mahogany floorboards polished to a mirror finish.

"And your name is?"

"You may call me Symmons."

"And you're the Mayor's flunky?"

"That would be one word. This way, please, Mrs McCrea..." he indicated the stairs.

Upstairs? The Mayor wasn't waiting for her in his bedroom, was he? She'd heard the stories, after all.

"Does everybody call you Symmons?" she was trying not to look too reluctant as they climbed the stairs, which were wide enough for them to walk side by side comfortably.

"Yes."

"Even your mother?"

"No," Symmons conceded, "she just called me a dumb halfwit. Mostly."

She glanced at Symmons to see if he was joking, but his face was as expressive as a brick wall, without even the flicker of what passed for one of his smiles inconveniencing his features.

"Halfwit?"

Symmons twitched a bony shoulder, "We were never close."

On the first-floor landing, Symmons indicated the nearest door, which he rapped a knuckle lightly upon and opened without waiting for a response. Standing aside, he nodded towards the room, "Thank you, it's been a pleasure."

Sweat was trickling down the back of her neck now, and she wished she'd put her hair up. Actually, she wished she'd stayed at home and poured more whiskey down her throat. She'd convinced herself that if the Mayor did want her dead, she'd be laid out beside Tom by now, and he wouldn't have gone to the trouble of giving her three months to settle her husband's debts.

That's what she'd thought when she'd been sitting in her own home, now...

The room was in shadow, light poured into the stairwell from a skylight and an ornate stained-glass window at the end of the landing, but the light seemed even more reluctant to cross the room's threshold than she was.

"Best not to keep the Mayor waiting," Symmons breathed, his lips suddenly next to her ear, "he's a very busy man." He placed his hand on the small of her back. She was sure he was going to shove her into the dimly lit room and slam the door shut, cutting her off from the light of the world.

"Well, if it isn't convenient-"

"Not at all, Mrs McCrea, please do come in..." a deep sonorous voice drifted out of the room and then Symmons did push her, though so gently it could scarcely be described as such. Not in a court of law anyway.

Faced with the choice of barging Symmons aside and rushing down the stairs like a little girl afraid of the dark or doing what she'd come here to do, she flicked a few strands of hair back, gave Symmons a smile tight-lipped enough for him to have patented and strode into the room with the air of a woman who knew what the fuck she was doing.

She was relieved Symmons left the door open behind her, and it was not, after all, the Mayor's bedroom but his study.

Wooden shutters barred the windows, allowing only smudged light to snick around the edges. Floor to ceiling bookshelves covered every wall, save for the windows and the door. A massive scroll top desk squatted before the windows. The desk was quite bare, save for the Mayor's booted feet, which were hooked up on top of it while he reclined in an upholstered chair large enough to consume him. It almost seemed some monstrous disembodied maw had swallowed the Mayor and only his legs remained to be gobbled up.

"Mrs McCrea, what a pleasure; I've been expecting you..." the Mayor made no move to stand or even remove his feet from the desk. It was his home, after all. His town, too, for that matter. The room smelt so strongly of sweet fragrant cigar smoke; blue-grey clouds should have been billowing about her, but the Mayor wasn't smoking, and there was no ashtray in sight.

"You have?" she bit back on a cough and glanced around. There were no other chairs in the room, forcing her to stand in front of the desk, hands clutched before her, like a schoolgirl sent to the headmaster's office to explain her poor behaviour.

"In my experience, when someone owes a considerable amount of money, they usually either run away or go to see their creditor. You haven't run away."

"Well, given the men you have stalking me, I couldn't run away, even if I wanted to."

The Mayor laughed, "Which you do, of course."

"I have family back east; I have a life to rebuild after my husband's... accident."

"There's nothing for you back east... there's nothing much for anybody, in fact. You should stay here. It's where the future is."

"I don't seem to have much choice. Which is why I'm here."

"I'm always happy to listen to my citizen's woes."

"And help them?"

"Of course," the Mayor smiled, his teeth brilliant white even in the gloom.

Despite the fact Tom had been working for the Mayor, she'd only met him a few times; still, it had been more than enough for her to decide she didn't like the man much. He was too neat for her liking, too fastidious, his suits always sharply pressed, his hair precisely greased back, his beard trim and carefully shaped. Then there was his eye. It rarely stopped moving; it rolled just around the socket, seldom settling on anything. She didn't know how he'd lost the left one, but she wouldn't have been surprised if it hadn't just popped out of the socket like a ball on an overspun roulette wheel. His eye patch was incongruous, too, an old, battered piece of leather fixed to his head with what looked like frayed boot laces.

Why go to the trouble of wearing immaculate, and no doubt expensive, suits, fine silk shirts and shiny boots if you were just going to tie a piece of leather that looked like it had been hacked from a blacksmith's second-best apron over your eye?

"I want to know why Tom bought prospecting provisions?"

"Really?" The Mayor seemed amused, "Now you do surprise me. I wouldn't have put money on that being your first question."

"What did you expect me to ask?"

"Oh, something along the lines of *I is just a poor helpless widow, this is nothing to do with little ol' me, can't you see your way to letting me off the money I owes. Pleeeease...*" he slipped his boots from the desk and partially extracted himself from his cavernous chair to rest his arms on the desk, "Maybe you'd even flutter your eyelashes at me and try to look all... oh, I don't know... vulnerable and needy?"

"That was going to be my second question."

The Mayor chuckled, "I like you, Molly, I honestly do..."

"I want to know why Tom bought prospecting provisions?" she repeated, her words slow and careful this time. She didn't like the way the conversation was turning. Had he expected her to flirt with him? Did he want her to? She wasn't that desperate yet. In fact, she'd throw her best whiskey bottle against the wall long before she got that desperate.

"Why else would a man want prospecting equipment? He thought there was gold in them there hills."

"There are no hills here... other than the one this town sits on anyway."

"You know Molly," he said, puckering up his lips and wagging an index finger in her direction, "if I'm honest, I always thought that was the flaw in Tom's plan."

"Yet you still gave him money?"

"I liked his zeal. I liked his get up and go. I encourage such qualities in my citizens. It's what makes Hawker's Drift what it is!"

A strange, messed up little town in the middle of nowhere.

The Mayor's eye stopped moving, fixing on her as if she had said or done something worthy of capturing his attention. Or thought something. She smiled at the Mayor as sweetly as she could and told herself to stop being silly. He was an unsettling man, but he couldn't read her mind.

"You've never been much taken with our little town, have you, Molly? Stuck away out here in the middle of nowhere..." the Mayor eased himself back into the maw of his yawning chair.

Her smile faltered, and she suddenly felt much less silly about believing the Mayor could hear her thoughts.

"More a case of the town not being taken with me."

"What could possibly make you think that? You are quite cherished."

"So cherished nobody came to my husband's funeral?" she snapped, feeling awkward, foolish, and patronised all at the same time. None of which were good for her temper.

"Well, the weather was quite awful – and you know how dangerous the storms can be out here. I believe Preacher Stone did recommend postponing, did he not?"

"I wanted to get away; I saw no point hanging around for some sunshine."

"Well, there you go then."

She blinked, "People didn't come because it was *raining*?"

"People didn't come," the Mayor corrected carefully, "because they felt insulted."

"Insulted! How?"

"Because you made it clear you were running out on us. We're a real close-knit little family out here, Molly. We have to be. People don't like being snubbed."

"Snubbed! They snubbed Tom and me!"

"Ssssh," the Mayor insisted, blowing his cheeks out and patting down the air in front of him with little flicking movements of his hands. His fingernails were spotlessly clean and buffed to neat, precise little crescents.

"Now, there's no need to get all uppity, and there's no need to worry either. Now you're going to be staying with us; I'm sure everybody will be prepared to overlook your previous discourtesy."

She was about to protest again, but the Mayor just talked her down, his eye roving over her as he spoke, "Though it would help if you dressed appropriately – you are a widow after all."

"Black doesn't suit me."

"My dear, black suits simply everyone…"

"I can see that," she stared pointedly at the Mayor's cream suit, upon which she couldn't see even the tiniest fleck of dirt.

"Well, if that will be all. I do have quite a lot of work to do," he swept a languid hand over his empty desk.

"So, you don't know why Tom wanted those provisions?"

"I think I've answered that already."

"And I don't suppose you know where they are?"

"No. I don't…" the Mayor was starting to sound bored, and his eye had returned to wandering around the room as if he were desperately looking for something more entertaining.

"Am I allowed to leave town to look for them?"

"You seem so preoccupied with getting out of Hawker's Drift. It really is quite disappointing."

"I don't have the money Tom borrowed off you, and I don't know what he did with the provisions!"

"How unfortunate."

"What will happen to me if I can't pay you back?"

His neat little beard split to reveal his white teeth, "Oh, there's more than one way to pay me back, Molly. I'm a man who accepts all manner of currencies…"

"And what exactly does that mean?"

Her tongue felt like it was sticking to the roof of her mouth from the sickly fumes filling the room; her head had started to throb too. Though that might just have been from the whiskey she'd drunk earlier.

"You will have a substantial debt to work off; you'll need to be flexible."

"How flexible?"

"Well, the customer's upstairs in *Jack's* always appreciate a flexible girl..."

"*What!?* You expect me to-"

"Symmons!"

"Yes, sir."

Symmons appeared at her side, his hand curling around her elbow.

"Mrs McCrea will be leaving now; please see her out."

"Yes, sir."

"Good day, Mrs McCrea; it's been a pleasure, but please do excuse me; I must catch up on my work," the Mayor smiled toothily before hooking his feet back up on his desk and fading away into the shadows of his chair.

She tried to protest but found herself back out on the landing, looking at the door Symmons had closed behind them.

"I hope you found the meeting satisfactory?" Symmons slid between Molly and the door.

"Well, I guess I know where I stand now," she managed to say without spitting.

Seeing no point in making a scene (she'd become terribly responsible in recent years), she followed Symmons glumly down the stairs.

"Well, good day; I'm sure we'll be seeing each other again soon," Symmons said.

"I don't think the Mayor wants me bothering him again."

"Actually, the Mayor is most accommodating. Always," Symmons insisted, "but that's not what I meant."

"Oh?"

"I shall enjoy seeing you when you're working upstairs at *Jack's*," Symmons said in the kind of tone you would use to discuss the weather before adding with the faintest ghost of a snigger, "I have a feeling you'll make a most fetching and comely whore."

With that, he gave a shallow nod and slammed the door in her face.

The Gunslinger

A little knot of people had gathered to gawp in the square.

He didn't have much time for gawpers; people should have better things to do than standing around with their jaws dangling in the air. However, as he crossed Pioneer Square, which was the official name of the mud patch housing the town's gallows, he found himself joining the slack-jawed timewasters watching Molly McCrea.

She was standing in front of the Mayor's grandiose pile of bricks, bent almost double as she screamed profanities at an apathetic and unresponsive front door.

The little gathering was shuffling about in the semi-solidified mud the sun had been gently baking, muttering like gossips at the back of a church congregation unable to hold their tongues till the sermon was over.

He hovered behind the townsfolk; their curiosity and amazement were making the air hum like overtightened guitar strings.

"Girl's got some temper," one of the gawpers commentated, spitting black chewy-looking phlegm at the ground, "...some mouth too..."

"I heard she owes the Mayor a goodly sum of money," a lumpy woman in a floral dress replied.

"I'm guessing she just found out the Mayor ain't for writing off what he's owed," the old spitter added with a chuckle that faded quickly when no one else took it up.

"Why should he?" The woman demanded, "just cos she's a looker don't see why she should get off owing money. Just ain't fair."

The old man nodded, "Mayor's always fair, gotta say that, good titties or not..."

His fellow townsfolk mumbled their agreement and made sure everybody could see how vigorously they were nodding their head.

"You folks here all like your Mayor?"

No one answered; a few glanced his way but most kept their attention firmly fixed on the foul-mouthed widow. He was reminded of the feeling that came just before someone went for their gun. Given none of the townsfolk were carrying anything more dangerous than a loaf of bread, he decided he was safe.

"Not so popular then..."

The old man swivelled sharply around, his eyes hooded against the afternoon sun, jawing furiously upon his chewing tobacco, "No one said that, son..."

"People don't seem to want to talk about him much," Amos remembered the way John X had grown silent when the Mayor had cropped up in their conversation.

"We just keep our business to ourselves in this town," the old man snapped, returning his attention to the redhead hurling curses at the Mayor's door.

"Anyone told her?" he nodded towards Molly, but when he didn't get a response, he pushed on. He usually liked being ignored, but something was gnawing at him about this town and its Mayor.

"Has he been Mayor here long?"

"What's it to you?" the florally decorated woman demanded, taut hostility in her voice.

"Nothing, just passing through looking for work. Thought the Mayor might be a good place to start."

The tension eased a little, and the woman's voice softened, "I think he's got all the help he needs."

"Ma?" A boy next to the floral woman tugged her sleeve. He was clutching an epic sandwich, two roughly hewn slabs of bread enclosing a great drooping lump of pink fibrous meat.

"Yes, dear?"

"What's a mother-cunting son of a pox-ridden cum rag?"

She gave the question some consideration before replying, "I'm not entirely sure, dear, but it sounds like she's met your father."

The boy nodded, bit into his sandwich, and eventually worried a chunk off.

And then they were gone. Like a sudden gust of wind whipping smoke from a fire, the only sound being the choking noise the youngster made as his mother dragged him across the drying mud.

The widow stomping across the square directly towards him explained the sudden dispersal, her face flushed to a furious red and hair flying like the mane of a charging lion.

He wasn't entirely sure if she was heading straight for him because she'd grown tired of insulting a wooden door and wanted to scream at something more rewarding, or he just happened to be planted in the middle of her wild trajectory between the Mayor's front door and her destination; which he figured, through a combination of simple geometry and the little he knew of her, was probably the saloon.

He took a few hurried steps to the left, and, as she hurtled by, her eyes flicked in his direction. He tapped a finger against his hat in greeting, "Yeah, I know, I'm an asshole."

At least she didn't shoulder charge him this time; instead, whooshing past in silence, leaving only a hint of lavender and whiskey in her wake to mingle with the mud and horse dung.

As he suspected, she *was* making for the saloon.

He'd been heading there himself but now wasn't sure whether to change his plans. Company was something he tried to avoid; a foul-mouthed liquor swilling widow shouldn't be any different.

Except...

He noticed two men sauntering across the square, not quite treading in her footsteps. They'd been lounging on a bench outside the livery, but it seemed they suddenly needed a drink too.

Despite the afternoon heat, they wore long, unfastened dusters that billowed enough as they walked to reveal their guns. They both strolled with arrogant casual ease and had roughly hewn, weathered faces softened only by stubbly half-formed beards. One of them had been in the saloon the previous day when he'd chatted briefly to the widow. He knew them well enough, or their type at least. Violent and not overly bright; he'd killed plenty just like them.

They noticed him watching; neither acknowledged the attention, but both let their eyes wash over him for a few seconds before dismissing him.

He watched them follow the widow into the saloon and then looked around Pioneer Square. The townsfolk were going about their business; two boys squatted by the gallows playing a game with coins, a wagon with a couple of farmhands trundled by, women carried groceries, old men chewed the cud on street corners, a man was grooming a horse outside the stables. Nobody seemed concerned about the two men who'd followed Molly across the square.

Two killers wearing silver stars.

The Mayor's Residence pulled his eye back. A man leant out of a first-floor window, arms braced on the ledge. He was leaning out so far that, for a moment, it seemed he was going to dive straight into the square.

He wore a cream jacket and an eyepatch. Hair slicked back, he sported a short, neat beard split with an ear-to-ear grin. Someone seemed singularly pleased with the world.

"Mr Mayor, I presume..."

The Mayor's gaze snapped down as if he'd heard his name. The grin slowly faded as his head cocked to one side. The gunslinger touched his hat in greeting. The Mayor made no response; instead, he slid back into the shadows after a few seconds as if he'd been lying on a wheeled trolley. The window slammed shut once his face had faded into the darkness.

Amos turned and headed for the saloon.

*

"You're all going to burn in hellfire and damnation!"

"No doubt," Monty Jack's hands slid up and down his apron, "but save your preaching for the church or the street corner or whatever fucked up circus you came from, not my saloon!"

Monty and his skinny young barman, Sonny, retreated inside, leaving the man sprawled in the mud. The pair had evidently dragged him out of the saloon and tossed him off the boardwalk.

"Anything broke?" he offered the old man a hand up.

"Nope," the man peered up at him, his expression more curious than suspicious, "Don't know you, do I?"

"New in town," he replied, hand still outstretched, "just passing through."

"Best not to linger in this godless place," the man accepted his hand and allowed himself to be hauled up. Despite his reticence when it came to touching people, he couldn't leave the man in the dirt; he was old, exceedingly fat and was wearing, what appeared to be, a clown's suit.

Thankfully, this time, nothing flooded his senses bar the smell of last week's sweat.

The old man went through the motions of brushing himself down, but his baggy yellow and black checked three-piece was so covered in dirt, dust, and stains of various hues that the only effect was to shift some of the grime around a bit. He wore a battered derby from under which bright red tufts of spiky hair protruded. A paper rose hung limply from his lapel. It had likely once been red, but the sun had long since faded it to a dirty pink; his face, however, appeared to have travelled in the opposite direction and was so red it fell only a little short of beetroot.

His face floated above several chins, and small restless eyes looked out from behind a nose that was unmistakably his own despite being red and bulbous. Comedy noses tended not to be covered in blackheads and crisscrossed by networks of broken veins.

He glanced at the old man's boots, which were worn, scuffed and down at heel, as well as elongated enough for the slightly curled up toes to be resting on top of his own more conventional footwear.

"Obliged!"

The man produced an oversized handkerchief that was too filthy to wipe a pig down. He dabbed his face. It wasn't immediately obvious whether it was his face or the handkerchief that got any cleaner.

"You're welcome," he replied, torn between asking the man why he'd been thrown out of the saloon and why he wore a clown's outfit.

The old man shoved his faded handkerchief away and grinned, "Anyway, must dash, parties to be hosted and sinners to be saved! If you ever need anything, do feel free to ask."

"I'll keep that in mind."

"Yes, you do that," he stuck out a hand from a frayed and grubby sleeve, "the name's Mr Wizzle."

"Wizzle?"

"'cos I'm a guy that's gotta lot a fizzle!" He pumped Amos' hand and held it tightly as he laughed heartily enough to send drool bombs rocketing from his big fleshy lips.

He smiled, the man was clearly not dealing from a full deck, but he seemed harmless enough.

"Anyways, I really gotta go, lotta souls in need of saving, don't want 'em spit-roasted on the devil's pitchfork before I get there. Do we, eh?"

Well, probably harmless.

Mr Wizzle's hand sprung open, and he waddled off down the street, whistling something tuneless, his hands still flapping at his jacket as if he could just pat it down hard enough, he might just get some of the dirt to fall off.

*

Inside the saloon, he let the miasma of smoke and warm beer fumes replace the stink of drying mud, horse dung and Mr Wizzle's body odour (in that respect, at least, he certainly did fizzle).

Molly the widow perched at one end of the bar; the usual suspects clustered together at the other end. It looked like they'd all either shuffled along to avoid her, or they'd convened an impromptu meeting of the local barfly steering committee.

Her two dark little shadows had taken up residence by the door. Neither were drinking, both were staring at the bar.

The more he looked at those two, the less he liked them. Their eyes were cold, feral, and almost unblinking. Predators stalking fresh meat.

The sensible thing would be to go to his room, take a nap, polish his boots, clean his gun while daydreaming about emptying the chamber into Severn's chest. Pretty much anything. He'd no need to get involved in the widow's business. But he really didn't like those two men at all; they made his brain itch. Itsy-bitsy spiders were scuttling about behind his eyes again...

And there was something about her as well, but he tried to ignore that.

She didn't look up when he sat next to her, though her eyes momentarily flicked in his direction. He got his beer and free whiskey from Sonny and slid the shot glass in front of her without asking.

"I'm off whiskey," she nodded at the beer in front of her.

"Very wise, that stuff gets folk drunk enough to cause a scene real easy. We wouldn't want that."

"No," Molly downed the whiskey in one before adding through her grimace, "not twice in one day."

"What was that all about, in front of the Mayor's?"

"I failed my audition for citizen of the year," her hands curled back around the beer glass, "I handle disappointment badly."

"There's always next year."

She snorted and half-turned to look at him, "Oh, I'll be eligible for all sorts of new categories next year," she was trembling slightly. Anger and fear buzzed around her like agitated wasps.

"Creative use of language?"

She smiled, just a little, and shook her red mane, "You should steer clear of me, follow the example of the rest of the town," she looked pointedly down the bar, "even the drunks have that much sense."

"Your beloved Mayor?"

"Yeah..." she twitched a shoulder and drained her beer, "he's a real piece of work."

"Tell me about him, and I'll get you another."

"Not a good idea," she forced a smile and started to slip from her stool.

"Be careful, Molly; those two men want to kill you," he said in a low voice before he could stop himself, nodding discreetly towards the deputies who'd followed her in.

She froze, one foot on the ground, eyes fixed on him, "They're just making sure I don't skip town; the Mayor has plans for me."

"Maybe that's what they've been told... but those kinds of men have a habit of doing what they want, eventually."

"I know well enough the kinds of shit inside men's heads. Don't mean they're ever going to do anything about it."

"Maybe... but be careful all the same."

"You got an interesting way of hitting on a girl, Mister," she forced a weak smile and slipped off the stool.

"I'm not hitting on you."

I'm not, am I? God help me...

"Just a good Samaritan? Or a guardian angel then?"

"No... I've just seen the things such men are capable of..."

She hesitated, fingers resting on the seat of her vacated stool as her eyes turned briefly towards the men by the door.

When she saw they were watching her intently, she looked sharply away, focusing on the bottles lining the shelf behind the bar rather than meeting Amos' stare.

"The one on the left is Blane, been a Deputy since Tom and I came here. Never spoken to him. Never actually seen anyone speak to him much, for that matter. The other one is new and hasn't been in town long, but they're both working for the Mayor now."

"Is everyone employed by the Mayor a killer?"

Molly shrugged, "Men with guns – all much the same. No offence."

He smiled in return but didn't feel the need to explain how he was different from the two men watching her.

She was scared enough already.

The Songbird

She held the last note long after the ratchety untuned piano had fallen silent.

When she finally peeled open her eyes, the crowd remained hushed, so quiet the only sound she could hear was her own heart; no murmuring, no clinking of glasses, no laughter, no tortured protests from the ill-fitting floorboards. Only rows of faces, hundreds of eyes fixed upon her, like a huge pride of lions surrounding an unfortunate gazelle.

Had they not liked her final song of the evening?

Then the applause started, not a ripple building to a crescendo as people joined in but exploding as if everyone in the saloon had been awaiting some specific instruction. Cece fought down the urge to see if one of the saloon girls had appeared behind her, holding up a whopping great placard with the word "APPLAUSE!!" written on it, which was a stupid notion for several reasons, most notably the fact most of the room probably couldn't read.

The clapping was accompanied by whistles, shouts, foot-stomping and palms slapping tables. Everybody was standing. Those at the back had raised hands above their heads; one particularly enthusiastic fellow was jumping up and down, arms flailing about as if engaged in maniacal star jumps.

Cece felt her cheeks redden and flashed an awkward little smile. She wondered how they would have responded to something more upbeat than a song about heroin addiction. Spontaneous combustion?

More people were in the saloon every time she sang. Monty had insisted she performed every night; he wanted his monies worth for the pokey little attic room and kitchen leftovers he was paying her with. Tonight, the place was stuffed to the rafters. She wasn't sure how many people would usually have been here, but she suspected it was an exceptionally good night for *Jack's* from the width of Monty's grin. The saloon girls looked equally flustered and busy, though not necessarily as pleased as Monty.

She recognised a few of the faces, though most were new to her. The farm boy, Sye, was at the front, where he'd been when she'd glanced down from the first-floor balcony almost two hours before she was due to start singing. He seemed very keen. Not just on her singing either, she suspected. At least he seemed harmless. Which she couldn't say about some of the men who'd been staring at her during the performance.

She closed her eyes, took a deep breath, and hoped she just looked like she was milking the applause. Why had she come here? *Really?* She could have said no after all. She could have done so many other things with her life, but she'd chosen to come here. To this dirty outpost of humanity. It'd seemed important, not so very long ago, now... now she was actually here, she wasn't so sure.

She'd felt so confident before, capable of handling anything this world could throw at her, but she'd her friends and family to fall back on then. And Quayle, of course, who she'd never expected to miss as much as she did. Now she was utterly alone and felt like a small lost little girl.

This was a dangerous place. Most of the men carried guns, and even the ones that didn't looked like they could break her clean in two with no trouble at all. Quite a few of them looked like they'd enjoy doing it too.

But that wasn't it; if anyone tried any nonsense, they'd get a very nasty surprise. It was the way they stared at her that unnerved her. She hadn't thought that would have been the biggest problem coming here. She'd had plenty of practice when it came to men staring at her, after all, and as much as she told herself men were much the same wherever they were, once you boiled off the manners, culture and learning at least, she couldn't shake the feeling the men here actually *were* different. Bestial, hungry, savage. Pick your word; they all unnerved her much the same.

She tried to ignore their stares, along with the haze of smoke burning her throat and the stink of warm beer and warmer bodies permeating the place. She'd heard about men undressing women with their eyes but had thought it just a saying. However, now she stood before the bellowing crowd, she felt at least half-naked, and she didn't doubt a significant proportion of the men in the place would happily finish the job with their rough bare hands given half the chance.

So, she'd concentrated on her singing and trying to get something vaguely in tune to come out of the old piano, using the music as a blanket to wrap around herself while her eyes slid across the crowd, not lingering on any one spot. That's what she'd tried to do anyway.

A man sat at the front, dressed in an immaculate black three-piece suit. He wore an eye patch, which didn't entirely make him unique amongst the patrons of *Jack's Saloon* given a number of men were missing body parts of one kind or another. He did stand out for being clean though, his clothes were spotless, his hair oiled and precisely combed back, his beard surgically precise.

Her gaze stubbornly refused to ignore him.

He'd arrived only a few minutes before she started to sing. The saloon had already been packed, but the crowd parted instantly, a chair conjured and placed before her piano. Even Sye had shuffled aside without complaint.

Although the chair was not exactly a throne, that's what it reminded her of. It was heavy and sturdy; whereas most of the chairs in the saloon would splinter to firewood if you threw them against a wall (or a fellow drinker's head), this one looked like it would go clean through. High-backed and thick-legged, it was clearly a special chair.

The one-eyed man wasn't alone. Two men had positioned themselves behind him. They were the only people, other than a couple of the saloon girls, who hadn't clapped during the entire night. They had remained blank-faced as their gaze continually swept the crowd. They wore silver stars pinned beneath the long coats they never took off despite the heat generated by so many bodies in one confined, smoky place. She supposed they were town deputies, though "goons" might be a more accurate title.

Neither of the men had said a word, they hadn't taken a drink and their hands never wandered far from the heavy functional gun belts slung around their waists. They were neither young nor old; weathered faces, hard and quite, quite expressionless. They looked like military men to her, though she knew there was nothing that passed for a military out here. They did, however, represent what passed for the law, and she suspected the law was whatever the one-eyed man said it was.

She didn't know the man's title, but king or emperor would pass as well as any other. Hawker's Drift was his domain. It might be small, remote, and worthless, but it was all his.

As the hubbub diminished and a sizeable portion of the crowd crashed against the bar in a thirsty wave, Sye appeared, eyes and grin about as wide as a human face could bear.

"That was incredible! You sound better every time you sing!"

Cece twitched her shoulders, "Well, I am a bit rusty; I haven't sung properly for a while."

"That's just a crime. Really... you should be on the biggest stage in the world!"

She laughed now; from most people, such gratuitous flattery would have smacked of ingratiation, but Sye's face was open and honest enough to believe he genuinely meant what he was gushing.

"Oh, I don't know about that... it gets me by."

"You should be doing more than just getting by!" He looked at an old, chipped brandy glass sitting atop the piano in expectation of tips, empty save for a couple of derisory coins, "You going to take that around?"

She pulled a face, "If people want to tip, they can, but I'm not going to beg. I get food and lodgings."

Sye snorted, "You're doubling Monty's takings; he should be paying you a damn sight more than that!" He suddenly looked aghast, "Sorry, Miss, I didn't mean to cuss."

"That's ok, really. I've heard worse..." she looked up at him before adding, "...and please, call me Cece, not Miss. I'm not a schoolteacher."

"Of course!" Sye beamed, "I knew that; all schoolteachers are kinda old and crabby."

"I don't think that's actually a requirement for the job."

"No? I guess you weren't schooled in Hawker's Drift then..."

"Can't say I was."

He grinned and spent an almost indecent amount of time looking at her before snatching up the glass, "Well, if you aren't going to get these skinflints to pay you your worth, I will."

"No, Sye, please..." she laughed as he began bounding around the saloon, thrusting the brandy glass in people's faces and demanding money. Hopefully, he knew what he was doing.

"He is right, you know; you are worth more than a few dimes..." she turned around to find the one-eyed man behind her. She hadn't noticed how incongruous his eye patch was from a distance; the saloon was only dimly lit. Up close she could see it was just a cracked and balding scrap of ancient leather fixed around his head with a frayed bootlace. It would have complimented their attire perfectly on most of *Jack's* clientele, but against this man's spotless black cotton suit, crisply pressed white shirt and meticulous grooming, it seemed singularly odd.

"People generally get what they're worth, in the end ..."

"People generally get what they take, Miss Jones," he corrected, his eyebrow clicking up a notch.

"You have me at an advantage; I have no idea what your name is?"

There was something decidedly odd about the man's good eye, she didn't want to be rude and stare at it, but it seemed to move constantly. Not randomly, but in small, precise, almost mechanical movements.

"I'm the Mayor," he said, claiming her hand and kissing it, "Welcome to Hawker's Drift."

Ah, the Mayor, but you think of yourself in grander terms than that, I bet.

"I still don't know your name?"

"Mr Mayor usually gets my attention."

"Mr Mayor? Does that mean your parents christened you with something terribly embarrassing? Like... Hubert Fartwangel?"

He was probably used to a little more deference, but he let out a bellowing laugh all the same, "Why, I think you are going to fit in here perfectly – we need a little songbird to brighten our lives, so far away from everywhere."

"I shall do my best," she didn't much care for the title "little songbird" but wasn't going to argue with the Mayor over his choice of words. He was a man, she decided; it didn't pay to cross.

The Mayor's attention slid to the sad old excuse of a piano she'd been playing, "That thing, on the other hand, makes an awful din."

"I've tried to retune it," she shook her head, "but it needs to be put down."

"Agreed," the Mayor flicked his jacket back and rested his hand on the butt of his holstered pearl-handled pistol, "will one bullet to the head do the job, or will it require all six?"

He stared at her impassively, his eye, for once, coming to rest upon her as if, finally, she had done enough to warrant his full and undivided attention. He cracked a glittering smile as his hand fell away from the gun. "I will have a word with Mr Jack; you should have the tools for the job even if he is too graceless to pay you your worth."

"Are good pianos easy to come by out here?"

"Everything is possible here; you just need to know the right person to ask."

"Would the right person be you, Mr Mayor?"

"Oh, I can get almost anything the heart desires."

"For the right price?"

"Of course, everything has a price," he cracked that smile again, and his eye seemed to sparkle.

She blinked; it hadn't metaphorically sparkled. For just a moment, it seemed to have *literally* sparkled as if beneath the goo of his eyeball, a diamond had caught the last rays of a setting sun. Which was silly, of course - the light was just poor here. Nothing else.

"And what would the price of a good piano be?"

"Oh, for you, not so very much. Perhaps you'll be kind enough to come over to my home one evening and sing just for me. I think I would like that."

To her ears that sounded like a euphemism.

"And your good lady wife? Does she enjoy music?"

"Alas," he sighed, "there is no Mrs Mayor."

"I find that hard to believe."

"Because I am so devilishly handsome and charming?"

"No," she shook her head, "it's just unusual for a man of your age to be single."

The Mayor threw back his head and laughed again

"Oh, Miss Jones, I can assure you I may be old, but I look very good for my age."

"If you get me a good piano, I will sing for you, Mr Mayor," she smiled. What was the harm? It wasn't a good idea to antagonise the most powerful man in town, even if the town was a backward pile of sticks in the middle of nowhere. Besides, the chances of him conjuring a half-decent piano out of thin air were, she reckoned, fairly remote.

"Splendid," the Mayor beamed, "I will see you again soon." With that he nodded, spun on his heels, and plunged into the milling crowd of drinkers. His two shadows lingered to examine her, their eyes cold, their lips unmoving before they too turned and followed their master.

I can look after myself; he's nothing I can't deal with. Just because he wears a clean suit it doesn't make him any different from the rest of these savages.

She turned back to close the lid on the piano. Sye was standing behind her, the brandy glass half full of coins. He'd been watching her talk to the Mayor and wore a strange look on his open face. It took her a moment to recognise the expression.

    It was anguish.

The Gunsmith

Ash Godbold was a punctilious man.

He arrived for work at exactly nine o'clock every morning except Sunday, took precisely fifteen minutes to eat his lunch on the back stoop of Hawker's Drift's only barbershop, and he was always back home for dinner at six o'clock every day bar Wednesday, when he took the family to eat at *Rosa's*. Rain, shine, snow, or any of the other freaky weather they enjoyed out here.

It was, therefore, something of a surprise to his wife, Kate, when he came home at a little after ten-thirty that morning. It was also a surprise, not to mention an inconvenience, to John X Smith, given Mrs Godbold was enthusiastically blowing him at the time.

"Oh shiiit!" she hissed as soon as her mouth was empty. She just knelt there looking up at him, blue eyes wide and cute mouth agape.

Damned inconvenient.

"You home, hun?" Her husband called from downstairs. To John's ears, which had some experience in these matters, he sounded distracted, but not furious. It was the voice of a man who'd come home early for some innocent and mundane reason rather than a man who knew his wife had been up to no good and was eager to put matters right with his fists. Or his shotgun. He did a terrific line in cut-throat razors too.

However, if the delightful Kate remained in her current position much longer, that might change.

Taking her hands, he hauled Kate Godbold to her feet, "Go down, tell him you had a bad head," he whispered before quickly kissing the end of her slightly upturned nose.

She spread her arms and looked down at herself. She was quite naked. The gunsmith had a look, too; he genuinely couldn't help himself at times. She was a little thick around the middle, perhaps, but not in bad shape at all, smallish pert breasts, long straight strawberry blonde hair, a few freckles across her cheeks. She looked younger than she was. He thought she was as cute as a button.

"Hun?!"

He grabbed the robe he'd pulled off her and flung it over the end of the bed five minutes earlier and pushed her gently towards the bedroom door.

"Up here, baby, got a bit of a head!"

John X indicated his only slightly shrivelling cock and winked.

You!!! She mouthed silently before calling out, "Something wrong?"

He nodded towards the window as he made himself decent. She shook her head frantically and pointed across the landing towards the kids' rooms with an urgent jabbing motion. Her room looked out over the front. He supposed it would be hard to explain a semi-naked black man shining down your drainpipe to the neighbours.

"Bad head too... think I'm coming down with something..."

He pulled on his shirt, which was the only garment he'd gotten around to taking off – if Ash had taken just a little longer to get home, things would have been even more inconvenient – and waited, listening as Kate went down and fussed over her husband.

Ash, bless him, wasn't the brightest star in the firmament; hopefully, he would put his wife's flushed complexion and tousled hair down to her being unwell. If he noticed her at all.

He'd learnt a long time ago that plenty of men hardly noticed their wives.

He could hear the Godbold's talking, too quietly for him to follow, but the voices soon faded as Kate led her husband away from the hallway. He looked down at his booted feet. Should he take them off? It would be quieter to pad across the landing in his socks, but he didn't want to hang around longer than necessary. Although Ash Godbold was a burly man, he wasn't known for having a temper; however, discovering your wife was cheating on you was usually an excellent way to find one.

He tip-toed across the landing and through the open door; thankfully, the floorboards weren't warped or loose.

The Godbold's eldest daughter's room was small and tidy; Kate was quite fastidious about tidiness when she wasn't busy being unfaithful. A few old stuffed toys sat on the bed's crisply folded sheets, awaiting the girl's return. The room smelt fresh and clean, and he felt the additional thrill of being somewhere he shouldn't be, doing something he shouldn't be doing. It made him feel alive, and there were few things still capable of achieving that feat after all these years.

He'd never been in the room before, Emily Godbold was only sixteen after all and, therefore, of little interest to him (in a few years, maybe, but not now), and he took a moment to be sure of his bearings. The window was open and looked out over the Godbold's backyard, which was small and shaded by a couple of cherry trees.

He could hear no voices; he hoped Kate had steered her husband to the front of the house. Yes, he was sure she would. She was bright enough to work that one out. He popped his head through the window; there was a sloping veranda beneath, then a short drop into the garden.

And with a single bound, he was free...

He checked the room again. Still empty and no sound of footsteps thudding up the stairs either. He sat on the window ledge, swung one leg outside, ducked under the raised window and brought his trailing leg over. Without pausing, he edged down the veranda. It didn't feel particularly solid; it was only a shallow roof covering the back porch of the house. He hoped Ash hadn't decided to clear his head by sitting in the shade to take some air while sipping lemonade. Although seeing the town's gunsmith suddenly falling into the backyard might make him forget about his sore head for a bit.

He made it to the edge of the roof and paused again. No sounds from the house or the porch below; nobody was in sight. It wasn't a long drop to the yard, but he really was far too old for such stunts. In and out of the bedroom, if he was going to be honest.

He looked over his shoulder and let out a sigh. A sprained ankle was a lot better than a shotgun wound...

He hit the ground and rolled in one movement before coming up in a crouch.

Maybe not so old after all.

His heart was thundering, but everything else seemed ok. The back door stayed closed, no curtains twitched. He scurried down the garden, bent half-forward in the manner of a man desperately searching for a toilet.

The yard was small, only twenty yards or so long, and other than two cherry trees at the back and a few piles of assorted bric-a-brac, the only thing of note was a clothesline from which Mrs Godbold's functional and unflattering underwear flapped in the breeze. In his humble opinion, she looked a lot better without the bloomers.

A shoulder-high wooden fence marked the end of the yard; it didn't quite qualify as rickety, but he put his chances of scaling it without it collapsing under him at no better than fifty-fifty. However, there was a latched gate in one corner (the latch was currently being left off several mornings a week), and he let himself out into the narrow alley running between the houses on Icke's Street and Low Street. Quite why the alley was there, he didn't know as it served no obvious purpose other than for dumping the junk even more unwanted than the stuff in the backyards.

That and allowing discreet access to the homes of married ladies, of course.

The passage was known as Cherry Lane, thanks to the trees lining the yards on either side. Dumped Junk Lane would have been equally accurate. Other than some of the local kids who used it as a playground and the town's small but hardy community of tramps who scavenged the garbage, nobody much used it, and it was rare to see anyone else on one of his "constitutional strolls" along it.

To walk straight into someone was a completely new experience.

"My, we are in a hurry!" A voice boomed after John had bounced off him.

Admittedly, he'd been half looking over his shoulder to make sure no irate husbands were about to come bursting through, shotgun in hand, but even so...

He'd been so certain Cherry Lane had been as deserted as normal that he let out a strangled, high-pitched cry as he staggered backwards and tripped over the half-rotted remains of an ancient pail.

"You know, a man rarely wakes up in the morning expecting to kick the bucket," the Mayor of Hawker's Drift grinned, resting upon an ivory-handled walking cane in the manner of a swanky gent out upon a promenade rather than a junk-strewn back alley.

"Mr Mayor!" he exclaimed, recovering from his surprise, "what are you doing here?

"Oh..." he looked about, nodding his head like a small excitable dog, "...I keep myself acquainted with all of the town, not just our fashionable square, throbbing Main Street and wide boardwalks, but the mean, dark little corners too. You just never know what you might come across..." he poked his cane at a pile of sun-bleached canvas. Something small and dark scurried away. He wrinkled his nose and looked at the gunsmith, "...though usually I just find rats here..."

"Vermin everywhere." he tried to sound casual; the Mayor had always unnerved him, the way his eye constantly moved, not the random meandering of malfunctioning muscle, but methodically, like anyone might look from place to place, just much faster.

"Yes... we have a perfectly good refuse pit out of town. You would think decent folk would prefer their trash there than at the end of their yards, but I suppose that's human nature; as soon as you can't see something, you stop thinking about it and don't even believe it's there. That's the trick, isn't it, Mr Smith? Making sure people never actually see you... that way, they never actually know who you are?"

"I suppose..."

The Mayor pulled in a great lungful of air and looked up at the overhanging branches, "You know, I'm quite fond of trees, not many of them out here on the plains, other than in our little island of civilization, of course. We should have more trees... don't you think?"

"You're the Mayor, sir."

The Mayor seemed to think about this before replying, "Yes, I suppose I am! Perhaps I'll get people to plant some more on Corner Park. I'd like that... So, Mr Smith, I'm here to enjoy what little foliage we have in Hawker's Drift. What about you? Tinkering, I suppose?"

"Tinkering?"

"That's what you do, isn't it? Or have you other hobbies now?"

"I make guns..."

The Burden of Souls

"Oh, guns! Pah, anyone can make a gun, can't they? I meant the other stuff. You still tinker with... what would you call them? Gizmos? Contraptions? Things that go buzz in the night?" He pronounced the word buzz like a child imitating a bee, his eye still flicking disconcertingly from place to place.

"Yeah, I mess about with stuff."

"Messing about? Yes, I suppose you do. Excellent! Curiosity, eh? Quite a virtue. We all need at least one of those." He smiled and tipped his hat, "Well, I must be going. Town business and all."

"Good day then, Mr Mayor."

"Indeed," the Mayor brushed past him; Cherry Lane was barely wide enough for two men to stand abreast, even if it hadn't been clogged with junk, and John felt the sleeve of the Mayor's jacket as he passed, while his nostrils filled with the smell of sweetly perfumed smoke.

The Mayor took a few paces before coming to a halt. He didn't look back as he spoke, "Ash Godbold has quite a collection of cut-throat razors, I believe, a steady hand too. A barber needs that, of course, one little slip when you're shaving a man and... well, it would be all quite unpleasant." He took another step before adding, "You might want to fix your shirt before you get back to Main Street, Mr Smith." With that, he headed off down Cherry Lane, whistling loudly.

John X looked down at his miss-buttoned shirt and cursed.

The Clown

Mr Wizzle settled himself down amongst the long grass, surrounded by the buzz and hum of little creatures. He took off his battered derby and placed it in his lap. From one of his jacket's many pockets, he eventually pulled a small brown paper bag that he placed inside the upturned hat.

Humming along with the insects, he fished out a pickled egg from the bag, which he ate with small precise bites while gazing at the sky. It was an hour or so from sunset, and mountainous islands of grey cloud, fringed with halos of silvery-white, speckled the otherwise dark blue vault.

It was a sky that promised a splendid sunset. Perhaps the scattered cloud would thicken to rain. Mr Wizzle usually liked rain in the evening, it washed the sweaty filth of the old day away, and the world would be clean and new again when the dawn arrived. Today, however, he would spend the night under the stars. He hadn't brought so much as a blanket, let alone a tent, so it would be a miserable night if it did rain. However, he'd prayed diligently about the weather, and he was confident he would be rewarded with a warm, dry night.

He didn't know if the angels liked the rain, though he'd seen them in most weather. He was sure they liked the dusk, though; they undoubtedly came more often at the end of the day, particularly after sunset as the last of the light bled from the world and the clouds were soft-washed by beautiful colours.

Mr Wizzle belched loudly after he finished his egg and wrinkled his nose at the smell. He wasn't sure what the angels felt about eggy breath. He suspected they didn't care too much, being above such mundane things; however, he tried not to take too much for granted when it came to the angels.

The sun was dazzling and warm, blanketing him in light. Once he finished his second egg, he was tempted to tip his hat over his eyes and take a little nap. The angels were unlikely to appear before sunset.

That, however, was lazy thinking. The angels, who obviously saw and knew everything, might not make themselves visible if they saw him snoring in the grass like some drunken bum who'd staggered out of the saloon. It wasn't respectful.

So, he stuffed his bag of eggs in his pocket before placing the hat back on his head. He climbed to his feet; his knees, which weren't what they had been, clicked in protest. He stretched out his arms and arched his back. He really was tired.

He looked about him, but there was nothing to see but grass.

He'd hitched a lift on the back of old Freddie Hooper's wagon out of Hawker's Drift, but his little farm was a fair few miles back now. Hooper had raised an eyebrow when he said he would spend the night out in the grass, but he hadn't said anything much. Fred Hooper had never been one for saying much anyway, but, like everybody else, old Fred thought he was utterly mad, so he had just shrugged.

He'd jumped from Fred's wagon where it turned off the road to his farm; he'd plucked a pickled egg from Fred's ear by way of thanking him for the ride, though he hadn't seemed overly impressed. Some people just didn't like pickled eggs.

He'd long since decided there was no accounting for the strangeness of folk.

After leaving Fred, he'd waddled north along the road. In truth, it was just a rough track between the grass, but people around here had always been partial to a bit of exaggerating. After a while, it disappeared, consumed by the encroaching grass. There was nothing much north of Fred Hooper's place warranting even a narrow track. He walked till he could see nothing but grass and sky; no trace of humanity save his own shoes.

The breeze rustled the grass while insects buzzed about their business, and that was about it. A man could just get swallowed up out here; there were no landmarks, no features, just dead flat land beneath an ever-changing dome of sky. It was quiet, peaceful, and nobody had gotten around to mucking up this little corner of God's Earth just yet.

Which was why the angels came here, he supposed.

Satisfied he was in the right spot, he settled down and watched the clouds parade across the sky, slowly changing colour as the sun fell towards the west.

And waited for the angels.

The Lawyer

"Is that you?"

"Yes, dear," he closed the door behind him and rearranged his face. Like he always did, he'd hoped that he'd got home late enough for Lorna to have passed out for the night.

"Well, keep the noise down," she shouted, "I've got a head!"

Guy Furnedge slid his case into its usual spot under the hall table as Amy came down the stairs. She looked flustered and grateful to be pulling on her shawl. The evening was warm, and the sun hadn't quite set, but Amy always seemed to pull her shawl about herself when she went out. Or at least when he was around anyway.

"I'm done for the day, Mr Furnedge," she announced, breezing past him.

"Well, goodnight, Amy," he tried to catch a glimpse of her behind, but her dress was as disappointingly shapeless as usual.

She paused by the door and looked back at him, flicking away a few strands of honey-coloured hair that had escaped her ponytail, "She's having a bad day..." Amy whispered unnecessarily.

Lorna never had good days anymore, but Amy's hangdog expression and flustered cheeks announced what kind of day his wife was having as clearly as a billboard.

"Thank you for all your work, Amy."

Amy came in four days a week to tidy the house, do the laundry, look after Lorna, and run whatever errands his increasingly incapacitated wife dreamt up.

None of which constituted the kind of work he'd put the girl to given half a chance.

"My pleasure, Mr Furnedge," Amy said in a flat perfunctory voice that suggested it was anything but.

What a pouty little madam; I should put her right over my knee...

Amy was nineteen, not the prettiest girl in town (he knew because he kept lists of all the young women in town, ranking their various qualities, including their prettiness. Amy was currently twenty-seventh on the prettiness list), but she was engaging all the same. He suspected she'd an intriguing little body under the shapeless smocks she always wore. Such a waste. If it were up to him, he'd insist she prettified herself before entering the house, but, of course such things weren't up to him. Not yet anyway.

He watched Amy let herself out and took a slow deep breath before entering the parlour where Lorna spent most of the day draped across an upholstered daybed, drinking bourbon and entertaining the sorry collection of dried-up old crones that passed for her friends. He thought of it as the Throne Room, though he never said so aloud. Lorna had lost her sense of humour a long time ago.

"Dragged yourself home then?" Lorna peered at him from behind a cloud of blue-grey fumes. His wife insisted on keeping the windows closed, and the drapes were drawn whatever the weather or time of day, resulting in the Throne Room being generally as dark, noxious, and over-heated as his wife's moods.

"Busy day, my dear; Malky Thurkettle is buying a big chunk of land from-"

"There you go again, droning on! Same as always, everything is about you!"

"Sorry, my dear," he took a breath and dived through the ring of smoke shrouding his wife to graze her pale, hollow cheek with a kiss, "how have you been?"

"Terrible, that useless girl you hired has just been making the most infuriating racket all day. I really don't know what she's been doing, but it's totally set my head off," she blew smoke towards him, "I should have known better and found an ugly girl to hire."

He retreated from the fumes and tried not to cough. Lorna hated coughing.

"Well, I'm sure Amy is doing her best..."

"Well, I can tell you, Amy is as hopeless as every other flea-brained piece of skirt you've hired to ogle since we came to this sorry excuse for a town."

"Well, she seems to be doing a splendid job to me."

And the chances of getting anyone else to work for us in Hawker's Drift are remote, given your reputation.

"You're too busy sniffing around her cunt to care," Lorna lifted an empty glass and pointed it in his direction.

Several responses came to mind, but he bit down on all of them. What was the point? Telling her she'd had enough to drink would do nothing but make her drink more. Telling her not to use such foul language would only make her swear more. Telling her he'd never ogled Amy or anyone else would only make her laugh. Telling her she was a miserable, bitter old harridan would just let her know she'd got under his skin spectacularly quickly this evening.

So, he poured her a generous measure of bourbon and then some more besides. With any luck, she'd soon be too drunk to talk anymore.

*

He'd once considered Lorna Allenby to be an attractive woman; admittedly, the attraction was largely due to the money her father had given him to marry her. For an ambitious young man, it had seemed too good an offer to pass up. After all, wealthy families looking to offload a daughter, along with a juicy lump sum bonus, to a young man struggling to make his way as a lawyer in an increasingly lawless world were not unduly common.

It had seemed like providence, a chance to escape the madness. Elliot Allenby wanted his oldest daughter settled, looked after, and taken as far away from the family home as possible.

They'd been a scandal, several he suspected, and for reasons best known to himself, old man Allenby had seen Guy Furnedge as a safe pair of hands. He'd agreed and

The Burden of Souls

Lorna, much to his surprise, had agreed too. He'd met her three times previously, and she'd spoken to him just twice.

He'd found out later her father had made it clear that if she'd refused, she would be out on the street and penniless, so being married to Guy Furnedge would be a far lesser evil than any of the alternatives on offer.

She'd seemed wild and headstrong, full of vitality and interested in everything. He was now embarrassed to admit that the young Guy Furnedge had been a little bit intoxicated by her. But that had been twenty years ago, and he'd long since worked out she wasn't wild and headstrong at all.

She was simply as mad as a bear with its head stuck in a beehive.

He sat and ate his supper alone in the kitchen; Amy had kindly prepared something for him, more out of pity than anything else he suspected. Given his wife survived on a diet of alcohol and tobacco, he usually ate alone. That and the fact she couldn't stand the sight of him.

Which was fine by him.

The house was quiet. He finished his meal, meat pie and cold vegetables, in peace. He hoped Lorna had drunk herself into a stupor; his evenings were always more pleasant then.

He would read for an hour in his comfy chair by the good lamp. Then a warm glass of milk before putting his pyjamas on and retiring to bed, where he would lie awake in the darkness, stroking his cock while he imagined how much better his life would be after his wife died.

"Where are you!!!?" Lorna screeched.

He took a deep breath, pushed his plate aside and rose to his feet; it looked like he wouldn't be allowed to unwind just yet.

The Widow

He was standing by the kitchen window drinking coffee, looking out across the yard.

She folded her arms about herself and watched him from the doorway. Her head was thumping, and the rest of her body wasn't far behind; her sleep had been restless and fitful, haunted by nightmares that had chased her back to consciousness to find her heart racing and her nightdress melded to her skin with sweat.

And that the other side of the bed was still empty.

The town would now consider her a shameless slut as well as a foul-mouthed drunk, of course. Her husband barely cold in his grave, and she'd brought a strange man home with her to spend the night.

Scandalous tramp!

Pity Amos had insisted on sleeping on the floor rather than in her bed. If everybody was going to think her a slut she might as well have had some pleasure from her shame.

Still, no need to worry; she'd soon have all the men she could handle...

She closed her eyes and took a deep breath. She already felt sick from all the beer and whiskey she'd downed the previous night. She didn't need to think about her enforced career change as well; then, she definitely would spew over the floor. Her new friend had already spurned her once; vomiting in front of him would hardly help matters along.

Help matters along?

What was she doing? Really? Did she think this stranger would save her from the whorehouse if she just got him into the sack with her? Was life really that simple?

She stepped back into the hallway and slid along the wall till she was out of sight.

Hadn't that been what she'd always done? Tied herself to a man, usually a violent, stupid man, in the expectation that, somehow, he would protect her from the world and all the shit engulfing it? She was scared and alone, so she'd reverted to doing what she'd always done and looked for salvation in a man.

It wasn't much of a plan; even last night, it hadn't seemed much of a plan, but she'd been drunk and attracted to this stranger, and when she was in that condition, all her plans tended to be drawn with an uncommonly broad brush...

*

The Mayor had arrived just before the girl was about to sing, two more of his long-coated henchmen trailing in his wake. If his freaky eye noticed her at the bar, he didn't acknowledge it, but, by then, the saloon had filled up, and she wasn't quite as obvious as she'd been a few hours earlier.

"Oily one-eyed cock weasel!" She glared at the Mayor's back.

Several of the nearby drinkers decided it was time to get a closer look at the new singer and shuffled away from her. Several more openly stared at her. They clearly weren't used to someone sticking it to their precious Mayor.

She was about to launch into another tirade when a hand clamped around her forearm.

"Just 'cos you bought me a few drinks doesn't mean you got the right to manhandle me," she protested, "I'm a widow, remember?"

"Don't cause a scene, Molly, it won't help you," Amos insisted; he leaned in and filled her vision. His eyes were the darkest brown, she noticed. Like wood polished to glass. Every other thing about his body was rough, in a worn and weathered kind of way, but his eyes, she realised, were very, very smooth.

Oh, stop it...

She wriggled free and pouted a little for the sake of form before settling back onto her barstool.

"Very well, I will behave. I swear I won't hurl any more insults at our beloved and resplendent Mayor..." she waved a finger vaguely over where she thought her heart was a couple of times, "...this side of midnight."

She looked back across the bar, but the crowd had parted biblically before the Mayor and allowed him safe passage to the front.

Fucker!

She smiled at Amos. She was fairly sure she'd only said that in her head.

She picked up her glass, which was disappointingly empty, and tipped it towards Amos to demonstrate the sorry state she'd inexplicably found herself in.

"If you're going to get a girl drunk, you might as well do it properly..."

She could see he was about to say he wasn't trying to get her drunk, every time she suggested he was hitting on her in some way he protested, but she was a woman of the world. She'd been here many times before with many men. Guys only plied you with booze if they wanted to get laid.

From town to town, from saloon to saloon; during the years she'd spent drifting along the open road between escaping Bert-Bert and finding Tom, she'd seen it again and again.

Hey, a stranger was trying to get her into bed. It was just like old times!

Amos ordered another couple of beers.

She peered at him; he was tall and spare, not skinny though, whipcord muscle. Hard, weather-beaten skin, darkened by years out in the sun. His hair was shaved short, a few flecks of grey peeking out of the stubbly growth around his ears. He was maybe ten years older than her, possibly less. Years in the saddle aged you, after all.

He carried a single pistol in his belt; she didn't think it was for show. He had an easy confidence. He didn't scare much either, she bet; he could handle himself. He kept talking to her, kept buying her drinks. He was interested.

A better bet than a life working in Hawker's Drift's only cat house.

How long has Tom been dead?

How long was one supposed to wait? She'd never been a widow before. In a perfect world, she would grieve for a respectable amount of time; months would be more acceptable than weeks and certainly days. But in a perfect world, she would have loved the man she'd married, and no sick one-eyed fucker would be trying to force her to work in a whorehouse to pay off her debts. Or rather the debts of the man she was supposed to be grieving for.

She knew nothing about Amos, save that he was a stranger to Hawker's Drift. Admittedly, that was a big tick in the plus column, but what else? His knuckles were heavily scarred; mementos from bar brawls or from knocking his women about? Maybe just from labouring or working on a ranch, but given she was attracted to him and her history with men, it would likely be the former.

He'd a distance about him that she hadn't probed too deeply, she'd enough of her own woes to occupy her after all, but he clearly didn't want to talk about himself. Did he have something to hide, or was he just modest? Some men were. She'd been told.

Did she need to know anything about him? If he could get her out of this shitty town, she would forgive him a whole steaming dunghill of faults.

She was sorry Tom was dead, truly; she even missed the damn fool, but he was gone, and nothing she could do would change that or even find out why he'd died. Maybe the Mayor had killed him, maybe it *had* been an accident; all that mattered was that he'd left her in an unholy mess. If she could find it in herself to forgive him, his ghost could hopefully forgive her for running off with another man.

All she had to do was convince Amos to help her.

The new girl had started to sing, something she noticed more from the unnatural hush that descended on the saloon than the music, though she clearly had a beautiful voice.

News of the young singer seemed to have brought half the town out to look at her. Even John X Smith was standing at the back of the crowd staring wide-eyed at the girl, and he hardly ever came into the saloon. She was young and pretty, and every man in the place was gawping at her. All the men save Amos; he was staring squarely at her.

She decided she knew how to convince him.

*

By the time the singing had finished, she was seriously drunk. It hadn't been a smart idea to switch from beer to whiskey, but that was a lesson she'd never quite got around to learning.

"I should be going," she made no move to slide off her stool.

"It's getting late..." Amos agreed. As the crowd ebbed and flowed along the bar, he turned to look at the Mayor, who was talking to the young singer.

Molly followed his gaze, "She should be careful..."

"I think she knows how to look after herself," Amos replied; still half-turned towards the singer.

"You can tell, huh?"

Amos swivelled back towards her, "Yes..."

"A special gift?"

He dropped his eyes, "I notice things."

"What else have you noticed?" she tried really hard not to lean forward too suggestively, but she wasn't entirely convinced the message from her brain had gotten through in time.

Amos coughed and looked back again, "Well... that young farm boy is quite smitten with Miss Jones."

"The one collecting the tips for her?"

"A-huh."

"Sye something or other... dunno... anyway, half the men in here were goggle-eyed watching her. Not really that perceptive."

"No," Amos insisted, "he really does think he loves her."

"Thinks?"

"When you're young, you can be in love with the idea of love. Which can be more dangerous than love itself..." he nodded back towards the young man who had just noticed Cece talking to the Mayor, "...see?"

Several expressions flitted across Sye's face; for his sake, she hoped the Mayor and his deputies didn't notice any of them.

The Mayor span on his heels; he was smiling as he turned, but it disappeared like water droplets flicked onto a hot stove once his back was to Cece.

"Now, if you can tell me what goes on inside that fucker's head, I will be impressed..."

The Mayor moved through the crowd, flashing transitory little smiles in response to greetings from those he passed; he was heading for the door but swerved at the last minute to join them at the bar.

"Why Mrs McCrea! I've been meaning to ask, just what is a cock weasel?"

She fumbled for a retort, but her mouth just flapped open, and nothing came but an unfamiliar heat in her cheeks. She must have been louder than she'd intended. Not the first time she'd been guilty of that, she supposed. She felt like she'd been caught whispering at the back of the class.

"Strangely quiet for once? Whiskey got your tongue? Make the most of it; you'll be selling it here soon. Among other things."

Amos slipped from his stool; for an instant, she thought he would punch the Mayor, which would have given her a moment of enormous satisfaction, but even she wasn't drunk enough to believe that was a good idea. The two deputies' heads snapped around in unison as he moved; both flicked their coats back from their guns.

"Leave her alone," Amos said.

The Mayor frowned and let out a little laugh, "And who might you be, exactly?"

"Just a friend."

"Yes..." the Mayor's eye scanned him up and down "...very civil of you."

"Not looking for trouble."

"Trouble? Oh, my dear fellow, there's never any trouble in Hawker's Drift. The four horsemen might be trampling over the rest of this world, but our town is a haven. A veritable paradise on Earth. I've worked hard to achieve that, so there will be no trouble here. I just don't stand for it."

"I've heard it's a peaceable town."

"Indeed, it is... well, enjoy your evening, Mr..."

"Amos."

The Mayor mouthed the word silently as if his lips needed to practice it, then he nodded and moved to turn away.

"And your name?"

He paused, head twisting back towards Amos, completely still save for his restless eye, "I'm the Mayor."

"That wasn't what I asked?"

"Be careful about lending her money; she's not good with settling her debts," he nodded in Molly's directions, "though if you get in quick, you can have her while it's still free."

The Mayor breezed past his two deputies who remained behind, their eyes not moving from Amos.

"Nice piece," one said, his voice low and hoarse.

The other glanced at his companion, "His gun or his cunt?"

They both laughed mirthlessly and turned after their boss.

She felt her hands shake. Actually, everything was shaking; she looked up at Amos, not sure whether he'd made things better or worse for her.

"If they knew who I was, they'd never have turned their backs on me," Amos whispered, watching the deputies push through the crowd.

"Who are you?"

"Something even worse than they are."

"Very reassuring..." she placed a hand lightly upon his arm, "...thank you, I think..."

"For what?"

"For taking my side. Nobody else in this shithole town has since Tom died."

Amos finished his beer, "The only side I take is my own, Molly."

"Then it would be better not to challenge the Mayor."

"I ain't challenging anyone," he looked sideways at her, "just can't stand assholes..."

"Sheesh... you really are in the wrong town."

She glanced at the table where Blane and the other deputy still sat. Watching her as intently as they had all night, ""I want to go home... will you walk me back... please?"

Amos took a moment to ponder; he didn't seem the spontaneous type. Finally, he nodded, "Sure, I'll see you home."

Nobody appeared to pay them much heed as they left, though she was sure it had been noticed and noted. Fuck 'em! Her reputation had already taken a battering today; she might as well let the town add easy virtue to her list of failings.

Once outside, Amos wrapped a hand around her arm and pulled her towards him. Perhaps he was more spontaneous than she'd given him credit for, and she half-closed her eyes in anticipation of his kiss as he pushed her gently against the wall. When no lips were forthcoming, she peeled open her eyes and looked quizzically at him as he stood next to her, back against the wall.

Her question never got past a frown as he put a finger to his lips. A moment later, the two deputies came through the saloon's door.

"Why don't you boys head home," Amos casually hitched his fingers into his gun belt, "you've had a long day."

The younger deputy jumped slightly, but Blane didn't show a flicker of surprise or any other emotion.

"Just doing our job," Blane's voice was deadpan to the point of lifeless.

"I'm sure, but you can leave it to me to get Mrs McCrea home safely."

"Much obliged," Blane continued to stare at Amos, who returned the compliment without blinking. Molly's own eyes flicked between the two, but she appeared to have become suddenly superfluous while they engaged in some kind of staring contest.

Then Blane was gone, without further word or comment, not even a facial gesture. He just turned and walked across the street, his partner a step behind.

"He gives me the creeps," she muttered, as much to herself as to Amos.

"You're a good judge of character."

"What was that staring thing about?" she asked, looking over her shoulder as they headed down the boardwalk despite herself. Blane and the other deputy were standing in the moonlit square watching them.

"He was trying to make me blink."

"And what were you trying to do?"

"See into his soul."

Her laugh petered out when she noticed Amos' distant expression; eventually, she asked in a hesitant voice, "And what did you see?"

"He hasn't got one..."

"Are you shitting me?"

Amos didn't reply; instead, he just flashed an enigmatic smile and shook his head.

She looked back again; the two long-coated figures were slowly following them along the middle of the deserted street.

They walked down Main Street in silence for a few minutes; other than a dog howling in the distance, Hawker's Drift was silent. It seemed everybody was either at home or getting drunk in *Jack's*. Save for two of the Sheriff's finest, of course.

"What did the Mayor mean about you selling yourself?" Amos asked after she'd turned back from looking at the deputies again.

"Just his fucked-up sense of humour," she stared at her shoes, the boardwalk didn't run this far down Main Street, but at least most of the mud had dried.

"Sounded more specific?"

She didn't want to discuss it with Amos; she barely knew him. It was one thing to take him to her bed, but it was another to tell him about the Mayor's threat to make her whore off her dead husband's debts.

Was she simply too embarrassed to tell him, or did she think he'd take off if he knew? Was she just being calculated? Wait until the right moment to tell him about the Mayor's despicable intentions to ensure he would help her. Would he be more likely to save her from the whorehouse if she let him have her? Tell him now, and he might not want to get involved, as if the prospect of having to prostitute herself already made her tainted somehow.

She shook the thoughts away. She'd never been adept at working out what she wanted, let alone how to get it. All she knew was that she didn't want to be alone tonight. If she hadn't run into Amos and spent the evening with him, she'd be walking home alone in the dark, with those two creeps in her wake.

Be careful, Molly, those two men want to kill you...

Amos' words had seemed fanciful in the bar. Her initial fear the Mayor wanted her dead had passed; now, she knew what he intended. But being followed along the deserted street in the darkness was another matter.

"What did you see when you looked in Blane's eyes?"

"You don't want to know."

"Yes, actually, I do."

Amos sighed, "He's quite mad and very dangerous."

She screwed up her face, "You *noticed* that?"

"Yeah, like I said, I notice things," Amos shot her an apologetic smile, "sounds... bullshit, I know. But I'm usually right."

They were approaching the corner of Baker's Street where they would turn off Main Street, a narrow road of compact wooden homes clinging to the slope that fell away to the surrounding Flats. It would be darker there as the moon was low and would be shadowed by the taller buildings on Main Street as they descended the hill.

"How mad?"

Amos looked uncomfortable, almost to the point of embarrassment. He wasn't trying to impress her or scare her. He really did think he could see something of Blane's character from just looking into his eyes.

"There's a stillness about him..." as they turned down Baker's Street, Amos looked back for the first time at the two deputies who were casually pursuing them. The low full moon side-lit them, their faces no more than suggestions beneath the shadows of their hats, "...but it's just like a mirrored lake reflecting back the sky. It hides what lies beneath."

"Which is?" She prompted when Amos once more fell into silence.

"Beneath the stillness is something... something that is slithering, snickering, jabbering, howling..."

"Fuck. You're right; I don't want to know."

She fought down the urge to look back up Baker's Street.

"You sound like one of those old women at a county fair, the kind that tells you you're going to meet a tall, handsome stranger and other unlikely shit."

"Yeah, I know what you mean," Amos snorted a little laugh, "...my mother did that."

"Oh fuck. Really?"

"Madame Mysterio."

"Your name is Amos *Mysterio*?"

"It was just a stage name for her act. *Obviously*. She told fortunes, prophesied the future. That kinda stuff."

"Did she get anything right?"

"Let's just say we didn't have much money to get by with when I was a kid."

"Like most people, I guess..."

The little house she'd rented with Tom was halfway down the hill; she stopped by the gate in the low picket fence.

"Here we are... will you come in?"

Why did she feel like a sixteen-year-old coming home from her first barn dance?

"I... shouldn't..." Amos stuck his hands into his pockets and made no move to leave.

Did she actually want this? Did it even matter one way or the other? If he could get her out of this mess... and even if he couldn't she didn't want to be alone in the house with nothing but memories of Tom and the knowledge that Blane and his friend were outside.

"Don't worry about my reputation."

"I wasn't."

"Thanks."

"Molly-"

"Please..." she could see two figures taking up position in the shadows along the street. Amos followed her gaze, "...I just don't want to be alone."

"I could just shoot them?"

"That's very kind of you to offer, but I'm already up to my fanny in shit." Despite everything, she couldn't help but giggle at Amos' expression, "Sorry, I've got a fucking awful mouth on me."

"It's endearing. Really. Reminds me of my mother..."

"Prophesying *and* cussing?"

Amos put on a deep and foreboding voice, "I see you are about to come into a great fortune, now cross my hand with silver or fuck off."

"I'm beginning to see why you had such an impoverished childhood."

He smiled, but it quickly faded when he gazed up the hill at the two figures now lounging against the side of a house; he appeared to be thinking again. He seemed to do a lot of that.

"I'll sleep downstairs and watch the door for you. Just in case."

Sure, you can sleep downstairs...

If he wanted to think he was a gentleman, that was fine; he could blame it on her in the morning.

She nodded and turned away, heart thudding hard. Had he noticed that? She felt queasy too, and not solely due to the amount she'd drunk. She wasn't sure if sex was one of the recommended ways of dealing with grief, but it might take her mind off things for a while, and she was sure, at the very least, she would feel safe in his arms while she slept.

Once inside, she fumbled to find the lantern in the darkness. Molly imagined returning to the house alone and wondering if Blane's colleagues were already there waiting for her in the shadows.

Be careful, Molly, those two men want to kill you...

She shut her eyes against the light as the lantern flared into life.

Nobody is going to kill me tonight. Amos is here; I'm safe. He'll protect me. Whoever he is...

She picked up the lantern and looked around for Amos; she'd hoped he would have followed in the darkness. To be perfectly honest, she'd hoped his hands would have been on her before she'd even got to the lantern.

He was still standing by the door, holding his hat before him. Looking awkward. Actually, he looked more than awkward; he looked downright terrified.

You sure this guy can protect you?

He'd faced the Mayor and Blane down without so much as a blink, but being alone with one *slightly* drunk, *fairly* horny, extremely vulnerable widow seemed to unnerve him enough to make him look scratchy in his own skin. Eventually, he followed her into the drawing-room. She put the lamp down on the little table by the fireside rocking chair.

Perhaps he's wondering if I'll scream and cry rape if he tries to kiss me.

She ran a hand through her long hair and smiled coyly. And then wondered if he'd scream and cry rape if she tried to kiss him.

"Would you like a drink? I have some whiskey left somewhere. I think..."

Amos shook his head and nodded towards the rug she was standing on. "No thanks, ma'am, I'll just settle myself down here while you go to bed."

"Ma'am?"

"Sorry... I don't want to be overly familiar. It's your home, and we only just met."

"It's Molly. I'm not a fucking dried up spinster – and you can be as familiar as you like!"

Amos shuffled his feet, then stared at them just to make sure he was shuffling them enough while wringing the brim of his hat so hard his knuckles had turned white.

Oh, for fuck's sake! How much shittier can my life get? I can't even get fucking seduced properly anymore!

Clearly, he needed some encouragement, and she was too tired and too drunk to want to play silly little flirting games for hours. She walked over and stood before him; his brown eyes were big and almost fearful. He couldn't possibly still be a virgin, could he?

"I don't want you to sleep on the floor," she said, holding his gaze and placing her hand on his left arm. He almost squirmed at her touch.

Amos looked around, "If you have a couch..."

"That's not what I meant," she reached up to kiss him, but before her lips could find his he'd staggered wildly backwards, dropping his hat and colliding with the wall. She stood aghast for a moment. Had he seen something in *her* eyes?

"I'm sorry," Amos looked around the room as wildly as a rabid dog trapped in a corner, "I just can't do that!"

She shut her eyes, shook her head, and bit her bottom lip. She hadn't often been rejected by men. Amos was trying to say something, but it wasn't registering, and she didn't trust herself to say anything either. She'd already had one screaming fit of profanities today, and she didn't need another. Instead, she just held up a hand to silence him.

When she realised nothing coherent was going to come out of her mouth, she stormed out of the room, took the stairs two steps at a time and slammed the bedroom door shut after her.

"Well, that was humiliating..." she sat on the edge of the bed with her face in her hands, waiting for the front door to slam after Amos.

She wanted to crawl into bed and erase throwing herself at Amos from history, but like all the other mistakes she'd made in her life, she knew that wasn't possible.

After a few minutes, she managed to regain a little composure. It was silent downstairs, but she didn't think

Amos had slunk away from the sex-crazed widow's house of vice yet.

She went to the cupboard to fetch a couple of blankets and a spare pillow for him. She was big enough to handle rejection magnanimously, she decided. As she bent down, her hair brushed against Tom's old coat. She reached out to stroke it, then pulled it to her face. No trace of her husband's scent lingered; it just smelt of old leather. It was the jacket he'd always worn before they'd come to Hawker's Drift; time-worn, cracked and faded.

A sob bubbled up her throat, and she found herself on her knees crying softly, her fingers caressing the seam.

"Damn you, Tom, how can I miss you so much when I never even loved you?"

She let the jacket fall away, pulled out the blankets and a flat sorry pillow that was her only spare and sank back onto the floor, cradling them. The pillow smelt musty, the blankets itchy on her skin.

She wiped her eyes and felt foolish. Was she crying for her dead husband or because the man downstairs wouldn't jump into the bed that still faintly carried the scent of Tom's sweat?

Wearily she pulled herself to her feet. Perhaps she should ask Amos to leave. It had been a stupid idea to bring him home. Disrespectful to Tom, who'd never so much as looked at another woman and who'd loved her completely with his big, stupid, soft heart.

She crossed reluctantly to the window and peered down the street. It looked deserted at first, till she saw a fleeting orange glow flare in the shadows. Someone was smoking.

Someone who was loitering in the darkness. Watching her home.

No, she decided, it hadn't been a mistake. Whatever else, Amos made her feel safe. He wasn't scared of Blane or the Mayor. That was something. At least.

She took the bedding downstairs, half afraid Amos might have slipped away while she'd been sobbing on the floor like a broken-hearted schoolgirl. She found him sitting in the rocking chair, fingers gripping the armrests tightly enough to whiten his knuckles. He didn't look at her. His eyes stayed fixed ahead, and his complexion had become ashen.

"Amos...?"

"I'm fine, Molly," he glanced up at her, "just leave the blankets on the floor. Thank you."

"Are you sick?"

"It's not your fault Molly. Just go to bed. You'll be safe."

His voice was a tortured rasp. When she took half a step towards him, he shook his head and looked away.

She put the blankets on the floor before retreating upstairs.

She really did pick the strangest men...

The Gunslinger

He pretended not to notice Molly watching him from the doorway. When she slipped away without saying anything, he continued to stare out of the kitchen window.

He should have known. Then again, perhaps he had? Perhaps some twisted part of his soul still wanted to know what it felt like for a beautiful woman to be attracted to him.

Perhaps.

Or maybe, it was just a blind spot. The Thin Rider's gift let him look into Blane's eyes and know what writhed around inside him, but he hadn't been able to figure out that a lonely, frightened, vulnerable woman might want him. Want him for sex, protection, comfort, and a way out of the hole her husband had left her in.

Yeah, that had been a real tough one for him to notice.

The tidy little kitchen looked out onto a small yard; it too was neatly kept. There were vegetables, a clothesline, a little outhouse and a fire-blackened metal bucket with what looked like the twisted remains of an umbrella sticking out of it. It was quiet, peaceful in the morning sunshine. It was normal, and he wished it was his.

He should leave. Pay his bills, get his horse and ride out of town. Life, for want of a better word, was easier when he was alone. There was trouble here, and he didn't just mean Molly kind of trouble.

He'd felt it for a while now, the way the air turns a certain way before a thunderstorm - heavy and sticky. He'd been trying to ignore it. He wanted to rest and get a little peace for a while. Just for a week or two. Small comforts away from his endless pursuit of a man he knew he would never find.

Then he'd met the Mayor and Blane last night...

Blane was a killer, the Mayor... he was something else. He'd looked into his strange, restless eye and had seen... what exactly?

He wasn't sure, and that made him uneasy.

At times, he could look someone in the eye and know them intimately, know their thoughts, fears, intentions, and ambitions. Know everything. More often he caught only tiny fragments, memories reflected in the splinters of broken mirrors. Occasionally he saw nothing but a bloodshot eyeball. But it was usually one or the other. It was something he'd been able to do from childhood, in a vague unrefined way, but since Severn had left him for dead, it had become more focused, more... *powerful?*

But the Mayor? He'd been different; he'd never experienced anything quite like it. He came away with no sense of the man at all... no sense other than a vast yawning darkness and the distant echoes of screams...

"Morning..." Molly announced, finally breezing into the kitchen with stilted cheerfulness.

"Morning," he replied, looking back and flashing a smile to conceal his own awkwardness.

The Burden of Souls

What on Earth must she think of him after last night? Whatever it was, it was preferable to the truth.

"There's coffee in the pot... I hope you don't mind me helping myself?"

"Of course not," she shook her tousled red locks and hurried to the stove. He returned to staring out of the window as she dragged out pouring herself a coffee for as long as possible.

She hovered by the stove when she was done, mug cradled in both hands beneath her lips. She didn't join him by the window or leave the room.

He finished his coffee in heavy silence. Molly was staring at him over the lip of her own mug.

"So, the Mayor wants you to work off your debts in the whorehouse then?" It seemed better to say something than nothing.

Molly sipped her drink by way of a reply.

"I kinda of figured it out, from what he said last night," he added.

And from what I saw in your eyes when you tried to kiss me. Among other things.

"You certainly know how to break an awkward fucking silence..."

"What are you going to do?"

"Get a sore fanny, I'd imagine."

"Molly..."

"What else can I do? I'm trapped here! I haven't got the money to pay off Tom's debts, and I don't know what he did with the stuff he bought on the Mayor's dime. And I can't even skip town with Deputy Dickhound following my scent up and down Main Street."

He pulled out a chair from under the kitchen table and sat down. Molly looked perplexed; as if she'd been expecting him to be heading for the door as soon as politely possible. Which was what he should be doing. Instead, he placed his elbows on the table, interlocked fingers and rested his chin in his hands while looking at Molly, with her sleep messed hair, shapeless over-sized shirt, and faded work pants.

He tried hard not to think about who she reminded him of.

"Is there anywhere left to look for the stuff?"

"Most of it could be sitting in any outhouse in town, not so many places you could keep a horse and two mules, though… I've asked around, but nobody knows anything."

"Could he have put them out of town?"

"There are plenty of ranches, farms, homesteads, but I can't leave town. Deputy Dickhound remember?"

"Nothing stopping me looking?"

"Would you?" She seemed surprised. Again.

"My horse needs some exercise. Gets skittish cooped up inside all day."

"Know that feeling…"

"What exactly did your husband buy?"

"Wait here," Molly put down her coffee and hurried out of the kitchen.

He sat back and looked out of the window. The sun was still shining; he could be out of Hawker's Drift in an hour. Less if he hurried. He closed his eyes and imagined kissing Molly; a stupid and pointless torment.

She hurried back to fan an assortment of bills and receipts across the table.

"A lot of stuff."

"No," Molly said earnestly, resting her hands on the table edge opposite and looking down at him, "it's a *fucking* lot of stuff."

"Sorry, ma'am, my mistake."

A faint little smile flittered across her face, the first of the day he noted for no obvious reason.

"Do you mind if I take these?"

"Be my guest – make sure you bring them back, though."

"Of course, you'll need them when you settle your debt with the Mayor."

"Nope," Molly shook her head as she replied earnestly, "I'll need em when I shove em up the Mayor's pale bony ass."

It was his turn to smile as he carefully folded the bills before slipping them into his jacket as he stood up, "I guess I'd better make a start on these then."

"Do you want some breakfast?"

"No, I'm fine," he smiled, his stomach rumbling faintly at the mention of food.

"Another time?"

"Sure... I'll pop by later; let you know what I've found."

"I reckon you'll find squat, but..." she let out a long sigh, "... I'm grateful. For everything."

"You're welcome."

They'd been edging slowly towards the door. He hoped she wasn't going to try and kiss him goodbye.

She rested her hand on the latch of the door, screwing up her face as her eyes slid past his, "I'm sorry about last night; I-"

He placed his hand over the one she was still holding the latch with. Her skin was smooth and warm, he could faintly smell lavender oil, and, for an instant, he could see her standing over her husband's grave, alone in the pouring rain feeling guilty that she'd never loved him.

He wanted to jerk his hand away as if he'd inadvertently picked up something glowing hot, but he didn't want to hurt her any more than he already had, so he left his hand there and felt the memory wash over him like the rain on Tom's grave.

"Really, don't apologise... it isn't you."

"Well, I know *that*."

He forced a smile and let his hand slip away naturally from hers. The echoes of summer rain, anger and sadness faded back into the colours of her soul.

She opened the door for him, "I guess you're married or something, huh?"

"Something."

She didn't pry further, which he was grateful for as he walked out into the bright morning sunshine.

"One thing, Amos," she called from the doorway, "I never got around to asking what you do?"

"Is it important?"

She shrugged to suggest it wasn't, but he knew otherwise. She wanted to know if he was the kind of man who could save her, which, of course, he wasn't. He considered her

The Burden of Souls

question and decided he didn't want to lie to her any more than he had to.

"I kill people."

She didn't look surprised or shocked. Molly had seen the bad side of life and become ensnared by it, Tom had saved her without her even realising it, and now she believed the only way to save herself from the Mayor was to find a man who was an even meaner excuse for a human being than he was.

He really wished he hadn't touched her hand.

Molly nodded, "I'll see you soon."

He nodded in return and walked out onto the street as she closed the door to her little house.

He stood in the gateway, took a long deep breath of the morning before placing his hat upon his head and tipping the rim to cut out the sun's glare. He looked up the hill, then down and back up again.

The street was quite empty. Blane and his buddies appeared to have slithered back into their holes.

*

"Yep, I sold the asshole a rifle, a good un too and yep, the Mayor paid for it," John mumbled between mouthfuls of the sandwich he was devouring. They were sitting side by side on the wooden steps leading up to the back of his store.

"You didn't like him much?"

John shrugged as he worked some gristle out from between his teeth with his tongue, "Can't say I knew him, but he'd gotten in a fair few brawls thanks to that temper of his. Drunk too much as well, which didn't help none."

"Any idea what he wanted the rifle for?"

"I dunno, shooting rabbits maybes..."

He raised a sceptical eyebrow.

"None of my business. Man comes into my store and wants a rifle; so long as he can pay for it, he gets a rifle."

"Or has sufficient credit with the Mayor."

"Mayor's credit is always good," John X took another bite of his sandwich, his eyes not rising from his feet as he chewed.

"He didn't say anything?"

"He wasn't much of a talker... and he seemed, I dunno, distracted..."

"Distracted?"

"Distant... had a kinda faraway look in his eyes. Thought he had a wicked hangover, which would have been fairly normal for him."

"Didn't hear any talk of what Tom McCrea was up to from anyone else?"

John stopped chewing, his eyes turning towards Amos, "I don't hear much, not really one for gossip. Why the interest?"

"Just trying to do a good deed."

"That so?" he nodded thoughtfully, "anything connected to seeing Molly McCrea home last night?"

"I thought you weren't one for gossip?"

"I'm not, but the whole town is talking about her stepping out of *Jack's* with a stranger, that would be you by the way, her poor husband still warm in the ground," he shrugged and returned to his sandwich, "Small towns…"

"Small towns…" Amos agreed. He'd hoped John would have been able to cast some light on Tom McCrea; despite the protests, he suspected he was the kind of man who knew an awful lot about what went on in town. So far, he hadn't been overly helpful.

He stared across the junk-filled yard out back of the gunsmith's shop.

"You collect a lot of crap."

"I like making things."

Assorted bric-a-brac, mostly machinery, filled the yard. Mostly old, rusted, and unidentifiable to Amos. Some of it might have been useful for making guns. He supposed.

"Keeps your hands busy, huh?"

"Keeps my brain busy; my hands usually occupy themselves."

He remembered the coffee-coloured children he'd seen running around town.

They sat in amiable silence till John X had finished eating. He pulled a bright red handkerchief from his pocket and wiped his lips clean.

"You gonna ask me about the Mayor again now, huh?"

Amos screwed his face up a little, "Thinking about it… but people here get kinda twitchy talking about him. You included."

"That's because my mamma didn't raise any fools. Actually, she barely raised me at all on account that she run off with my Uncle when I was two, but you get my drift."

"I know you're not a fool, John. In fact, I think you're smarter than most people in this town. A lot smarter..."

John swivelled his head and stared at Amos, narrowing his eyes, "I'm just a small-town gunsmith, son. Nothing else."

He didn't meet his gaze; instead, he fixed his eyes on a battered tin bath sitting in the yard, full to the brim with cogs and wheels of all shapes and sizes.

"Stupid people spend their lives in fear because their ignorance fills the darkness with monsters. You're not stupid, John, but you are scared of the Mayor. So, tell me, what scares a clever man?"

"Philosopher too, huh?"

"Just wondering..."

"Take my advice, Molly McCrea is a nice lady, if you can get past that damn mouth of hers, but she ain't worth crossing the Mayor for, my friend. No one is. If you're looking for some female company, there are a lot of ladies in Hawker's Drift who'd be much less trouble than Molly."

"I'm not looking for female company."

John looked perplexed, "She paying you to help her?"

He let a little chuckle escape his throat as he shook his head, "Nope, if she could afford me, she'd have enough to pay the Mayor off."

"Then why are you helping her?"

"It's complicated."

"Gonna get a helluva lot more complicated if you piss the Mayor off."

He continued to stare into the junk-cluttered distance. It wasn't a question he could readily answer himself. It wasn't

The Burden of Souls

like him to get involved in someone else's business unless he was well paid to do it. Actually, he *could* answer it, but he knew he'd just sound foolish if he uttered it aloud, so he said nothing instead.

"Tom McCrea worked for the Mayor, didn't he?"

John nodded, "So I heard."

"Doing what?"

"Some stuff out on the Mayor's ranch, I think, don't know exactly, but the Mayor paid him well enough. The pair of em rolled up in Hawker's Drift with barely a change of clothes between em; three months later, they were in a nice house on Baker's St, and she was wearing some quite lovely dresses. I did notice that..."

"Where is the Mayor's ranch?"

John X shook his head, "As I'm the closest thing you've got to a friend in this town, discounting folk with long red hair and fine-looking breasts, I'm gonna do you a big favour and not answer that question."

"I'll find out anyway."

"Don't go poking around there, Amos, seriously..."

"Then tell me why I shouldn't?"

"I gotta get back to work..." John let out a long sigh before rising to his feet; he patted Amos' shoulder a couple of times as he turned before walking up the short flight of stairs to the back door of his store.

Amos raised a hand in acknowledgement before closing his eyes and saying in a soft, hoarse little voice before he could stop himself, "She reminds me of a woman I once... knew, back when I was still a righteous man..."

"And is that enough?"

"Enough for what?"

"Enough to die for."

A rueful smile played across Amos' face, "Oh, I died a long time ago."

"Be careful... else you might end up dying twice."

"There's always that..."

He heard the door open and the floorboards inside creak under John's boot, but the door remained open. He could feel the gunsmith's eyes on his back.

"Amos."

"Yeah?"

"The clever man is scared when he knows the monsters are real..."

The door clicked shut, leaving him alone to stare across the junk-filled yard.

The Sheriff

A noise, urgent and unfamiliar, pulled him awake. He peeled open his eyes. The scuffed metal tip of a walking cane was a few inches from his nose.

"Sleeping on my dime, Sheriff?"

It was a depressingly familiar voice. He lifted his head from his arms to find the Mayor standing over him, his cane tap-tap-tapping upon the desktop.

"I've been here since six this morning..." Sam Shenan growled, slowly sitting up. His back was stiff, his skin damp with cold sweat.

"I'll see about a bonus then," the Mayor eased himself into the chair opposite.

"Is there a problem?"

"Other than your narcolepsy?"

"Narco what?"

"There are always problems," the Mayor took off his fedora and placed it upon the desk, obscuring some of the papers scattered across it.

He folded his hands in his lap, sat up and tried to look attentive. Blane was lurking in the doorway as he often did. Like most of the town deputies, he'd been hired on the

Mayor's advice, and, like most of the Mayor's men, he scared him more than a little.

He was too old to be scared; he just wanted to retire, work a little homestead out of town, grow pumpkins, keep a few chickens, sit on the porch in a rocking chair and watch the clouds tumble across the sky. To dream about Elena and wait to die.

The Mayor, however, had other ideas. He knew why of course; he just wished he had the courage to tell him where to go. He was tired of being the Mayor's fop.

"The McCrea widow..." the Mayor was still tapping his cane against the edge of the desk.

He tried hard not to sigh. Another of the Mayor's little projects that had very little to do with law enforcement.

"We're watching her, just like you wanted."

Or at least two of the monosyllabic head cases you made me hire are watching her.

"I asked you to keep an eye on her, make sure she didn't skip town," the cane was still tap-tap-tapping. He tried hard not to look at it or show how irritating it was.

"Which we've done."

"No!" The Mayor slapped the cane down hard enough to make Sam flinch, "You're having her stalked! Twenty-four hours a day!"

His eyes flicked in Blane's direction, "We like to be diligent."

The Mayor forced out a little smile. It wasn't the slightest bit reassuring.

"Very commendable, but she is just one little girl in a small town with few easy ways out of it. Just keep an eye on her; the stagecoach, the stables, what she is up to. *Discreetly...*"

"Discreetly?"

"Yes, I don't want people to notice she is being followed. It might upset them."

"And the other things that happen here don't?"

The cane stopped tapping, "People see what they want to see, especially if they think they're free and happy. That's all people want, after all. To think they are free to do as they like and to have all their little comforts, all their petty desires sated. They just want their tummies scratched and to have the bars of their cage far enough away for them to pretend there aren't any."

"I'll see my men are more discreet."

"You do that."

They both knew who the town's deputies worked for, but the Mayor seemed happy to promote the myth that the Sheriff was more than just a figurehead, a fat old man with an easy smile. Someone who wouldn't scare the decent folk of Hawker's Drift; someone who was, after all, just one of them.

"And how long do we need to tie men up keeping an eye on Molly McCrea?"

"Until I have her where I want her," the Mayor replied unhelpfully. He was used to his boss' habit of never quite answering a question, particularly when it came to his little games. He'd once suspected the Mayor had some dark purpose, some scheme, some plan. Now... now he thought it was no more than a game to him; a little diversion to amuse and distract him. He could be wrong, of course, but, frankly, he'd stopped giving a shit a long time ago.

"Well, now we have resolved that little wrinkle..." the Mayor reached for his hat and began to rise.

"There is something else,"

"Really?"

He considered mentioning the stranger Molly had been seen with a few times, but he was sure the Mayor already knew all about that. He'd a habit of knowing things, though, in this case, it would be because Blane had told him directly rather than anything arcane.

"I want to retire."

The Mayor blinked as if he didn't quite understand the point Shenan was making.

He decided to rephrase the statement, "I'm going to retire."

The Mayor eased himself back into his seat, "Well, I honestly don't know about that, Sam..."

"Town Sheriff is up for re-election in a couple of months, as I'm sure you know being such an advocate of democracy an all. I'm not going to be standing again."

"Why ever not? You've headed up our fine Sheriff's office for so long; how could we possibly maintain the peace without you?" the Mayor said, with as much sincerity as a shyster trying to sell a lame horse to a blind man.

"I'm old, I'm fat, I'm owed..."

"Owed?"

"I've been loyal, done everything asked of me. I just want to see out my days in peace."

"We had a deal, Sheriff."

"And I've honoured it. Let young Blane have it; he'll do an outstanding job."

For a cold-blooded, murderous sonofabitch anyway.

The Sheriff glanced toward Deputy Blane. If he was surprised or grateful for the recommendation, the fucker was doing an excellent job of hiding it. His face was as expressionless as it usually was. The man was like a frying pan; a cold, unresponsive piece of iron unless you applied some heat, then, Sam suspected, he could burn you badly.

"You're Sheriff of Hawker's Drift," the Mayor shook his head, "till the day you die. That's what you wanted, remember…"

"Yeah, I remember, but that was a long time ago."

"A deal's a deal. There's no statute of limitation on it."

He shuffled in his seat; the only thing more disconcerting than the Mayor's roving eye was when it stopped roving and fixed on you.

"I just want to retire…"

"We can't *always* get what we want, Sheriff," the Mayor flicked the tip of his cane over his shoulder, "Deputy Blane has many admirable qualities, not least his diligence, but he lacks, for now, the necessary interpersonal skills required for the job. Wouldn't you agree, Blane?"

"Yep," Blane drawled, which was about as verbose as the man ever got. His murky hooded eyes, however, said something else entirely.

"I need you, Sheriff; Hawker's Drift needs you. So, you'll be the only name on the ballot. Same as usual." With that, the Mayor rose smoothly to his feet.

He wanted to protest, but the words drained away. Arguing was futile. No one changed the Mayor's mind, save the Mayor himself.

Once the Mayor had settled his hat upon his head, he tapped his cane on the desk one more time, "There's a newcomer in town, a gunslinger. Keep an eye on him; he looks... *insolent* to me."

"Discreetly?"

"Yes, discreetly," the Mayor nodded at him and then Blane, "Good day, gentlemen."

Once his boss had strolled out of the office, Sam's eyes turned back to the papers spread before him until he realised Blane was still in the doorway, leaning against the frame, thumbs hitched in his gun belt, watching him.

"You heard the Mayor? About the McCrea woman?"

"Yep."

"So, start watching her *discreetly*; like I told you to in the first damn place, stop following her everywhere. There's no need to scare the girl witless. She only owes some money after all."

"Yep."

His eyes rose from the desk when Blane continued to loiter in the doorway, "Is there anything else?"

Blane considered the question before slowly shaking his head, "Nope..."

"Then get outta here!"

It might have been his imagination, given the deputy was usually as expressive as a corpse, but the cold ghost of a smile seemed to touch Blane's face before he sauntered off to make someone else miserable.

Blane didn't say much. His range of expression was not significantly wider than the mannequins in the window of *Madame Fontaine's* on Main Street, but he knew well enough the younger man wanted to swap his silver star for a gold one.

He'd been the same once. So eager to be the Sheriff of Hawker's Drift, he would have done anything to get the job. He closed his eyes and thought about Donny Bildt.

Whatever became of him?

They'd been best friends growing up together. Not quite brothers, but they'd been damn close as kids. They'd both become town deputies, then they'd drifted apart a little, they'd both wanted the same job, and the same girl; few friendships survived such things intact.

"Donny Bildt..."

He should have gotten the Sheriff's job all those years ago, should have married Elena May Thompson too. He was the better man, after all. He'd always recognised it. They both had, which was one reason why their relationship became strained towards the end.

Still, Sam Shenan had been the one the Mayor had come to and offered a deal. Bildt would be leaving town, and he would have a free run at both the sheriff's job and the girl. All he had to do in return was stay loyal. Do as he was told. Don't ask awkward questions.

Hadn't seemed so high a price to pay then.

He'd shaken the Mayor's hand, looked into the man's single fucked up eye, and told him he was his man. Forever.

Dumb sonofabitch...

Two days later, Donny Bildt had been accused of raping and beating a 13-year-old girl half to death.

Donny Bildt?

The guy who'd helped at the school in his spare time, the guy who was the first to organise a collection when someone fell on hard times, the first in line with his toolbox if someone's roof got taken off in a storm. The guy whose jokes everybody laughed at, the guy every eligible girl in town made eyes at.

Donny had been one of the most decent and law-abiding men he'd ever met, but Nancy Klass swore he'd dragged her behind *Casson's Livery* and beaten her black and blue with his studded leather belt before raping her. A mad-eyed beast, that's how she'd described the man who'd been taking flowers to Elena May Thompson those past three months. The man, he was fairly sure, Elena loved and wanted to marry.

A mad-eyed beast...

They'd both been town deputies when old Sheriff Kolman dropped dead in the street from a heart attack. He and Donny had been the only names in the hat to take over. Sam Shenan and the most popular man in town, it would have been a walkover for Donny. To be fair, nobody else would have given him much of a contest either, save for possibly Jesus H Christ, and even that would have been a close-run thing.

So, when the Mayor had come and asked if he wanted the job, he'd said yes. The Mayor had asked him if he would be loyal and do whatever was required of him? He'd said yes. When he'd asked about Donny Bildt, the Mayor's eye had stopped roaming around its socket and fixed on him. He could remember the feeling clearly; it was the first time he'd seen it happen. It felt like having a rifle trained on him and staring plumb down the muzzle.

"Well, you just let me worry about that little cocksucker..." Shenan swore he'd heard a round going into the breach.

Two days later, some asshole raped young Nancy around the back of *Casson's Livery*.

He never got to hear Donny's side of the story, he fled town before the other deputies or the lynch mob could get hold of him. He was never seen or heard of again. He'd led a posse to track him down, but they never found a trace of the man. He'd learnt over the years, from bitter experience, that men could have all kinds of shit inside them, stuff the world rarely got to see. Most men have secrets, most men have shit, but Donny Bildt was no rapist.

The Mayor had offered him a deal, and he'd grabbed it with both hands without reading the small print. His friend ended up being chased out of town by a braying mob.

Still, he got the job he wanted, and six months later, he'd married Elena May Thompson. So it all worked out in the end, eh?

The Sheriff stared at the ceiling of his office; it was overdue a lick of paint, there were small dark splatters in several places.

He'd been thinking a lot about Donny Bildt lately and how the Mayor had gotten him removed. Maybe he'd just known Donny's dark secret; that the most popular guy in town liked young girls. Maybe, but he doubted it. He knew a thing or two about the Mayor now that he hadn't known back then.

The only people who knew for sure were Donny and Nancy. No one had seen Donny since he'd left town, and Nancy had died a few months later. A heart attack, out of the blue. The kind of heart attack that happened quite a lot in Hawker's Drift; the kind that could strike down the young and healthy as easily as the old and infirm.

Yeah, he'd been thinking a lot about Donny and Nancy. About Elena as well. She'd died three years back. Rotted away from the inside, everything good and pure eaten away till nothing remained but puss, bile, pain, and heartbreak.

He couldn't help but think much the same had happened to Hawker's Drift.

Yes, he'd been thinking a lot lately. More than was entirely healthy for a man. He wanted time to think some more; he wanted to give back the star he'd sold his friend to get; he wanted to find some peace.

He thought about all those things, but what he thought about the most was that it was over thirty years since the Mayor had offered him that deal. When he'd taken his hand and looked into that unmoving eye, that reminded him of a rifle muzzle.

Thirty fucking years.

And the Mayor hadn't aged a day since…

The Farmer

After unloading the last of the cheese around the back of *Pickering's General Store*, Sye sat in the wagon and stared along Main Street towards Pioneer Square. He was only a couple of minutes away from *Jack's Saloon* and Cece, but he might as well have been sitting on the moon.

He had to get back home. Ma always got nervous on days he delivered produce to town and picked up their money. Today it was the cheese she'd made from the milk their small dairy herd produced. She didn't trust him, really; that was what it boiled down to. Every time he went into Hawker's Drift, he was sure she expected him to come back with no more than a bag of magic beans for their labours.

Main Street was about as busy as it ever got, which meant he could see about a dozen people. Sadly, none of them were Cece Jones.

He could just pop into *Jack's* for a quick beer. Just the one. It wasn't as if he was in danger of becoming a booze fiend or anything. He was, after all, looking for a wife, which Ma should have approved of. She wouldn't, of course.

He'd parked the wagon on the corner of the side street next to the store. If he set off home now, he'd just about make it back to the farm before dark; home in time for his dinner... and his evening chores. Then another restless night followed by getting up with the dawn chorus to milk their cows.

He looked up at the cloud-flecked sky and thought of the big wide world beyond the plains. He envied Cece, whatever her story was. She'd given little away about her past when they'd talked, but he was entranced anyway; she was a beautiful troubadour, moving from town to town, no limit on her imagination bar the horizon.

She might spend a day in Hawker's Drift or a year, but she was free to leave whenever she chose and let the road take her on to some other place, with other people and other lives. On the other hand, he would be chained here, to the farm, to the land, to those wretched, stupid cows and the vegetables they grew in the rich black soil. Till his back and his spirit were broken, and he no longer dared to even dream about a different life.

All his mother cared about was the farm. Protecting the family inheritance, producing an heir, like a feudal monarch desperate to secure their legacy and throne. That was Sye Hallows fate; the King of the Cowsheds.

He looked up and down Main Street, but there was no flash of blonde hair, no sparkling smile to lift his soul and offer something more than the drudgery that had been mapped out for him since birth.

"My, my, what a glum face!" A voice declared, startling him from his thoughts.

He looked down to find himself being inspected. Without invitation, the Mayor hoisted himself up and plonked himself alongside.

"Is something... wrong, sir?"

"I think there surely must be..." the Mayor placed his cane between his splayed feet and wrapped long fingers around the handle "...so why don't you tell me what it is?"

"*Sir?*"

"You look like you have all the troubles of the world on your shoulders, young man, and on such a glorious day too..." he leaned in closer "...remember, I make all the rules in this here town; and that just isn't allowed. So why don't you tell me your woes?"

"Oh... it's nothing really," he squirmed and felt much as he did when Ma caught him dozing in the barn when he should have been working.

"I think otherwise." The Mayor's single dark eye looked him up and down; he couldn't shake the feeling the man was trying to memorise every last thing about him as if someone would be asking him a list of questions about Sye Hallows later.

"Has the bottom fallen out of the cheese market perhaps?" The Mayor demanded when he remained silent.

Sye shook his head, "We got a fair price... as always."

"Good to hear; I'm very partial to your mother's cheese," the Mayor licked his lips in a manner far too theatrical and sensuous for a conversation about dairy produce.

"Really? I didn't know..."

"Oh yes, your Mother's wares are delicious... she's so creamy."

Obviously, the Mayor had meant her *cheese* was so creamy, but he thought better of correcting him.

"Must be girl trouble then? Nothing casts a young man's

face down more readily than girl trouble. In my experience."

It felt like a gigantic oven door had swung open in front of him. Beads of sweat erupted from his skin while the Mayor's sweetly perfumed scent caught the back of his throat.

"Any particular girl?"

He glanced away. He'd the uncanny feeling the Mayor could look right inside his head and see all his dreams.

"You were talking to our new songbird the other night, I noticed. Miss Jones?"

And I noticed you talking to her too.

His eyes darted back to the Mayor; he wore a knowing little smile. Was that why he was here? To warn him off? Everyone in town knew the Mayor was partial to a bonny face; it was one of a number of things nobody talked about.

He nodded without knowing what he was acknowledging, but he didn't trust his tongue just then.

He'd assumed the Mayor had wanted Cece for himself that night he'd been scampering around rustling up tips for her. He'd also assumed she would want him. He was the richest and most powerful man in town, and any chance he had with her had evaporated the moment the Mayor's dark and baleful eye fell upon her.

Whatever had passed between the Mayor and Cece, she'd acted no differently to him afterwards. She was still friendly, in a non-committal way. He didn't know if she noticed him, or the way that she made him feel alive, or how much he'd been around the saloon when she was performing. He guessed she had. He didn't believe for a second she was stupid.

But if the Mayor wanted her... then it didn't matter what

he felt, or even particularly what she felt or wanted either. Hawker's Drift was the Mayor's town, in every possible sense.

"She seems very... nice..." he spurted when the Mayor continued to stare at him.

"Nice? I suppose she is. Such a dull, unimaginative word, isn't it? *Nice?*"

He agreed, but he lacked the courage to utter words like beautiful, wonderful, or captivating.

"Have you told her yet?"

"Told her what?"

"That you think she is... *nice?*"

Sye shook his head and looked away. This was even worse than Ma's interrogations.

The Mayor let out a long sigh and settled back on the wagon's wooden bench, "In these matters, it is best not to dally. Otherwise, someone else, someone *less deserving*, will beat you to the prize."

He hadn't been aware courting advice was one of the Mayor's civic responsibilities.

"I suppose."

"There's no suppose about it, my lad!" The Mayor rapped the floor with his cane, hard and unexpectedly enough to make Sye jump, "one must strike while the iron is hot!"

"One must..." he could feel the Mayor's eye boring into him again.

"Then we are agreed!"

"We are?" He shuffled in his seat to look at the Mayor, who was still far too close for his comfort, "If you don't mind me asking, sir, why are you interested?"

"Because I'm interested in the well-being of all my constituents, of course!"

He was going to point out that as he lived beyond the town limits, technically, he wasn't one of the Mayor's constituents but decided against it. The Mayor might not be able to milk a cow, but he certainly knew more about who his constituents were than Sye did.

"Thank you, sir; I'm flattered."

The Mayor slung an arm around the young man's shoulders and leaned in close to his ear; Sye hoped the smell of cheese and sweat didn't offend him.

"The problem is…" the Mayor said in a conspiratorial whisper "…there just aren't enough pretty girls in this town. In fact, if truth be told, there are far too many ugly ones, so if we have the opportunity to brighten up the scenery with a lovely young maid, I think we are all beholden to do our utmost to ensure she stays here and puts down some roots. Lovely girl like her really shouldn't be flitting around from town to town. It just isn't right, is it?"

"I suppose not…" he replied, equally conspiratorially.

The Mayor's breath had the same overly sweet, perfumed scent as his skin. Did he gargle cologne? He fought down the urge to giggle. It seemed utterly absurd that the Mayor of Hawker's Drift, who he couldn't remember ever speaking directly to before, should saunter over to his wagon and throw a fatherly arm around his shoulders as he gave him advice about girls. Perhaps he'd misjudged him; if he wanted to warn him off Cece, he was going about it in the most peculiar manner.

"Then you need to be bold because, believe me, some

The Burden of Souls

other less deserving fellow *will* help himself sooner or later. It is the way of the world. There is always some less deserving fellow after what you want. After what is *rightfully* yours? Isn't that just so, lad?"

He found himself nodding. The Mayor was right; everything he'd ever wanted in his life, from Barney Deeb's bay foal to a kiss from Katy Keener behind the school outhouse, had ended up going, as the Mayor put it, to some less deserving fellow. And deep down, he suspected Cece would be the same. Maybe he'd been wrong about the Mayor, but he knew plenty of others who did want her. Hadn't he seen it in all those hungry eyes watching her sing and not a one of em able to hear the beauty in her voice the way he did?

"Yes..." he muttered before looking deep into the Mayor's single eye that was so deep and perfectly black at the centre it seemed to drink in all the light of the day. "Yes!" He repeated more forcefully.

"That's my boy!"

He felt giddy. He wasn't sure if it was from the thought of Cece actually being his, in a way he hadn't quite visualised before, or that the air seemed to have become so thick and viscous with the Mayor's syrupy scent that he had to chew it as much as breathe it.

"If you want her, boy, you gotta go out and take her! Then she'll eat out of your hand... and anything else you want besides."

"I want her, sir, more than anything."

"Anything?"

He blinked; of course he wanted her more than anything!

"Yes."

"Is she your heart's one desire?"

Sye nodded.

"Then you and I must do what is required," the Mayor grinned, his teeth white, bright, and almost feral.

"What is required?"

"To keep Miss Jones here, in Hawker's Drift. With you..." the Mayor leaned in so close his lips brushed against Sye's ear as he breathed one final word.

"...*forever*..."

The Songbird

"Well..." Monty wiped a grubby little towel across his sweaty pate as he looked up at her, "...I hope you're pleased with yourself, young lady?"

She'd paused halfway down the stairs, staring at Monty, Sonny, and several burly men she didn't recognise gathered around a huge piano they'd clearly just manhandled into the saloon.

"Where on Earth did that come from?" she frowned, continuing down.

"The Mayor or Santa Claus, I'd guess..." Monty shook his head as if it were the dumbest question he'd ever heard. Though that hadn't been quite what she'd meant.

"Of course, the Mayor..." she grinned at Monty as she ambled over; she was happy to play dumb when required.

She slid a finger over the black lacquered top. It was flawless. Not a mark upon it and polished to a near mirror finish. It looked like it had just come out of the factory gates.

"It's a beast, ain't it?" One of the men she didn't recognise announced, leaving greasy handprints on the piano as he patted it. He was bare-chested, though so hirsute it hardly mattered. He seemed to be grinning somewhere beneath the tangles of a copious black beard while equally long dark twists hung to his shoulders. All he needed was a fire-hardened spear, and he would have looked much like a caveman standing proudly next to the corpse of a freshly killed mammoth.

"It's a grand piano."

"Yep, it sure is pretty."

She forced a smile.

"You'll have to excuse Sniffy," Monty explained, "he ain't here for his brains."

"Sniffy?"

"It's Gordi, really," Sniffy grinned again (probably) and wiped a sweaty palm on the wiry dark rug of his chest before holding out his hand, "Gordi Smelts,"

"Nice to meet you, Gordi," she accepted his hand, which engulfed hers entirely.

"It's alright; everyone calls me Sniffy anyhows. It's kinda funny. Sniffy *Smelts*... see?"

"Like I said..." Monty ushered Sonny back towards the bar with a playful flick of his towel.

"What happened to the old piano?" she looked around the saloon.

"It's out back; it'll still be useful... gets cold here in winter," Monty explained, half turning away before adding, "Oh, before I forget, this came with your new toy..." he handed her a small white envelope before following Sonny to the bar. The rest of the men dispersed, too, save Sniffy, who continued to stand and stare at her.

"What's it say?".

"It's private," she turned the envelope over.

"I understand, Miss; I won't tell anybody what it says."

She looked pointedly at the big man, but he clearly wasn't the type to take a hint, and it wasn't worth being abrupt with the guy. He seemed harmless enough, even if he shared the habit most of the men in the town had of staring excessively at her.

She tore open the envelope and unfolded the note inside.

I hope the piano meets with your approval. You have Wednesday night off, so come and sing for me...

"Who's it from?" Sniffy peered over the top of the note.

"The Mayor," she stuffed the note back into the envelope, "apparently, I have a night off, which is news to me. And Monty, too, I expect."

"Oh..." Sniffy shuffled backwards.

"He would like me to sing for him."

"Oh..."

"I suppose I should be flattered."

"S'pose..." Sniffy shuffled a bit more before leaning in and adding in a lower voice, "You gonna go?"

"It would be rude not to... wouldn't it?"

"S'pose..."

Cece eyed him before asking in an equally low tone, "Is there anything I should know about the Mayor?"

Sniffy pondered the question before replying in a measured and flat voice, "He's a wonderful man who has done great things for the town. Everybody says so; Preacher Stone, Mr Jack, Sheriff Shenan, Dr Rudi. Everybody... well everybody save Mr Wizzle, but nobody pays any heed to him on account of him being soft-headed and all. That and being a clown..."

"The Mayor's a real diamond. I get that."

Sniffy nodded his head and added in a loud voice, "Yep, the Mayor sure is a great guy," before looking around; when nobody paid any attention, he leaned in close again. She held her ground despite the greasy forelocks brushing her face.

"You seem real nice, Miss, just be a bit careful... around the Mayor."

"Careful?"

The hair filling her vision convulsed; there may have been a frown somewhere, "You being pretty an all."

The man in charge has an eye for the ladies. What a surprise.

"I can look after myself when it comes to men."

Sniffy looked like he was going to say more, but Monty shouted at him before he could. "Sniffy! Get back to the yard, or I'll have to pay Norris for your time. I'll have a couple of beers on the house for you tonight!"

Sniffy's eyes lit up, and he cracked a smile wide enough for a few yellowing teeth to emerge from the undergrowth, "Free beer!" He chuckled and wandered off towards the door, whatever he'd been trying to tell her quite forgotten.

Men really were the same wherever they were ...

The Barber

Like every other Wednesday, Ash Godbold closed his barbershop at four o'clock on the dot. Everybody in town knew he closed at four o'clock on Wednesdays, as that was the day he took his wife and daughters to have dinner in *Rosa's*, which was, by a long and winding country road, the best place to eat in Hawker's Drift.

Or rather, everybody in town knew except Audley Cobham, who invariably came in for his weekly shave precisely at five to four. Every Wednesday.

"I'm closing in five minutes," Ash looked up from the broom he was sweeping the offcuts of Barney Deeb's and Chester Budoch's hair up with.

"Yep," Audley nodded and settled himself into the chair, jutting his chin forward to inspect himself in the large mirror that had belonged to Ash's grandfather.

He put the broom to one side, "You know you could come in at three o'clock for a change..."

"Nope... gotta feed me chickens then. They're darned particular. Don't lay right less they get fed at the same time every day. You can ask any chicken man that."

"Creatures of habit, eh?" he wrapped a towel around Audley's shoulders and resisted the urge to strangle him with it. Might as well argue with the north wind as with the ol' coot. He'd considered closing ten minutes early more than once just to teach him a lesson, but it wasn't worth it. He really would never have heard the last of it.

"Yep. Pesky critters."

He glanced at the clock hanging above the mirror; he hated being late, even though he wouldn't be keeping anyone waiting. Kate knew old man Cobham ensured he never got to close exactly at four o'clock, so she and the girls wouldn't be on time for their pre-dinner soda either.

He whipped some lather up in his soap jug before working it into Audley's scratchy grey whiskers, only half listening to him yap about the town's goings-on. As well as a keen chicken man, Audley Cobham was an incessant and insatiable gossip.

As soon as the clock clicked onto four o'clock, he put the soap jug and shaving brush down, crossed to the door and turned over the "*Closed*" sign.

"Taking the family to *Rosa's*?" Audley's eyes followed him back to the chair in the mirror.

"It's why I close early... *every* Wednesday..."

"Family..." Audley nodded sagely.

Ash held a dish under the old man's chin.

"Spit it out."

"I ain't finished yet!"

"You want to chew that nasty stuff, that's your business, but I'm not taking a razor to your throat with that jaw of yours worrying away at it. I hate mopping up blood; it's bad for business."

Audley worked his jaw a bit more before reluctantly spitting out a black gob of chewing tobacco.

"Why can't you just smoke the stuff, like a civilised man?" he wrinkled his nose and slid the dish away from him along the dark wooden counter running along the wall beneath his grandfather's mirrors.

"I prefer a good spit," Audley chuckled, his thin bony shoulders twitching beneath the towel.

He flicked open his razor, gave it a couple of swipes along the leather strap hanging beneath the counter and gently pushed Audley's head to one side.

"Did you see that McCrea woman the other day?" Audley cackled, twisting around to look up at Ash just as he was about to put the razor against his skin.

"Jeeez Audley! They call these things *cut-throat* razors for a reason, you know!"

"Sorry... always forget," Audley sniggered softly and settled back. He suspected the fool jigged about in the chair so much because he actually wanted to be cut just so he could run around town showing off his scar and telling everybody what a cack-handed oaf Ash Godbold was.

"Well, did ya?" Audley repeated, less animatedly, as soon as he scraped off the first swathe of stubble.

"Nope... heard about it though," he paused, razor in mid-air, to look at Audley in the mirror before continuing in a lower voice, "...bad-mouthing the Mayor?"

"Yep... never heard the like. I was standing plumb in the middle of the square meself, and I heard her as clear as day, screaming like some demented banshee outside the Mayor's front door. Which you knows is a goodly way away."

Wouldn't be the first woman to come out of that house screaming...

He kept the thought to himself.

"Strange woman..." he said instead and managed to get his razor out of harm's way before Audley started nodding vigorously in agreement.

"Her and that foul-tempered husband of hers – God rest his soul – made a fine pair of uppity no-goods."

Ash grunted his agreement, he'd never had much to do with the couple, and Tom McCrea had always been passable enough when he'd come in for a haircut. However, he wasn't going to argue the point with Audley Cobham, especially given the collected wisdom of the majority of Hawker's Drift's council of miserable, sanctimonious old gossips was that the McCreas were trouble.

He sometimes wondered what the good folk of the town said about him behind his back...

*

"Mr Cobham?" Kate asked once he'd kissed her cheek. He rolled his eyes by way of a reply.

"Sorry to keep you waiting," he grinned at the girls.

"We're kind of used to it," Emily replied, pursing her lips in mock annoyance.

Lord, she's growing up so fast...

"I know, I'm a terrible father," he ruffled Ruthie's hair and winked. Ruthie stuck out her tongue.

"The worst!" Emily insisted.

"Yep, that's why I'm going to make *you* pay for dinner this time, young lady."

"Not possible; I have no money. I'm quite the pauper."

"I'm sure Rosa has plenty of dishes needing washing."

"Rosa isn't that cruel to children," Emily replied, "whatever you say!"

He smiled and looked at his eldest daughter, standing on the corner of the square in the warm afternoon sun, her dimpled infectious smile and eyes as big and blue as the endless sky above. She was wearing her second-best dress, and Ash couldn't help but notice it was straining to contain her breasts; he was sure the dress had fitted her just fine only a few weeks ago. He had a vague feeling of wrongness that his little girl even had breasts.

Young Euan Rudi, the doctor's boy, ambled past, clutching a package. He grinned and touched his cap in greeting, though his eyes were fixed solely on Emily, who smiled in return, blushed faintly, and tried to both look away and stare at Euan at the same time.

Ash suspected he wasn't the only person who'd noticed his daughter's new breasts...

He ushered his family inside *Rosa's* before anybody else could get an eyeful of his daughter. He would have a word with Kate about getting Emily a new second-best dress.

Rosa Fawn greeted them in the same way she did every week, which was to say, in the manner of a woman reunited with a close relative whom she'd heard had died years ago.

She was a big blustery woman with red cheeks and grey hair who insisted on hugging almost everybody who came into her restaurant. After Rosa made a fuss of the girls, she hugged Kate then Ash, who found himself semi-crushed in a particularly fierce bear hug.

"How are you all!" she beamed finally, "it's been too long, far too long. I've missed you all so much!"

It had been precisely a week since they had last been in, and, unforeseen calamities aside, it would be precisely a week before they came in again, but Rosa never seemed to have grasped the concept of time. Absolutely everything was too long ago, be it a year or five minutes.

They settled themselves into their usual stools at the counter. Later they would eat at one of the check-clothed tables along the window so they could look out and see who was about in Pioneer Square, but the girls had always liked to sit on the high wooden stools along the dark rosewood counter first. From there they could eye the cakes laid out under glass dishes and catch occasional glimpses of Rosa's husband through the swing doors, toiling in the steam and noise of the kitchen as they drank their sodas.

Even when *Rosa's* was empty, the kitchen was still full of steam and noise. When they were still young and breasts had not been a concern, he'd told the girls that there were enormous iron cauldrons in the kitchen which were continually kept on the boil and stirred by Harry Fawn's kitchen trolls. They'd once been naughty little boys and girls who'd been sent to work in the kitchens by their exasperated parents when nothing else could be done with them, but the heat and noise had disfigured them until they were hunchbacked, scarred and pitiful little creatures.

Kate had never approved of the story, afraid the girls might say something to offend Rosa, but it had kept them quiet, their eyes fixed on the swing doors to the kitchen in the hope of catching a glimpse of one of Harry's trolls.

Of course, they knew he was only joking, though, given Harry Fawn's sour disposition, cold eyes, and mirthless expression, he looked like the guy who *might* keep a troll or two in his kitchen.

Quite what Rosa had ever seen in him, he couldn't imagine. They seemed about as mismatched a pair as you would ever come across.

He glanced at Kate, who was inspecting the cakes with Ruthie and smiled. He guessed not everybody could be as lucky as he'd been.

Lucky? More like blessed! A beautiful wife, not one, but two beautiful daughters, a good business, a comfortable home. If all he ever had to complain about was Audley Cobham, he truly was a fortunate man.

He'd never believed his life would turn out like this, that he'd ever make anything of himself. Perhaps some people would say being a barber in a town so remote the rest of the world seemed to have forgotten about it didn't amount to a great deal, but so what? He was happy, his family were happy, life was good.

Big, bumbling Ash Godbold, with his mismatched face and slow tongue. Not good looking and not bright. No money, nothing much going for him. He'd washed up in Hawker's Drift near on twenty years ago, nothing in his wagon save a couple of chairs and his grandfather's mirrors. A young man going nowhere. Now he'd everything he could ever want. Now he was happy.

He sat at the end of the counter and watched his wife and daughters giggling as they sucked their sodas through brightly coloured paper straws. The sun was streaming through the large plate-glass windows, fringing their blonde hair with halos of gold. Emily and Ruthie had taken their looks from Kate rather than him, something he was sure they were all extremely grateful for.

He glanced along the counter to see if their usual table was free, the one in the corner by the window, where they could sit and look out over the square and see everyone in the restaurant too.

It was still early, and they shared *Rosa's* with only two other customers. Eudora Dewsnap was scratching away in her journal between distracted stabs at a slice of one of Rosa's fine fruit pies and Deputy Blane, who sat in the back corner, mechanically sipping coffee.

Blane sat in the only part of the restaurant where the rays of the afternoon sun did not reach. He still wore his hat, ensuring his eyes were lost in shadow, but he got the impression he was staring intently at them all the same.

He tried to shake the feeling off; he didn't really know the Deputy. He seemed a quiet and solitary man with a singularly inexpressive manner. He'd never been much of a talker himself and wasn't usually inclined to hold that against a man, but with Blane, it seemed to run deep enough to suggest he was actually disdainful of other people.

He turned his attention back to his family; Ruthie had finished her soda with a final prolonged slurp and was looking terribly pleased with herself.

"Such a piglet," Emily sighed, shaking her head at her little sister.

The Clown

Mr Wizzle peeled open his eyes and looked into a cloudless cornflower sky. He'd fallen asleep. Now he'd woken up. He tapped his fingers against his generous belly. He had only meant to close his eyes for a moment, he'd been watching the first stars emerge from the dusk, and now it was morning.

He must have plum tired himself out with yesterday's long walk. Even here, in the middle of nowhere, it still took an effort to get away from folks. He yawned and shut his eyes again. Never mind.

He'd slept well and obviously needed the rest; he wasn't a young man anymore. God had wanted him to sleep rather than see angels. Who was he to complain?

His mouth was dry, but he felt so at peace stretched out on the ground that he couldn't face sitting up and finding his canteen of water.

No, just a little longer. He would lay and feel the morning sun warm his skin and listen to a silence broken only by the grass sighing upon an occasional kiss of wind. Even the insects were quiet; the morning was still too cool for them to be about their business.

The Burden of Souls

Everything was perfect. He was alone and at peace with the world, away from the filth and noise of Hawker's Drift and all its Godless shenanigans. Just the sun and sky and grass and Mr Wizzle. A slight smile played across his face. He felt content, which he only ever truly did when he came out onto the grass and looked for the angels.

Perhaps they'd come while he slept, dancing about him, ephemeral and translucent, lighting the sky with their angelic glory. Or perhaps he'd have seen nothing but the occasional falling star. It didn't matter. He would spend the next day and night here; he'd food, water, Hobart's old Bible and a pack of playing cards to practice his tricks with. So, what was the hurry? Everything was perfect.

He tipped his hat over his face; maybe he'd nap more and enjoy the silence.

"Mr Wizzle! Mr Wizzle!"

Eyes snapping open, he sat bolt upright, battered derby tumbling into his lap.

He blinked and looked about him. He could see nothing but the vivid green grass, which would have been above his knees if he'd been standing, stretching from horizon to horizon.

"Oh my God! It really is you, isn't it?"

The voice, which was female, was coming from behind him. He twisted around to find an elderly woman standing in the grass; she was wearing a loose robe and clutching a peculiar looking bottle to her chest.

Her skin was a deep, rich sepia, crumpled and fissured by age; her hair was short and grey, thin enough for the morning sun to show the black of her scalp beneath.

Once he'd turned to face her, she clapped her hands delightedly and revealed her teeth, which looked near perfect despite her obvious age, with a dazzling smile. Mr Wizzle couldn't help but return it, even if he didn't have the faintest idea who the old woman was.

"I'm sorry, ma'am, do I know you?" he struggled to his feet despite the stiffness in his legs.

"Why, surely you do! I'm Amelia. Amelia Prouloux! Well, Amelia Cooper, I suppose, but I never really liked that name. Dead common, and I'm sure Frank's kin never had much doing with making barrels anyway, so I kinda gone back to my old name since Frank passed on."

He looked at her blankly.

"Pleased to meet you, Amelia Prouloux," he reached up to doff his hat but found only tufts of his spiky red hair as he'd forgotten his derby had fallen off when he'd sat up, "I'm Mr Wizzle."

Amelia leaned in closer to him, "I know who you are, silly. I've never forgotten you."

When she continued to stand there staring at him, he fished a bag out of his pocket and offered it to her.

"Pickled egg, Amelia Prouloux?"

She added more wrinkles to her broad nose, "No thanks, hun."

Mr Wizzle picked one out for himself. It was breakfast time, after all.

He looked around to see if the strange old woman was with anyone, but the grass was as deserted as it usually was. He wondered where she'd come from, given she looked like she'd just gotten out of bed.

"Where did you come from?" He decided to ask.

"Mississauga."

"Huh?"

"Ontario."

Mr Wizzle didn't know what those words meant; he assumed they must be where she came from, though he'd never heard of them. He decided to try again.

"I meant, where did you come from out here?" He swept an egg-free hand out over the grass, "Are you with a wagon train?"

Amelia just smiled, "Never mind all that, you just help me with my sitting down. My legs ain't much good for standing on these days..."

Amelia seemed sprightly enough despite her age and soon hunkered down next to him, still clutching her peculiar bottle, which was bright pink, flat, and wide and appeared to be made from rubber.

She took a deep breath of air and lifted her face towards the sun, "God, everything smells so clean out here."

Mr Wizzle followed suit. Amelia was right, of course; it was always good to start the day with a prayer.

"God, everything is so beautiful out here, and we thank you for your infinite bounty."

Amelia laughed and looked away. Mr Wizzle couldn't quite see the joke, but it was a kind laugh, not like the nasty little sniggers he got back in Hawker's Drift when people shouted bad names at him.

The smile faded, and Amelia turned bright chestnut eyes on him, "Am I really here again, or is it just a dream?"

"You're not having a dream," Mr Wizzle frowned, "well, not unless I'm having a dream too."

"Not sure we can both be dreaming, hun?"

Mr Wizzle agreed; that didn't seem entirely likely.

"Sure you don't want a pickled egg?" Mr Wizzle rustled the bag in Amelia's direction.

"No, they give me wind, dear."

"Me too," he replied with a shrug as he fished another one out.

They sat in silence for a while. Mr Wizzle still didn't have a clue who Amelia was, but she seemed like a nice old lady, even if she didn't like his eggs, so he was happy to sit with her and watch the grass swaying all the way to the edge of the world.

After a while, when he'd eaten enough eggs, he looked over at Amelia; two fat, silent tears were running down her hollow cheeks.

When she noticed him looking at her, she wiped a hand across her face and smiled, "Look at me, crazy old bird, crying over silliness."

Mr Wizzle didn't know why Amelia was crying, but he held up his hand and snapped his fingers in front of her nose, and as she blinked, a paper flower appeared in his hand, which he handed to her with a little nod of his head. She squealed and clapped her hands in delight.

"Thank you... it's beautiful," she declared. Mr Wizzle knew it wasn't; it was just an old and faded paper rose like the one he wore in the lapel of his jacket. But it was kind of her to say all the same.

She played with the flower, twisting it back and forth in her hand, "I was just thinking how much I wish I could have brought my Frank here; he so would have loved these big clean skies."

"Why didn't you?"

"Cos after I found my way home, I stopped believing in this place. I stopped believing in everything and everyone, tried to make myself forget what was to be and what I must one day come back and do..." she looked up from the paper rose and stared at him with big wet eyes, "...and as for the Devil. I stopped believing in him too..."

The Gunslinger

He didn't see her until he'd rounded the remnants of the old homestead; she was sitting on an upturned timeworn bucket, her attention flicking back and forth between a book in her lap and the distant flat horizon.

She was so engrossed in what she was doing that she didn't notice him until his horse whinnied and shook its head.

"Afternoon," he dismounted at the same moment Cece shot up from her improvised seat, eyes widening as the colours of her soul flared in vivid alarm. The image of the ball of her palm connecting with the bridge of his nose flashed behind his eyes. He didn't come any closer.

"Sorry to disturb you," he nodded at the thin little book she was clutching to her chest.

"That's ok..." she glanced down before quickly stuffing it into the satchel slung over her shoulder "...I was just drawing the view..."

"Not much to see."

"Oh... the sky is beautiful."

He looked up; a handful of small cotton wool clouds littered an otherwise blue sky. There didn't seem much for someone to draw, especially when they weren't holding a pencil...

"Sure is..."

She'd tethered her horse to the remains of a fence post poking above the grass twenty feet or so further on. She was munching on the long green grass and seemed much less bothered about his appearance than her rider.

He patted the neck of his own mount but made no move to approach the girl. He could understand her skittishness, they were a couple of hours' ride west of Hawker's Drift, and there wasn't a soul in sight.

"Your horse is going lame," he nodded towards the animal.

"It is?"

He led his horse over and tethered it next to Cece's, "Hope you didn't pay much for her?"

"Just hired her for a few days."

He ran a hand across the animal's haunch; she was a docile old thing, "She'll get you back to Hawker's Drift so long as you don't ride her hard, but get another horse the next time you want to come out here. Sorry, old girl."

"I'm neither old nor a girl," Cece's mouth hardened.

"I wasn't referring to you," he patted the mare's neck, "she prefers being out here in the fresh air and the grass to being cooped up in the stables where it's hot and dusty, but she's way too old for anything but walks around the town with a kiddy on her back. Or the glue pot. How much they make you pay for her?"

"I got a deal..."

"I bet."

"She tell you all that?"

He just smiled.

"I'm Cece," she said, still looking skittish.

"I know."

"You do?"

"You sing at *Jack's*; I'm staying there too."

"Oh... I thought you looked familiar," she lied. She didn't know him from Adam, but why should she? He was just another rough-handed stranger.

"Amos."

"Pleasure."

"You mind if I take a quick look around?" he waved a hand towards the shell of the old homestead.

"You thinking of buying it? Needs a bit of work; nice view, though."

"If you like grass," he took a wide berth around her to the ruin; she still wasn't entirely convinced he wasn't going to rape and kill her. Even if she didn't have a gun, it was best to get out of her way as quickly as possible. He didn't like making women nervous.

The homestead was just a burnt-out shell, a stone chimney surrounded by charred timbers poking out of the grass like a pile of blackened matchsticks.

He'd spent the day following the road west of town, checking the farms and homesteads, but none of the residents knew anything about Tom McCrea or his dynamite. He'd spotted this ruin from the road and had made his way across the ghosts of fields all but washed away by the grass that had flowed back after the farm's abandonment.

Cece and her old horse had been on the far side, and he'd gotten no sense of her till he'd rounded the remains of the farmstead.

He poked through the timbers, looking for signs of disturbance. Why Tom would have wanted to bury his provisions out here, he couldn't imagine, but in the featureless landscape of the vast grass plains surrounding the town, if he'd wanted to hide them – and presumably find them again – then the abandoned farm would be a good choice.

It took only a few minutes to work out it was another dead end. The grass was growing through the charred wood; nobody had been around in a long time.

"What are you looking for?" Cece stood in the doorway, one hand tightly clutching the strap of her satchel.

There seemed little reason to lie to her; the word that he was helping Molly would get back to the Mayor soon enough anyway.

"Dynamite."

Cece raised an eyebrow, which had been plucked into a perfect arch.

"Other stuff too..."

"What makes you think it'd be here?"

He crouched down to peer beneath some charred roof beams.

"Just a guess..." he straightened up and winced slightly at the sound of his knees clicking, "...and not a very good one, it seems."

"Is there a lot of missing dynamite in Hawker's Drift?"

He tipped back his hat; it was cooler in the shade of the farm's remaining walls; the faint scent of damp decay lingered in the air. Sadness, too, like the echo of broken dreams. "I wouldn't know; I'm not a local. Just passing through."

"Me too."

"You gonna be riding around much in the next few days?"

"Planning to, I only sing in the evenings... the days are mine."

"If you happen to notice anything odd..."

"Like a box of dynamite?"

"Provisions. Anything looking like it might have been hidden. Or abandoned... forgotten... could you let me know?"

"Sure..." Cece shrugged "...why are you looking for this stuff?"

He went back to poking about with the toe of his boot but only unearthed the fire-cracked head of a wooden doll, "Helping out a... friend. Her husband died without paying his bills, and the Mayor's trying to collect from her. If I can find the stuff he bought, it'll make life easier for her."

"If I see anything, I'll let you know," Cece nodded, her brow creased into a frown before she turned and wandered outside.

He didn't expect to find anything but nosed around for a few minutes more before following Cece. She was leaning on the remains of a fence, chin in her hands as she stared over the swaying grass.

"Have you met the Mayor?" She asked without turning back to him.

"Briefly."

The Burden of Souls

"What do you think of him?"

He stood at her side, careful not to get close enough to unnerve her. She was wearing riding pants, a too-large shirt and a wide-brimmed hat tied under her chin. She also had a long thin blade held in a wrist sheath that wasn't particularly well hidden beneath her baggy sleeve.

"Not sure..."

"I've got to go and sing for him tonight, in his monstrous pile across the square."

"On your own?"

"You want to chaperone me?"

He glanced at her wrist, "Oh, I think you're capable of looking after yourself." She followed his gaze and quickly lowered her arm to her side.

"I find him... creepy."

He'd gotten no read from the man when he'd met him, but he'd heard something, or thought he had. The sound of screaming or at least something *like* screaming, though he was starting to think he might have imagined it, it wasn't at all how he usually picked things up about people.

"I wouldn't trust him."

"I don't," Cece glanced at him and smiled, "he's a man..."

He smiled back and hitched his boot up on the first bar of the fence. They stood for a while in silence, just watching the grass and the clouds. He felt comfortable with Cece. She was young and beautiful, thankfully too young and too beautiful to be interested in him. He also knew if he put a finger on her, she would try and slice him open with the blade she had strapped to her wrist. Which made for more comfortable company than Molly.

191

That and the fact Cece Jones looked nothing like his dead wife.

*

He'd been surprised when Cece asked if he would ride back to town with her. He'd been planning to turn back anyway, so he agreed with a curt nod.

"Be glad of the company," he lied.

"Just in case this old beast keels over on me... I don't want to keep the Mayor waiting."

"We'll be back in town well before dark... plenty of time to make yourself beautiful."

"Fat chance," Cece snorted, vaulting effortlessly into her saddle. She didn't know much about horses, but the girl seemed comfortable in the saddle. Athletic to boot.

"Not going to dress to impress?"

"Not something I do..." she wheeled her mount around to come alongside. Her skin was flawless, and her eyebrows were carefully plucked, for someone who didn't care about their appearance...

The horses plodded through the grass towards (what passed for) the road. He looked back to the farm once they were on the packed earth.

"Fertile soil here..." he muttered, "...but it's been a good few years since that farm burnt down."

"You'd think there would be plenty of people in town looking to take it on."

He agreed, another year or so, and they'd be nothing poking up above the grass save the stone chimney breast, one more marker for the death of someone's dreams.

There were a few other buildings scattered about, but not many. Even so, the distances involved meant it would take a long time to check all of them. How long did he want to stay in Hawker's Drift? He knew the answer, but he had the nagging feeling he might be around a lot longer.

"What brought you out here... to Hawker's Drift?" Cece asked after a while.

"Nothing, just looking for work."

"Out here?"

"As good a place as any. If there's none, I'll just move on. It's what I do."

"Just a drifter, huh?"

"I guess."

"Don't want to put down any roots?"

Amos glanced over his shoulder before answering her, "Did once... not again."

"Married?"

"I was."

"Kids?"

"You ask a lot more questions now you don't think I'm going to jump you."

"Well, if you were going to, you would have done already, so I might as well make the most of your honourable nature."

He smiled at that, "Honourable? I don't think so."

"You're helping a woman in distress; you didn't try to rape me. Makes you a saint around here."

"You haven't got much regard for men, have you?"

"Just speaking from experience."

Cece wasn't far past twenty to his eye. How much experience could this young slip of a thing have? Then again, the world had fallen to pieces.

"Anyway, you didn't answer my question?" Cece said, watching him from the corner of her eye as they rode side by side.

"What question?"

"Kids?"

"Oh, that question."

"Something you don't want to talk about, huh?"

He shook his head and swivelled in the saddle again.

"So, what happened? With your wife and kids?"

"I definitely preferred you when you thought I might be trying to jump you."

Cece smiled sweetly. It was hard to resist her bright, infectious smile. It was the kind that could open a lot of doors for a girl, or get one into a helluva lot of trouble...

"My wife's dead. No kids."

"Oh..." Cece's smile faltered to a grimace, "...I'm sorry."

"It was a long time ago."

"It can help to talk about these things... if you want?"

"I don't," he shot her a look colder than she deserved, "...and it doesn't."

"I didn't mean to pry."

Of course she meant to pry. It was human nature, after all. Generally, he didn't have to ask questions to find out what went on in someone's head, but most folk weren't like him. Which was for the best.

"What about you?" Counter-prying was the best way of deflecting her questions.

"Me?"

"What are you doing here?"

"Much the same as you," she lied. Again.

He kept his gaze forward; he didn't want to look too closely in case he saw something he didn't like.

"Just drifting too, huh?"

"Yep."

"Aren't you a little young for the road... not to mention too pretty."

"It *is* a knife I have up my sleeve, by the way."

"Just a compliment... and a question."

Cece tipped her hat back and stared out over the grass towards another homestead, this one not burnt to the ground.

"Just seeing the world," she said finally. He had to stop himself frowning. That didn't sound like a lie.

"Where you from?"

"Back East. You?"

"Down south, originally."

"Whereabouts?"

"Little spit of a town, nothing but dust and heat, wouldn't be surprised if it's shrivelled up to nothing now. Like a cow shit left in the sun."

"Sounds like a nice place."

"Yeah. Regular little Eden. Running away or looking for something?"

"Sorry?"

"Everyone who's out drifting along the road is either running away from something or looking for something. At least to begin with. Eventually, it becomes a way of life... you drift along because you don't know what else to do. But you're too young to have gotten into that sorry state yet, so, running or looking?"

Cece pursed her lips before replying, "Looking..."

"For what?"

"For the end of the world..." she winked at him, then kicked her old mount into a surprised trot.

He kept his own steady pace, glad she'd moved ahead so he could look back on the road again, which ran, more or less, in a straight line. He could just about make out the chimney top of the ruined farmhouse. There were two specks at the far end of the road, a pair of riders, dark in the afternoon sunlight. He'd half expected Blane or some of the other deputies to have followed him out of town, but his tail had been empty all day. Now, after meeting Cece, other riders had appeared on the road.

It might just have been a couple of hands from one of the ranches further to the west of Hawker's Drift heading into town for the night. It might have been, but he didn't think so.

He could feel the spiders scurrying behind his eyes again...

*

"Having trouble keeping up?"

Cece had pulled her mount to the side of the road after she'd gotten a couple of hundred yards in front. He was mildly surprised she'd stopped to wait for him. He supposed it showed she trusted him, not that it mattered.

"You shouldn't push that horse..." he dismounted in one smooth movement.

"Problem?" Cece looked down at him.

"Maybe."

He gently patted her horse's rear as he walked around the animal to examine her left hind leg. It wasn't the one about to go lame, but it afforded him a view back along the road.

The horse shuffled as he made a show of running his hand up and down her leg. He crouched on his haunches. The two riders were still too far away to make out clearly, but they seemed to be wearing long canvas dusters, just like the deputies back in Hawker's Drift.

He eased himself back up and tried not to wince at the sound of his knees cracking again. Just how old was he now?

He took off his hat and glanced up at Cece, but she was staring out towards the horizon; banners of grey cloud were sweeping in from the north, their shadows darkened swathes of rippling wind-tossed grass.

"It's so beautiful here," Cece whispered, "I don't think I've ever been anywhere quite like it."

"Don't travel much, huh?" He returned to his own horse and took a long slow swig from his canteen. After wiping the mouth on his sleeve, he offered it to Cece, but she shook her head and continued to watch the cloud shadows.

He took a good while to fix the stopper back securely, his eyes continually flicking between the canteen and the two riders. They'd stopped in the middle of the road. Watching them.

"Is this old thing likely to die on me?" Cece asked.

"You mean the horse or me?"

Cece smiled and slowly wheeled her mount around as he heaved himself back into the saddle.

"As I'm not planning to ride you home, the horse is of more concern."

"Same advice as before; don't ride her hard... unless you have to."

She raised an eyebrow as they continued along the road, "Oh, don't worry about those two; they've been following me all day. If they were going to do anything, they would have done it by now."

The girl was no fool.

"Town deputies?"

"Think so."

"Any idea why they're following you?"

Cece shrugged, "Maybe they want an autograph."

He glanced at her, not entirely sure what the remark meant, but although she'd said it flippantly it didn't fool him. She was trying to hide her fear; the fact that she was being followed scared her... and yet she'd remained out here on the grass alone. He'd no idea what she'd been doing, but he was damn sure it wasn't drawing clouds.

"Strange little town, don't you think?"

"Town seems normal enough... it's just the people who are odd."

"Like the Mayor?"

"Example number one..."

Cece laughed, "Everybody seems... I dunno... reluctant to talk about him."

"Yeah, I noticed. Never anything bad anyway."

"A politician nobody bad mouths..."

"Like you said, it's a strange little town."

Cece nodded back towards the two riders behind them, "You think the Mayor sent them?"

"He runs the town... besides, he has history."

"History?"

"You're not the only woman in town his men are keeping an eye on."

"You think I shouldn't go?"

"What do I know?"

"Probably not much, but you're an outsider, like me, so at least your opinion is honest."

"He's the big man in town; best not to offend him unless you're planning to leave soon."

Cece narrowed her eyes against the glare of the afternoon sun as she looked out over the dancing grass, "No... I think I'll be here for a little while yet."

"Go sing for him then..." when Cece glanced across, he added, "...but keep that knife up your sleeve. Just in case..."

*

The shadows were long and soft by the time they trotted back into Pioneer Square. Amos noticed their other shadows had faded away once they had reached the town limits. He would have been back in town much earlier if he'd been riding alone, but Cece's half lame old nag had dictated the pace. He should have left her to it, but her company was bearable, and he was curious as to why the Mayor was having her followed too.

Curiosity had, after all, always been one of his biggest failings.

Once they'd stabled their horses, he explained to the protesting stable boy that Cece's horse was good for little more than glue, and she should get a mount less likely to die on her the next time she went out riding.

"I think you scared him," Cece noted with a fleeting grin after they'd emerged back into the square.

"He's a smart lad…"

"Thanks for your help."

He shrugged as they crossed the square. He seemed to be developing a habit of helping women, which was a thought that returned Molly to his mind. She would be expecting him tonight, he supposed.

Perhaps he would camp out on the grass for the next few nights as he searched the surrounding plains. It would be more efficient, he told himself, and it would make it much harder for her to try and kiss him again.

A few men were drinking outside the saloon, enjoying the warmth of the sun's farewell. They were mainly involved in spinning yarns or staring into their beer the way men tended to do. Two, however, were watching them intently.

"Your friend is waiting for you," he noted without looking at Cece.

"Friend?"

"The young farmer."

"Oh, Sye? I doubt he's waiting for me."

Now he did look at her; her cheeks had flushed ever so slightly. And so had her soul. Yes, she knew what he'd meant.

As they mounted the steps to the saloon's boardwalk, Sye doffed his hat and smiled broadly at Cece while his eyes flicked over Amos.

Cece returned his smile and introduced him, explaining that he'd helped her with her lame horse out on the grass.

Sye had given him a curt nod before spluttering a volley of questions about what she'd be singing tonight. Considering himself dismissed, he bid them a good evening. He was tired and hungry; he hadn't slept well at Molly's for several reasons, only one of which had been the hardness of the floor. He just wanted to grab some food and sleep.

Hopefully, it would be a quiet night for the girls working upstairs.

Cece flashed him a smile and said she'd see him soon, which was something that seemed to unsettle both Sye and him.

He was about to push open the saloon's doors when the second man who'd been watching them intently stepped in front of him.

"Come with me," Blane folded his hands in front of his lap as if he were concerned that Amos might be thinking of kneeing him in the balls. Which was quite astute.

"I'm sorry."

"I said, come with me," Blane repeated, his voice a low emotionless monotone.

"I meant I'm sorry, I'm not coming with you."

Blane frowned, slightly and momentarily, as if bemused by the reply.

"Why won't you come with me?"

"I'm tired and hungry – so unless I've done something arrestable, which I'm pretty sure I haven't, I'm going to eat and sleep.

"I'm not arresting you,"

"Good," he moved to step around the deputy.

"The Mayor wishes to see you," Blane moved in unison to block him off.

"And why should I want to see him rather than my bed?"

Blane produced a hint of a smile, just a cold little twist of the mouth, but a smile, nevertheless.

"He wants to make you an offer…"

The Widow

Amos paused outside her front gate, looking back and forth before heading towards Main Street. She resisted the urge to follow him. Instead, she pressed her face against the window. Neither Blane nor any of the town's other long-coated law enforcement dickhounds seemed to be around.

She hurried through the house and peered out of the kitchen window. A narrow lane ran behind the house, but it was empty too.

Had Amos scared them off?

His coffee mug sat alone at the bottom of the shallow stone sink. She wrapped her fingers around it before springing them open and turning hurriedly away. She was being stupid. Again.

After double-checking she'd locked the front door, she trudged upstairs, kicked off her shoes and pants and crawled back into bed.

Her temples throbbed. She'd long since lost count of how many times she'd decided to quit drinking. Probably every single morning she'd woken up with a lousy head and a queasy stomach, which added up to a heap of broken promises over the years.

The occasional passing voice floated in from the street, but other than Bruno, Mrs Firth's beloved crossbreed hound (part wolfhound, part rancid old cheese), howling at a disinterested world, nothing disturbed the peace bar her own thoughts.

She could be doing numerous things; some of them might even have been useful, but given her recent track record, staying in bed for the day was the smart move. It was far harder to make either a complete fool of yourself or a bad situation even worse if you just pulled the sheets over your head and told the world to go fuck itself.

Besides, perhaps Amos would appear in the evening loaded down with dynamite, guns, mules, and the rest of the shit her husband had bought for no obvious reason. It wasn't very likely, but if he managed it, she would be extremely grateful. She'd give him a big wet kiss no matter how much he protested.

She turned onto her belly and pushed her face into the pillows; they faintly smelt sweat. Laundry hadn't been one of her main concerns since Tom had died, especially as she'd planned to take the first stage out of town and leave the old sheets for someone else to worry about.

Molly spent a few minutes trying to figure out what had happened with Amos the night before but soon drifted off into a fitful doze pursued by long-coated men with dead slack faces.

*

Knuckles were rapping on the coffin lid as they tried to bang it down on her.

She sat bolt upright, sweat-soaked the sheets, and her heart was pounding. She took a deep breath and shook long unkempt hair from her eyes. Blane had been putting her in a coffin. His usually cold, expressionless face contorted with glee as he forced her down, pushing her face against the silk lining, all the while telling her to be a good girl in Bert-Bert's raspy pant as other hands pressed the coffin lid in place and the darkness engulfed her.

"Shit... I gotta get outta this town..."

She jumped as the knocking sound came again, even though she knew, this time, it was just someone rapping on her front door.

She wrapped her arms around her knees and remained seated on the bed. The coffin had just been a nightmare, but whoever was banging her front door was real enough.

What if it was Blane come to fetch her? Perhaps the Mayor had decided in the end he didn't want to give her three months to pay Tom's debts, some men could be a bit touchy about a woman standing outside their home screaming every obscenity imaginable at the front door.

Were they here to drag her off to the whorehouse?

She took a deep breath. Whoever it was, she didn't want to see them. The knocking, however, kept on coming – they didn't seem to be buying the idea she wasn't in. Maybe they'd checked the saloon already.

"Oh, go and fuck a big fat duck..." she rolled her eyes, pulling herself out of bed and creeping over to the window. She tugged the curtains aside a fraction, but whoever it was must have been standing right against the door as she couldn't see anybody.

The knocking came again.

She shook her head and made her way downstairs; she still wore an old, crumpled shirt; her legs were bare, but she couldn't be bothered to pull anything else on. If they were going to drag her off to the whorehouse, she might as well go half-naked anyway.

"Alright! I'm coming already!" she yelled to the sound of more frantic knocking.

"Please be Amos..." she mumbled as she finally got to the door, unlocked it, and threw it open.

"Mr Furnedge," she said, trying to sound neither disappointed nor relieved.

"Mrs McCrea! I came as soon as I heard!"

The lawyer breezed past her without waiting for an invitation, his little leather briefcase swinging agitatedly in time to his scurrying stride.

"It won't do; it just won't do at all!" His usually slitty little eyes were wide behind his thick spectacles.

Oh fuck, is the Mayor suing me for slander as well now...

Why on earth had she let rip at him in public? Apart from it feeling bloody good, of course.

"Come, come, we must discuss this at once!" Furnedge beckoned her into her own home with a flick of his wrist before disappearing into the drawing-room.

She stared out into the bright sunny street and wished Amos was there with a couple of horses, but Baker's Street was quite deserted. She supposed she should be thankful

The Burden of Souls

there wasn't a crowd. She was providing the best free entertainment in town these days.

Fighting down the urge to bolt outside, Molly closed the door and trailed after Furnedge. The little man was inspecting himself in the mirror above the fireplace.

"Mr Furnedge?"

Still patting down his thin, greased back hair, he spun around and stared at her, "My dear!" he gulped, "you're quite... *undressed...*"

The shirt she wore was one of Tom's cast-offs; old, shapeless, and almost long enough to reach her knees. She didn't consider it in the slightest bit alluring, although the way Furnedge's Adam's apple was bouncing up and down, it seemed the lawyer might think differently.

She hoped he wasn't going to pass out.

"I'm sorry," she ran a distracted hand down the shirt to make sure everything remained buttoned up, "I was asleep... I can get changed."

"No! No need to go to any trouble for me... this is your home, after all." Furnedge deposited himself into one of the fireside chairs before pulling out a white handkerchief and dabbing his brow.

"How can I help you, Mr Furnedge?"

"Help? Oh... of course. I came once the news reached me. I must say it is an absolute scandal. An outrage!"

She stared glumly at the lawyer, had he burst into her home to give her a lecture about moral standards. For fuck's sake, she hadn't even slept with the guy!

"Is this really any of your business?" Molly crossed the room and sat opposite Furnedge; she got the feeling he was staring at her legs. If she was going to get a ticking off, she didn't see why she had to suffer an ogling at the same time.

"Why, of course. As your lawyer... and as your friend... I must say, the Mayor's conduct is quite, quite despicable. Something must be done, Mrs McCrea; something most indubitably must be done!"

She tried not to frown, "The Mayor?"

"I have only just learned of his... *proposal*. That he should stoop so low!" Furnedge spluttered and put the handkerchief back to work. He was sweating profusely.

"Oh, that..."

"You are taking it all very calmly, Mrs McCrea. A most admirable attitude, I must say."

"I wasn't quite so calm yesterday," she muttered, "how did you hear about the Mayor's... proposal?"

"I was with the Mayor's man Symmons this morning, just some papers requiring the Mayor's John Hancock, council business, very yawn-yawn, but the wheels must turn. Anyway, Symmons, a most disagreeable fellow I have to say, just between the two of us of course..."

"Of course."

"He divulged to me the... method of restitution the Mayor has in mind if you cannot resolve his debt. Frankly Mrs McCrea, I was horrified."

"I was none too pleased myself," Molly said evenly.

"It cannot be allowed to happen; I will intervene on your behalf with the Mayor... if you would like me to?"

She leaned forward, "Do you think you could change his mind?"

The Burden of Souls

"I've always found the Mayor to be a most reasonable and fair man. I cannot imagine where this has come from, expecting a young woman of your quality to demean herself in so base a manner simply to settle a debt? The man quite simply cannot be himself. I'm sure I can reason with him."

She blinked and tried not to smile, not entirely convinced she'd heard the lawyer correctly.

"You'd talk to the Mayor? For me?"

"Of course... if you would like me to? I doubt I can get him to write off your debt, not all of it anyway, but I'm sure we can come up with something more... befitting? The thought of you in such a place..." Furnedge actually seemed to shudder, "...it is just too horrid!"

"That would be... very kind, Mr Furnedge," she'd never particularly liked the little lawyer, and she'd assumed he thought no more of her than the rest of the town did. Perhaps she'd misjudged him; he certainly didn't need to go out of his way to help her.

"Not at all, I am only too glad to be of assistance... do not worry yourself, this can all be sorted," he smiled, leaned over and patted her knee, his fingers were sticky with sweat "...and please, call me Guy..."

Molly returned the smile and slid her knee away from his touch as casually as she could.

Under the circumstances, slapping his face might not be the best idea.

The Preacher

"Is it wrong to hate your own flesh and blood, Preacher?"

"It's wrong to hate anyone, Martha; we should find it in our hearts to forgive all trespasses; after all, who amongst is perfect?"

"That no-good boy of mine certainly ain't..." Martha Cripps spat and shifted herself on her pillows in search of a more comfortable position.

"You should forgive him. It is what God wants."

He sat by the old woman's bed, crouching forward slightly, a closed Bible encased between long slender fingers. He felt he was engaged in an exercise of stating the obvious, with as much likelihood of success as telling a wall to stop standing about doing nothing.

"God ain't gotta live with the little shit..."

"Martha..." he sighed, which was as close as he let his exasperation get to the surface.

She grimaced, "Just cos I'm dying, I don't see why I gotta start being nice to people."

The Preacher gave her a weak smile.

Can't really disagree with that one...

"You're not dying; you just had an accident and busted your ankle. You'll be fine."

The Burden of Souls

She screwed her face up, "Weren't no accident, know I didn't leave those shoes at the top of the stairs..."

"You think your son did?"

Martha settled for chewing her lips with her gums by way of an answer.

"Why would he do such a terrible thing?"

"He'd boil my old bones and sell em for glue if he could get a good enough price!" She shouted, her venom sufficient for droplets of spittle to moisten the air.

He sat back. Martha Cripps had been claiming her son was trying to kill her for years. Before that she'd believed her husband had been trying to kill her, right up till the day he'd staggered out of *Jack's* drunk as a skunk and walked in front of a stagecoach. It had been an impressive, if unfortunate, feat of timing given the stage only passed by twice a week.

He looked around the sparsely furnished room. Other than a simple unfussy double bed, there was a nightstand that looked like it might revert to firewood if someone left the front door open on a windy day, a cupboard knocked together out of mismatched planks and a threadbare rug of an indeterminate colour. The rest of the small house, rented from Judd Proctor for little more than the cost of a couple of turnips a week, was no better furnished. In other words, if Hector Cripps wanted his mother dead, it sure wasn't to get his inheritance early.

"You think he's after your money, do you?"

"Why else would the ungrateful lil' weasel want me dead, eh?"

He might have been able to think of a few reasons, but it would have been singularly unchristian of him.

"Perhaps this is something you should discuss with Hector; I'm sure it's all just a misunderstanding."

"I should have wrung his scrawny neck as soon as I'd shat the wretch outta me. But it's too late for that an all," Martha folded her arms across her chest and stuck out her bony chin, "An it ain't no misunderstanding neither!"

"I suggest you pray for guidance... I'm sure God will show you the way."

"I'm sure..." her eyes followed him as he stood up, "...you going, huh?"

"I have several other people to see... is there anything else you wish to discuss?"

She shook her head, "Nah... just make sure Sheriff Shenan goes knocking on Hector's door when they find me with me neck broke one morning."

"I'll bid you good day then," he nodded, conjured a smile, and left the old woman to fester in her own bile.

Hector Cripps sat downstairs by the fireplace in the house's one good chair. With his legs stretched out, he looked rather comfortable. Hopefully, he wasn't so desperate for the chair that he'd kill his mother for it.

"She still bellyaching about me?" Hector Cripps wanted to know, making no move to rise from the chair. He'd spent most of his adult life perched on the copious folds of his behind and had long since made loafing his main vocation in life.

"She is in some pain; she-"

The Burden of Souls

"Aww, don't fall for that. She just rolled down enough steps to get some bruises and sympathy. That's all she ever wants."

"You should not speak so ill of your mother."

Hector snorted, "If ever a babe was found beneath a bush, it must have been me! Don't look like my parents, don't sound like my parents, not one solitary thing in common with either of them."

Apart from an extraordinary talent for moaning, of course...

"Hector, your mother is old and frail. Whatever has gone between you should be left in the past. You do not know how much time you have left together. Make the most of it; else you may live to regret such harsh words and deeds."

Hector muttered something under his breath that he couldn't quite catch, though it sounded a lot like it had ended with the word "off."

"Tend to your mother, Hector, and may God go with you."

He let himself out without waiting for a response or a farewell from Hector, who was just as bitter and poisoned as his mother. No wonder Maxwell Cripps had ended up such an incorrigible old drunkard.

He stood in the street and let the smell of horse dung wash the bitterness and bile of the Cripps house from his mouth and nostrils. The house was on the South Flats, at the foot of The Tear, after which Hawker's Drift became little more than a collection of single-storey cabins, shacks, huts, and sheds built with no particular thought or plan scattered about the warehouses and yards that the Mayor had ringed the town with.

He slipped his Bible into one pocket and pulled a small notebook, where he summarised Martha Cripps wild accusations and her son's vitriolic rants from the other. Quite why the Mayor was interested in all this petty gossip, he couldn't imagine, while the ethics of passing on what the sick, desperate, poor, delusional, and just downright stupid folk of Hawker's Drift told him in confidence was something he didn't dwell on too much.

Once he'd summarised the Cripps' bitterness, he put his pocketbook away and looked up the long tapering tail of The Tear, where the South Road climbed up the hill to become Main Street. He blew his cheeks out; it was a long walk back to his church in Pioneer Square. Despite what he'd told Mrs Cripps, he didn't have any more engagements.

His hand slipped into his pocket, and curled around the little black bottle, just to make sure it hadn't fallen when he'd fished out his notebook. He wanted it. Badly.

No one was around except a down at heel woman hanging grey laundry out on a line, but her back was to him. Nobody would notice, and even if they did, what would they see? Preacher Stone swigging from a bottle. He wouldn't be the only man taking a discreet nip in this town, though his bottle didn't contain whiskey. He didn't even know what it did contain.

Sweet, black candy...

The washerwoman turned and saw him; she waved and smiled. It was Mrs Calbeck; she had a son with a twisted leg and a husband who liked to spend his money on Josie Sonsoma upstairs in *Jack's*.

The Burden of Souls

He waved and smiled back. He also hoped she'd go inside and leave him in peace. Instead, she returned to hanging out her laundry. Phyllis Calbeck wasn't much of a talker, though she liked her Bible and occasionally questioned him about it. She seemed to like the Old Testament stories the best; it was one of the few times her flat tired eyes ever seemed to sparkle, which deep down he thought was unspeakably sad.

He could walk further into the South Flats, which was about as rough as Hawker's Drift got, but nobody would bother a man of God in broad daylight. He could find a quiet spot away from prying eyes and take a sip, just a little one, just to steady his hands and keep the fire from slow broiling his guts.

In the distance, he could make out the gloomy pile of Old Beevoir's place, slowly rotting to ruin in the sunshine. It was one of the few large houses down here, and it had been empty since its reclusive owner had died. There would be no prying eyes to see him in there.

He licked his lips. It would be stupid. He knew well enough what the little bottle did to him. He couldn't risk being seen, but part of him craved it too, feeling the air on his skin and the sweet candy in his throat. The decadent, debauched beauty of it.

He let the bottle slip from his fingers and pulled his hand reluctantly from his pocket.

No, he couldn't; there might be questions. Wagging tongues spread town happenings up and down The Tear like a summer firestorm, and the gossips would simply love such a juicy morsel. The Mayor wouldn't be happy about that. The Mayor had told him to be careful. So, he would go back to the church and his little house around the back. He would sit with the shutters closed and the curtains drawn. He would take a sip in the darkness, just the tiniest nip of sweet, black candy and let it make him feel whole again... even though he knew he'd feel disgusted with himself afterwards.

The Mayor had also told him only to take a sip in the morning and the evening. No more. But that was just one of several things he refused to think about as he began the long, slow walk up The Tear towards Pioneer Square.

The Gunsmith

The corner of Main Street and Leaning Lane offered a fine view; it was to the north of the Square, just before Main Street dropped down the northern slope of The Tear. Several of the buildings at the top of Leaning Lane had burnt to the ground years ago, a couple of people had died, and the houses had never been rebuilt. It wasn't really a park, just a little patch of scrubby grass dappled with a sprinkle of wildflowers in the spring, but everybody in town called it the Corner Park now. It was preferable to the-place-where-some-folk-got-burned-to-death, he supposed.

People sometimes came to eat here and look out over the endless prairie stretching away to the distant horizon. In one of his occasional acts of civic benevolence, the mayor had put a couple of simple wooden benches in so folk could sit and watch the sunset, which out here could be spectacular.

John liked to plonk himself down from time to time and watch the weather. Great mountains of cloud could boil up almost out of nothing and disappear just as quickly. Curtains of hazy rain could mist the horizon as they cascaded from near black skies while the sun still shone fiercely above the town. Rainbows like freshly painted banners could form enormous arcs while the wind tossed the grass heads into a churning sea of molten green or gold, depending on the time of year. The land was like freshly ironed linen in winter, every feature masked in white; clean, crisp, and unending.

Today, however, the weather was unremarkable. The sun was still hours from setting. The clouds were patchy and ill-formed; grey-white abstracts smeared across the sky without form or beauty. So, he just sat and watched the grass move. The surrounding farms stood out, patchwork squares of cultivated ground stitched upon the land, tiny little doll's houses here and there, all but lost in the vastness of the wild restless grass, occasional pebbles strewn over the great expanse of a sandy beach.

He loved it here. Despite everything. He enjoyed a kind of peace he'd never expected to find again. A peace he didn't deserve given all he'd done, but the past was the past. He'd come here looking for a woman he loved, but it'd been so long ago he was barely the same man. He'd never found her and had long since given up hoping he ever would. Or even really wanting to, if truth be told. Fear could do strange things, particularly if you gave it long enough to simmer your soul.

Funny how the universe had a way of screwing up your expectations.

"Enjoying the view?"

He looked up, startled by the voice.

"I'm sorry. I didn't mean to make you jump," the way Kate Godbold's eyes twinkled suggested that was exactly what she'd intended to do.

The Burden of Souls

"Yeah... I am enjoying the view..." a slow smile spread across his face as he stared up at her.

"Bad man..." Her voice dropped a little, though no one was around. Young couples might come in the evening to do their courting, and women, fortunate enough to have small children to play with, in the morning, but at this time of the afternoon, they had the place to themselves, though the Corner Park was too exposed to passers-by on Main Street for them to do anything but talk.

"Just happen to be passing by?"

"Nope... hoped I might find you here."

"We have to be careful."

"I know..." she flicked a strand of hair the wind was whipping about her face away, "...but I like taking risks. It's exciting."

He sighed inwardly but didn't say anything.

The last thing he wanted was excitement, outside of the bedroom anyway. He sometimes wished he'd grow out of women, he'd given up a lot of things, but he doubted that particular vice would be one he'd be able to kick while he still had breath in his body.

"There's no need to look so worried; I'm not going to try and straddle you on the grass," she winked at him, "as much as I want to."

He felt a stirring down in his pants. Nope, not anytime soon...

"You've got more to lose than I have."

Kate shook her head, "Nah, I'd just get kicked out of my home, lose my family, have my friends spit in my face and be chased out of town as a nigger-loving whore, whereas you, my love, would likely get lynched by Ash and his buddies."

He shuffled uneasily on the bench, not sure whether the prospect of being lynched or Kate calling him "my love" unsettled him more.

"Ash has never struck me as a violent man."

"He's not, but I think it would be what is expected of him under the circumstances. And Ash always likes to do what is expected of him. He's boring like that."

"Even more reason not to be seen together then."

"True, but I wanted to let you know Ash will be out tomorrow night. *All night.*" She emphasised the last two words with a significant pout of her extremely kissable lips.

"Where's he going?"

"Playing cards with his buddies, they do it from time to time. Not often enough, sadly."

"And he won't be back?"

"Not till morning – they're playing out on the Doherty farm this time. They'll be up till dawn drinking and talking horseshit; like guys do."

"What about Emily and Ruth?"

"I'll come to you."

"And they won't notice?"

"Ruthie is staying over with her little friend Gillian. Emily goes to bed early; I've got some pie dishes to take back to *Rosa's*. If she wonders where I am before she goes to sleep, she'll just think I'm talking horseshit with Rosa; like girls do."

"I dunno... it's safer if I come to you in the daytime."

"Like when Ash came home with a bad head?"

The Burden of Souls

"But if anyone sees you—"

"They won't; I'll sneak around the back of yours once I've finished with Rosa and be home long before Emily's up. It's not like she's a little girl who cries in the night for her mommy anymore."

"But why take the risk?"

Kate pursed her lips and raised her head to stare out over the plain.

"I married Ash when I was eighteen; I'd never been with a man before and have only been unfaithful with you – and every time with you was in my bed. I've never had sex anywhere but my own home. I want to do it somewhere else. Not a good reason, I suppose, but it's what I want."

"It's much the same wherever you do it," he could see by the way she pressed her lips together that he wouldn't persuade her otherwise, "Ok... just be careful, huh? No one can see you."

She looked back down at him and smiled that big radiant smile of hers, the one where she wrinkled her nose at the same time. It was a smile that could make him do just about anything. Still...

I shouldn't be doing this, not now, not anymore...

"Well, you manage to sneak into my place without anyone noticing. I'm sure I can do the same."

He thought about mentioning bumping into the Mayor but decided against it. The Mayor wasn't interested in their little affair, he guessed...

"See you tomorrow?"

"I'll look forward to it. I might even iron a shirt especially.

"That..." Kate said with a little laugh, "...would be an awful waste of your time as you won't be wearing it for long."

With that, she turned on her heels and walked back up the slope to Main Street. He watched the sway of her hips before turning back to stare across the plains.

And tried to shake the feeling he'd just made a terrible mistake.

The Farmer

He didn't like the way the stranger had ridden back into town with Cece or how she'd flashed her dazzling infectious smile at him when he'd said goodnight. He'd liked her saying she would see him again soon even less.

The stranger had a brutish look about him. A cold, hard man. The kind of man who always took what he wanted as if he had a God-given right to it. He knew the sort alright, and he was worried Cece was interested in him. He didn't understand why a beautiful, intelligent young woman would be attracted to a rough, weather-beaten man old enough to be her father, but he was the first to admit he understood what went on inside the minds of his dairy herd far better than he did any woman's.

Am I going to lose her to him?

That was what usually happened. It was how his world worked; as the Mayor had so succinctly put it, some less deserving fellow always ended up getting what was rightfully his.

Well, perhaps *rightfully* was too strong a way of putting it, but he knew they were meant to be together. She was perfect; she would make him happy. Even the Mayor could see that. He wasn't sure he wanted to stay in Hawker's Drift with Cece as the Mayor had suggested, he yearned to see the world and get away from his wretched farm, but he would endure that muddy little life willingly if he could live it with Cece.

He'd known her for such a short time, but he already couldn't imagine being without her. That was what being in love felt like, he supposed.

Cece kept looking at the stranger as he talked with Deputy Blane in the saloon's doorway. She looked distracted and concerned, more interested in the gunslinger than his questions about her songs.

She loved music and had a voice God himself must have given her; he was being interested and attentive, showing he shared her passion, which was just one of a whole heap of reasons why they should be together, yet his words washed over her as she kept glancing past his shoulder.

Perhaps the Deputy was going to arrest the stranger for something. He looked like the kind of man who must have done plenty of stuff worth being thrown in a cell for; maybe they'd string him up, though that was probably too much to hope for.

Whatever Blane wanted with him, Amos eventually turned away from the saloon and walked in silence with the Deputy across the square. Towards the Mayor's Residence rather than the Sheriff's Office, though. Which was a pity.

"What that's about?" Cece watched the pair walk away.

"Dunno," he replied, he hoped, disinterestedly, "Perhaps he's done something wrong; that's usually why the law takes an interest in a man. Perhaps you should be careful of him."

"I'm careful of all men," Cece smiled. He wasn't sure if she'd meant him as well, though he couldn't see why she would.

She turned away and headed inside; he paused before following her as a thought struck him. Perhaps the Mayor wanted to warn the stranger off Cece. He'd seemed keen to help after all.

Sye didn't know as he'd never had one before, but he guessed it never hurt to have friends in high places.

He shook the thought away; it didn't matter. The only thing he wanted from the Mayor was his advice. He was a strange coot, but he'd been right about Cece. He had to be bold. He just hadn't quite figured out how you went about being bold yet.

"You were out riding?" He asked once they got inside.

"Yeah..."

"Why?"

She frowned and turned back to face him, "Why not?"

"There's not much to see."

"It's beautiful... maybe you don't notice because you grew up here. Where I come from there's nothing..." she flicked her wrist towards the world outside the saloon "...like this."

"You don't have grass and cows where you come from?"

Cece laughed, which always made the blood rush from his head, "Yeah, we have grass and cows, but here... it's all different. Clean and unspoilt."

"You should visit my cowshed; that might change your mind."

Cece wrinkled her nose, "Very tempting, but I gotta sing tonight."

"Some other time... maybe?"

"To see your cowshed? Is that a euphemism?"

He chuckled. That sounded like something medical. He made a mental note to ask Dr Rudi if he got the chance.

"Well, not exactly the cowshed. If you want to see the countryside, I can show you. I know near every blade of grass around these parts." That wasn't technically true, obviously, but given every blade of grass looked much like any other, he didn't think it was far off the mark.

Cece pursed her lips and looked thoughtful. Sye's heart sank; she was trying to think of a way of letting him down gently.

"Sure, why not," she said with a little toss of her head.

He felt like he might faint. Was this what happened when you were bold? He didn't know as he'd never tried it before.

"When are you free?"

"Tomorrow?"

"Ten o'clock, I'll be at the livery finding a less lame horse..." she grinned and turned away "...sorry, but I have to get changed for tonight. See you!"

He watched her hurry off up the stairs, his mouth still hanging open long after she'd disappeared from sight.

The Gunslinger

"I wasn't sure whether you'd come," the Mayor looked up from his book.

"Your man is very persuasive," he nodded towards Blane, who'd moved to stand a couple of discreet paces behind his boss, muddy eyes not leaving him for an instant.

"One of his many virtues..." the Mayor opened his palm and indicated the chair opposite, "...please, take a seat."

The Mayor sat at a small cast-iron table in the garden to the rear of the Residence, a pitcher of iced lemonade before him. He poured a second glass and pushed it towards Amos.

"You look thirsty... I would offer something stronger, but I rarely partake of alcohol."

"No free whiskey here then?"

The Mayor smiled, "The mere mortals do so like their little pleasures, and I'm happy to indulge a few minor sins."

The lemonade was cold enough to hurt his teeth but otherwise pleasant enough.

The table sat upon a square of flagstones shaded under arches of honeysuckle and jasmine. Their scent rose with the evening to sweeten the air.

"A beautiful garden," he said when the Mayor continued to regard him in silence. He didn't really know if it was or not but assumed it was to his host's taste

"Ah, a man who can appreciate the world's beauty."

"I've seen enough of its ugliness."

"Of course, we all have; it's the way the world is, unfortunately... but would anything be truly beautiful without the ugliness?"

"If you've asked me here to discuss philosophy, you may be disappointed. It's not really my speciality."

"And what is your speciality?"

"Putting lead into flesh."

The Mayor regarded him over the rim of his glass, "More useful than philosophy, I suppose, in days like these at least."

"The pay is better."

"Quite," he sipped his drink and put it down before adjusting the cuff of his shirt beneath the cream linen jacket he wore.

Careful, fastidious, meticulous.

"I feel I should apologise," the Mayor continued once the cuff was to his liking, "I believe we may have gotten off on the wrong foot last night. Mrs McCrea can be quite bothersome."

"She's scared."

"She owes me a lot of money; she's entitled to be. Still, screaming insults outside my front door was... excessively unpleasant."

"I'm sorry she troubled your sensibilities, though if you were trying to force me to work in a whorehouse, I might be tempted to swear at you too."

"If I wanted her to work in the whorehouse she'd be on her back earning me dimes right now," a coldness crept into the Mayor's voice, "I've given her three months to pay the debt off by more agreeable means, or return the goods her husband procured on my credit. A more generous settlement than many would offer."

"Just why was her husband buying prospecting gear?"

"I didn't invite you here to interrogate me."

"I didn't think you did, but as I'm here..."

"You thought you'd help the merry widow out a little more?"

"If you can cast any light on the matter, then Mrs McCrea might recover the goods and return them. Which would be a more... agreeable solution for all parties?"

"Of course, it would! And if I could, I would, but as I explained to dear Molly, I can't. I don't know what her husband wanted the provisions for. He didn't tell me."

Amos nodded and pursed his lips, "Are you in the habit of lending men money without asking what they want it for?"

"You're interrogating me again."

"Yep."

The Mayor smiled, "If a man thinks he has discovered gold, he tends to keep the fact to himself. Tom McCrea asked for money, he was a trusted employee, and I was paying him well enough to repay the money, plus a little interest, in a reasonable amount of time. It wasn't my fault he went and fell off his horse."

Molly thinks otherwise.

He was about to ask exactly what Tom had done for the Mayor, but he held up his hand before he could get the question out.

"I'm delighted you're helping Mrs McCrea. Truly, but I didn't ask you here to discuss that matter. My time is somewhat limited; I'm a very busy man after all."

"I can see that," he glanced at the book, old and leatherbound, sitting in front of the Mayor.

The Mayor smiled thinly, "Tell me, Mr Amos, how good are you?"

"At what?"

"Gun work."

His eye flicked towards Blane's impassive face and back to the Mayor, "I could kill you both in the blink of an eye."

"That's quite a boast; Mr Blane is an accomplished gunslinger himself."

"I'm better."

"I do so love a confident man!" The Mayor clapped his hands together and beamed, "Would you care to demonstrate?"

"Wouldn't you object to me killing one of your employees?"

"Terribly. However, I was thinking of a more inanimate target," rising to his feet he ushered him out onto the lawn, Blane sauntered behind them.

The lawn was immaculate, smooth as a silk carpet. A dozen paces away from the table, the Mayor pulled an apple from his pocket, "Think you can hit this?"

He nodded.

"Very well, on the count of three, I will toss the apple in the air, and we will see," he stared at the gunslinger when he remained motionless, "are you going to draw your weapon?"

"I can draw and shoot in one. No need for a count either; just throw it when you're ready."

"Very well," the Mayor's eye remained on him as he turned sideways and held out his arm. In turn, Amos rested his hand on the butt of his revolver.

He stared at the Mayor rather than the apple. He could usually get a sense of a man, what he was thinking, what he would do, what he was feeling. They were things that seeped from the soul, allowing him to react almost before someone had even acted. It was a talent he didn't understand, but it had kept him alive for years, kept him able to do the Thin Rider's dark work long after he'd stopped even wanting to be alive.

Everyone was slightly different but similar enough for him to anticipate, but the Mayor... it was like standing in the mouth of a vast cave. He could feel the size of the space before him and knew it was immense, but he could see nothing of its dimensions or what was inside, other than something lurked there, something hungry and malevolent; something watching him with curious eyes. Something screaming.

The Mayor threw the apple in the air.

It had only cleared his head by a couple of feet when his gun boomed, and the apple exploded, showering the Mayor in pulp.

"Sorry about the suit."

"Impressive," the Mayor flicked a piece of apple off his shoulder.

He holstered his gun despite the nagging sense that he should have blown the Mayor's head off while he'd had the opportunity.

"Thanks."

Usually, he would have taken the apple much quicker, but the Mayor was harder to read than most men and he'd had to rely on his more mundane senses. No need to tell the Mayor that, though.

"You really do have a gift – are you so accurate when it comes to men?"

"They tend to be a bigger target."

"True, but fruit rarely shoots back,"

"Neither do the men I kill."

The Mayor nodded and slipped his hands into his trouser pockets, "I am always on the lookout for talented men. These are dangerous times; the world is full of renegades, bandits and assorted scum looking to destroy what's left of civilisation to sate their petty needs and desires. My deputies help keep them away from Hawker's Drift. Good steady work, lots of perks. Excellent prospects. Interested?"

"I've never really seen myself as a payroll kind of man. I'm more interested in short-term contracts."

"I can be flexible in my terms, exceedingly generous too. Whatever your heart desires, in fact. Ask any of my employees."

Like Tom McCrea?

"I appreciate the offer, but I'm not planning on sticking around here long."

"Oh, I'm sorry to hear that..." he felt something come rolling out from the cave's depths, the first clear sense of the man he'd got. The Mayor felt relieved.

"Besides, I already have a job. Once that's done, I'll be moving on."

"A job?"

"Yeah," he smiled, "not my usual line of work, but I like to try my hand at different things from time to time, but when it's done, I'll be on my way."

"And what exactly is this job, if you don't mind me asking? I'm curious to know who can offer better terms than me in Hawker's Drift?"

"It's no secret, Mr Mayor. I'm working for Molly McCrea, and I'll be in town until I've kept her out of the whorehouse..."

He touched his hat before turning his back on the two men.

"I'll see myself out ..."

The Widow

"Ma'am," Amos said, taking off his hat as she opened the door.

"Hey, Mr Mysterio!"

"Mysterio isn't my name."

"And mine isn't *ma'am*," she stepped aside.

"I just stopped by to let you know what I found," he made no move to come in.

"I know what you found... jack shit," she cocked her head to one side; "if I promise not to throw myself at you, will you come in?"

Amos didn't look convinced, so she reached out and yanked him towards the door. She'd decided he was a man who had trouble taking a hint. Or he really did think she was a sex-crazed vixen out to corrupt him. Either way, she had no intention of discussing her predicament on the doorstep.

As enthusiastically as a bullock being led into an abattoir, Amos trudged down the hallway, sitting down by the fire only when she told him she didn't want to get a cricked neck looking up at him.

"No dynamite, huh?"

Amos shook his head, "Not so far, but I'll go out again tomorrow... there's a lot of land to cover, so I might spend a few nights sleeping out... wastes a lot of time coming back and forth to town."

"I don't have a great deal of money, but you must let me give you something for your time."

Amos waved her down, "I don't want your money."

You don't want my money, and you don't want to fuck me, so what the hell do you want?

She decided it best to rephrase the thought slightly.

"So why are you doing this?"

"I'm not really sure, to be honest."

"That's reassuring," she said. It sounded like a lie. Men didn't go to this much trouble without a good reason, not in her experience anyway.

"I just wanted to let you know I might not be around for a few days; I wouldn't want you to think I'd run out on you."

"Thanks, but please be careful out there, huh? People have a tendency to fall off their horse around here."

"I can look after myself."

She sat back in her chair, "It might not be necessary; Mr Furnedge called today. He said the Mayor was being outrageous and would speak to him on my behalf."

"Furnedge?"

"He's the town's lawyer. I'm not entirely sure I can trust him, though."

"Why not?"

"He's the town's lawyer."

"Other than his choice of profession?"

"He's a creepy little fuck ass who undresses me with his slitty little eyes every time he comes near me."

"You don't like him much then?"

She blew out her cheeks and pushed her hair back. She really should get around to washing it sometime soon.

"I dunno, maybe I've misjudged him... This morning, he seemed genuine enough, all spit and fury about the Mayor. So, he can't be all bad."

"I saw the Mayor this evening."

Her eyebrows rose, "You did?"

"Well, he saw me. Blane was waiting when I got back to the saloon."

"What did he want?"

"Offered me a job."

"A job? Doing what?"

"Town deputy, I think."

"Why would he do that?"

"He appreciates my talent, and I suppose it would save on manpower watching you."

She flashed him a tight-pressed smile, "Haven't seen the dickhounds today, not that I've been out. I almost feel neglected. Did you take the job?"

"I'm fussy about who I work for; besides, I told him I already had a job."

"Doing what?"

"Keeping you out of the whorehouse."

"How'd he take that?"

"I'm not sure. I don't think he's used to being turned down."

"The pay would be better, given you won't take a dime from me."

"Your terms are preferable... and so are the bonuses," Amos added quietly, meeting her eye before quickly looking away.

Fuck. Was that some cack-handed attempt at flirting?

"The only bonus I can offer you is some cold leftover meatloaf. However, I did make it with my own fair hand..." she grinned before adding, "...which is probably why it tastes shit."

"Sounds better than anything the Mayor could ever offer."

*

Amos didn't so much eat the meatloaf as savage it, venomously driving his fork into it before working off great chunks to shovel into his mouth. He swallowed each lump so quickly she feared he might add yet another problem to her list of woes by choking to death on her kitchen floor.

She sat opposite him, cradling a mug of coffee. She'd eaten earlier and really couldn't stomach any more of that shit. She'd had to let Annie, the girl who'd come in to clean and cook for Tom and her, go; she couldn't afford to keep her on without any money coming in, so she'd had to revert to her own cooking, which seldom rose above awful.

Tom had always said her cooking tasted far better when he was blind drunk; the rude ungrateful fucker that he was.

Had been, she quickly reminded herself, looking down into her coffee.

Amos, however, was eating with enthusiastic gusto and, as far as she could tell, appeared to be completely sober.

Either he was being exceedingly polite, or something had gone terribly wrong with his taste buds.

After clearing the plate, he wiped the back of his hand over his mouth, "That was great. Is there any more?"

"More?"

"Oh, sorry – didn't mean to eat you out of house and home."

"No, it's not that... you don't have to force it down to be polite; I know it's barely edible."

Amos frowned and pulled a surprised little face, "But it's really good!"

Molly shook her head and took his plate. Over the years, she'd come to realise most men loved her body and hated her cooking.

This guy was clearly even more screwed up than she'd thought.

After watching him scoop another plateful of indigestible slop into his mouth, she asked him if the Mayor had said anything about her. She'd thought it safer to wait until Amos had finished swallowing before asking.

"I asked him a few questions."

"And?"

"I don't think he was impressed by your cussing."

"You don't say."

"He also said if he wanted you to work in the whorehouse, you'd be there already... who knows, maybe your friendly lawyer can persuade him."

"Fingers crossed..."

However, if Guy managed to pull off that particular trick, she had a hunch he'd expect her to express her gratitude by means other than meatloaf ...

The Lawyer

He hated waiting, or rather being *kept* waiting.

He always managed to be punctual, and he was an exceptionally busy man. An important man. The whole town would grind to a halt without him, the cog that turned the wheel, as he liked to think of himself. He barely had a moment to himself! When he wasn't getting business done, he was at home looking after his mad bitch of a wife. And yet he was never late, not once, ever. Nor did he keep people waiting.

If somebody had an appointment to see Guy Furnedge at one o'clock, then at one o'clock, they would most certainly see Guy Furnedge, not a minute sooner, not a minute later. It was simply good manners.

He pulled out his pocket watch again and checked how long the Mayor had now kept him sitting in the little anteroom next to his office. Seventeen minutes!

He took a deep breath to calm himself. He must not show any irritation, this *was* the Mayor, and he supposed the normal rules didn't apply. He was here for Molly, after all. This was important, and he didn't want to ruin his one chance by somehow upsetting the Mayor. No, he would be courteous and professional. Just like always.

The Burden of Souls

It didn't particularly help that he knew exactly what the Mayor was doing while he waited. The rhythmic *thud-thud-thud* coming through the wall, intermingled with a woman's occasional muffled cry, was quite distinctive. It might even be two women.

He took off his spectacles and rubbed each lens vigorously with the little soft cloth he always kept in his inside left jacket pocket. He tried to stay calm. He tried not to show his irritation; he tried even harder not to feel jealous, though he was not entirely successful quashing either. Which was unusual.

After all those years around Lorna, biting his tongue and heroically not throttling her, he'd come to quite pride himself on his self-control. Lately, however, things had slipped a little. He supposed that it was understandable, given how close he was to getting what he wanted and the rewards he deserved. So damn close…

"The Mayor will see you now," Symmons appeared at his side suddenly enough to make him jump.

"Very good, Mr Symmons," he put his spectacles back on and, after folding it neatly in half, slipped the little soft cloth back into the inside left pocket of his jacket. Picking up his case, he followed Symmons out of the anteroom.

"Please accept the Mayor's apology for keeping you waiting," Symmons said in a dry clipped tone without looking at him, "but something important came up."

"It is no problem; I had paperwork with me," he replied evenly, "I understand how it is when… town business comes up."

"Actually, I was talking about his cock," Symmons opened the door and ushered him inside.

"Mr Furnedge for you, sir," Symmons announced.

He looked back at the Mayor's vulgar little aide and noticed two women, dressed in nothing but short satin robes, disappearing up the stairs. He didn't recognise either of them in the moment before the door closed in his face.

"Guy, what a pleasure!" The Mayor was slipping his jacket back on as he strode across the room to shake his hand vigorously. His fingers felt sticky.

"Thank you for seeing me, sir."

The Mayor slapped him lightly on each shoulder, "Anytime! Anytime!" He indicated the single hard-backed chair in the centre of the room as he retreated behind his vast empty desk. He was being favoured; most visitors to the Mayor's office had to stand. He thought it was a good sign, resisting the urge to try and discreetly sniff his hand.

"I saw Mrs McCrea earlier," he said once the Mayor had settled himself back into his chair.

"And how was the poor woman?"

"Quite fraught."

"And no nearer to paying me back?"

"It would appear not..."

The Mayor nodded and eased himself into the chair, the leather squeaking softly as he leant backwards.

"She has someone helping her, you know?"

"Other than me?" Furnedge tried not to look surprised.

"Amos."

"Who?"

The Burden of Souls

"He's new to town. A drifter and gunslinger. A Travellin' Man, I believe such souls are called."

"I don't know him... is he a friend of Mrs McCrea?"

"He is now, I believe."

He shifted uneasily in his seat, "A problem?"

The Mayor steepled his fingers in front of him, "I believe so. A dangerous man, I would say."

"Why is he helping her?"

"I can't imagine. Why would any man help an attractive vulnerable woman after all...?"

"You think he has... *designs!?*"

"He spent the night at her house, I understand."

"But... she is in mourning! Her husband has only just gone to his grave!"

"It is quite the scandal. I'm surprised you haven't heard. She walked out of *Jack's* with him, bold as you like, in front of the whole town. She's quite the brazen little hussy it would appear."

"Perhaps... he just walked her home?"

"My dear Guy," The Mayor smiled thinly, "I'm afraid I do not believe that he is a gentleman."

"But-"

"He didn't leave until the morning. I've been keeping an eye on her, as you know."

He didn't know what to say.

"It would appear you have a rival."

"This must be stopped – he could ruin everything!"

The Mayor waved him down, "What is life without problems? Things rarely go smoothly, especially in matters of the heart."

"Indeed..." If such things ran smoothly, he wouldn't have ended up married to a drunken lunatic, "What is to be done?"

"I will have to deal with him; he claims he intends to leave town. Which is good, but not before he has kept Molly McCrea from the whorehouse. Which is not good. It is also strange; he doesn't strike me as an honourable man..."

"He is a fly in my ointment Mr Mayor... in our *arrangement*."

"Don't fret. You will be rewarded. You've been a dutiful servant to me. I am always generous to those who serve me. You know that?"

"Of course. We have an understanding."

"Indeed, we do. You have no second thoughts. I take it?"

"None at all."

"And in return you will be my man, always."

"I am already your man."

"In mind, in body... and in soul? Forever?"

He nodded vigorously, "I just want to be happy, Mr Mayor. It's the only reward I desire for my labours."

"Of course, it is only what every man deserves."

"But if he *can* help her?"

The Mayor raised a hand, long fingers splayed wide, "He will not. I will hasten his departure from town; now I have run my little eye over him, I know he is dangerous, and not just to our understanding. He will be gone, one way or another. I will make arrangements."

"That is reassuring, sir."

"We will proceed then."

"Splendid!"

"It is only fair I give you one last chance to change your mind. I would not want you burdened later with... *regrets*."

"My life as it is... it is intolerable. It cannot continue."

The Mayor gave the faintest of nods, "Then we shall proceed to the matter of your wife."

"Good..." he felt his heart thumping fiercely.

"And her money?"

"Yes, her money. My dues for the service I have given her, the sacrifices I have made... still, it's not my primary concern. As you know, Mr Mayor, there are more important things in life than money."

The Mayor smiled, his eye sparkling as it fixed upon him, "Indeed, Guy, there are..."

The Songbird

Her first thought was that the Mayor had moved his piano back from the saloon to his home. It looked *exactly* the same; brand new, immaculately polished and totally out of place in this remote back of beyond little town.

She ran a finger along the keys; it was perfectly tuned.

"Is this one to your liking too?"

She raised her eyes; the Mayor was still sitting expectantly in his leather upholstered chair, a knowing smile dusting his lips.

"It's beautiful."

"As good as the one I sent to *Jack's*?"

Before answering, Cece played a few notes, "You just happened to have two identical grand pianos?"

The Mayor's mouth twitched with amusement, "Well, you never know when you might need a spare. I like to be prepared for all eventualities."

"You're a music lover?"

"I'm a lover of many things."

"You play?"

"I've been known to fiddle now and then."

She watched him, unsettled by the way his single eye flicked over her, seeing more than perhaps it ought to. A woman entered the room, pulling her attention away from the Mayor. She was young, blonde hair tumbled down her back, and she wore a white silk dress, cut low enough to make the saloon girls back at *Jack's* blush, drawn tightly about her slim waist. It was. Her figure was so perfect there had to be some serious corsetry at work beneath the silk.

"Our entertainment for the evening," the Mayor was still sitting and watching Cece intently. She wasn't sure if he was talking to her or the newcomer.

The girl glided without acknowledgement to stand behind the Mayor; she placed a hand on his shoulder and stared with big languid blue eyes. She looked bored.

"Cecilia Jones, please meet Felicity, one of my companions..."

"You have a spare of her too?" she asked before she could stop herself.

The Mayor laughed; Felicity didn't.

"Would you care for a drink?" Felicity floated to a decanter next to the Mayor, her tone wasn't exactly hostile, but it was flat and cold as if she considered the whole business a dull little chore to be endured.

"I don't drink alcohol."

"Very wise," the Mayor's eye flicked to watch Felicity pour herself a generous measure before returning to stand behind the chair once more, "I prefer a clear head too..." his hand reached up to take the glass from Felicity, "...most of the time..."

"So..." she shifted on her stool ",...this is where I have to sing for my new piano?"

"Don't worry; I have no intention of taking it back."

"What would you like me to sing for you?"

"Oh… surprise us with something."

She started with a ballad; she tried to keep her eyes front as much as possible. Somehow being scrutinised by the Mayor's one restless eye and Felicity's two cold disinterested ones was more unsettling than a couple of hundred drunks undressing her in their heads.

When she finished the first song, silence greeted her, save for the sound of Felicity sloshing more booze into her glass. Rather than look up she moved on to another song. And then another.

"Most beautiful," the Mayor said at the end of the third song, "an angel's voice, don't you think, Felicity?"

Felicity sniggered over the rim of her glass; she was less standing behind the Mayor's chair than draping herself over it.

"Thank you, sir."

"Are you sure I can't fix you a drink? Some iced water, at least? Lemonade, perhaps?"

"I am a little dry; some iced water would be nice, thank you."

The Mayor retrieved the whiskey glass from Felicity's dangling hand and shooed her off to fetch some water. She sauntered past the piano without acknowledging Cece.

"Please forgive her," the Mayor said once the girl had left the room, "she can be a little aloof at first. But trust me; she does warm up quite nicely…"

"There is nothing to forgive, really," she played with the sleeve of her blouse, which sported modest frills down the front and cuffs. It was by far her most flattering piece of clothing, as it made her look neither like a boy nor a scarecrow. Given the Mayor's obvious importance in the town, she'd decided she should make some kind of effort with her appearance.

"You know how some girls are when presented with another as pretty as they are? They can feel a little threatened."

She was starting to wish she hadn't.

She swivelled on her stool so she was half facing the Mayor for emphasis, "There is nothing for her to feel threatened about, truly."

The Mayor didn't reply, but the way he smiled suggested he thought otherwise.

The Mayor sipped Felicity's whiskey; his eye seemed to be moving about less than usual as if Cece were the only thing of interest in the room, and the Mayor's eye had decided to settle solely upon her for the time being.

"Tell me Cecilia, where do you come from? Exactly?"

"Back East..." she replied, "...and people tend to call me Cece."

"I think I prefer Cecilia, and as I am not most people, I like to be indulged."

"Of course... it just makes you sound like my father."

"Well, I'm sure we can live with that; Cecilia is just more... refined. I prefer things that are both beautiful and elegant around me. Before Felicity came to me, some people used to call her *Flissy,* would you believe? Quite dreadful. I had to put a stop to that straight away."

"Do you object to people calling me Cece?"

"Of course not, unless you're thinking of moving in too?"

She shook her head and looked down at the piano keys, "No... I'm not."

"Pity..."

"Would you like me to play another song?" She said after an interminably long silence filled only by the ticking of a grandfather clock accompanied by her own thudding heart.

"Why, of course, but let us wait until Felicity returns with your water. I wouldn't want to deny her the pleasure of you."

The Mayor slowly rose to his feet and came over to stand at the end of the piano, it was a large piano, but he was still too close for comfort.

"Where did you say you came from, back east?" He asked after another long pause, his gaze flicking back and forth between the whiskey he sloshed around the glass and her. He looked like he couldn't decide which one he wanted to taste first.

"Nowhere you'd have heard of; just a tiny little place by the sea."

"I'm exceedingly well-travelled; it might surprise you to know some of the places I've been – ah, here's the lovely Felicity..."

The young woman ambled over and placed a long glass of water filled with roughly hewn chunks of ice atop the piano.

She smiled her thanks before sipping the near-freezing water, staring at the ring of condensation on the black lacquered piano top rather than how Felicity poured herself over the Mayor as she retrieved the whiskey from his hand.

"Did you enjoy your ride today?" The Mayor casually slipped an arm around Felicity's waist.

"Yes..."

The Burden of Souls

The Mayor laughed, "Do not look so concerned, Cecilia; I'm not having you watched."

"You seem well informed of my movements?"

"This is a peaceable corner of the world, particularly given the rack and ruin surrounding us. You've travelled a fair way to get here, Cecilia, so you must have seen a thing or two in that regard... but even here, all manner of undesirables occasionally wash up, so I have men patrol the surrounding land, just to make sure. They told me they saw you on the road. Even close to town, it can be dangerous for a woman to ride alone."

"I can look after myself."

"You came across a gunslinger, I heard."

"You're very well informed."

The Mayor pulled a little face, "It pays to be well informed... and I do pay well to be informed. What was Mr Amos doing out on the grass?"

"Riding."

"More specifically?"

"I didn't ask."

"Ah... and I would have put you down as a girl of a more inquisitive nature... wouldn't you, Felicity?"

"Best not to be..." Felicity gave the barest of shrugs, "...curiosity gets kitties killed, after all..."

"Well, there is that, I suppose... why the interest in Amos?"

"See? I told you, Felicity, she is inquisitive."

"Poor dead kitties, rotting in the sun..." Felicity pouted as she looked down at Cece.

251

"He's a dangerous man, I think," the Mayor said as Felicity slipped away from his grasp to fill her glass again, "you should be careful."

"He seemed fine to me."

"Oh, I can assure you, Cecilia, I'm an excellent judge of character when it comes to bad men."

Felicity giggled behind her.

"Thanks for the advice; I'll keep it in mind."

"I'm sounding like your father again, aren't I?"

"A little."

"How is young Sye?"

Cece cocked an eyebrow, "Are you sure you're not watching me?"

"Of course not; the whole town has noticed the big puppy eyes he makes every time he is around you."

She felt her cheeks flush, which irritated her deeply.

"Is he dangerous too?"

"Oh, goodness no, he's a sweet boy."

"I'm sure he would be delighted to be described like that."

The Mayor let out a low laugh as Felicity draped herself over the piano. She did have a remarkable amount of cleavage.

"He's been looking for a wife for a while…"

"I'm not the marrying kind," Cece replied curtly. She hadn't quite known what to expect from the Mayor, a fumbling attempt at seduction would have been her best bet, but she wasn't sure what he was up to.

"What kind of girl are you then?"

"The kind that plays songs."

The Burden of Souls

"You've travelled a long, long way just to play songs, Cecilia. A *very* long way, I think."

"I like to travel."

"Very commendable."

She brushed her fingers across the keys, "Should I play something else for you?"

"That would be delightful, perhaps something more up-tempo?"

"Very well…"

The Mayor held up a finger to stop her, "There is one song I like in particular; maybe you know it?"

"Perhaps. How does it go?"

The Mayor started snapping his fingers; after a couple of clicks, Felicity began banging her palm on the piano top in accompaniment. The Mayor threw back his head and began to belt out the song. Felicity hummed along, tossing her head from side to side. She was pounding the piano forcefully enough to make the ice in Cece's glass tinkle.

A cold hard stone formed in the pit of her stomach.

"I'm afraid I don't know that one," she said after the Mayor's rough deep voice faded away.

"Really?" The Mayor bestowed a bright, vivid smile, "I thought that old one was well known back east?"

"New to me."

"I believe it's called *I Can't Get No Satisfaction…*"

She kept her face blank and shook her head.

"You do surprise me; I'd have thought a wanderer like you would have come across it somewhere…" the Mayor loomed over her, and she fought the urge to shy away as he leaned

253

forward, his eye burning dark and fierce, "...but I guess no moss grows on a rolling stone, eh?"

Who the hell is this guy?

Distantly Felicity giggled…

The Clown

He was meandering back to town, though he was trying to take as much time to get there as possible. He always felt reluctant to leave the grass, but he couldn't stay out here forever.

He'd thought about it more than once. There was no shortage of empty land out here, plenty of room for a man to build a little cabin for himself away from all the noise and hullabaloo, where he could just listen to the grass whisper and talk to God.

Unfortunately, souls needed saving back in town, and as nobody else was doing much in that regard, as far as he could see, it fell to him to give them the Lord's word. If he could just persuade them to stop drinking and whoring for long enough anyway.

Maybe one day, he'd just come out here and stay. Truth was, he didn't have enough money to build himself a place. Wood was expensive with so few trees about. Of course, he could just bring a tent, his needs were decidedly modest after all, but the winters were too harsh for that. Beautiful, of course, but harsh. Mr Wizzle didn't really like the cold.

He was walking through the long grass, occasionally, he would let his fingertips brush the tops of the stems, and he kept his eye out for anything new. Anything that might be a sign from God, or just that people were about changing things. People had a habit of never leaving alone. He'd noticed a new barn on the Rodgers place as he'd skirted by the cornfields. Big and bright red. *Bright red?* He could understand why a man might need a new barn, but bright red? It stood out here, between the lush green of the grass and the vivid blue of the sky. Garish and thoughtless.

He'd considered knocking on old man Rodgers' door and pointing out a *red* barn was entirely inappropriate, but he'd decided against it. It would have meant a long detour unless he trampled through the farmer's crops. He somehow doubted old man Rodgers would appreciate that. He didn't want to get shot at again after all.

Instead, he ploughed across the wild grass, heading for, if his bearings were right, Drake's Crossing, where he could get a ride on a wagon back into town.

He'd tried to talk Amelia into coming with him, but she'd laughed him off and said she could barely walk to the end of her yard anymore.

They'd talked for hours, though he hadn't really understood what she'd been reminiscing about. She seemed to think they were old friends and he knew all the people she was referring to. He didn't like to be rude unless someone was involved in Godless shenanigans, but Amelia seemed like a nice, if somewhat deluded, old lady, so he'd just nodded and smiled and kind of drifted off as he'd watched the grass sway and listened to the soft purr of Amelia's voice.

Most people had voices that annoyed him sooner or later. The world would be a better place if people just shut up and listened to the wind a bit more rather than rabbiting about nonsense, but Amelia had a sweet voice. Soft and soothing, he'd found he liked its cadence; it reminded him of someone reading a bedtime story to a child, all soft and warm and with no bad words. He didn't like bad words.

Like bright red barns, they were entirely unnecessary.

Anyway, he'd found Amelia's voice so soothing in the warm sunshine his eyes quickly drooped and his head dropped despite his best efforts to stay awake. He hadn't wanted Amelia to think him bored as she'd seemed so genuinely pleased to see him. Whoever she was.

He didn't know how long he'd been asleep, but he'd awoke with a start to find Amelia gone. He'd jumped up and looked around, but she was nowhere in sight. He was sure he'd only nodded off for a moment, and there weren't exactly a lot of hiding places between him and the vast horizons, but there was no sign of the old lady.

He'd sat down, munched an egg for lunch, and thought about it. Perhaps he *had* been dreaming; it seemed a strange and vivid dream, but it would explain why he didn't know her, and she knew him.

You got odd stuff like that in dreams.

The Gunslinger

The day had been long, hot, and utterly pointless.

He'd ridden out of town before dawn, with only the faintest smear of light on the eastern horizon and the stars still shining coldly overhead. Hawker's Drift had been deserted, and he hadn't seen or sensed another soul.

Perhaps he wasn't pretty enough for the Mayor to bother having followed.

He'd struck out north of the town and, as he had the previous day, rode slowly while scanning the long flat horizons for possible hiding places and trying not to think about Molly.

By late afternoon he'd failed spectacularly in both regards.

He'd intended to sleep out for the night; the air was warm and the sky clear of all but a few unthreatening fluffs of scattered white cloud. It would be a fine night to sleep under the stars, not that such a thing held any mystery to him, given he'd slept outside most nights since he'd ridden away from the burnt-out shell of his home in search of Severn and his men all those years ago.

The Burden of Souls

By the time he'd sat in the grass and eaten his lunch of bread and ham, he'd become less enamoured with the idea. He was paying for a bed; it would be a waste to have it lay empty in favour of a night on the hard earth.

And he'd be able to see Molly if he went back.

He'd lost count of how many times he called himself a fool, but the more time he spent with her, the more she reminded him of Megan, save for the cussing. Megan had never had much time for bad language.

It was her hair mostly; if Molly had been blonde, he'd barely have noticed the resemblance, but she had the same wild, fiery locks spilling down her back that he'd so loved about Megan.

He knew he was torturing himself. Molly wasn't Megan, and he certainly wasn't the man who'd married her all those long years ago. No, he was something else entirely now. Jacob Severn and the Thin Rider had seen to that.

All he had in him now was bitterness and hatred. It kept him alive, kept him moving on from one ramshackle little town clinging to the world to the next, forever following but never catching up with the Thin Rider and his weary grey stallion.

He should just keep riding, not just for one night, but every night. He should not be getting involved with Molly, he shouldn't be helping her, and he certainly shouldn't be thinking about her.

He was still glumly trying not to think about Molly when he came upon a crossroads; he'd ridden across country and stumbled on a road cutting up from a cluster of distant buildings, all but lost in the haze. He'd sat on his horse for a few minutes looking to the north; he could check the buildings out or follow the road south, which would return him to town and back to Molly.

Eventually, he'd pulled his horse to the south and followed the road till he reached the crossroads. Two intersecting rutted little tracks of no particular note save for a tubby man in a faded and worn yellow and black checked suit and a battered derby hat, who was sitting in the grass eating, what appeared to be, an egg.

"Mr Wizzle," he pulled his horse to a halt, "you're a long way from town?"

Mr Wizzle swallowed the last of his egg, pulled himself to his feet and doffed his hat, "I've been looking for angels," he explained before picking egg crumbs off his jacket's lapel.

"Angels?"

"Yes, you can see them out here, though they didn't reveal themselves to me this time. I did meet Amelia Prouloux, though, which was nice. Care for a pickled egg?"

He declined the crumpled bag the old man produced from his pocket.

"I don't believe I know her."

"Me neither, but she was very nice," Mr Wizzle repositioned his hat and stepped forward before adding in a lower voice, "though I think she might be a little bit mad."

Amos stopped himself from commenting there was a lot of that about in Hawker's Drift.

"Where are you heading?" he asked instead.

"Back to Hawker's Drift, just waiting for a farmer's wagon to hitch a ride on."

"I'm heading back to town; my horse can manage both of us," he offered before considering what the pickled eggs might have done to Mr Wizzle's breath.

"That's terribly kind," Mr Wizzle beamed, "but, unfortunately, I get a bit nauseous on the back of a horse, all that swaying and up and downing, I think."

"Well, if you're sure."

"No, really, I wouldn't want to sick up eggs all over your back."

He nodded, smiled, and decided not to offer again.

He swivelled around in his saddle; no one else was coming down the roads in any direction.

"Do many wagons pass this way?"

"Oh plenty, one or two a day at least."

"And if there isn't another one today?"

"Then they'll definitely be one tomorrow. I'm in no hurry. I still have a couple of eggs."

He noticed the small canteen slung across Mr Wizzle's chest, "Do you have any water left?"

"I'm afraid not," he said glumly giving the canteen a little shake.

Amos pulled off one of the two large canteens strapped to his saddle and handed it over, "I've got plenty, fill yours up; you don't want to spend a night out here without water."

Mr Wizzle beamed and accepted the canteen, "You see! God will always provide whenever you are in need, either through nature's bounty or the kindness of strangers!"

As he waited for Mr Wizzle to fill his canteen, half a dozen crows erupted from the grass, startled by some critter or another.

Mr Wizzle followed his gaze as the birds circled overhead and wrinkled his nose, "Not terribly nice," he sighed, "even if they are God's creatures it did spoil my day a little when I stumbled across them."

"You don't like crows?"

"It's what they are doing I'd rather not have seen. It tarnished the beauty of my day somewhat…"

"What are they doing?"

Mr Wizzle pulled a face as he handed the canteen back.

"Eating the dead horses…"

*

The air was thick with flies and the stink of rotting flesh while the cawing crows taunted him like Severn's maniacal laughter.

"Who would do such a terrible thing?" Mr Wizzle stood a pace behind his shoulder, languidly waving his hat back and forth in front of his wrinkled nose.

"I can't imagine…"

I could make a fair guess, though.

The crow's feast consisted of a horse and two mules. Each animal, as far as he could tell, dispatched by a shot to the head. It was hard to say exactly how long they'd been dead, but given the amount of flesh stripped away and the degree of decay, a couple of weeks seemed about right.

Around the same time Tom McCrea had fallen off his horse, in other words.

A man might shoot a horse with a broken leg, which wasn't unusual if you were riding hard across country, but the chances of three animals all breaking their legs at the same time were so high as to be non-existent. People didn't kill horses and mules without a damn good reason; they were far too valuable.

So why else would three healthy animals be killed?

Because if they were ever taken back to Hawker's Drift, someone might recognise them as the animals sold to Tom, and a dead man's horse turning up with someone else might raise awkward questions.

He couldn't think of another explanation as much as he tried.

He walked a slow wide circle around the dead animals, scanning the grass for anything that might give a clue to whoever had done this. A silver star, for instance.

"Are we looking for something?" Mr Wizzle trailed in his wake through the grass.

"Just wondering what kind of a fool kills three good animals?"

"It's a terrible world. People do all kinds of things that make no sense..." Mr Wizzle muttered, "...like old man Rodgers painting his barn *bright* red!"

He didn't ask.

They'd almost completed a full circle when something in the grass caught his eye. At first, he thought it was just a bit of old wood until he remembered there were few trees out here.

"Is that a rifle?" Mr Wizzle asked as he pulled the blackened and twisted remains of the weapon from the grass.

"It used to be..."

The butt had burned away, leaving only the scarred remains of the barrel; he kicked around in the grass for the trigger guard and lever but found nothing more.

Destroying a rifle made even less sense than killing horses and mules.

The livery might recognise the animals, and he suspected John would know a rifle he'd sold; he seemed like that kind of man. The other provisions Tom had bought (shovels, pans, food, etc.) would have been much less incriminating to dispose of.

There was no fire-blackened grass, so whoever had burned the rifle hadn't done it here. Someone had led the horses out into this unfarmed grassland where they were unlikely to be stumbled upon anytime soon and killed, the rifle remains tossed away into the grass too. Given the endless plains surrounding the town, whoever had killed them could have found a more remote location; they were only a hundred yards from the crossroads, after all. Perhaps they didn't think they needed to be careful or were just lazy.

"It's a bit of a mystery, isn't it?" Mr Wizzle asked once they started back to the road and his horse, which he'd tethered to a marker post.

Amos stared at his feet pushing through the long, unbroken grass stems before replying, "Best you don't mention this to anyone back in town."

"Oh, no one really listens to anything I say, even when I give them the Lord's words."

"Even so..."

"Somebody didn't want the poor horses and rifle to be found?"

He looked at Mr Wizzle, with his tufts of red hair sticking out from under his battered derby and his faded clown's suit.

He wasn't as stupid as he looked.

"I think so."

Mr Wizzle tapped his nose, "Won't say a word; it'll be our secret."

"Sure you don't want a ride back to town?" he asked when they got back to his horse, and he'd stowed the ruined rifle in his blanket roll. He still didn't fancy getting eggy sick down his back, but Mr Wizzle might be in danger if the wrong person came by and found him so close to the carcasses.

"Thank you, but no. A wagon will come along soon enough. The Lord will provide for me, as always."

"Take care, Mr Wizzle," he hoisted himself back into the saddle.

"And you too, your kindness will not go unrewarded!" Mr Wizzle pulled off his hat and gave a little wave; "By the way, I don't believe I know your name?"

"It's Amos."

"Amos?" Mr Wizzle frowned, "Amelia said something about an Amos."

"Amelia?"

"Amelia Prouloux, the nice, slightly mad, old woman I met out on the grass."

"I doubt she was talking about me."

"I guess... she said Amos was a very brave man."

"Nope, definitely not me then."

"I did ask her why he was so brave."

"What was it? I'm sure I'd remember every brave thing I've done, given they've been so few."

"You're a modest man, Amos. I like that..." Mr Wizzle screwed up his podgy face, "...now what was it she said about her Amos. Oh yes, that was it. She said... he was brave because only a brave man picks a fight with the Devil..."

*

"You think it's Tom's?"

He rubbed his chin and stared at the ruined rifle he'd laid out on Molly's kitchen table.

"Yeah... I think so. I'll take it to John tomorrow and see if it matches what he sold."

"He'll be able to tell?"

"I can ask, he seems a smart fellow, so I'd imagine so."

Molly sat looking at the gun, her shoulders slumped and her brow furrowed. It wasn't the kind of news he'd hoped to bring her.

"I don't suppose it's exactly in a returnable condition, is it?"

"The rotting horse and mules certainly aren't."

Molly sighed deeply, sat back, and looked at him with wide green eyes. He didn't need any gifts to tell her mood.

"So, that's that..."

"Don't give up; we'll think of something."

Molly returned her eyes to the gun, "They killed Tom and destroyed the provisions he'd bought."

"Seems that way... at least the gear that might be recognisably his."

"Why?"

"I've no idea... I'll keep going out and asking questions."

"Thank you," Molly ran a finger along the blackened barrel before adding, "...please be careful; there's no need to take these risks for me. I wouldn't want to see you... end up like Tom."

"I don't fall off my horse easily."

She gave him a wan smile and ran fingers through her tousled hair. "I guess I'd better start getting ready for the whorehouse..."

He wanted to reach over and take her hand but managed to stop himself in time; instead, he leaned forward and crossed his arms on the table.

"That's not going to happen, Molly."

"Isn't it?"

"We'll think of something... is there no way you can get enough money in three months to pay off the Mayor?

She shook her head emphatically, "No, I haven't got any particular talents that could earn that much. I could get a job, but it'd only be something menial, nothing that would pay enough."

Leaning back, she blew out her cheeks, "Ironically, the only thing I'm actually any good at is fucking."

Molly stared at him before letting out a half-suppressed laugh and glancing away.

"What's so funny?"

"You look surprisingly sweet when you blush..."

He dropped his eyes to the table. Megan had often called him sweet; he was damn sure no one else had since she'd died.

He let the thought slide away; it wouldn't do either of them any good.

"If nothing else works, I'll get you out of town," he fixed her a hard stare, which he hoped looked as unsweet as possible, before adding, "You're not a whore, Molly. And you never will be."

"You know, that's possibly the sweetest thing a man's ever said to me..."

He forced a weak smile. He clearly needed to work on his not being sweet a bit more.

"How would we get out of town?" She asked after a long pause.

"I'd just need to get another horse."

"We couldn't just use yours? I don't weigh much."

He shook his head, "Only as a last resort. I reckon if we skip town, the Mayor's men will come after us, I doubt my horse could outrun them carrying two... if we were in the mountains, I'd be able to lose them, but here everything is so flat, we'd be seen for miles. There's nowhere to hide."

"Yeah, that's what I thought... and I bet if you go and buy a horse in the livery, the Mayor and his dickhounds would get to hear about it pretty quick."

"I'd imagine. At least the deputies don't seem to be following you around anymore."

"Not seen them today, though I haven't been out of the house," she shrugged, "I decided there was less chance of me making an exhibition of myself if I stayed at home."

The Burden of Souls

"Best you keep indoors as much as possible from now on."

"There's no need to agree with me!"

He smiled, "Let them get used to you being out of sight; it'll buy us more time when we make a run for it."

"When not if?"

"Last resort."

"Only resort?"

"Maybe."

"What'll happen if they catch us?"

"There'll be more vacancies for town deputies opening up."

"I don't want anyone to die for me, Amos; not even that creep Blane."

"I'd better get you a fast horse then. You can ride?"

Molly nodded.

"Good," he pulled himself slowly to his feet, "I should be going; I want an early start tomorrow."

"Is there any point?"

"There were buildings a couple of miles from where I found the gun and carcasses; I want to see if anyone there saw anything."

"Would that help?"

"I dunno, but I also need to see what farms have horses I could borrow easily as well."

"They hang horse thieves here, you know?"

"I suspect they hang people who help folk flee their debts too."

Molly made no move to rise; she sat looking up at him before saying, "You don't have to go, you know?"

"Your floor's not that comfy, and I need a few hours sleep."

"I wasn't talking about my floor."

He shifted from one foot to the other.

Oh, that again...

"Well, at least you're not climbing up the wall this time."

"Molly, I can't..."

She pursed her lips and let her eyes slide back towards the rifle, "Most men I understand easily enough, but you... you I don't get at all."

"It's really not that complicated."

"Amos... why are you helping me? You don't want money, not that I have any, you don't want to sleep with me, and I'm damn sure my lousy meatloaf ain't the way to any man's heart!"

He rested his hands on the back of the wooden chair and thought about it. Did he owe her an explanation? Why couldn't she just accept he wanted to help her? Accept that the tide of the world had washed him up here and be grateful he was offering her a way out.

He could feel the confusion coming off her in waves. No, that wasn't going to work. He sat back down again.

"My wife, Megan..." he began in a hesitant voice, each word reluctantly hauled from somewhere deep and broken inside him "...I loved her very much. It was a long time ago."

He stared at his fingers; he was rubbing his thumbs over them without knowing why. Molly was silent.

"We had a farm, the land wasn't good like here, but we managed. We were happy. One day some men came, they... they raped and killed her in front of me. Left me for dead. I couldn't save her; I haven't even been able to avenge her. I've spent thirteen years looking for the men who did it, but I've never found them. I couldn't save her..." he looked up, "...but I can save you..."

Molly's eyes were wide, pained sympathy etched her beautiful face; she reached over and placed her hands upon his writhing fingers, stilling them. He didn't really want her to touch him in case he saw more than he wanted to, but nothing came bar the softness of her skin. He was grateful for that. He considered telling her the rest, but what was the point?

She didn't need to know just how broken he really was.

The Widow

She rolled over again and stared at the ceiling. She didn't much like sleeping alone, she decided.

The world outside her window was silent. Even Bruno wasn't howling at the moon tonight. After blowing the candles out, she'd cautiously peered up and down the street, but it had been as deserted as when Amos left. No dickhounds.

She thought about Amos.

Thirteen years searching for the men who'd killed his wife. Thirteen years, driven by the need for vengeance, but that wasn't all. He still loved her; he couldn't even stand the touch of another woman. The way he squirmed when she'd suggested they spend the night together had made that obvious enough.

Thirteen years.

How long had Tom been dead? Less than two weeks, and she wanted to have sex with another man. Would she have felt like that if she'd actually loved Tom? She couldn't imagine.

She screwed her eyes shut and tried to push the thoughts away.

It didn't work.

The Burden of Souls

Whatever the reason he was helping her, she didn't entirely buy the line about him wanting to save her because he couldn't save his wife. It was noble, she supposed; perhaps that was why she didn't believe it. Not entirely anyway. Somehow, she just couldn't accept Amos had spent thirteen years saving women from the clutches of adversity. There was something else. Something he wasn't telling her. She could see it in his eyes. She might not have his talent for reading another's soul, whatever that bullshit was about, but he'd a way of looking at her sometimes like he saw something he couldn't quite believe.

She would have called it attraction or lust if it weren't for the fact he'd twice spurned her advances. The first time he might not have wanted to take advantage of her because she was drunk (it did seem a bit far-fetched, admittedly, but she supposed some men might be like that), but tonight her desire had been quite whiskey free.

Whatever his motivation was, she could deal with it later; for now her only concern had to be getting away from this crazy little town and its whorehouse. Not to mention the slimy one-eyed fucker who ran it.

It wasn't like she had any other choices after all...

*

Guy Furnedge smelt of peaches today; rotting, rancid peaches left out in the sun for a dog to piss over, but peaches all the same.

They were sitting at the table; she'd manoeuvred him into the kitchen under the pretence of making coffee for them. At least here, she could open the backdoor later to clear the air, which was better than having to put up with his peculiar smell lingering in the drawing-room for hours afterwards like she'd had to following his last visit.

"The Mayor is somewhat aggrieved," he announced after asking her how she was in half a dozen different ways.

"I've really pissed him off, huh?"

He flinched. Just the tiniest little spasm pulling at his face. He did the same thing every time she swore. He probably considered it unbecoming for a lady, which only encouraged her to cuss all the more. The asshole.

"That is certainly one way of putting it; your little... outburst the other day hasn't helped matters, I must confess. Not that I consider that a justification for the Mayor's actions, of course."

She thought about pointing out her swearing fit had come *after* she'd found out the Mayor was going to send her to the whorehouse to work off her debts but decided to keep her mouth shut for once. She got the impression the lawyer wasn't fond of being corrected.

"He wasn't prepared to change his mind?"

"No, in fact, he was all for calling in the debt immediately."

"Oh fuck."

Her big mouth had made things worse. What a novelty.

Furnedge flinched again but held up his hand and gave a smile meant to look reassuring, "I did manage to dissuade him in that regard at least. The Mayor has always been a man of his word, and I pointed out, in quite the strongest terms, that it would not be becoming of him to change the conditions of your agreement retrospectively."

I didn't agree to any damn thing!

She managed to stop her mouth again and instead conjured a smile that she hoped looked a bit sincerer than his had done, "Thank you... Guy, I do appreciate that. Really."

"I am happy to do anything I can to help you... Molly."

This was all getting a bit too intimate. She took a long slow sip of coffee, which at least made her feel a bit less queasy.

"So... what happens next?"

"Perhaps the Mayor will relent once he's had time to reflect a little more. You've had no success in finding your late husband's provisions?"

She shook her head; she had no intention of telling him about the carcasses and rifle Amos had found. Her mouth wasn't *that* big.

"They appear to have disappeared off the face of the Earth – I have no idea what Tom did with them."

"It's a mystery."

She noted the way his eyes narrowed more than usual. He dropped them quickly to stare into his coffee.

"Who knows, perhaps I can still find them."

"Let us hope," he took a dainty sip of coffee and returned the mug to the table, "This man... Amos?"

"What about him?" she returned, too quickly.

"He is helping you?"

"He is looking for the provisions out on the grass as, you know, I am not allowed beyond the town limits."

"Without success?"

"There is a lot of land to cover out there."

"Indeed. A lot of time and effort in searching it, I would imagine. You are paying him?"

"No."

His eyebrow raised a fraction, "You have some other arrangement, perhaps?"

She didn't like his tone, adding it to the long list of other things she didn't like about the man.

"No... he's just a friend."

"There has been talk, Molly..."

I bet there fucking has.

She took a breath and counted to three to stop her mouth from running off again.

"I couldn't give a shit, to be honest."

Perhaps she'd try and count to ten next time.

"People are questioning your reputation, my dear."

"The same people who couldn't be bothered to come to my husband's funeral. I can live with it."

"Well, that was unfortunate, but the weather was rather inclement."

Her fingers tightened around the mug, and she fought down the urge to hurl it at the lawyer. Money was tight, and she couldn't afford to waste a perfectly good mug, no matter how much she'd enjoy it.

"Yes, it was very inconsiderate of Tom to die when he did. He was always doing things like that..." she eventually managed to say through a tight-lipped little smile.

"Sarcasm is really not required. I only have your best interests at heart."

"I know you do, Guy, and I do appreciate it."

She hoped he didn't notice the gritted teeth.

"All I am saying is that you should be careful; this man is a stranger... who knows what his motives might be?"

She couldn't argue with that.

"I am in a difficult position; I'll take whatever help I can find. Anything is preferable to the whorehouse."

"There are always alternatives," Furnedge smiled. She couldn't decide if the smile was sly or oily. Either way, she didn't like it.

"Alternatives?"

He finished his coffee without replying and rose to his feet.

"You must excuse me, but my dear wife is quite poorly. I really should be popping home to see her."

"Oh, I didn't know she was ill?" she said, still thinking about "alternatives" as she showed him out.

"The poor woman is getting frailer by the day; I fear the worst."

She hadn't seen Mrs Furnedge in a while; she'd heard talk that Lorna just sat indoors all day drinking herself into oblivion, which was precisely what she'd do if she'd the misfortune to be married to Guy Furnedge. Actually, it wasn't far off what she was doing anyway.

They paused by the door, and Guy took the chance to place a clammy hand gently on her forearm, "Do not fret, my dear; I will continue to argue your case. I am sure there is a way out of this predicament."

"I hope so."

"I am very fond of you, Molly," he blurted, "I will do anything to keep you from that despicable place."

She tried not to stare too pointedly at his hand upon her skin, which seemed to be trembling slightly.

"I... am appreciative, Guy... you have been a good friend."

He squeezed her arm slightly, "Friends... yes, we are. Good friends!"

Before she could do anything, he raised her hand to his mouth and not so much kissed it as slobbered over it.

"Until next time..."

After seeing him out with a smile and a little wave, she hurried back to the kitchen to throw open the back door and find some soap to scrub her hand with.

The Preacher

The porcelain vase had been smashed. It was not just broken but shattered into so many tiny slivers and shards that it looked like someone had taken a sledgehammer to it.

The morning was warm, the air sticky and close already, but Preacher Stone shivered all the same. It slowly dawned on him that he was naked.

He couldn't remember breaking the vase, but nobody else had been in the house. At least he didn't think so. Who'd creep into his bedroom just to destroy a vase anyway?

Nothing else was damaged as far as he could tell.

The vase was cheap and held no sentimental value, just a little thing he'd picked up simply because he liked how the roses wound around it. He'd always been fond of roses; they reminded him of his mother's garden. Now it was nothing at all. He must have hurled it against the wall; it would never have shattered like that if he'd just knocked it off the table.

But why?

Of course, there was no why; it was simply the Mayor's candy. It made him do things like that. Things he couldn't remember. Pointless, stupid things. He closed his eyes and shivered again. He wanted more already. He usually felt too disgusted when he finally came back to his senses, but not this time. He ached for it.

The little black bottle still sat upon the bedside table. He hadn't hurled that wretched thing against the wall. Inanimate, silent, unremarkable. Apart from the way it sang to him. Not out loud, but in his blood. It wanted him. It wanted to be poured down his throat and spread through his body.

And his body wanted it too.

He placed a bony hand on the soft spare meat of his hollow stomach. The pain had gone. No bubbling, gnawing torment. No mocking whispers of impending death echoed up from his bowels.

That was why he drank it, wasn't it? It took the pain away; if it kept doing that, couldn't he live with it washing his senses away for a little while? It was a small price to pay, wasn't it?

He wiped a hand across his face, his breath catching as he lowered it. Blood smeared his fingers.

He stared at his hand, holding it out before him. Blood reddened his fingers and nails, but none covered his hands or lower arms other than a few elongated smudges.

There would be more if I'd killed someone, wouldn't there?

It was a strange thought. He'd never been a violent man; he couldn't remember hurting anyone since he'd punched Bobby Henniker on the nose, but as he'd only been nine at the time, and Bobby Henniker had been bullying him for months, he'd forgiven himself that lapse long ago.

His gaze fell to the vase debris decorating the floor. No, he'd never been a violent man...

The Burden of Souls

He turned to the little square mirror hanging on the wall by the door. His one concession to vanity, though he'd long since tired of seeing the wizened and sour-looking face he barely recognised living inside it.

Vivid slash marks raked across his chest and abdomen.

Had someone attacked him in the night? His finger traced one of the marks running from his left shoulder down to his nipple. The skin was broken, but the cut wasn't deep. The blood had dried to scabs. He pressed a little harder against the wound.

It didn't hurt at all.

He pulled his finger away and stepped back sharply from the mirror.

There was dried blood under his fingernails; he'd been meaning to cut them for days, but, like many of his little chores lately, he hadn't gotten around to it.

At least he hadn't hurt anyone, but why'd he hurt himself?

He glanced at the little black bottle again.

Resisting the urge to go to it, he poured water into the enamel bowl on his nightstand and used a thin sliver of unscented soap to clean the blood from his hands. He washed his chest with a damp cloth, revealing the red slashes cut into his flesh.

He thought of himself thrashing about in the darkness, a demented soul tearing at his own skin, and closed his eyes. Had he screamed? Had he babbled like a lunatic? Had he smashed the vase before scampering out into the square and howling at the moon like a rabid coyote?

He guessed not. Even in the small hours someone would have noticed, and he would have woken up in one of the cells beneath Sheriff Shenan's office. At least he lived alone; there was nobody for his torment to wake in the night.

Mrs Sibinski would come to clean this morning. It would be easy to dispose of the vase. Even if she noticed it was missing, he'd just say he'd knocked it over in the night. Clumsy old man, she'd scold with a shake of her head and an exasperated smile. He liked Mrs Sibinski; she vaguely reminded him of his long-dead mother, big, blustery, and permanently smelling of laundry.

Laundry?

He checked the sheets, they smelt of sweat and forgotten dreams, but there was no blood.

He straightened up. The water in the washbasin was now a dirty pink from the blood and soap. If he'd clawed himself in bed, surely there would be some blood on the sheets. So... he must have done it elsewhere?

The image of his naked self, writhing in the square, came again as he hurried from the bedroom into his little study in the next room. Everything was as he'd left it. No damage, no blood; the letter he'd been writing to his niece in Bridgeton still sat, unfinished, upon his scuffed old roll top desk.

He walked through to the modest drawing-room he only used to see his parishioners and listen to their problems and concerns.

"Oh no..."

The words escaped his lips as he balled his hands into fists, consumed by a profound despair, he simply wanted to curl up on the floor and sob.

Shreds of paper littered the room, pages of a book torn from their binding and ripped into long thin strips before being scattered like autumn leaves across the entire room.

Sinking to his knees, he picked up the nearest scrap. He didn't need to look too closely; he already knew what it was.

"Father's Bible," he choked.

The most precious thing he owned. It had been his greatest comfort as old and dog-eared as he was. Not just from the scripture but also from his father's words inside. "*To my beloved William. For when I am too far away to guide you, Your loving father, James.*"

His father had died when he'd still been a young man, and barely a day had passed without him thinking of him; James Stone had been such a kind, loving and generous man.

"A better man than I…" he let the scrap fall from his fingers like discarded confetti.

Pulling himself to his feet, he stumbled back into the bedroom and grabbed the little black bottle; he raised his arm above his head and held the cursed thing aloft. Willing himself to smash it like he had that hapless vase. It was evil, whatever it was.

Maybe it did take his pain away, maybe it did make him, briefly, feel like he was soaring above the clouds, but what else was it doing to him? What was it turning him into? A beast and a madman, a base animal with no control, a man who would destroy his most cherished belonging, his only reminder of a man whom he'd loved so deeply that he still missed him forty years after his death.

What else would he do if he kept taking it? What if the next time he awoke, not just his own blood soaked his hands? What if he found it was something even worse than a bible he'd torn to shreds in his dementia.

His arm shook; he willed it to cast out the devil in the bottle, to smash it and let the vileness it held seep out and be gone. He sobbed and thought how disappointed his father would be if he could see the wretch his son had grown into. To see how far he had wandered from the path of righteousness, how far he had staggered away from God.

He tried. He tried so very hard to break that awful bottle.

Instead, he crumpled to the floor and cried, for he could not do it. For if he did, he knew he'd be down on all fours, his face amongst the shards of glass desperately licking up the thick, sticky, and so, so sweet candy before the floorboards could soak it up.

Eventually, without really knowing, he pulled the stopper from the neck and lifted the bottle to his lips once more...

The Lawyer

By the time he got home, Lorna had passed out, an empty bottle of bourbon at her feet and flecks of vomit on her chin.

"I tried to clean her up, but she just started screaming at me," Amy explained as they stood in the doorway of the Throne Room. She looked pointedly at him, "By the way, I don't get paid enough to be called a fucking dumb whore."

"I'm sorry... my wife is very unwell."

"And she's getting worse... she never used to pass out till the evening!"

He considered reprimanding the girl, it wasn't an entirely appropriate way to address your employer, but he let it pass. She was, after all, quite correct.

Instead, they half-dragged, half-carried Lorna up the stairs between them and deposited her on the large brass-framed bed he'd used to share with her until it became too intolerable, and he'd moved into the spare room. Like many things in their marriage, it hadn't been discussed; she'd never complained about it, though, which was surprising as his wife complained vehemently about everything else.

Lorna had mumbled a few unintelligible words as they laid her on the bed, but she hadn't come around.

Once they had her settled, he led Amy out onto the landing and apologised for his wife's behaviour. Again. He placed a hand on her arm as he spoke. She was upset and frayed. An almost sulky little pout played across her face. He found it terribly attractive.

He left his hand on her arm longer than he should have done, but he enjoyed touching women, they would assume he was just being friendly, which he was, but it excited him that while he touched them, he was thinking all the time about what he'd really like to do to them. It didn't excite him as much to touch Amy as it had Molly, but then no woman excited him as much as Molly did. Still, he yearned to find Amy's small young tit all the same and squeeze it through her shapeless smock till she squealed...

"Amy, I know how trying it is here with her all day; I appreciate your hard work."

"Thank you, Mr Furnedge... but it's difficult sometimes."

She was looking up at him with large brown eyes, and she hadn't pulled away from the fingers resting on her arm like she sometimes did. He liked that.

"I will stay and look after her this afternoon; why don't you take the rest of the day off. As a thank you from me..." he nodded towards the closed bedroom door, "...and an apology from her."

"Thank you, sir... that's very kind."

He imagined her dropping onto her knees and showing him exactly how grateful she was, but he just nodded and let his fingers slip reluctantly from her arm, "Can you pop into my office on your way home and let Miss Dewsnap know I won't be back today as Mrs Furnedge is unwell."

"Yes, of course, sir, it's on my way home," she smiled, no doubt relieved to be given the day off. And she would remember why too.

"My wife is unwell," he repeated, "it's important Miss Dewsnap knows that. I wouldn't want people thinking I am just malingering from my duties."

"Your wife is unwell," Amy nodded her understanding before hurrying downstairs to fetch her shawl and be off to do whatever she did when Lorna wasn't shouting at her.

He stood on the landing and smiled. He hoped Amy would get the message right, it was simple enough after all, but it was necessary because once Eudora Dewsnap knew something, half the town would hear it soon too...

*

Guy sat by his wife's bed for a while, just watching her. She was out cold. He could have been hammering Amy over the dresser, and she wouldn't have woken.

He should have drugged her bourbon years ago.

Taking out the little black bottle the Mayor had given him from his pocket, he turned it over slowly in his hands. He had no idea what it was, but the Mayor had been very specific; use half the bottle, no more, no less. Do not spill any on your skin, do not inhale it and definitely don't taste it.

It had seemed thick and viscous when he'd poured it into Lorna's bourbon bottle that morning. An uncharacteristic curiosity had almost made him wave the bottle under his nose until he remembered the Mayor's instructions. The little glass bottle was opaque, and the liquid inside poured like syrup, making it hard to judge when he'd tipped exactly half of it into the bourbon.

Whatever it was, Lorna hadn't tasted it; she'd polished off the entire bottle by lunchtime. Which was some going even by her standards.

The Mayor had assured him it would knock Lorna out cold, though an entire bottle of bourbon would do that to most people anyway. She looked quite peaceful now that he'd dabbed the vomit from her chin with a damp flannel.

He placed his palm on her forehead; perhaps she was a little warm to the touch, but nothing unusual. He plumped up the pillows and made sure the sheets covered her slender frame, then sat back down and held her hand. It was just skin and bone. All she did was drink and smoke. He supposed she had to eat occasionally, though she never did when he was in the house. Amy had told him that as often as not, she didn't touch her lunch unless it was to throw it at Amy if the girl had done something to upset her.

He remembered when the touch of her hand had excited him. There'd still been blood in her veins rather than just booze and bitterness back then. He'd loved her once; at least, he thought he had. For a little while, he'd believed they might even be happy together, but he supposed she'd just concealed her resentment better back then. Blaming him for the loss of the privileged life she'd enjoyed rather than her own actions and the father she'd driven to distraction.

Resentment had led to bitterness, and that hellish union had begat hatred, an offspring she'd succoured on bourbon until it consumed her.

He'd tried, unquestionably he had, and it hadn't been solely for her money, not at first anyway, but he knew he'd given up a long time ago and accepted being trapped by their marriage of inconvenience. He should have walked away, but if he divorced her, he got nothing; if he were ever unfaithful, he got nothing, and if she died in unnatural circumstances, he got nothing.

Did he even actually need the money anymore? He'd done well for himself since they'd come to Hawker's Drift, Lorna hadn't wanted to come, of course, but they'd had little choice but to move after she broke the jaw of the preacher in the last town they'd lived in.

He'd heard the local lawyer here had been looking for a younger man to bring into the business with an eye to taking over when he retired. Theo Fitzsimmons had immediately seen his potential, intelligence, and appetite for hard work (so he'd assumed) and had given him the job. With Lorna's money, they'd built a fancy new house just off Pioneer Square, and eighteen months later, when Fitzsimmons had keeled over with a heart attack, the business had become his.

Yes, things had gone well for him here, but didn't he deserve her money? After all these years of suffering? He'd given his word to her father that he would look after her, and he'd given his word to God that he would be her husband; he had forsaken all others and cared and provided for her. He'd protected her from the world. As he had promised he would.

Till death do us part...

*

"How is Lorna?"

He gave a little cry, and half rose from his comfortable chair by the unlit fire. All bar one of the candles had gone out while he'd unexpectedly dozed, encasing the study in shadow.

A figure stood by the door. Although the sole remaining candle only dusted the man with light, he recognised him well enough from his voice and how he rested easily upon his cane.

"Mr Mayor!"

"I'm sorry I startled you."

"I must have fallen asleep," he began to climb to his feet, but the Mayor waved him down.

"I let myself in, I hope you don't mind, but I thought it best."

"No, you are always welcome," he spluttered. He thought he'd locked all the doors as he hadn't wanted to be disturbed. Obviously, he hadn't.

"Under the circumstances..."

"Under *any* circumstances."

The Mayor gave a slight nod of acquiescence.

"You gave your wife the bottle?"

He shifted in his chair and lowered his voice in case Lorna might have woken up.

"Half... just as you told me to."

"And?"

"She'd drunk the whole bottle of bourbon I poured it into by lunchtime; she is out cold."

"It has that effect when taken to excess."

"What exactly is that stuff?" He could sense the weight of the little bottle in his pocket, which seemed ridiculous because it was such a small thing. Unless what he actually felt was his conscience, of course.

"Just my own little concoction. You didn't try it, did you?"

"Why would I do that?" he rose to his feet and crossed the study before adding in a tortured little hiss, "It's poison, isn't it?"

The Mayor smiled, "It is many things."

"I don't understand?"

"You don't need to..." the Mayor held out his hand, palm upturned under Guy's nose, "...just give me the bottle."

He did as he was told, though he felt a strange nagging reluctance to drop it into the Mayor's palm.

"Do you still want me to do this for you?"

He nodded, his gaze unable to rise from the little bottle dangling from his fingers towards the Mayor's eye, "I could just give her the rest of this myself... I can..."

"Of course you can, Guy, but it takes a little more than just this..." he curled his hand around the bottle before plucking it from the lawyer's fingers like ripe malevolent fruit from a twisted tree.

"It does?" his eyes snapped back to the Mayor as soon as it disappeared into his jacket pocket.

"It has to look natural, doesn't it?"

"So her will stipulates, I don't suppose she's changed the one her father drafted for her before our marriage."

"The perfect wedding gift."

"He was a practical man."

"And this will can't just..." the Mayor reached out and wriggled his fingers under Guy's nose "...disappear?"

"It is with Carson in Fellowes Ford."

"And Mr Carson will come running to confirm matters?"

"He is a most diligent man, and my father-in-law's estate pays generous fees to ensure he remains that way."

"You would think your father-in-law didn't trust you?"

"He just wanted to ensure his daughter was looked after, which I have done to the best of my abilities for many years."

"And now you have had enough?"

He fought down his irritation. It was never good to show such a thing, least of all with someone who was going to the trouble of murdering your wife for you.

"We have discussed all this before."

"I know that, Guy..." the Mayor placed a hand on his arm and squeezed it gently, he supposed it was intended to be reassuring, but he felt like a piece of meat on a butcher's slab being tested for tenderness before purchase, "...I just want to know that you're sure. It's one thing to desire a death; it is so much more to actually make it happen."

"I know what I want. Lorna has suffered long enough. This is a mercy for her."

"And for you."

He dropped his eyes and replied in a small voice, "I deserve to be released from my suffering too."

"And to reap your reward? To receive your due for all the care you've bestowed upon your ailing and tormented wife."

"Indeed!!"

The Mayor nodded and pursed his lips, "Then go and sit and I will do what is required."

"She... will not suffer, will she?"

"We all suffer, Guy... but no, she will not wake from her sleep, from her dreams. She will pass peacefully, and you will have your heart's desire. Your freedom and her money."

"And Molly?" he hissed, "That's the most important thing!"

"Of course..." the Mayor nodded before slowly backing out of the room and closing the door gently in his face.

He stood there, listening to his pounding heart as the Mayor's boots squeaked upon the stairs.

"At last..." he whispered, raising a shaking hand to his face, "...thank God, at last."

Though he knew who he was really thanking wasn't God at all.

The Farmer

Cece was waiting for him outside the livery; she was wearing loose pants, a baggy shirt with a satchel slung across her chest and a wide-brimmed hat tied under her chin. She'd braided her blonde hair into a long ponytail. It was about as unfeminine a look as she could have chosen.

She looked almost unbearably beautiful.

He smiled at her and hoped he'd managed to wash the stink of cow dung off. He'd been up long before dawn to milk the herd and get the chores he couldn't leave done, then wash, gobble breakfast and ride hell for leather into town; all without, he hoped, looking like he'd been dashing about like a madman.

"Morning," he grinned, trying not to sound too breathless. He'd had to ride hard to get here on time and had only reined in his horse as they'd galloped up the Tear towards Pioneer Square.

"Morning," Cece tipped back her hat slightly as she looked up at him.

"Ready for a ride?" he tried not to wince at his own words, which sounded utterly inane and slightly lewd. Small talk had never been one of his strengths, which he put down to spending far too much of his time entirely in the company of cows.

Cece answered by hoisting herself smoothly up into the saddle.

"So, where do you want to go?"

"North," Cece said with a purposeful nod.

"What's out there?"

"You tell me," she wheeled her horse around.

"Grass, cows, farms... much the same as every other direction."

"Perfect."

"We could ride out to Hayliss' Creek," he offered tentatively.

"What's that?"

"Just a little stream; it's kinda pretty, though..."

"Is it North?"

"More to the east, I guess."

Cece stared ahead as they trotted down Main Street, "I want to go north."

He'd long ago concluded girls could be quite strange in the way their minds worked, even more so than cows in fact, so he didn't argue. He'd brought a picnic and thought Hayliss' Creek was a lovely spot to eat, drink, laugh, look into each other's eyes and... who knows what else while listening to the water bubble over the smooth grey rocks scattered along that part of the creek.

He felt a momentary irritation she'd dismissed his suggestion out of hand, he'd been thinking of what to do and where to go from the moment Cece agreed to ride out with him, however, it didn't actually matter. He pushed his irritation aside. The sun was shining, he was with the most beautiful girl in town, and he didn't have to milk another cow until tomorrow. Cece could go anywhere she wanted, and he'd happily follow her because, just for once, no less deserving fellow was going to spoil things for him.

*

"What do you know about the Mayor?"

They'd left Hawker's Drift behind them, the town no more than a smudge on the hazy horizon. Cece had said little, she hadn't been rude or dismissive, but she seemed preoccupied. She'd half swivelled in her saddle several times to look back along the road.

"Don't really know him."

"But you know *of* him?"

"Well, yeah, of course, he's the most important guy around here. I'm his first port of call if he needs advice on shovelling cow dung, but otherwise…"

Cece nodded, and he looked away when she didn't smile at his little joke. Maybe he shouldn't overplay the shit shovelling gags; not all girls saw the funny side of cow dung after all.

"Has he been Mayor long?"

"Oh, forever…"

"Forever?"

He laughed at how Cece was frowning at him as if he'd meant *really* forever.

"Well, not literally, but since before I was born."

"And how old are you?"

"Twenty-three."

"And how long was he Mayor before you were born?"

"I dunno."

Cece pursed her lips in thought.

"Why all the interest in the Mayor?"

"I had to go and sing for him last night – just curious."

The land to their left belonged to the Skellings, a miserable bunch of inbred halfwits according to his Ma, and a small herd of their cows were grazing close to the road. If he didn't know better, he'd have thought they were sniggering.

"Oh…" he eventually managed to say, "…how did that go?"

"He was…"

Charming? Witty? Handsome? Rich? Not whiffing of cow shit?

"…a bit odd."

"Really!?"

Cece looked across at him, "You haven't noticed?"

"I've barely spoken to the man."

Apart from discussing you, anyway.

"Not even at election time when he's whoring for votes?"

He didn't entirely approve of the phrase, but he let it pass, "No, we live outside the town limits, so we wouldn't get a vote, even if there ever was an election."

"The Mayor isn't elected?"

"Sure he is. Unopposed."

"Nobody *ever* stands against him?"

"What would be the point? He's popular; town's doing well… would be a waste of everyone's time."

"Hard to believe nobody's ever stood against him."

"Well, Hogg Perkins did stand years ago; I was just a boy, so didn't pay much attention."

"And the Mayor won, I take it?"

"Oh, no one got to vote. Perkins dropped dead of a heart attack a week before polling day; died in his sleep apparently. Guess the stress of the election must have been too much for him."

"Must have been..."

He jumped into the pause between Cece's questions, "So, how'd it go with the Mayor?"

"Fine."

The Mayor had seemed so keen to help him, had it all been some kind of ruse? A distraction while he seduced Cece for himself? But why would he do that? He was no competition after all.

"Did he like your singing?"

"I think so."

"Did you stay long?"

"A couple of hours, I suppose. I sung, they drunk, I went back to *Jack's* they... did whatever."

"They?"

"The Mayor and his... companion, Felicity."

"The Mayor has a companion?"

"I got the impression he has several. You haven't seen her?"

"Must have done around town, but I don't know her."

"She's quite striking."

"Really?"

"And a little unhinged, I think."

"I'd heard stories... about women, but..."

"What stories?"

"That he had women in his house and his ranch... you know, women... like the girls in *Jack's*, but more... *expensive.*"

"You mean whores?"

He shifted in his saddle; he really wished she'd stop using that word.

"Dunno, I don't really listen to gossip."

"The Mayor has a ranch?" Cece asked abruptly, "Whereabouts is it?"

He looked glumly ahead.

"North of town..."

The Doctor

"Is she dead?"

It was an unnecessary question. Lorna Furnedge's complexion was pale grey, her flesh cold, eyes wide and lifeless. However, more than anything, it was the complete silence that pointed to the poor woman's passing. During his increasingly frequent visits to attend her, Mrs Furnedge had never been silent. Even when she wasn't complaining about her ailments, her husband, or the world in general, the rasping dry breath that rattled around her chest before escaping the confines of her body, usually accompanied by a cloud of smoke, was enough to assure she was very much alive.

Now there was only silence.

"She is far beyond my help," Dr Rudi straightened up.

Guy Furnedge stood in the doorway; he was wringing a handkerchief in his hands and looked only marginally less pale than his deceased wife.

I'd have thought he'd be doing cartwheels.

He clamped down on that particular thought. The ties binding people together could be unfathomable sometimes. Lorna had been a difficult woman. Actually, that was being polite, he could think of quite a few words that would have been more accurately descriptive, but he'd never liked to speak ill of the dead.

"I... found her this morning... I was bringing her coffee..."

Dr Rudi looked down at the shattered cup and the dark stain upon the entangled vines weaved into the thick rug at the foot of the bed.

"She must have passed during the night."

"Did she suffer?"

"It would have been quick."

Furnedge nodded and wrung his handkerchief some more, "Better she passed in her sleep, I suppose. Best way to go... if there is such a thing."

He was going to point out people didn't tend to sleep with their eyes wide open, but there was no need to dissuade Furnedge of that small comfort. Instead, he reached down and passed his hand over her eyes to close the lids.

"Indeed..." he muttered.

She was meltwater cold.

"When did you last see your wife... alive?"

"Yesterday... I came home at lunchtime to check on her. She was unwell. Amy and I had to carry her to bed."

"You didn't think to call me?"

Furnedge grimaced and pulled off his spectacles, "It wasn't the kind of illness you could have helped her with."

"What kind of illness was it?"

"The bottle of bourbon by lunchtime kind of illness."

"I see..."

"Her drinking has been much worse lately... I should have seen this coming... I should..."

He walked over to Furnedge and patted his arm, "There is no point blaming yourself. There is only so much abuse the human body can take. If she was drinking that much, then this was just... inevitable, I'm afraid."

"But I could have stopped her drinking..."

"I knew your wife... I don't think anyone could have stopped her doing what she wanted to do."

Furnedge didn't look entirely convinced. Poor chap no doubt blamed himself; it was the natural thing to do. People liked to assign blame to such things, whether to themselves or to others. Of course, in reality, it was just a combination of God's will and Lorna's own demons, which Dr Rudi guessed were considerable.

"So, it was the drink, in the end?"

People liked to know, too, even if it did them no good. They liked to think he knew too, which was a notion he never disabused anyone of.

"In part... a heart attack is what I suspect. Brought on by the abuse of hard liquor."

"Is that what you will put on the death certificate?" Furnedge looked odd without his spectacles on, blinking like some little critter caught in the open.

"A heart attack, that's all I shall say... there's no need to mention the liquor."

"Oh... yes. I'd appreciate that, Klaus. Thank you."

"I've seen enough of em after all."

"You have?"

Dr Rudi turned back to the bed, "Yes, we seem to get a lot of bad hearts in Hawker's Drift."

The Burden of Souls

"We do?" Furnedge's voice wavered a little. He hoped the poor man wasn't going to start crying. He always found that difficult.

He stared down at Lorna's lifeless face, "Indeed we do. The human heart can be a frail vessel; all manner of things can stop it dead. Liquor abuse is one reason; overwork, worry, bad food, the simple wear and tear of passing years can all cause heart attacks too."

"And do we have a lot of that here?"

"So it would seem, for example, your old boss, Mr Fitzsimmons, he keeled over in the street as I recall."

"He was quite elderly."

"Always seemed fit as a fiddle to me... just goes to show."

"Show what?"

"That you can never tell. There's something out there waiting for all of us, I suppose. There but for the Grace of God..."

"Indeed."

He heard Furnedge shuffle a little in the long silence that followed as he remained motionless, staring at Lorna Furnedge's corpse.

"So... what happens now?"

"I'll let Charlie Molloy know; he'll pop by later to collect the body. You'll need to make the funeral arrangements with him. He is the only undertaker in town."

"Of course..."

The front door opened and shut with a bang.

"Amy... I'll have to let her know," Furnedge explained, "she's our domestic help."

Dr Rudi knew her well enough. Having to wait on Lorna Furnedge ensured the girl had the sympathy of the whole town.

"Best you go down and tell her, there is no need for her to see the body."

"Yes, it wouldn't do to upset the poor girl unnecessarily."

"I will finish up here."

Furnedge hovered before nodding his agreement and hurrying downstairs.

Dr Rudi lifted the sheet to cover Lorna's face. Her cold dead eyes were staring up at him. Strange, he was sure he'd closed them. Not that it mattered; they would never see anything again either way. Her features were not entirely slack. Her mouth was slightly open, the lips pulled back to reveal her yellowed teeth; her eyes were unnaturally wide too. Perhaps that was why the lids had rolled back up. In fact, her eyes seemed to be slightly bulging. It almost looked like she had died halfway through a stifled scream.

Liquor abuse, overwork, worry, bad food, the simple wear and tear of passing years could all cause a heart to stop. So too could terror.

He pulled the sheet up over the poor woman's face and tried not to think too much about that. After all, it wasn't the first time death had etched such an expression onto a corpse's face.

Not in this town anyway ...

The Gunslinger

"Where'd you find this?" John demanded.

Before he could reply, the gunsmith hurried to the window and flipped the CLOSED sign over.

"Actually, don't answer that!" he barked, returning to whip the remains of the rifle off the counter and dropping it unceremoniously into something that sounded like a metal bin. "I really don't want to know!"

"At a crossroads, north of town."

"I said I didn't want to know."

"Next to the carcasses of a horse and two mules."

"You having trouble with your hearing?"

"Think they'd been there a couple of weeks."

"Best see Dr Rudi; he might be able to help you with that."

"In other words, about the same time Tom McCrea died."

John continued to stare at him, his lips pressed into a thin dark line and his gnarled fingers splayed on the countertop.

"At least you didn't say murdered."

"About the same time he was helped off his horse."

John X rolled his eyes, "Why are you bringing this shit to me?"

"Is it the rifle you sold to Tom McCrea?"

"Hard to say."

"Why's that?"

"Because it's just a burnt-up piece of junk; I sold Tom a rifle of this type, but I can't say if it's this specific rifle."

"You sold many others like this?"

"One or two..."

"We both know this is the rifle you sold to Tom..."

"Amos, what does it matter?"

"A man died."

"Men die all the time, and most of em, just like Tom McCrea, you don't know from squat. And frankly, if you had known him, I doubt you'd have been mightily taken with him. Let's at least be honest; this hasn't got anything to do with justice for Tom McCrea. Has it?"

"Not a great deal."

"Well, at least you're not claiming to be some kind of justice-seeking avenging angel. Something I suppose."

I've spent thirteen years trying to be an avenging angel. It turned out I'm crap at it...

"I just... don't want Molly to end up in the whorehouse."

"You're in the minority with that son; from what I hear, she will be a real takings booster for Monty."

"People have heard?"

"These kind of things get around."

"Gonna be a lot of disappointed folk in town then."

John sighed before his voice softened, "You're... fond of her, aren't you?"

"It's more complicated than that."

"Yeah, it always is," John leaned in closer, "whatever damn thing you want to call it, be careful; *fondness* can get a man killed just as easily as a rifle slug in the back. Or falling off your horse..."

"You going to give me that rifle back?"

"Nope, I got a little furnace in the yard; I'm going to melt the barrel down for scrap. Only thing it's good for."

"It's evidence."

John laughed, "You ain't thinking of taking this to the Sheriff, are you? I know you're not *that* stupid."

Amos nodded; the gunsmith was right. There would be no trial for Tom McCrea's murderer; justice didn't work like that out here. Actually, it didn't much work like that anywhere. He should just concentrate on getting Molly out of here if they couldn't raise the money to pay the Mayor off.

But then what? Where would he take her? He was used to being alone; he generally shunned the company of men, let alone women. If he got her out of Hawker's Drift, he couldn't just dump her in the next town with no money and a stolen horse to fend for herself.

Could he?

*

Mr Wizzle must have found a ride back into town as he was no longer at the crossroads. Amos glanced over as two more crows swooped down to join the continuing horsemeat banquet. The day was roasting hot, and there wasn't a scrap of shade out here on the grass. He squinted against the sun's glare towards the buildings he'd seen the previous day.

He nudged his horse and continued on.

He wasn't entirely sure what he was looking for, answers he supposed, but to what question? Was he really just trying to help Molly, or was there something else? A wrongness hung about Hawker's Drift, something vague and unfocused, but that whispered unease had been much louder around the Mayor and his deputies. He'd visited some sorry excuses for towns during his travels, and Hawker's Drift seemed a world away from all of them. It was peaceful and prosperous, but something wasn't right.

So what?

Did it matter? Would it help him find Severn? Would it bring him peace?

He was sure the answer to all those questions was no. So why get involved? Why allow a town he didn't care about or a woman who reminded him of his dead wife to distract him from his search?

Severn was getting further away all the time he spent here; the bastard's laughter still echoed around his head. That braying, interminable, hysterical screech in his ear, spraying spittle over his cheek, coarse stubble scratching his skin as Severn held his arms and one of his men pressed a pistol hard into his temple as they made him watch Megan being raped and then killed.

He spat.

Further away? *Really?* He'd found not a trace of that piece of shit and his merry band of killers in thirteen years; they might as well have gone to the moon for all the good his searching had done.

Perhaps that was why he was helping Molly. He just needed an excuse to give up. To admit defeat and accept

Megan would never be avenged. That *he'd* never be avenged. Better that than ending up in some backwater saloon drinking himself into oblivion or riding on till he simply keeled over and fell off his horse through old age and exhaustion, his last memory of life being the sound of crows waiting to peck out his eyes, their hungry contemptuous caws so much like Severn's laughter. Mocking him till the very end.

Had he given up?

He suspected he'd given up on life a long, long time ago. Was it time to give up on Severn too? He'd had no sense of the man for years, no word, no hint, no clue, no trace. Nothing. He'd likely been face down in an unmarked grave for a decade. If so, he hoped his death had been slow and painful, but it gave him no sense of closure to think the bastard had died at someone else's hands.

He'd failed Megan in so many ways, and now he'd failed even to avenge her.

*

A gate barred the road a few hundred yards from the crossroads.

The surrounding land appeared unfarmed, the grass stretching away as far as the eye could see to the horizon. Nothing much caught the eye other than a few cows slowly ploughing through it. Just the road, the distant buildings barely visible atop a gentle, low rise, the gate and a simple barbed wire fence stretching away as far as the eye could see on either side of the road. That and the two horses tethered to the gate and a man leaning on a post, staring off towards nowhere in particular.

"Afternoon," Amos finally said when the man continued to keep his back turned after pulling up at the gate.

The man jumped and spun around; his attention had obviously been a long way off. It was the young farmer from the saloon, the one who was always moping around Cece.

Sye Hallows, the name came after a moment. He seemed to recognise Amos far quicker than he'd recognised him.

He didn't look particularly pleased to see him.

Two horses. Of course, he was with Cece.

"You looking for something, Mister?" Sye was leaning back on the gate, trying to look nonchalant. He wasn't making a particularly good fist of it.

"Kind of..." he couldn't see Cece around, and there were few places to hide unless she was hunkered down in the grass. He dismounted and led his horse to the gate; a roughly painted sign Sye had blocked from his view was nailed to it.

KEEP OUT.

"Friendly folk live up there then?"

When Sye just looked at him blankly, he nodded at the sign and then towards the buildings shimmering in the distant afternoon haze.

"Oh, the Mayor's ranch... he likes his privacy when he's out here, I guess," Sye peered at him curiously; "...you got business with the Mayor?"

"Not exactly... you ever been up there?"

"Me? No... the Mayor's never even spoken to me."

He swivelled to look at the young man as the lie washed over him, "Is that so?"

Sye's discomfort glowed around him. He wasn't a particularly convincing liar... which was something in his favour, at least.

"I just run a little dairy farm with my Ma..." he said, truthfully this time.

"You out riding with Cece?"

Sye's eyes narrowed, "How'd you know?"

He nodded towards the two tethered horses, "The larger one, the bay mare, she's yours, right?"

"Uh-huh."

"The other one is the second lamest horse in the livery... so you must be riding with Cece."

He smiled at the young man's confused expression.

"Where is she anyhow?"

"She went off to... you know."

"Piss?"

"I guess."

"Well, I'll stick around to say hello, then be on my way."

Sye looked both irritated and relieved, "I'm sure she'll be back soon."

"Ladies do take their time when it comes to... *you know.*"

"Sure..." Sye grunted, "...thirty minutes already."

"Thirty minutes?" he looked around, but there was nothing to see but gently swaying grass.

"Yeah, she must have a helluva bladder."

"Seen anyone else about?"

"Nope."

"Were you followed from town?"

"Followed? Why would anyone follow us?" Sye snorted.

Amos didn't answer. Nobody took thirty minutes to do their business, but Sye would have noticed them approaching if anyone had grabbed Cece. He looked back at Sye, who had half turned away to pick his nose with his thumbnail.

Surely?

"Why you out here?"

"Are you Cece's father or something?" He could see the ire flickering in his soul. For some reason, the boy felt threatened.

"Nope... just a friend."

"And you just happened to turn up here. Today? While I'm with Cece?"

"Why would that be strange?"

"Cece wanted to come here... she must have mentioned it to you."

"Why'd she want to come here?"

"I dunno, you're her *friend*, surely, she's told you? I wanted to have a picnic at Hayliss' Creek..." he looked dejected, a man watching a long yearned for day unravelling before his eyes and was thrashing around for someone to blame.

A less deserving fellow...

The phrase popped into his head.

"She wanted to come to the Mayor's Ranch?"

"She just wanted to ride north," he shrugged, "and here we all are..."

They stood awkwardly in silence, Amos trying not to feel either Sye's resentment or his own unease. He was considering how to suggest they go and look for Cece, without it sounding like he thought the young man was a complete idiot to think a girl took more than thirty minutes to take a piss when she suddenly emerged from the grass.

He'd been looking at the ranch but caught her in the corner of his eye; she must have been squatting down about a hundred yards from the road, near to the barbed wire fence cutting across the grass to his left.

Perhaps he didn't know so much about the toilet habits of girls after all.

She smiled and waved at him as she meandered back towards them, one hand pressed against her hat as the wind picked up to set the grass shimmering about her. She didn't look entirely surprised to see him, which he was sure Sye noticed too. She was dressed much the same as before and was fumbling something into her satchel as she walked back towards them. He thought it was the thin little notebook she'd said she'd been drawing in when they'd first met, though he couldn't be absolutely sure.

"Amos!" She beamed once she made it back to the road; for one awful moment, he thought she would reach up and peck him on the cheek. Which he was sure would be enough to make Sye explode with rage.

He settled for a nod and a touch of his hat.

"What you doing out here?"

"Just riding. You?"

"Just riding… with Sye."

"How'd it go with the Mayor last night?" he nodded towards the ranch in the distance.

"He's stranger than I thought."

"Did he do anything he shouldn't have?"

"Are you my father?"

"That's the second time I've been asked that question in the last five minutes," he nodded towards Sye, who was making a noisy show of mounting his horse, which provided a much loftier perch for sulking.

Cece gave him a knowing smile, "He was a perfect gentleman."

"Really?"

"Yes, I was surprised too."

"He's dangerous."

"I know."

Amos' attention drifted off to the distant buildings, "Any particular reason you came out here to look at his ranch?"

"Who said that's why I'm here?"

"There's nothing else out here."

"Much the same in every direction."

"But you wanted to go north."

Cece glanced at Sye, who was trying hard not to stare impatiently at them.

"Yeah, I wanted to go north."

"You're not going to tell me why, are you?"

"I think we've already established you're not my father."

"It's getting late," Sye called.

"I'd better be going; see you around Amos," she grinned.

"Just be careful around the Mayor, huh?"

"I am," she half turned away before looking back and winking at him, "and no, I didn't sleep with him... or any of his friends."

"Friends?"

"He has his own little harem; I met one last night. Charming girl, but... not my type."

"The privileges of power, eh?"

"Quite..." she grinned and patted his arm lightly as she passed,

...a city without end, countless people toiling beneath bleached sulphurous skies, buildings disappearing into the clouds, noise, bustle, congestion, blank, faceless people, everybody communicating, but nobody listening, strange metallic smells, incoherent noises, reflections upon reflections, glowing multi-hued lights, blaring, screams, constant movement...

"...thanks for the concern all the same."

"You're welcome..." he managed to reply. Cece smiled at him once she was back in the saddle; Sye didn't. The pair wheeled their horses and headed back down the road.

He stood watching them slowly shrink towards the horizon, all the time wondering why, when Cece had touched him, he'd seen a vision of hell itself ...

The Widow

She hadn't been sure whether to go and see Guy or not.

She'd almost been grateful most of the town chose to ignore Tom's death; it would have been even harder to bear if she'd had to glad-hand a succession of neighbours knocking on her door to demonstrate their communal grief and mock sympathy.

However, not everybody else was like her.

She didn't like the little lawyer, but, in reality, other than Amos, he was the only person in town who'd even tried to help her or show they gave a jot of concern for either her loss or her current predicament.

So, after thinking about it for half a day, she changed into something suitably sober and headed up to the Furnedge's home behind Pioneer Square.

A few glances came her way as she walked up Main Street. More than a few, truth be told. Most varied between withering contempt and degrees of lechery. The former mostly from women no doubt appalled by her scandalous behaviour, and the latter from men looking forward to finding out just how scandalous she really was when she took up residence in *Jack's*.

"Is Mr Furnedge available?" she asked the bedraggled looking girl who answered the door of Furnedge's home.

The girl leaned out of the door towards her, "You've heard about his wife?"

She nodded, "Yes, I just wanted to give him my condolences... but if he isn't receiving visitors, I quite understand."

"I'll just check... it's Mrs McCrea, isn't it?"

She nodded a second time. She vaguely recognised the girl from around town but didn't have the faintest idea who she was. Not having to introduce yourself was clearly one of the benefits of notoriety...

She stood on the step and waited. It was an impressive house, not as grand as the Mayor's, but a fair size all the same. White clapperboard behind a small lawn and a picket fence, it sat on the western side of The Tear, just before the hill plunged towards the surrounding flats.

Not long after she and Tom had rolled into Hawker's Drift, she'd asked one of the locals why they called the hill the town sat upon The Tear. The old drunk (inevitably, they'd been in the saloon) had told them the story went that when God had finished making the Earth, he'd looked down upon the great grass prairie and wept at the beauty he'd created, one of God's Tears had solidified to form the small hill upon which the town had been built.

It seemed more likely that God had gotten bored and hadn't quite completed this bit; like when you were painting a room, and you didn't bother to finish the corner where the dresser would go because nobody was ever going to see it.

Although slightly drunk, she'd managed to keep that thought to herself.

She had, however, asked why the fuck, when surrounded by mile after endless mile of flat land, they'd built their damn town atop the biggest hill they could find.

"Because we like the view," had been the frosty response. Her relationship with the locals had gone nowhere but downhill from there on.

The girl reappeared at the door and ushered her in with a harried little smile; the master of the house was waiting for her in the hall.

"That will be all, Amy," Furnedge shooed the girl away. Amy gave her a curious look before hurrying off.

"Mrs McCrea, is something wrong?" Guy Furnedge's concern stretched across his face.

He's thinking of me, even at a time like this.

She wasn't sure whether to feel touched or unsettled.

"No... I'm fine, but I heard about your wife, I..." she flapped for the right word; she'd never been quite sure what people were supposed to say at times like this, something that actually meant a damn anyway "...I just wanted to say how sorry I was."

Guy blinked and looked as if he were going to burst into tears.

Oh fuck.

"That is so kind," he said, stepping forward to take her hands, "your kindness is so much appreciated, my dear..."

The first thing she noticed was that his hands were clammy. She resisted the urge to pull free so she could rub her palms on her skirt. The second thing was he didn't smell of anything in particular. Was that one of the things grief did to men? Stop them pouring shit cologne over themselves?

"It must be a terrible shock; I know Mrs Furnedge had been unwell, but even so..."

"Very unwell..." he nodded vigorously, "...but as you say, a terrible shock." He continued to stare, his clammy hands still gripping hers, before adding in a blurted torrent, "I found her; I was taking her morning coffee up, she hadn't called, which was unusual, but I didn't think anything of it at the time... I went in, and there she was... quite dead."

"What happened?"

"A heart attack, according to Dr Rudi... I don't know, but that's what he says," he squeezed her hands more forcefully.

"Poor thing..."

"I will manage, in time..."

She'd meant his wife but didn't correct him. She was more concerned with getting her hands back.

"I'm sure, but we will all miss her; she was such a... a *character!*"

"Yes, she was that. I... did you know her?"

"Well, I couldn't say that we were close, but I always enjoyed talking to her."

"I didn't know you'd even met her?"

"It's a small town."

She'd run into Lorna Furnedge in the saloon on a couple of occasions. It turned out they had enjoyed a common interest in hard liquor and bitching about their husbands.

"I suppose it is, strange that you can share your life with someone and not even know a thing like that."

From what she remembered Lorna saying about her husband, the only thing they'd shared had been a mutual loathing for each other, although, to be fair, Lorna might well have gone away with much the same opinion about Tom and her.

"I would ask you to stay, but some of Lorna's friends are here; they are quite emotional, I'm afraid."

"No, no," she shook her head, "I don't wish to intrude; I only popped in to offer my condolences."

"And it is much appreciated."

She took a step back from the door, though her hands remained firmly ensnared; the last thing she wanted was to spend the afternoon surrounded by Lorna's friends. From what she remembered, Lorna's opinion of them hadn't been much higher than of her husband.

"Well, good day then... and if there is anything I can do?"

The lawyer looked like he was going to blurt something out but managed to contain it with a nod and a smile.

"That is very kind... though I hope I will soon be able to do something for you."

"For me?"

"Once my late wife's affairs are settled... well, shall we say it will alter my own circumstances somewhat."

"Really?" she smiled thinly, not sure what the little man was getting at.

"I can't say too much, but I hope I'll be able to help you out of your predicament."

"You think you can persuade the Mayor after all? There's really no need to worry about me at a time like this."

"I worry about you constantly, Molly, really, I do."

"Why... thank you..."

"I will come to see you when matters are in hand. Then everything will be resolved."

"That will be a great relief."

"To us both, Molly, to us both!"

She tried to extract her hands from his grasp, but Furnedge was having none of it and, instead, raised her right hand to his lips and kissed it as lightly as a starving dog would a bowl of offal.

"Until then," she badly needed to rub her hand on her skirt now.

He reluctantly let her go, and she turned and managed to get the front door open before he could slobber over any other part of her.

"Good day, Mr Furnedge; I hope you manage to come to terms with your loss."

When he smiled, it was not the kind of smile normally associated with the recently bereaved.

"I assure you everything will be quite *tickety*, my dear... and please, please call me Guy..."

As the door closed, she caught Amy peering out of the window, the curtain falling back the moment she glanced at her.

If she'd stayed at the window a second longer, the girl would have seen Molly virtually running down the garden path.

The Songbird

"Do you have to do that!" Monty Jack hissed, throwing his hands out in exasperation.

"I did warn you," she favoured him with one of her sweeter smiles.

"Just cut it out; it's bad for business!"

"That's the first guy I've had to slap tonight!"

"Plus the three last night and the five before that!"

"See?"

"See what?"

"Less every night. They're learning. I bet I won't be getting pawed at all by next week!"

Monty glared at her; she suspected he was worried the reduced pawing opportunities might hit his takings.

"You're welcome!" She beamed and slid away before he could give her any more customer relations advice.

She made her way back towards the piano; her break was almost over. The saloon was as busy as it seemed to be every evening. It was a small town, and there was nowhere else the locals could go to drink themselves into oblivion, gamble away their earnings and fondle fallen women under one roof - and all now with the added bonus of having their drinking/gambling/groping accompanied by Cecilia Jones and her swanky new piano.

It didn't seem her patron slapping had had any more detrimental effect on Monty's customers than her refusal to wear more appropriate attire for a saloon had. She'd quickly worked out "more appropriate attire" was Monty-speak for "dress like a slut."

She took her stool and sipped water, the novelty of her first few appearances had worn off, and there would be no silence to fill with her voice anymore, though the general hubbub at least dropped below its normal level, which was usually somewhere just shy of raucous.

She was grateful the Mayor was not present; his visits to the saloon appeared to be more fleeting and irregular than most of the men in town, but then he did have Felicity to keep him entertained at home, of course.

Her visit to the Mayor's ranch had revealed as much as she had expected it to; there was undoubtedly an awful lot of resonance, but she would need to get much closer. Which meant going back alone.

She'd thought getting Sye to ride with her would provide a plausible excuse for being out on the grass, though she hadn't anticipated how difficult it would be to slip away from him to work. It was lucky the grass was long enough for her to hunker down out of sight during her toilet break, as that was the only time he left her alone.

What had she expected?

He followed her around so doggedly she'd considered taking a bone with her to throw for him. He was harmless enough, by the standards of Hawker's Drift at least, but a whole day of him had been tiring. Still, if people thought they'd been out riding and spent the day cavorting in the grass, that was preferable to questions about exactly what she had been doing.

She wasn't sure he'd have been any help if the Mayor's men had decided to do much more than keep an eye on her. At least she now had an idea why the Mayor was showing an interest in her and had her followed that first day she'd gone out riding.

Though how could he have known?

It wasn't supposed to have been like this; she was supposed to blend in, be unremarkable, not attract attention to herself while she did what she needed to do. She wasn't sure whether or not singing in front of several hundred people every night quite fitted in with that brief, but what else was she supposed to have done? It counted as initiative in her book.

Get a job and become part of this community, they'd said. She didn't know if she'd been naive about the kind of employment opportunities available to a young woman here or whether she'd been the butt of someone's idea of a joke. There were plenty who'd argued this was no work for a woman in the first place.

Idiots!

Monty was making a circular motion with his finger. Break over.

She'd exhausted the repertoire of songs she knew by heart and was reaching the bottom of the ones she could muddle through, although it wasn't as if anyone was going to know if she got the words wrong anyway. Apart from the Mayor, at least.

She tried to push *that* particular thought from her mind, though it kept resolutely bobbing back up to the surface. Just who the hell was he, and more to the point, how had he gotten here?

Several possible answers presented themselves, none were particularly palatable, but she had to find out.

As she sang, she noticed Sye appear from the crowd; he looked wistful and doe-eyed. She fought down the urge to slap him.

Instead, she caught his eye and smiled; he looked like he might explode with happiness.

She let her eyes slide back to the keys, ignoring the twinge of guilt. She didn't want any emotional entanglements, they weren't recommended unless required to complete the job, and she had no physical itch that needed scratching. But he could be useful, so she would use him as required; that was what they'd taught her.

You'll be travelling light, so learn to live off the land and use whatever tools come to hand.

Besides, she *was* still engaged, even if Quayle was an awfully long way away. And if she ever saw him again, there was no guarantee he would be the same man she'd left.

She thought of him standing on the beach that last night together, the waves pounding the shore on the edge of a quicksilver sea. A fucking beach under the moonlight; that was just so typical of Quayle. They couldn't have just said goodbye over a drink like other people did. No, goodbye had to be a statement – look at what you're leaving behind. Silly girl.

She'd started playing a mournful ballad without even realising it. Monty didn't like her playing sad songs; he insisted they were bad for business.

But Monty was an idiot.

The Mother

It was late.

Kate hurried along the deserted street, taking the less direct route home. Best not to be seen; she didn't want anyone gossiping in Ash's chair about seeing his wife scurrying home in the early hours.

She wished she could have stayed until dawn; that would have been even more exciting. Creeping home as the sun came up after a whole night of... she smiled and pulled her light summer shawl more tightly around her shoulders.

What a wicked woman...

John had whispered that in her ear, among other things, several times; each hoarse, breathless word thrilling her more than the last.

Kate had long since stopped asking herself what she thought she was doing; it excited her so far beyond care it didn't really matter anymore.

She'd only been seeing John for six months, but she couldn't remember what her life had been like before that clearly, and the things she did remember she didn't like terribly much.

The slow, repetitive drudgery and routine of the loyal wife and doting mother. So selfless, so supportive, so commendable, so unutterably, soul-crushingly boring.

Now her life had excitement and colour in it. Yes, she liked having a life with a little colour in it... and she liked having a little colour in her too...

Kate laughed aloud and looked about in embarrassment; no, nobody had seen the crazy giggling woman sneaking home. The crazy, giggling, *adulterous* woman sneaking home.

Raised voices briefly disturbed the night, a husband and wife's bedtime squabble by the sound of it, but, otherwise, the world was quiet, the town deserted.

It had been a stupid risk to take, but it had been worth it. God, it had been worth it! The things that man did to her, the way he made her feel. Her legs hadn't quite solidified again yet; she still feared they might yet buckle and deposit her in the dirt. A squealing, giggling and immensely satisfied mess.

However, the closer she got to home, the more apprehension and unease tinged the excitement. What if Ash's poker buddies had called their game off? What if Ruthie had thrown up her dinner and Mrs Milligan had brought her home? What if Emily had been unable to sleep and had come down searching for hot milk?

Her mind played over all the things that could have gone wrong; they made her heart pound a little faster with each step. Strangely, it seemed to make the excitement more intense, as if her fear were somehow focusing the excitement, the way a magnifying glass might focus the sun's rays till they were strong enough for flames to erupt.

The Burden of Souls

She slowed her pace and took several deep breaths, forcing the memory of John away; the sound, sight, feel and taste of him.

For an instant, she thought a figure was loitering in the shadows near her house and a missed heartbeat restored her wits. Hawker's Drift was mostly a safe town, certainly by the standards of every other place she'd ever heard about. After all, there was still law here, but she was still a woman alone at night. Things happened, even here.

She slowed her pace and stared. Cloud had swept in while she'd been with John, and the sky was a featureless black vault. The street ahead was just differing shades of darkness, but she saw no movement, and her breathing eased. It must have only been her imagination painting pictures with the shadows.

Picking up the pace again, she kept glancing at the dark silent houses of her neighbours, looking for the glow of a lamp or the twitching of a curtain, but each house slumbered, the windows no more alert than the blind eyes of sleeping dogs.

She paused by the gate to her own home, her heart quickening again. The house was dark and still. If someone were awake, she'd see the light of a lamp or candle, wouldn't she?

Nobody was about; Emily was asleep, Ash was probably half drunk and still playing cards, Ruthie was with the Milligans, the neighbours were all tucked up in their beds. She'd done it, gotten away with it.

So why did she feel someone was watching her?

There was no chill in the air, but she pulled her shawl tight all the same.

Across the street, the houses were higher up The Tear, and they loomed over her. Anyone could be watching from a bedroom window. A sleepless child, a wife waiting for her husband to stagger back from *Jack's,* someone who knew what she'd been doing...

But no. Instead, her eyes slid away from the houses opposite and rested on the corner of Grover's house, two down from her own, where a little path ran on to Cherry Lane. Was that a figure standing there? Watching her?

The shadow was almost absolute, black on black, but it did look like a tall slim figure. Unmoving. Silent. Staring.

She jumped as something moved outside her house.

Magda, next door's cat...

Kate forced a smile at her own skittishness. When she looked back towards Grover's place, there was no figure. Just her imagination... and maybe a little guilt?

No! Why should she feel guilty? She deserved something for herself. After all those years, all those long, dry, passionless years. Damn right she did.

She hurried to her door and let herself in as quietly as possible, shutting the door behind her with the faintest click of the latch. The house was silent. Her only welcome were its familiar smells; beeswax, dried lavender, her husband's pipe smoke. She padded through the downstairs, still half-expecting Ash to be waiting for her, his usually placid face flushed with hurt, anger, and incomprehension, but everything was as she'd left it.

Slipping off her shoes, she tip-toed up the stairs in the darkness; no need to light a candle, she'd lived here half her life now. She knew every crack, warp, and weave in the fabric of the place. She'd cleaned it a million times; she knew well enough the position of every chair, table, rug, and candlestick. No mysteries hid here. No excitements...

She lingered outside Emily's door, resisting the urge to look in; she wasn't a baby anymore. No light snuck under the door, no sound of restless to-ing and fro-ing, no questioning voice asking her where she'd been all night. She'd preferred to have heard her daughter snoring, but Emily had never been much of a snorer unless she had a cold.

Kate smiled and moved on to her room; she should wash, but Ash would not be home until late morning, and she would clean herself when she woke. She wanted to snuggle down in the sheets with the memory of John lingering on her; the feel of his lust dried upon her skin, the scent of their passion still between her legs.

She stripped slowly, far slower than earlier in the evening, and crawled quietly into her empty bed.

She'd done it. Nobody would know save her and John. She thought she would lay there for hours, feeling her heart beat faster as the memories washed across the ceiling, but she drifted off into a dreamless sleep within a few minutes.

*

She awoke early and with a start. Grey light pushed its way around the curtains; the world beyond muted and distant. She smelt of sex, vague and fuzzy as a dream. She stretched, smiled, thought about John for a few delicious minutes and resisted the urge to let her hand find its way between her legs.

Instead, she yawned and reluctantly pulled herself from the bed. Best she sorted herself out before Emily woke and Ash and Ruthie got home. After tidying up the clothes she'd left decadently strewn over the floor the previous night, she washed herself thoroughly with soap and a wet flannel, before pulling on a tired unfussy dress that made her feel like the dull, faithful little wife and homemaker she usually was.

She tied back her hair and patted down the loose strands till the mirror confirmed she looked nothing like a wicked woman.

The house was still quiet, Emily hadn't risen, and it would be a while yet before Ruthie got home; she doubted the silence would last much longer.

She set about making porridge, which she'd sweeten with honey, and tried to stop thoughts of John sneaking back into her head. Did she love him? No, she wasn't that stupid. She knew John's reputation; perhaps it was part of the reason she'd been so attracted to him in the first place. That and the boredom.

Whatever else, she didn't feel bored anymore.

Once the porridge was done, she shouted to Emily, "*Breakfast!*" Followed a moment later by, "*...then chores!*"

She felt a moment's anxiety about facing her daughter, afraid Emily might confront her errant mother about her nocturnal comings and goings. She'd felt much the same after the first few times John had stolen in through the backyard, almost certain her husband and daughters would see exactly what she'd been up to, the shame and guilt so visible upon her flushed cheeks. Instead, they'd asked her when dinner would be ready, if their clothes had been ironed yet and had she had a chance to pick up some fresh bread from Mr Calhoun?

Just the same as every other bloody day.

It wasn't a bad life. She was lucky; she should be grateful. She'd a decent (albeit dull) husband, two beautiful daughters blessed her life while childlessness and misfortune blighted so many other women's, she'd a comfortable home, food, money, safety. She *was* grateful. She just wanted something more, something that made her heart gallop now and again; hanging the rugs on the clothesline and beating the dust out of them once a week just didn't cut it anymore.

"*Emily – your porridge is getting cold!*" She shouted from the kitchen doorway. That girl was getting downright slovenly.

Sitting at the table, she slowly spooned down her porridge. What would she do when the girls had grown up? Still a few years yet for Ruthie, but Emily was practically a woman; the local boys had certainly noticed even if Ash hadn't. It wouldn't be long before she'd be married off; Ruthie was just as pretty as her older sister and could be gone in what? Five or six years. Kate's spoon hovered over the porridge; how old would she be then? Thirty-Eight? Thirty-Nine?

Just her and Ash rattling around the house forever. Of course, they'd be visits, son-in-laws, extended families, maybe grandchildren in time.

Grandchildren?

The spoon plopped into her half-finished breakfast. She'd lost her appetite.

She stared at the uneaten bowl of porridge opposite. "*Emily!!*"

When there was still no answer, she stomped up the stairs, her good mood evaporating as it would until she saw John again, or she ended up shouting at Ash and the girls about something utterly trivial and unimportant. Like her life, for example.

"Come on, Miss – up now!" she stormed into her daughter's room, crossing to pull back the curtains without pausing.

The only response from the bed was a small wet moan.

She turned to the bed, "You're not sick, are you?"

The bright morning sunlight fell directly upon Emily; the sheets had been pushed aside, and she was quite naked; blood had run down her face and caked to dried-up crimson streams. Her eyes were swollen and bruised, her mouth twitched, and a bubble of dark drool popped upon her lips. Bruises covered her body, too, the kind of bruises left by a fearsome beating, and as Kate's eyes took in her daughter's body, she noticed the stained sheets and the blood that had dried between her legs.

"*Emily!*" she managed to cry.

Then she screamed.

The Lawyer

By any measure, the funeral had gone exceedingly well; there had been an excellent turnout, the day had been pleasantly warm, everybody had sincerely expressed their sympathy, and absolutely nobody appeared to think he'd murdered his wife.

Molly had looked particularly fetching too.

He'd made every effort not to stare at her or single her out for particular attention. That would have been unseemly and, possibly, suspicious; still, it hadn't been easy.

She'd flitted around the back of the funeral service, looking somewhat awkward and out of place until they'd returned to his house for the wake. Where she'd looked completely awkward and out of place.

Few people talked to her. Clearly, she wasn't approved of. The rumour that the Mayor had been angry with her husband before his death, which had kept people away from Tom's funeral, had only been compounded by her outburst of profanities on the Mayor's doorstep; the good folk of Hawker's Drift kept their distance from Molly, perhaps fearing her a little mad or a lot godless.

That, of course, would all stop once they were married.

He tried not to linger on the thought. It wouldn't do to smile too broadly or display an inappropriate bulge in his trousers; neither were seemly at a wake.

Instead, he moved from room to room of his house, shaking hands, giving thin, brave little smiles and small attentive nods of the head. Everybody told him how sorry they were, how much of a loss to the town Lorna's death was, how much they would miss her.

In other words, everybody lied through their teeth.

Lorna had been a bitter, drunken, harridan, with a vicious temper and a spiteful tongue, but today everybody loved her.

Molly didn't stay long, which was understandable. He didn't say anything about her predicament, not with so many ears around to overhear. He'd simply smiled when she came to say goodbye, thanked her, squeezed her hand and hoped his heart would not explode with the excitement of her touch.

He heard the nasty little whispers about her when she'd gone. That she was for the whorehouse, and it was the best place for her. She was a drunk, she was a foul-mouthed good for nothing, she was a slut and a brazen fornicator.

Naturally, it had riled him, though he saw the irony too as they waxed on about the sainted Lorna in almost the next breath. The people of Hawker's Drift, he decided, were lousy judges of character.

He caught the Mayor watching him. His eye was at rest for once as he sipped tea with two of Lorna's withered cronies who would have to find some other dark lair to curl up and avoid the sun in now Lorna's Throne Room had been aired,

The Burden of Souls

fumigated and was, after today, out of bounds to gossiping old prunes.

The Mayor was noting how he behaved. Seeing if he could be trusted, ensuring he was being appropriate, especially around Molly. He wasn't worried. He'd waited a long time for this; he wouldn't risk it all by fawning over Molly now. Matters would soon be settled, and he would have his reward.

He would have his due.

*

The house was empty; silent, still and at rest. It was wonderful.

It had taken an age for the last of the mourners to leave. While free booze and food remained on his table, the hangers-on, none of whom had known Lorna particularly well as far as he knew, had attached themselves like limpets to the furniture.

He'd wanted to tell them it was high time they staggered off home, but that wouldn't have done. Appearances mattered, and so he'd remained the gracious and stoic host, displaying his grief for all to see.

After the last of the freeloaders had finally swayed unsteadily out into the night, he'd helped Amy and the other girls he'd hired for the wake tidy up. Not because he felt obliged, such mundane chores were far beneath a man of his station, but because he wanted to be close to them, to feel them brush past him as they hurried back and forth to the kitchen.

This would be his life now, surrounded by women. For a little longer, he'd have to content himself on imagining what he would do to them, but soon Lorna's money would be his, all legal and *tickety*. Then he could do whatever he wished.

Molly would marry him, it was what he wanted, what he deserved, but their marriage would be markedly different to the one he had endured with Lorna. This time he would hold the upper hand. He would save Molly, and she would be grateful; he would give her a better life, comfortable and secure, and in return, he would have his dalliances. He would have his just desserts. Hadn't he deserved that?

After she'd finished tidying up, Amy had asked him if he still needed her to come and look after the house now that he was alone. He'd said that he did, and she'd looked relieved. No doubt she needed the money, and he was happy to keep her on. Obviously, the exact terms of her employment required renegotiation, but so long as she was willing to take on one or two new responsibilities (he couldn't seriously think of what he had in mind as chores), then she would find him to be an exceedingly generous employer.

He'd wanted to suggest it to her there and then; he wanted to reach out and squeeze her pert little titties, to make her do all the things he'd dreamed of. He wanted to see what she kept hidden under those shapeless smocks of hers. It was so close he could almost taste her in his mouth, all young and fresh and eager to please him.

However, he'd simply bid her good night and pushed a little extra money into her hand as a thank you for all her help and support. She'd beamed at his kindness, and he'd bit down on the urge to explain to her just how much more generous he could be.

Once he was alone, a grin had spread across his face. At first, it had been flickering and uncertain, but it had soon bloomed into a big, goofy, ain't-the-world-just-great kind of smile. It was the one he'd felt twitching under his skin all day but had been unable to let out.

It was late, but it didn't matter; he wouldn't be going to work tomorrow. Everything was still too raw; he grinned and poured a small whiskey. He'd never been much of a drinker and seeing what the stuff had done to Lorna had further reduced his appetite for booze, but, once in a while, a small whiskey or two was acceptable.

When he had something to celebrate.

*

His sleep was fitful and teasing; every time he felt himself nodding off, it danced away like a flirty maid leaving him frustratingly awake.

Perhaps he'd had one whiskey too many.

He rolled onto his side. Instead of sleep, he thought of women and money. Carson would arrive from Fellowes Ford in a few days and once matters were resolved, his new life could begin. Or rather, he could start to actually have a life.

There was nothing for Carson to be suspicious about; Lorna had been a sick woman who'd passed away in her sleep. It was a formality; she'd died of natural causes, and once the will had been read and executed, every last cent Lorna had would be his.

He didn't exactly know how much his late wife was worth, but she'd been receiving money from her father's estate every year, as Mr Allenby had stated when he'd agreed to marry his wayward daughter. They'd used the money to build a respectable house and live in comfortable style, but there must be plenty left for him to inherit. That had been the understanding, look after my daughter, and I will look after you. Allenby might be dead too, but a deal was a deal.

It was time for his reward.

Hawker's Drift wasn't a big town, but it was more than a wide place on the road. Between his own business, Lorna's money and the Mayor's patronage, he'd soon be the second richest and most powerful man in town. In just a few short years he would have climbed higher than any of the local landowners, ranchers and merchants whose families had been toiling out here for generations.

He would have money, power, and influence, which was only right and proper, but with those gifts came women, which he wanted more than anything. He could not remember the last time he'd been with a woman. He hadn't dared while Lorna was alive; one whiff of infidelity and her money would be snatched from his grasp. He should have killed her years ago, but he didn't know how to do it, he didn't want to raise suspicions, and he didn't want her to suffer. In the end, he'd thought she'd drink herself to death soon enough anyway; however, bourbon had proved to be a disappointingly slow poison.

Then the Mayor had suggested something else...

He didn't know how the Mayor had done it, and he didn't want to know. He supposed it had been quick at least, though he still felt perturbed by the expression on Lorna's corpse.

He'd taken her a morning coffee, just like he always did. Even though he knew she was dead, he took it anyway; best to stick to the routine. He'd planned to leave the cup on the bedside table, a little piece of evidence to support his story when Dr Rudi came; instead, he'd dropped it in shock when he'd seen her face, her mouth stretched and eyes wide as if frozen halfway through some ghastly scream.

The smashed cup on the floor proved a much better touch.

Initially, he'd been concerned by the expression; would it make Dr Rudi consider foul play? As innocently as he could think how he'd asked him about it, but the Doctor reassured him it wasn't unusual. Lorna may have awoken during her heart attack, confused and frightened. She may have tried to call out, and death had preserved her cry. Rudi had assured him it would have been quick. Lorna wouldn't have suffered.

He was glad, even if he couldn't help but think he'd been suffering for years…

He turned over and let out a frustrated sigh; if Molly or Amy were here, he wouldn't be so eager to fall asleep. He smiled at that. Maybe he could have them both together; the Mayor did with his little companions; it would be an appropriate reward for a man of his stature and importance. He smiled even more and gently squeezed his swelling cock. Molly, Amy, and as many other women in town as he could.

He knew he couldn't have them all; he wasn't a fool, but money and power could get you a lot, and the Mayor had intimated where that wasn't enough, other ways existed. He was eager to learn.

As he stroked himself, he thought of the Godbold girl. Pretty little thing, how old was she now, fifteen, sixteen? Obviously, someone had considered her old enough. It was an outrage she'd suffered such a terrible beating; there was no need for that. Who'd ever done it would deservedly swing from the town gallows if she ever regained consciousness and named the monster who'd dared to climb into her bedroom and rape her while her mother slept in the next room.

Still, he couldn't help but feel excited by the idea of sneaking into her bedroom and helping himself to her young sweet little body, though personally, he would have liked the mother as well. He sniggered in the darkness

He was pumping hard on his cock now, his mind imagining young Emily under him, although *he* wouldn't need to hit her because she would be loving it far too much to struggle.

Clink.

He stopped; he was sure he had heard something like a bottle tinkling on the side of a glass.

The room was empty, of course, the whole house was empty. He half sat up in bed. The curtains were heavy and let in little light, but nothing, from what he could see, looked out of place. The door remained shut; he was alone.

He sank back into the pillows and found his cock as he tried to visualise young Emily again, but the moment was lost, even when he got her mother Kate to join them.

He turned onto his side and thought all kinds of things, but the day seemed to have caught up with him, and he began to drift off again.

You always were a sick little fucker, Guy...

"Lorna!"

He sat up in bed. The room was silent, the shadows unmoving.

He fumbled with a match and lit the oil lamp by his bed, its yellow light spilling out across the room once the wick caught. The room was empty, the door closed, and his dead wife was in her grave. He shook his head and let his heartbeat slowly return to normal.

Of course, it had just been a dream, one of those vivid ones you can have as you pass from consciousness to sleep. Perhaps it was guilt whispering from his soul. He'd never had anyone killed before, so he didn't know about these things.

Just a dream, of course. Still, he left the light on. As he stared at the ceiling, he told himself the faint acrid odour he could smell was just the lamp burning rather than the reek of old tobacco that had always hung around Lorna...

The Barber

He was constantly pacing. He was sure it was irritating, it was irritating him, but he needed to do something; he couldn't just sit there. So, he paced. Back and forth. He felt their eyes following him; Kate, Ruthie, Preacher Stone, and the Sheriff as if mesmerised by some frantic human metronome.

He stopped as a door closed upstairs. A moment later, he heard the sound of Dr Rudi's footsteps on the stairs.

Funny that he could hear the Doctor close a door and walk down the stairs, yet his wife hadn't heard a damn thing while their daughter was raped and beaten. He looked at Kate; she was colourless save for the vivid red rings around her eyes. She hadn't slept since she'd found Emily, bleeding and unconscious, in her bedroom. She had been crying almost continuously since.

He looked away. It wasn't fair to blame Kate; she'd always been a deep sleeper, easier to raise the dead he'd used to joke back when there had been things to laugh at in the world. There was only one person to blame, but until (he preferred *until* a lot better than *unless*) his daughter regained consciousness and told them who'd done this, then he didn't have anyone other than Kate to blame.

"Well?" he demanded as soon as Dr Rudi entered the room.

The doctor offered a faint smile all but lost beneath the abundant moustache flowing into his formidable sideburns, "There is no change. It is difficult to say when there will be; the superficial wounds appear to be healing as well as one might hope, but..."

After he left the word "but" hanging in the air, Ash fought down the urge to scream at the man.

"But.... w*hat,* Doctor?" Kate jumped in and asked, somewhat more politely than he was going to.

Dr Rudi held his little black bag before him, both hands clutching the handles. Ash wondered what was in it; he suspected it was no more than a sandwich and a bottle of whiskey.

"There is nothing life-threatening about her physical injuries; as distressing as they are, she will recover from them, but inside..." he let his words drift off; the Doctor had a habit of not finishing his sentences.

"When will she come around?"

He'd paused his pacing at the window; outside, neighbours and gawpers bunched together in tight knots on the street. Gossiping. Blaming this on him and Kate, no doubt; not directly, of course, but in muted little tuts and head shakes and knowing silences.

And with sentences they didn't finish.

"I don't know," the Doctor said bluntly, "the trauma to the head concerns me most; she could be remaining unconscious because of the shock of what has happened to her, or it could be because her brain has been injured. Her heart is strong, there is no blood in her lungs, she is breathing normally. I'm afraid all we can do is wait for her to recover."

"And pray," Preacher Stone mumbled. He was sitting next to Kate, staring at his entwined fingers.

"Of course," Dr Rudi smiled thinly again.

Kate and Ruthie looked terrible, pallid-faced, and bleary-eyed; Ash doubted he looked better. Preacher Stone, however, looked worse.

He appeared, somehow, to have lost weight. He'd always been marginally skeletal; but now there was little more to him than paper stretched over bone. His eyes were restless and bloodshot. His remaining hair lifeless grey straw while his bony hands shook whenever they weren't writhing together.

It was his tongue that kept drawing Ash's eye, however.

When the preacher spoke, or occasionally it flicked out to lick his dry, cracked lips, it appeared bloated and discoloured, like a dead fish left in the sun to rot and blacken.

He might have inquired about the man's health in other circumstances, but thoughts of Emily and what she'd suffered filled his mind, pushing out all other concerns, leaving only room for despair and anger.

"Well, if there is nothing more..." Dr Rudi announced, edging towards the door, "...I will call again in the morning."

Kate rose to show him out while Ash managed a nod. It didn't seem the Doctor had been able to do anything for Emily; he could witter on about the injuries being superficial

The Burden of Souls

as much as he liked; the bruises on her face and body didn't look superficial to Ash.

Once the Doctor had left, he turned his gaze on Sheriff Shenan, "Have you anything more helpful to say?"

The Sheriff came over, his voice lowered so only he could hear, "We'll find the bastard, trust me."

"You'd better find him before I do."

Sam ran a hand through his remaining hair, "Don't do anything rash."

"Rash?" He snorted, "I'd just like to be able to do something... *anything!*"

Kate and Ruthie stood up, followed, laboriously, by Preacher Stone, "We're going to pray," Kate said quietly, "with Emily."

He gave his wife a curt nod but didn't say anything as she ushered Ruthie upstairs. The Preacher followed, swaying slightly in their wake.

"Is he drunk?" Ash demanded.

"Couldn't smell anything... well, not liquor anyhow."

Ash raised an eyebrow.

"Just that sweet, syrupy smell... I don't think he's drunk."

It didn't really matter if he was drunk; it wouldn't make his prayers any more or less effective. God wasn't paying the slightest attention to any of them.

"I'd best be getting back to work..." the Sheriff edged towards the door.

"This has happened before, hasn't it?" The question stopped the older man in his tracks.

"What has happened before?"

"With girls in this town?"

"Pretty girls... things can happen anywhere. You know how some men are?"

He nodded. He knew how men were right enough; men talked, shit even he *talked*, about what they'd like to do to this woman or that woman, but a long, long road stretched between the crap men shot at each other over a beer and what had happened to Emily. So sure, he knew how men were. Just not the kind of man who'd raped his daughter.

"Still... this is a quiet town mostly. No trouble. But kids... stuff happens. Sometimes they just plain disappear, like Holly Schubert did and Clara Pierre and..."

Sam shuffled from one foot to the other; he looked like a man who wanted to be somewhere else, anywhere else, "Things happen, no rhyme or reason, Ash."

"Yeah, things happen, but nobody really sees them, do they?" He jerked his head towards the window, "Everyone's yapping away about Emily out there, but in a few days, no one will be talking. Everything will be forgotten."

"Everything will be forgotten..." Shenan put a hand on his arm, "...after we hang the bastard who did this."

He shook off the Sheriff's hand, "Until the next girl..."

"What the fuck are you suggesting, Ash?"

What *was* he suggesting? He wasn't entirely sure, but a lot of strange shit had gone down in this town since he'd come here and met Kate. Not often enough to panic people, but more often than it should. He'd visited some rough towns before washing up in Hawker's Drift. Towns where guys died in bar fights, towns where whores got beaten and raped, towns where horses got stolen and banks got robbed.

Bad shit, but normal bad shit. The kind of stuff that hardly ever happened here.

No, in Hawker's Drift, it was young people, girls mostly, disappearing. Every now and then... and nobody ever talked about it.

The Sheriff knew it too; it was in his eyes. He'd been in Hawker's Drift a lot longer than Ash had, all his life as far as he knew. And Sam Shenan wasn't stupid either.

"I'm not suggesting anything," he said finally, "just saying what I've seen."

"This kind of shit happens all over, believe me. Hawker's Drift hasn't got any kinda monopoly on assholes and perverts. We'll get the guy... and that'll be the end of it," the Sheriff put his hat back on before giving Ash a final nod, "if Emily comes around, let us know, we'll need to talk to her as soon as possible. One of my men will be outside for the time being."

"When," he said quietly.

"Sorry?"

"*When* Emily comes around."

"Of course... that's what I meant." The Sheriff gave another awkward nod before letting himself out.

He watched him walk off down the street, the little knots of neighbours outside falling silent as he went by.

Probably wondering why the Sheriff hasn't arrested me yet.

He snapped the curtains together. There were hours of daylight left, but he'd no desire to see either sunshine or neighbours. The shadows were softer and more comforting.

He stared across the empty room, nothing out of place, nothing missing, save the daylight, everything as it should be. Save for some monster sneaking in and half killing his beautiful little girl.

He wanted to break something. Anything. He clutched his hands tightly together and brought them to his mouth. He must control himself. He mustn't lash out. He mustn't be stupid. Kate and Ruthie needed him. Emily would need him. He was the man. He was supposed to know what to do. To be in control, to look after and protect his girls.

Something he'd failed miserably to do.

Stupid fucking card game. A bunch of drunken fools bragging and talking shit. He didn't even really enjoy it, not anymore anyway. It was just part of his routine. Something he did. Like clockwork.

As anyone who knew him would know.

He gently bit his fingernails. Was it someone he knew? How would a stranger know he wouldn't be home? He was damn sure he would have heard something if he'd been home. He was much easier to raise than the dead.

How many people knew he wouldn't be home that night? Dozens, at least. It was hardly some big secret after all. He peered through the curtains at the gossips, well-wishers, gawpers, do-gooders and do-nothings. Was he out there? The bastard who had hurt his girl. Was he out there tutting and headshaking with the others and all the while laughing inside?

He fought down the urge to go and start questioning them.

Instead, he walked slowly upstairs to Emily's room. He knew his place was by her side, but it was the last place he wanted to be on Earth. It made him feel small and selfish, but he didn't want to see his little girl bruised and broken.

The Burden of Souls

He didn't want to see what had been done to her, knowing nothing he could ever do would make it right. Even if he could get the bastard who'd hurt her alone in a room, even if he could break every bone in his goddamn worthless body, it would never be enough to give Emily back what she'd lost. It wouldn't even be enough to make him feel like a father again.

He stood in the doorway; Kate was sitting by Emily's bed holding their daughter's hand, Preacher Stone behind her, bible still clutched in one hand, the other resting lightly on his wife's shoulder. Ruthie must have gone to her room.

Emily was as he'd seen her last, eyes closed, breathing slowly, peacefully even, you might think if it wasn't for her swollen lips and black eyes. He'd seen the welts on her body briefly; he never wanted to see them again.

Kate glanced in his direction; she seemed to look straight through him before returning her gaze to Emily.

He moved next to the Preacher, who smelt of stale sweat and something sickly sweet and unfamiliar that made him think of refuse rotting quietly in the swelter of a summer's day.

"Who would do such a thing?" he muttered to no one in particular; it was a question he'd been asking ever since he'd come home to find his distraught wife and Dr Rudi tending Emily. Sometimes the question was just ricocheting around his head; other times he muttered it aloud. Sometimes he didn't know which it had been.

When the Preacher turned cloudy distant eyes on him, he was fairly confident this time he must have spoken them aloud.

"A beast..." Preacher Stone said simply.

"Yes..." he replied, for want of anything else to say.

"A beast that takes the form of a man, a beast that walks upright and talks and dresses itself in the clothes of a man – but a beast nevertheless."

There was a certainty in the old man's voice like he knew exactly who was responsible. Although Ash recognised it well enough as preacher's rhetoric, he asked all the same.

"Do you know who did this?"

Preacher Stone fell silent, his eyes fixed upon Emily until he finally offered a reply so quiet, he barely heard it despite standing next to the man.

"Only the beast and God know who did this... and God is not talking to me."

He bit down on his irritation; the last thing he wanted was vague twaddle that was neither a comfort nor a help. He guessed the old man was just trying to do his job, but the preacher seemed so distant and almost tormented that he couldn't be entirely sure what he was trying to do.

"Emily!" Kate cried, suddenly leaning forward. At first, he thought his wife was just trying to wake their daughter again, but his breath caught in his throat as her bruised eyes flickered open.

"Mom..." Emily's voice was little more than a strained whimper.

He rushed to the opposite side of her bed and gently swept the hair away from his daughter's face. He should comfort her, tell her everything was alright, that she was safe, he was here to protect her now, and nobody would ever hurt her

The Burden of Souls

again. He should tell her he loved her. He knew that was what he should say. Instead, he said something else.

"Emily sweetheart... who hurt you?"

"Ash..." Kate hissed, "...*later!*"

He stared at his wife. Later? Why later? Give the bastard who'd done this more time to get away? He didn't think so. Ignoring his wife, he pressed on.

"I'm sorry, honey, but do you remember what happened?"

Emily swallowed and gave a rasping cough before nodding weakly. Tears welled in her eyes, breaking his heart all over again.

"Who was it, sweetheart? Who did this?"

She turned her head and looked up at him. Before she spoke, her tongue flitted out to lick her dry lips. It was black. The Preacher let out a strangled little cry, but Ash paid no heed as Emily gave him a name.

The name of the man he was going to kill...

The Gunslinger

"I thought you might have run out on me?"

"I thought you'd agreed to keep your head down?"

"I am..." Molly replied earnestly, "...I haven't insulted *anyone* today."

They were at a corner table in *Jack's*, a spot that was about as discreet as the saloon could offer without renting a room. He'd found Molly sitting alone at the table; he wasn't sure if she'd plonked herself down there to wait for him or she'd just decided to get drunk. Whichever it had been, she'd managed to achieve both.

"Turned over a new leaf?"

Molly stuck out her tongue.

It was a gesture that made her look like a little girl. He let his eyes drop to the beer he was cradling. Megan had used to do that too.

"You find anything?" Molly lounged casually in her chair, one arm hooked over the back while she twisted curls of red hair around her fingers. He, on the other hand, was sitting up ruler-straight and trying not to catch her eye. He suspected she was being flirtatious; drink seemed to have that effect on her.

Surprising really...

"That damn grass gets everywhere when you sleep on it."

"I can imagine..." More hair twisting.

Definitely flirtatious.

"Three days of nothing much; I rode around the perimeter of the Mayor's ranch, checked out the surrounding farms in every direction."

"And?"

"The Mayor has a *very* big ranch."

"Worth sleeping on the ground for that?"

"You never know what you might find."

He'd found precisely nothing, or at least nothing that meant much. He'd stayed beyond the barbed wire marking the perimeter. It would have been easy enough to get through the fence on foot; it was just a couple of strings of wire running from post to post; fine for keeping cattle in, but not a sufficient obstacle to deter a snooper. However, he'd chosen to remain outside for now.

The buildings had only really been visible close to the road, disappearing from view as he'd followed the fence around. They'd been nothing else to see but grass, cows, and a couple of distant wind pumps.

It had taken him the best part of two days to circle the ranch, and he hadn't seen another living soul.

The second night he'd settled on a spot close enough to make out the ranch buildings but far enough away from the road not to have been visible as he sat in the grass while his unsaddled horse could be mistaken for one of the ranch's out grazing. As far as he could tell, nobody had seen him.

He'd sat quietly, watched the sunlight fade till all the colour bled from the day and the only light was from the stars, cold tiny diamonds sown across a black velvet sky, and from the ranch itself.

There had been a lot of light from the ranch.

The Mayor must burn a ton of lantern oil; at times, so much light seemed to spill out of the ranch it momentarily appeared to reach up towards the stars themselves in a pale translucent column before fading away to darkness. The buildings didn't appear any brighter than one would expect; the light seemed to be coming from beyond the structures he could see, a courtyard or another building masked from view.

No sounds carried from the ranch other than the occasional bellow of a cow. The light was eerie, faint but quite discernible; sometimes, it seemed to twist about itself, although he wasn't sure whether that was just his imagination as it never lasted for long and could disappear altogether for hours at a time.

Part of him was tempted to sneak under the wire and find out exactly where the light was coming from. Instead, he'd sat and hugged his knees uneasily. He could feel a sense of foreboding rolling out from the ranch, as faint and ephemeral as the column of light but equally wrong.

Something on that ranch was best left alone.

He'd slept little and had left as the first hint of dawn turned the eastern horizon from black to dark blue. He'd no idea what it meant and whether it had anything to do with Tom's death, but he didn't intend to mention it to Molly. She no doubt thought him strange enough as it was. He'd spent another night on the grass after searching further east but had found nothing.

His eyes slid past Molly as he noticed Cece picking her way across the saloon.

Talking of strange.

Was it a coincidence she'd turned up outside the Mayor's ranch? And just what had he seen when they'd touched? He needed to speak to her again. Or get as far away from her as possible. He hadn't decided which yet.

"Amos!" Cece called and waved, a bright smile lighting her face. He nodded in return before turning back to find Molly peering at him.

"New friend?" she asked, perhaps a touch frostily.

"Not particularly."

Molly sipped her whiskey, held the glass to her lips, and then tipped the rest back in one shot, "She's got a great set of lungs..."

"She was out by the Mayor's ranch."

"That must have been a surprise."

"The Mayor's been keeping an eye on her too. You have anything in common?"

Molly frowned and stared at Cece before her green eyes flicked back, "Most of the men in here want to sleep with both of us?"

"I doubt that's it."

Molly smiled, "Except for you, of course."

He shifted in his seat.

"Unless you've changed your mind?"

Molly played with her hair some more.

He squirmed some more.

"Molly..."

"I think I have another suitor, by the way."

"Suitor?"

"Mr Furnedge."

"The lawyer?"

"Uh-huh. His wife died."

"So?"

"He's expecting to inherit some money; it was all hers, apparently."

"And he's willing to pay off your debts?"

"He didn't say so outright... but he intimated it."

"Very generous of him."

"I think he would expect some reciprocation."

"What would he want in return?"

"Oh, Amos, come on. Not all men are like you!"

Well, that was certainly true...

"How... do you feel about that?"

Molly raised an eyebrow, "Delighted, obviously."

"Do you like him?"

"Are you being serious? He can't possibly be inheriting that much!"

She shook her head and poured another shot.

"Not tempted?" All of a sudden, he had an urge to go find this lawyer, Furnedge and punch him in the face.

Curious...

"The only difference between what he and the Mayor are offering me is the variety. I'd still be whoring myself."

"It might not be what he meant. Grief can do strange things."

"He seemed to be coping with his loss remarkably well," she shrugged, "still, not something I have to worry about if you still want to help me." She glanced towards Cece.

Something was wrong with Hawker's Drift, with the Mayor, the deputies, the ranch, even with Cece Jones. It was a wrongness that nagged him, but not enough for him to want to stay and get to the bottom of it. In the end, it meant nothing to him; it wouldn't help him find Severn. It wouldn't help him find peace. Neither, of course, would helping Molly, but he'd no intention of leaving her here, and it had nothing to do with the fact she reminded him so much of Megan.

And if he kept telling himself that, maybe he'd eventually start believing it.

"I still want to help you."

She leant forward and lowered her voice, "Then let's get out of this fucking town."

"We'll discuss that in private... too many ears here."

"Shall we go back to mine?"

She was twisting her hair again.

Before he could think of a plausible excuse not to, the saloon's doors crashed open, and a tall, heavy-set man rushed in, looking wildly about. He didn't recognise him, but he veered in their direction as soon as the man's eyes fell on them.

"You Amos?" the man bellowed, not breaking stride.

He put down his beer and nodded.

"Uh-huh."

"Bastard!" the man screamed, raising a cut-throat razor as he came at him, the blade making a wild arc towards his face.

Amos pistoned out of his chair, head down, shoulder ramming into his assailant's midriff. The man made a startled whooshing noise as he straightened up and sent him somersaulting over his shoulder to crash onto the floor.

By the time he tried to regain his feet, Amos had drawn his gun and swivelled around to stand over him.

"I really wouldn't..."

The man was still clutching the cut-throat; wide-eyed with fury and panting hard. The hatred, hot, hungry, and pungent, blazed off the man bright enough to make Amos squint. Even staring down a pistol barrel might not be enough to stop him trying his luck.

He cocked the gun.

"Drop that pistol!" A voice roared from behind him, "and stay on the fucking floor, Ash!"

"What do you say?" he asked Ash.

Furious eyes still locked on his, Ash's fingers slowly unpeeled from the razor, and it fell from his grasp. Amos nodded and lowered his weapon. Looking around he found the Sheriff and his deputies fanned out behind him, all with guns levelled at him.

"I said drop it!" the Sheriff repeated. There was no other sound in the saloon. Molly was on her feet, backed into the corner; she nodded furiously at him.

"Ok..." he slowly placed his gun on the table and raised his hands.

"Get him out of here, Vasquez," the Sheriff ordered one of his men, nodding towards Ash, still sprawled on the floor.

"Leave this fucker to me, Sam... *please*," Ash begged as Vasquez hauled him to his feet.

Shenan grabbed his arm, "You're damn lucky we got here in time; otherwise, I might have had to string you up instead of him. Now go back to your family. They need you. Vasquez!"

Ash nodded as Shenan scooped up the razor, closed it and handed it back. Amos thought he would try to come at him again, but after a pause, he slipped it into his pocket. As the deputy led Ash past, he turned and spat in Amos' face.

"I'm going to do that to your corpse after they fucking hang you!" he hissed.

He wiped a sleeve across his face as the deputy pushed Ash towards the door. Once the big man was gone, he looked at the old Sheriff.

"Anyone feel like telling me what that was about?"

The Widow

"We need to speak to you about the assault and rape of Emily Godbold," Sheriff Shenan announced while Blane dangled a pair of cuffs in front of Amos' nose, "are you going to come quietly?"

"Are you fuckin' serious?" she demanded.

Sam ignored her, though one of his men did raise his shotgun a little in her direction.

Amos' eyes flicked across the other deputies, all of whom were wearing their long canvas coats despite the warmth of the evening and all of whom were either carrying shotguns, rifles or had their hands resting on holstered revolvers. Amos looked more like he was weighing up an invitation to play cards than a man who'd just been accused of rape.

Does he only ever get in a flap when I make a pass at him?

The saloon was silent; all eyes turned to their little scene in the corner. The Sheriff had spoken loudly enough once Ash had gone, deliberately, she suspected, for everyone in the place to hear what was going on.

A few of the men had already risen to their feet, the ones usually attracted to trouble.

The Burden of Souls

News of the attack on Emily had spread rapidly around town, and there would be plenty of volunteers happy to take justice into their own hands.

"This is bullshit!" she protested again. Nobody paid her much attention, save the deputy with the shotgun, who inched up further.

"I don't even know who Emily Godbold is," Amos said evenly, "and I certainly didn't rape her."

"Then you've nothing to worry about," Blane told him and jangled the cuffs again. The Sheriff shot an irritated look at his deputy but didn't add anything.

"It doesn't appear I have much choice."

"You don't."

Amos nodded, eyes never leaving Blane's. They regarded each other before Amos held out his hands. He really didn't have a choice, but she felt sick to her stomach. She didn't think he was a rapist for a second, even if Emily's father clearly did, but she wasn't sure she'd ever see him alive again if he went with the Sheriff and his men.

Blane put on the cuffs none too gently. Amos flinched slightly, his first real reaction to any of this.

"Sheriff?"

"Stay out of it," Sam Shenan growled at her, "Bad business…"

The Sheriff was fat and old, his face crumpled beneath a scratchy beard. He carried himself wearily, as if everything required just a little more effort than it was really worth. She didn't know him particularly well, but unlike most of his deputies, he at least came across as being human.

Blane took the gun from the table before pushing him towards the door, "Do I get a receipt? I'll want it back."

"Sure, we're a real by the book town..." Shenan said as they led him away.

"He didn't do anything," she insisted, trailing after the lumbering Sheriff, along with half the saloon. A few of the hotter heads were hurling insults, but she wasn't really paying them any attention; she just needed to get Shenan to listen to her.

"He really didn't do anything!" she said more forcefully as they burst through the saloon doors. A small crowd was waiting outside. At least Ash Godbold wasn't part of it. The deputies formed a loose circle around Amos as they moved towards the Sheriff's Office across the square.

Few things irritated her more than being ignored. She had to fight the urge to start screaming at the Sheriff and manhandling his deputies.

"He didn't fuckin' do anything! Why won't you assholes listen to me!"

Amos glanced back over his shoulder at her and grinned. She supposed he was trying to be reassuring, but it just managed to irritate her more. She slowed down and let go of the skirts she had been holding up as she'd scurried in the wake of Hawker's Drift's lawmen.

She became aware of the voices behind her and turned to look at the townsfolk who'd appeared in the square. Some were scampering past her in pursuit of the deputies; one oaf caught her hard with his shoulder. If his gleaming wide eyes were not so avidly fixed upon Amos, she might have suspected he'd done it on purpose.

"Hey!" she cried, before noticing the remainder of the crowd weren't staring at Amos, but at her. Their eyes were cold in the warm evening air as they squinted into the low sun's glare; the harsh guttural shadows cast across their features made them seem, momentarily, inhuman. A few were muttering; the words she could make out were not pleasant. All of them looked angry, snarling mad angry. All of them bar one slight figure at the back who she only noticed when Bradley Cloun turned to whisper something to Audley Cobham while keeping his dark hooded eyes firmly upon Molly.

It was Guy Furnedge, dapper in a new pinstripe suit; he didn't look angry at all.

He looked like a cat fully expecting to get its cream.

*

"Mrs McCrea, perhaps it would be best if I escorted you home?"

Guy had appeared at her side, and the way he gripped her elbow, as much as the cold stares, made her feel she had little more choice than Amos.

"My, people do seem a little het up tonight," he tipped back his derby slightly once they were off down Main Street. Did he think it made him look a bit rakish?

She glanced back, relieved to find that none of the crowd (rapidly becoming a mob) had decided to follow them. However, a steady trickle of people headed up Main Street towards Pioneer Square; news spread quickly in a small town.

"He didn't do anything!" she insisted, as much to herself as to Furnedge, who, she was dimly aware, still had a hand upon her elbow.

"Who?"

"Amos!"

"The chap the Sheriff arrested?" Guy was a lousy liar; she was sure he knew exactly who Amos was.

"Well, I'm sure it's all just a misunderstanding. Everything will be fine and *tickety* by morning."

"Tickety?" she snapped, "They're going to fuckin' hang him!"

"We do things properly in this town. They'll be a trial and everything." Furnedge appeared to be trying hard not to look pleased, "They'll only hang him if he's found guilty."

"He isn't guilty!"

"How well do you know him?"

"Well enough," she fixed a cold look upon the lawyer.

"Men can be…"

"Amos isn't like that!"

He shrugged.

She yanked her arm out of Furnedge's grasp and stomped down Main Street fast enough for the little lawyer to have to scurry to keep up with her.

Just how well did she know Amos?

Not very, she supposed, but he'd nearly climbed up the wall when she'd offered herself to him, hardly the behaviour of a rapist. Unless mouthy widows putting themselves on a plate just weren't his thing. Perhaps he preferred younger game…

How could she be so sure he was innocent?

Lord alone knew she'd spent enough of her adult life tagging along with one kind of degenerate or another. Why should Amos be any different? Wasn't she just doing what she always did, ignoring a man's demons in the vain hope he could protect her from the bigger monsters in the world?

But Amos is different...

She simultaneously felt guilty for doubting him and foolish for trusting him.

"Well, how are things otherwise?" Furnedge was panting slightly from the effort to match her stride.

"Apart from my friend being falsely accused of raping and beating a girl and my husband being dead, not to mention the money I owe the Mayor and the prospect of the whorehouse?" she spun on her heels to face the lawyer. "Well, I guess I'm just fuckin' *tickety!*"

Furnedge winced and fiddled with his sleeve, letting her cool before dipping his toe in again.

"Well, I'm sure the matter with the Mayor can be... *resolved.*"

The Mayor...

Tom had been up to something with the Mayor, and he'd died, Amos had been sticking his nose around the Mayor's ranch and generally into his business and now...

Of course, how could she have been so soft-headed! This was that creepy patch-eyed fucker's work. With Amos out of the way, she was trapped in this wretched town, with no way out but the cat house or Furnedge. If she'd understood him right.

Would the Mayor go to so much trouble just to keep her in town? It seemed unlikely, but Amos had been looking into

Tom's death; he'd found those dead horses and the burnt rifle. The Mayor might not frame a man and hang him just to keep one loud-mouthed widow in town but to dispose of someone who might be able to link him to murder?

Yeah, that hat fit real snug.

Her attention snapped back to the lawyer as his words sunk in, "How exactly would they be resolved... Guy?"

She was tired of Furnedge dancing around her, she had a pretty good idea, but it was time to find out exactly what he wanted. As they walked, she drew a little closer to him, not close enough to be inappropriate but close enough to fill her nostrils with the smell of almond paste and boiled cabbage.

"Well..." he cleared his throat and flushed slightly, "...this may not be the most opportune moment to discuss matters. I can tell you're distressed."

"I am... I'm also very resilient."

Furnedge stared at her, wheels clicking furiously away somewhere behind those narrow little eyes, before answering. "Well, I shall soon be a man of some means once the obligatory paperwork is completed, you understand?"

She nodded and tried not to breathe more than was absolutely necessary.

"I would then be in a position to discharge you from the Mayor's debt."

"That would be very generous, but why would you do that?" She looked at him with wide, unblinking, and, she hoped, quite innocent eyes. It was a difficult look for her to pull off, but she thought she nailed it.

"Well..." his eyes were growing uncharacteristically wide behind his spectacles, "...you must know I am fond of you..."

Ah, I knew it...

"Very fond if you want to pay off my debts, they are not inconsiderable..."

"You are worth every cent!" Furnedge spluttered.

She smiled, just.

"And this would be a purely financial arrangement? Is there anything you would want... in return?"

"As I said, I am very fond of you. We are both alone... I am sure we can be happy together, not to mention comfortable. *Exceedingly* comfortable, actually..." Furnedge finished the sentence with a knowing little smile as he ran his fingers down the lapels of his jacket. It was actually a nice suit and clearly more expensive than what he normally wore.

Sadly, it didn't make him any less of an asshole.

She'd thought he just wanted a fumble or two in return for helping her out, but he wanted more. Oh God, did the poor sap actually think he loved her?

"You are only very recently widowed?"

"We would have to be discreet, of course! To begin with!"

He was getting rather excited.

"Of course..." she let her eyes slip away. She was nearly home.

"Are you... conducive to the proposal?" he stumbled over the words as they gushed out of him. His cheeks flushed deeply again.

"You have been kind to me..." she replied carefully "...perhaps it would be good for both of us."

"It would! It would!" he spurted, eyes widening even further as a big beaming smile split his face. He looked so happy she felt a momentary pang of guilt.

"I would need to think upon it, of course..."

"Of course!"

"Though this business with Amos is... quite upsetting and distracting."

"Well... indeed, but it will be sorted quickly, I'm sure."

Yeah, with Amos dangling in the breeze if the Mayor gets his way.

"You're a lawyer; perhaps you could look into it for me?"

Furnedge screwed up his face like a child presented with a plate of greens when they'd been expecting ice cream.

"Well, it's a criminal matter. Not my field at all."

"I would be very grateful..." She stared at him evenly and resisted the urge to flutter her eyelashes. No need to lay it on too thick.

"I'm sure," his voice carried a coldness she hadn't heard before, "but really, there is nothing I can do. Justice will out, my dear."

They'd reached her house; she hoped he didn't want to come in.

"Well, here we are!" he exclaimed, bright and puppyish again.

He wanted to come in.

He'd no interest in helping Amos; her womanly wiles would only get her so far, even with Guy Furnedge. Inevitably he saw Amos as a rival for her affection; he wasn't to know her affections just gave Amos the jitters. Him being locked up was something the little lawyer probably considered convenient. A hanging would be even more convenient.

It was all, she realised, *very* convenient.

"Would you like me to come in?" Furnedge asked hopefully, "just to see you settled?"

I'd rather eat dirt from the fireplace.

"That would be lovely... but I need some time to think things over," she forced a sweet little smile, "perhaps they'll be other times for coming in..."

He almost swooned.

She wanted to tell him exactly what she thought of him but decided it was best not to burn all her bridges just yet. He still might be useful somehow.

If they hang Amos...

She pushed the thought away, leant forward, pecked Furnedge on the cheek and hurried up to her front door before he could grab too large a handful of her ass.

He waved enthusiastically at her, and she kept her warmest smile on until she closed and latched the door behind her. Then she slowly slid down the door and sat with her back against it, hands over her mouth.

They were going to string Amos up; she was sure of it. The Mayor had somehow framed him. Like Tom, he wanted him out of the way. Furnedge would be no help, and half the town looked on her as some kind of accomplice in the assault on Emily Godbold.

She had to help Amos get out, not only because she liked him and was certain he'd never hurt that girl, but because if she didn't, she would have only two choices left, both of which were equally unpalatable.

Become a whore or become Mrs Guy Furnedge ...

The Deputy

The man, Amos, stretched out on the cot, one booted foot hooked over the other, hat drawn down over his eyes.

He didn't look particularly concerned, which Blane couldn't understand given his circumstances. Perhaps it was just bravado, some men did things like that to mask their fear, either that or the man had faith in the local justice system, but that seemed unlikely. Amos didn't strike him as that big a fool.

Three cells filled the basement of the Sheriff's office. Save for the occasional drunk, they were usually empty; there was surprisingly little crime in the town. They'd put Amos in the furthest of the three; the Sheriff wanted him to stew for a few hours before questioning him, which was a waste of time in Blane's opinion. Not that Shenan was ever interested in his opinion on anything.

As soon as they'd arrested the gunslinger, a crowd had gathered outside, and it had grown steadily since. They were eager for the hanging, and, as far as he could see, there was little to gain by keeping them waiting.

He was picking at a bag of sunflower seeds, methodically cracking open one at a time between his teeth, leaning back against the brick wall of the corridor outside the cell. He was supposed to be watching the prisoner. Making sure he didn't do anything stupid, like hanging himself without permission, Amos appeared to be dozing lightly, with no more care than a man with too big a dinner in his belly.

Amos didn't appear to be much of a talker; he'd said little since they'd hauled him out of *Jack's*. No squeals of outrage, no protestations of innocence, no threats, no tantrums. In other words, little entertainment.

Generally, he preferred people who didn't talk a lot; they tended not to expect much from him in return. He'd never understood the infernal need to chatter that afflicted so many people; incessant yacking, endless jawing, lots of noise, but little meaning. Small talk, they called it. Pointless talk, he called it.

He only talked when there was a purpose; to buy a drink, order dinner or scare someone shitless, for instance. A few well-chosen words whispered in the ear could be very rewarding, but mostly he kept his mouth shut and wished the rest of the world could figure out how to do the same.

The conversations in his own head were far more entertaining and stimulating than almost anything he could have with another human being. However, he was smart enough to know most human beings would be horrified by the things he discussed in his head, so he kept them to himself until somebody needed frightening.

He cracked another sunflower seed and continued to stare at Amos, wondering what might scare the tall, quiet man. People usually scared easily enough in the end. He liked it when people begged before they died; it was one of the few things in life that genuinely excited him. He doubted Amos was the begging kind, though anyone could blub when they felt the noose tightening around their neck.

The sound of raised voices floated down the corridor; he paused, a sunflower seed on his lips, listening. Perhaps he should go and see what was happening; Amos was proving poor sport after all. Shenan had told him to stay down here; however, he knew it had little to do with making sure Amos didn't do anything stupid. Shenan didn't like him much and preferred to keep him out of his sight when he could. Shenan was scared of him. It was the only thing about the fat old fool he liked.

Shenan would beg, he was sure; he'd beg loud and sweet.

He'd considered killing the old fuck several times; there was a fair chance he'd be Sheriff once Shenan had the decency to croak, after all. The Mayor liked him. He knew he was a man who could be trusted to do what he was told and take care of business. But the Mayor wanted Shenan to carry on as Sheriff, and he didn't think he could kill the old man without the Mayor knowing he'd done it. He'd been in town long enough to know the Mayor was nobody's fool.

He liked the idea of being Sheriff. Being a lawman wasn't something he'd ever have aspired to, but he'd taken to it since he'd turned up in Hawker's Drift. He'd only planned to spend a few weeks in town, just long enough to find someone interesting and amusing to kill before moving on. That was the only life he'd known since he was sixteen and had run away from home after raping his cousin, which was something he'd come to bitterly regret.

The Burden of Souls

He should have killed the bitch afterwards and dumped her body down the old mine shaft at the end of Henderson's Road.

Still, he'd been young, and he'd learned from his mistake while drifting from town to town, searching for the dark thrills that were the only things that ever made his heart beat faster.

That's what he'd expected in Hawker's Drift. He'd arrived one January morning, the air almost too cold to breathe and the land coated so deep in frost it looked like everything in the town would snap in half if you pulled it hard enough. The ground had crackled beneath his boots with every step he'd taken.

He'd shared the stage into town with a mother and daughter who'd spent the journey shivering under a blanket together and trying not to notice how he looked at them. Over the long rattling hours, he'd developed quite a fancy to rape and kill them together.

Instead, he'd found the Mayor, who'd offered him something better.

Still crunching sunflower seeds, he ambled back upstairs, Amos wasn't going anywhere, and he was curious to see what the fuss was about.

He found the Sheriff perched on the edge of his desk trying to look authoritative while the McCrea woman shouted at him. She'd quite the talent for it. He glanced at Vasquez, who was sitting in the corner, shotgun across his lap, leering openly at the woman, and raised an inquisitive eyebrow.

"We got the wrong man," Vasquez grinned, "apparently…"

The only other deputy in the office was Royce, leaning on the counter, scribbling in a ledger. Royce liked to record things. He was meticulous in his dullness.

"Where's everybody else?"

"Outside," Royce didn't look up, "there's quite a crowd, and they're in a bad mood."

"They think we got the wrong man too?"

Vasquez laughed. He liked Vasquez, as much as he liked anyone. He was a man who could take care of business too.

He sauntered over to the open door of Shenan's office and leaned on the frame to watch the Sheriff getting chewed out. The old fat fuck hated it when he came and loitered outside his office, looking in but saying nothing. So he did it as often as possible.

She was working up quite a froth, and Shenan's only response was to turn progressively redder. The fool should just slap the bitch and throw her out. Too soft by half. He didn't know why the Mayor wanted to keep him on, but the Mayor was smarter than he was, so he let it be.

There weren't many people Blane considered to be smarter than him, but the Mayor was one clever cookie. One of the many lessons he'd learned while drifting along the road was that a fellow, particularly a strange tricky fellow like him, should know his limitations if he wanted to keep out of trouble, not to mention out of a noose.

So, he didn't try to second-guess the Mayor, or think he could be cleverer than him, or try to play him for a fool. Tom McCrea had tried that, and look where that had gotten him. He suppressed a smirk.

The Burden of Souls

He liked to keep his emotions on the inside; he didn't understand why people were happy to wander around with their thoughts and feelings plastered all over their dumb gurning faces. Why tell the world what was going on inside you? Admittedly, most people didn't have the same kind of shit going on inside their heads as he did. Well, not as much anyway.

Like him and the Mayor, the smart fellows kept the world guessing about what was ticking away deep inside the meat. The Mayor didn't keep his face blank like he did, but nobody could tell what he was really thinking and feeling. He wore a mask just the same, maybe it was a wilier mask than Blane's, one that moved and pulled expressions and made fools think they knew what might be going on his head, while Blane's was just a piece of painted lifeless wood, but they did the same thing.

They hid their monsters from the world.

The Sheriff

His head had started to throb.

Molly McCrea was in full flight, and now Blane was loitering outside his office. Again. He was trying to focus on what Molly was saying, or rather shouting, but Blane, who was eating sunflower seeds and spitting the husks onto the floor, kept drawing his eye. Like everything else he did, it was mechanical, methodical, and slightly creepy; a de-husking automaton spewing out shredded husks at precise intervals determined by some clockwork mechanism hidden from view.

He thought about telling Blane to use the wastepaper bin. He thought about telling Blane to go take a flying fuck at the moon too, but his deputy would respond to either suggestion with an equally blank look and carry on doing whatever he felt like, and it would just antagonise Molly more. Which would make his headache even worse.

"Molly..." he held up a hand as he retreated behind his desk to slump into his chair.

"I'm sorry..." she blinked "...are we on first name terms now?"

"You're not helping the situation."

The Burden of Souls

"The situation you caused by arresting an innocent man! You know you've got a fuckin' lynch mob out there, don't you?"

"Yes, I do... Mrs McCrea, that's why my men are outside; they'll be no lynching in my town."

Blane spat another husk onto the floor.

He glowered at the man. Was he smirking? No, of course not; that would suggest something went on behind those cold empty eyes of his.

"Well, I nearly got lynched coming in here!"

"People get emotional when incidents like this happen, and most people are aware of your association with the accused."

"So, I get spat at when I walk down the street?"

"If you want to make a complaint, I'll get one of my boys to-"

"No! I don't want you to get one of your *boys to do anything!* I want you to let Amos go."

"He is accused of a serious crime. If I let him go now, he'd be beaten to a pulp before he got halfway across Pioneer Square regardless of his guilt."

Another husk hit the floor.

"So, you just gonna keep him locked up here, are you?"

"Until I get to the bottom of things, yes."

"Well, he didn't hurt that girl."

"And how do you know that, Mrs McCrea?"

"Because the night she got attacked, Amos was with me," she leaned in slightly towards him before adding, "All. Night. Long."

He stared up at her, standing over his desk, hands on her hips, almost daring him to ask her more. God, how he wished he was still young enough to spend a whole night with Molly McCrea.

He sighed deeply.

"And what were you doing all night long?"

"We were fucking. What do you think we were doing?" She glanced at Blane in the doorway, "Spitting sunflower seeds at each other?"

"Molly... Mrs McCrea, Emily Godbold has clearly said that... your friend raped her. She was certain it was him."

Molly planted her hands on the edge of his desk and leaned forward, "Did she name him?"

"Yes," he was trying not to lean back in his chair despite the way Molly loomed over him.

"How the fuck does she even know who he is? Amos has hardly been in town five minutes?"

"Well, it was long enough for you two to become... *acquainted.*"

"He certainly didn't rape me; he's not the type," she looked pointedly at Blane, "I can usually tell the kind that would."

Blane didn't break stride from his seed processing, duly spitting another husk onto the floor.

"Are you *sure* he was with you?" he asked once Molly's attention had returned to him.

Just how did Emily know his name?

"Of course I'm bloody sure! Contrary to what the half-witted gossips in this town might say, I don't sleep with that many men."

"If you're lying, it's a serious matter."

The Burden of Souls

"I'm not lying. Ask Amos,"

"I intend to," he rose to his feet and tried not to groan with the effort. Damn, he was tired. A little farm, a rocking chair, pumpkins, and not having to deal with shit like this anymore. Was that really too much to ask?

"You haven't even questioned him yet?" Molly's face creased in astonishment.

"Not yet."

"Why not?"

He was being interrogated in his own office. How had his life ended up sucking so much?

"Mrs McCrea, don't presume to tell me how to do my job, just like I wouldn't presume to tell you how to… do whatever it is you do!"

She stood her ground and glowered at him. He straightened up and looked her in the eye. She was very pretty, irritating, but pretty. A little farm, a rocking chair, pumpkins and… well, that would be a nice retirement.

Sorry, Elena…

"Ok, tell you what, we'll both go down and see what he's got to say about your night together. And if it turns out you're lying, you *will* be spending the night together. Right in the next cell."

He swivelled and walked to the door, not waiting to see if Molly followed him. Blane was still in the doorway littering his office floor with damn chewed up sunflower husks.

"Should we search her?" Blane made no move to get out of the way; his voice its usual flat, emotionless monotone.

"Search her?"

"She could have something to help him escape."

"I think we should have enough to keep this wild-eyed desperado in check. Don't you, Mr Blane?"

Blane said nothing, his sludge-grey eyes unblinking. Instead, he spat a sunflower husk on the Sheriff's boot.

The headache was definitely getting worse.

The Gunsmith

The crowd had been building ever since the Sheriff marched Amos out of the saloon and across Pioneer Square. A fair few had followed them as far as the boardwalk outside the Sheriff's office.

They'd been told to go home, and half a dozen deputies had strung themselves along the boardwalk to emphasise the point no one was going any further.

He'd watched from his doorway for a while.

Damn fool.

He liked Amos; in his own quiet way, he seemed a decent man. Well, as decent as a man who made a living from guns could be. He'd tried to warn him, but some men refused to listen. He expected the next time he saw him, Amos would have a rope around his neck.

He'd hoped the crowd would dissipate after a while. There was going to be little to see till the hanging, but as soon as a few men wandered back to the saloon to retrieve their abandoned drinks, others appeared to take their place, dribbling out of Main Street as news of the arrest spread. The tongues of gossips were quicker than a swallow's wings.

After an hour or so, Ash Godbold arrived and became the crowd's focus. Kate wasn't with him, thankfully.

He'd been expecting Ash to come knocking on his door ever since he'd heard about the attack on Emily, but she must have decided to keep quiet about where she'd been while her daughter was being raped.

He sat outside his shop and stared at the crowd churning around Ash. He tried to figure out why he felt vaguely guilty about the whole sorry business. It wasn't his fault; he'd known nothing about what was going to happen.

It had no more to do with him than, he suspected, it did poor Amos.

Monty Jack, a man who rarely missed a money-making opportunity, had sent Sonny out with a handcart of beer to flog to the crowd. That would help things along nicely, he thought, with a shake of his head.

How long would it be before people started haggling over the best spots to watch the hanging?

He let his eyes drift over the crowd and stared at the saloon. Maybe it was time to move on. He'd turned a blind eye to a lot of things because he was safe here. Besides, if he did stay, then, sooner or later, he would have to confront his past. Strange that the thing that had brought him here in the first place was the thing he was now hiding from...

"There is something about tragedy that brings out the worst in human nature, don't you think?"

He'd lived in Hawker's Drift long enough to know the Mayor had a habit of appearing unexpectedly if you stopped looking at a particular spot for long enough. It still made him jump all the same.

"It depends on the individual..." he replied, letting his eyes slide away from the Mayor, who was leaning nonchalantly against the doorframe of his store.

"Some are worse than others, I suppose," the Mayor conceded with a sniff.

"And I suppose you're here to appeal to their better natures?"

The Mayor just smiled.

"We haven't had a hanging for a while," his attention remained on the crowd, swirling slowly around Ash. Grief and anger could be as hard to resist as gravity sometimes.

"I suppose not. We're quite a peaceable town at the end of the day."

"And the girls usually just disappear. No crime, no one to hang."

"That is not true," the Mayor moved to sit next to him, dangling his booted feet over the boardwalk, "boys disappear too, sometimes."

"Strange, huh?"

"People come, people go, people have their motives..." he glanced across, "...and people have their secrets, too."

"Yes, some people do," he looked back at the Mayor, holding his gaze for a few seconds. He felt his stomach tighten before returning his to the crowd. What was he doing? Above all other things, he was a coward, and the Mayor of Hawker's Drift was not a man to challenge.

The Mayor of Hawker's Drift, however, appeared more amused than challenged, a distant little smile flickering over his face the only reaction.

"This man Amos, he's a friend of yours?"

"I know him... wouldn't go so far as to call him a friend."

"Friends! Who needs em, eh? Especially when they go and do something heinous!"

"I'd have given you the same answer yesterday... I'm not really a people person after all."

"What did you make of him, this non-friend of yours?"

He let out a long slow breath. He should never have offered to fix Amos' rifle. Good deeds were seriously over-rated.

"Seemed ok."

"Very insightful, Mr Smith."

"Didn't strike me as a rapist, though..." he replied, needled by the Mayor's sarcasm.

"Who can tell? Many people are not necessarily as they seem; take Kate Godbold, for example. I'm sure most everyone would consider her a loyal wife and devoted mother..." he tipped back his hat and grinned, "...everyone apart from you and me anyway."

He hauled himself to his feet, "Think I'll be closing up the store... just in case the crowd gets ugly later."

"Oh, no need to worry, Johnny; I'm not going to breathe a word of it. I wouldn't want people getting the wrong idea. Especially if it turns out this Amos fellow is innocent."

"What does that mean?"

The Mayor rose to his feet and leaned in close to the gunsmith, "Well, under the circumstances, people might jump entirely to the wrong conclusion if it were known you were seen climbing out of Emily Godbold's window just last week. You know how folk are?"

"I-"

The Mayor patted his arm, "Just keep that in mind if Amos' guilt is questioned…"

"If someone wanted me to vouch for him, for instance?"

The Mayor smiled broadly, his teeth perfectly white and straight. Just like a good politician's should be.

"Just so, Mr Smith, just so," the Mayor winked and hopped down from the boardwalk, straightening his cuffs as he headed towards Ash Godbold and the nucleus of the crowd.

John X watched him before swivelling on his heels and hurrying inside to busy himself with closing up. He'd pull the shutters down just in case things got ugly; once done, he'd inventory his stock and check his books were up to date.

He wanted to keep himself busy tonight so he wouldn't have time to wonder how the Mayor knew the window he'd seen him jump out of when Ash had returned home unexpectedly had been the window to Emily's room…

The Preacher

The church was dark and silent, save for the faint hum of voices drifting in from the square. He ignored them as he tried to hear God's voice, but if the All-Mighty was listening in on his desperate prayers, he was not responding. In fact, Preacher Stone suspected the Lord was hiding, the celestial equivalent of crouching down behind the biggest piece of furniture in the house and pretending you were out when someone you wanted to avoid was rapping frantically on the front door.

He'd been kneeling before the altar for hours. His knees ached, and his stomach throbbed, though neither came close to the aching pain in his soul. Or at least where his soul had once been before he'd sold it for the Mayor's black candy.

He should leave. Just walk off onto the grass and keep going until his wretched life ended. He had failed God, he had failed his father, and he had failed himself. The last of those failings was the least important, but it was the one that hurt the most. Dreams were ashes, hope spent, good intentions withered. The man he'd always intended to be shrivelling to a cold dark cinder.

All for a little black bottle containing he knew not what.

Whatever it was, it wasn't medicine. He'd been a fool to ever think it was. Sure, it took the pain in his guts away for a while, but it replaced the pain with something worse.

It gave him joy.

That wasn't quite right, but he couldn't think of a better word. It took not only his pain away, but his senses too; he became a creature of weakness and desire. A wretched thing so far removed from God and the world that he'd become something less than a man. And the more of the stuff he drank, the more he wanted, and the more he wanted, the further he travelled from himself. Yes, it gave him joy, but it was a dark, twisted unholy joy, an abomination rotting away his immortal soul.

Then there was the girl.

He prayed again, screwing his eyes shut till they hurt. Begging for guidance, for a sign, for forgiveness and the Lord's redemption. Nothing came bar the distant voices on the square eager for the vengeance of the gallows.

Her tongue had been black, just as his became after he drank the candy. How could that be?

The little bottle in his pocket was empty, and the Mayor hadn't come to give him more. He'd had half a bottle left, and now it was gone. The last time he'd drunk from it, he'd blacked out and woken naked on the rug of his drawing-room, the dawn light pushing at the windows and the little bottle tightly gripped in his hand.

An empty bottle.

Had he raped her? Is that where his candy had gone? Had he poured it down her throat and defiled her? Surely not? Please, God, not.

When her father had asked Emily who had attacked her, he had, for one awful moment, expected her eyes to turn accusingly upon him, peering fearfully through swollen flesh as she raised a shaking figure.

He'd wanted to run, to scream and flee the room, but he'd been unable to move. Instead, sweat erupted from his body, and he'd begun shaking uncontrollably.

Ash and Kate Godbold had been too distracted by their daughter to notice, at least he hoped they had, for he'd felt like a guilty man and was convinced he must have looked much the same.

Instead, with a dry croaking voice, she'd whispered, "Amos... the gunslinger... he did it..."

He'd felt relief proportional to the rage that flowed through Emily's father.

Ash had jumped to his feet and hurried out of the room. Kate had half risen and called out after her husband, only sitting back down once she heard the front door slam shut.

When his attention returned to Emily, he found her eyes had closed again, and the poor girl had drifted off to sleep.

He'd stayed a while longer but had slipped away once Kate too had fallen asleep, her hands still entwined with her daughter's.

Returning to his church, he'd tried to find sanctuary in prayer, but all he could feel was a deep sense of guilt. He kept seeing the shredded remnants of his father's Bible and poor Emily's blackened tongue. He couldn't remember hurting the girl, and she herself had said this Amos fellow had attacked her, but the fear he was somehow responsible wouldn't leave him.

The Burden of Souls

Ever since he had begun supping the Mayor's black candy, he'd felt something writhing inside him, a desire he'd not suffered for many, many years. Naked flesh haunted his dreams, leaving him slick with sweat when he awoke in the morning, his crotch sticky with spent lust.

The candy made him want to rut like a beast; it filled him with dark, monstrous desires. Every time he saw a pretty woman, the urge to reach out and touch her was almost irresistible. To feel her, use her, and defile her in the basest of ways. It sickened and excited him in equal measures. He found no respite no matter how hard he prayed or how studiously he read his Bible.

Like floodwaters held by an old sun-baked mud dam, his desires were rising inexorably.

Only his faith had saved him from succumbing to temptation, but he needed more, and God was giving no help. He felt alone, abandoned, and forgotten. Had that been why he had destroyed his father's precious bible? And what else might he do when he lost himself to the candy? Even if he hadn't hurt the Godbold girl, he was terrified if he took the candy again, he would wake and find a naked woman next to him and, maybe, like his father's bible, she would be torn to shreds too.

He hadn't had any candy for days. He hadn't gone to the Mayor to ask for more, to beg as he had previously. The pain in his guts was now worse than it'd ever been, but he'd rather suffer that than what the little black bottle did.

And yet...

He wanted it so badly his very core writhed in torment. He had hoped if he could last a few days without it, the desire would fade and with it the terrible yearnings they fuelled, but the waters had yet to subside. If anything, they were still rising, and the dam of his faith was buckling under its remorseless pressure; cracks were starting to appear and when it broke…

Better he walk out onto the grass. Better that he die.

He grimaced and let out a low rumbling groan as he rose slowly from his knees. His frozen joints and numb legs nearly buckled from the strain, stumbling forward.

"You're in pain, old man."

The Preacher, still half bent and panting, did not look around.

"The church is closed."

"Really? I thought the doors to the House of God are forever open."

"They are closed to you."

The Mayor chuckled.

Straightening up and fighting to keep the pain from showing, he turned to find the Mayor sitting in the front pew, one immaculately polished boot hooked over his knee. He wore a black suit over a black vest and a black shirt. It seemed entirely appropriate, given his heart was the same colour.

The pew was less than two yards back from where he'd been kneeling, but he hadn't heard the man come in and settle himself down. Perhaps he'd been praying too hard.

"I brought you something for the pain," the Mayor held up a little black bottle between his thumb and forefinger, twisting it back and forth.

"I don't need it."

His mouth instantly filled with saliva.

"Of course you do... it takes your pains away, remember?" the Mayor said in a sonorous voice that echoed about the church, the little bottle still twisting back and forth. It seemed to catch the candlelight as if diamonds floated in the black goo it held.

"The pain is easier to bear than what that stuff does to me," he insisted, though he found his traitorous legs had taken him to stand over the Mayor. His eyes followed each little twist of the bottle.

"Oh, come now, there is no need to be so dramatic with me... you know you like the way it makes you feel."

"It's turning me into a monster!" he hissed, biting down so hard upon his teeth he feared he would shatter the few he had left.

"What nonsense! It is simply putting you in touch with your desires... that's what you want, isn't it, Preacher Billy? Deep down. To know all the things you've forsaken for your calling?"

"I forsook those things willingly so I might better hear God's words and do his work. I have no regrets."

"You cannot lie to me, Billy; nobody can lie to me. You do not hear God at all anymore, do you? But this? Oh, you hear this well enough; it sings to you..." the Mayor's grin was wide and his eye still, "...my black candy sings to you, Billy, loud and sweet and clear."

The Mayor reached up, still holding the little bottle delicately between thumb and forefinger, still twisting it as you might a toy to catch a kitten's eye.

He meant to swipe the wretched thing from the Mayor's hand and send it spinning across the church; he swore he had. Instead, the Preacher found it resting upon his palm, the glass strangely warm against his skin. He rubbed his thumb up and down it, transfixed by the thick, slow sloshing of the candy inside.

"Have a little nip; it'll do you good…"

He remembered his father's bible shredded on the floor and poor Emily Godbold's black tongue flicking between split and swollen lips.

He blinked away a drop of sweat.

"…that old serpent, called the Devil, and Satan, which deceiveth the whole world: he was cast out into the earth, and his angels were cast out with him!"

Preacher Stone drew strength from the familiar words where he had none himself. He hurled the bottle at the floor. When it failed to break, he brought his foot down upon it. The glass exploded beneath his heel. The black viscid potion spurted out as if he had stamped on some giant diseased beetle.

The Mayor pursed his lips and leaned forward slightly to examine the remains of the bottle as the Preacher staggered backwards.

"I think you'll find that stain will be a bugger to get out," he raised his single eye and added, "both from the floor and you…"

"Be gone!"

"My, you are in a tetchy mood this evening, Billy; just why is that?"

"Because I see you for what you are! A peddler of misery and deceit!"

"Are you casting me out too? Don't you need some holy water or something for that?" the Mayor gently stroked the bristles beneath his chin.

"I am not blind to you."

"Isn't that an insensitive thing to say to a man with only one eye?"

Preacher Stone shook his head and tried to ignore the voice in his skull, pleading with him to get down and lick up the candy before it soaked into the scuffed floorboards, "Perhaps, but in a town where everyone else is blind, the one-eyed man is king."

"I'm certainly no king, if that is what you are implying, Preacher, I think it would be fairer to say that in a town of the blind..." the Mayor smiled as he rose smoothly to his feet, "...the one-eyed man is God..."

"Is that what you think you are? You are not God, just a manipulative blasphemer!"

"Good night, Preacher Billy," the Mayor gave him a nod as he brushed past him and headed up the aisle towards the doors, "do come and see me when your pain becomes too great and you change your mind."

"I will not beg for your poison again!" he shouted, "it's evil and unnatural, it's the Devil's brew, and God will smite you for all you have done!"

The Mayor paused and turned back, hands outstretched, "*Really?* What have I done other than try to take away your pain? To give you your heart's desire?"

Preacher Stone stared at him; he was wheezing, his heart thundered, and he could feel his foot sticking to the floor as if the black candy was in no mood to let him go yet.

"I've seen the girl..."

"Which girl?"

"Young Emily, of course! I saw her tongue, black like mine, black from this abomination!" he shouted, pointing at the floor and the shards of glass scattered around him.

"I understand the poor girl was beaten quite badly," the Mayor said evenly, "her tongue was likely bruised – perhaps she bit it during her ordeal. Such things can happen."

"No, you had something to do with this, just like you have something to do with everything rotten in this damn town!"

"Everything, Billy? I really would need to be a god to do that. Wouldn't I?"

"God will strike you down for your blasphemy and your evil works."

The Mayor laughed, a deep booming roar that filled every corner of the church; when it subsided, he inclined his head to the left and took a single step back down the aisle.

"Shall I tell you about God, Billy? God is a senile old fool who lost interest in this world and the lives of the simple little apes who scurry across its surface a long, long time ago. I, however, find you all rather fascinating and amusing..." the Mayor's right hand was tapping against his thigh as if keeping time to a tune only he could hear, "...so I decided to take up the slack."

"You're quite mad..."

"Aren't all gods?"

The Burden of Souls

He winked his one good eye before striding down the aisle; he looked back again as he opened the doors. His voice was low, but despite being at the opposite end of the church, the Preacher heard him as clearly as if he'd been standing close enough to whisper in his ear.

"Oh, and don't mention such nonsense about the poor Godbold girl again. That wouldn't be wise..."

He watched him disappear into the night, where he suspected the one-eyed man felt most at home.

He stood alone, shaking in the soft candlelight, trying to find peace in the quietness of his church. When he took a step back, the candy stuck to his shoe. He stared at it, a thick black puddle spreading out from the crushed remains of the bottle. His eyes filled with tears as his legs buckled.

He found himself kneeling before the remains of the bottle in much the same way he'd earlier knelt before the cross. His shaking hand snuck out in frantic spasms, inexorably drawn down towards the spilt potion by some malign force he could not resist.

It felt oily and ever so slightly warm as it stuck to his fingers. It was repulsive, like something excreted from a monstrous bug. Still, he could not stop rolling his finger in it till it glistened darkly in the candlelight, any more than he could stop himself taking his finger into his mouth and sucking furiously upon it.

The sweet, sickening, irresistible candy set first his tongue, then his throat and then his stomach afire.

Later his blood would sing, and his cock would become like iron. After that, he would remember nothing but the rush towards the light and the release from all his cares and burdens.

He smeared more candy onto his fingers, ignoring the tears cascading down his face as much as the booming laughter rolling through the church...

The Gunslinger

He didn't open his eyes when he heard boots clicking on the worn flagstones, but his heart did beat a little faster for an instant. Why? He wasn't afraid of dying, though he'd feel a bit pissed to hang for something he hadn't done. Still, he'd done plenty of dark work a man could deservedly swing for; funny how life had a way of evening itself out in the end.

He'd prefer a bullet to a noose, but was that enough to wake the fear coiling around his guts? He couldn't remember the last time he'd felt fear. He hadn't felt anything much in a long time save his burning hatred for Severn and his crew. He hadn't cared for anyone in a long time either. Perhaps the two were connected?

Should he have gone for his gun? He could have taken a few of them out. Killing Blane would have been a generous parting gift to the world. Maybe if Molly hadn't been there, he would have, but he hadn't wanted to put her in danger, so he'd come meekly. A lamb ready for slaughter.

"I have a few questions..."

It was the Sheriff.

Blane would have little time for questions or other niceties. He wanted him dead, and not just for the fun of it either, but the Sheriff? He seemed different to the men who worked under him; he'd sensed that when they'd arrested him, among other things.

"I've never heard of Emily Godbold."

He was still stretched out on the thin, sweat-stained straw mattress draped over the musty cell's single metal cot; hat pulled down over his face.

There was a drawn-out sigh, the kind born of both tiredness and exasperation. It didn't sound like the Sheriff of Hawker's Drift was having a good day – although, as his own one had taken a dramatic turn towards the plughole, he couldn't muster much in the way of sympathy.

"It's in your best interests to be co-operative – you do realise how much trouble you're in, don't you, son?"

"You hang rapists in this town?"

"Yep."

"Then I know how much trouble I'm in."

Another sigh.

"You having a bad day, Sheriff?"

"Oh, for fuck's sake, Amos, stop farting around!"

Now he did push back his hat and look up.

"Molly? What are you doing here?"

"Well, someone's got to try and sort this mess out before you get strung up, and as you're making a fuckwit's ass of the job, I guess it's down to me to save your sorry hide!"

The Sheriff, face crumpled into a pained grimace, was holding up a hand trying to hush Molly with as much effect as a man flapping his arms about in front of a charging bull. Good luck with that.

"Mrs McCrea, please don't talk to the prisoner," Shenan insisted, half turning to glower at her.

She pouted and glowered right back at him. If there was going to be glowering contest, the winner wasn't going to be wearing a star.

"I'm trying to save your time too – while you've got him locked up in here and your men keeping the mob out - the asshole who did this is free as a bird. Probably stalking some other poor girl while you lumps are showing off who's got the biggest fucking pair of balls."

"Another word, and I'll lock you up too!"

"But-"

"Blane!"

Molly glanced at the deputy as he took a step toward her. He was as expressionless as ever, though he'd a feeling Blane would consider locking a woman up a perk of the job.

"Shutting up..." Molly muttered before pouting. Silently.

"Ahhh... blessed hush."

"Send her home," tossing his hat aside, he swung his legs off the cot to sit on the edge.

"You think I haven't tried?"

Molly stifled a retort. It didn't look like something that came naturally to her.

"You *are* the Sheriff."

Shenan tapped the star on his jacket, "This carries only so much weight."

He suppressed a smile, and Molly looked like she wanted to spit.

"She shouldn't be here."

"No, she shouldn't," Shenan glanced at the unnaturally quiet Molly, "but there's a mob outside, so she's safer in here for now."

"Molly didn't do anything."

"No... but the folks outside want to lash out at someone, and with you in here, she's the next best target given your... *friendship.*"

He looked at his feet and thought about pointing out they *were* only friends, but he didn't suppose that would mean much to Shenan and even less to the townsfolk outside. It didn't take much for people to get ugly, and a hurt girl was a better motive than most. In their eyes, his arrest assured his guilt, and anyone associated with him would make a suitable second best if they couldn't get their hands on the accused themselves.

The Sheriff took a step forward, close enough for his belly to press against the bars of the cell.

"Where were you on Thursday night?" His tone became colder.

"I don't know Emily Godbold, I don't know where Emily Godbold lives, I've never met Emily Godbold..." he rose to his feet and crossed to the cell bars too, "...and I didn't rape Emily Godbold."

"That wasn't what I asked."

"I've told you; he was with me!" Molly insisted, two minutes of silence clearly the most she could manage in one go, "All night. In my bed. With me!"

"Be quiet!" Shenan snapped.

Molly looked pointedly at him, ignoring the Sheriff as she slapped her hands onto her hips, "Go on, tell him!!!"

He felt a fuzzy sense of gratitude that someone would go to the trouble of lying through their teeth for him. She must like him a lot.

Molly was, he decided, really rather odd.

"Well," Shenan demanded, giving up on the idea of keeping Molly quiet, "were you?"

After a moment, he shook his head, "No, I wasn't."

"For fuck's sake, Amos, if you're trying to protect my honour, it's too damn late for that!" Molly shouted, her face so flushed with anger and indignation he momentarily had to think whether he actually had spent the night with her. Which would be quite a trick.

"Where were you then?" the Sheriff demanded.

Poking around the Mayor's ranch because your boss had her husband killed...

Yeah, that would get him out of here real quick.

"I was out riding."

"Riding? All night?"

"No, I slept out."

"Any particular reason?"

"I've spent the last thirteen years in the saddle – I don't sleep too good in a bed and don't feel comfortable around people. I went riding to clear my head and slept under the stars because that's what I prefer."

That sounds lame even to me...

"Anyone see you, while you were... clearing your head?"

He thought for a moment before nodding, "That singer from the saloon, Cece and the young fellow who's been following her about."

"Sye Hallows?"

"Yeah, I bumped into them; we spoke for a few minutes."

"When?"

"Thursday afternoon."

"Where?"

"North of town, fifteen miles maybe."

The Sheriff shifted his weight from one foot to the other and pursed his lips.

"Near the Mayor's place?"

"I dunno; I'm not from around here."

Blane was staring at him intently. Molly, meanwhile, was just looking pissed.

"Plenty of time to get back into town and attack Emily."

"If I had, why on Earth would I have come back?" he gripped the bars separating him from the Sheriff, "It's one thing to be a sick bastard; it's another to be a complete fool. I have no reason to stay here; I could have been long gone by now."

"In my experience, people do all kinds of crazy, particularly the really sick ones."

"I told you, I don't know this Emily girl, and I didn't rape her."

"Then why does she say you did?

"What did she say? That some tall stranger attacked her? What makes you think it's me?"

"Because she named you. She said it was *Amos, the gunslinger.*"

The Sheriff wasn't lying. He got no sense of deceit coming from the man. He might get a clearer picture if he touched him, but he didn't think Shenan would take kindly to being grabbed through the bars. However, they were only inches apart, close enough for the man's soul to wash over him as pungently as his breath.

He'd eaten pickles recently, and he wasn't yet entirely

The Burden of Souls

convinced Amos was guilty.

"You heard her say this?"

"No... but her parents and Preacher Stone did, and they were all quite clear about what she said."

He shook his head, "I've been in town for a week or so; I've barely spoken more than a few words to anyone other than Molly... Cece, Sye, John the gunsmith... the Mayor, your deputy over there... but nobody else, how would she even know my name, let alone how I make a living?"

"That's what I told him!" Molly chipped in.

"It's a small town; people have been talking about your relationship with Mrs McCrea, you might not realise it, but you're quite the celebrity," Shenan said.

The Mayor? He was thinking.

"Are young girls usually included in the town's gossip?"

"It's a small town... and Emily's sixteen, old enough to pick up on her elder's chitchat."

"I wouldn't know her age, given I've never met her."

The Sheriff gave a little snort.

"What happened to her?"

"You know what happened to her."

"Tell me exactly."

Shenan mulled it over before replying, "Someone got into her room while she was asleep, this... *someone*, beat and raped her and left her unconscious. Her mother found her in the morning; she came around this afternoon and told her parents you did it."

"Was there a lantern on in the room?"

"No, she was asleep."

He steepled his fingers as if in prayer as he spoke slowly,

"So, she was woken in the middle of the night, beaten, raped. She's sixteen; she would have been terrified, and it would have been pitch black. And yet she recognised *me*? A man she's never met, a man, at most, she may have heard of, may have passed on the street? Does that sound likely?"

"She said it was you," the Sheriff insisted, but his voice didn't carry much conviction and his thoughts even less.

"Sounds like bullshit to me," Molly offered.

"Blane, lock her up!"

"Hey!" she wailed as Blane gripped her arm and pulled her towards the cell furthest from Amos,' "you can't lock me up for speaking my mind!"

"Nope, I can't," Shenan agreed, "but I can lock you up for providing a false alibi."

"Sheriff..." Amos pleaded.

"You can listen to her for a while; my goddamn ears need a rest," Shenan said as Blane slammed the cell door on Molly.

"She's only trying-"

"I know exactly what she was trying to do," Shenan snapped before adding in a softer voice, "I'll kick her loose tomorrow morning; the crowd will have gone home by then. Hopefully."

The Sheriff turned towards Blane, "Go sort out some food for our guests."

Blane gave Shenan a lingering look, which pretty much encompassed his full range of reactions, before heading up the stairs, keys jangling on his belt.

Once he was out of earshot, the Sheriff asked, "You said you'd spoken to the Mayor?"

The Burden of Souls

"I had the pleasure."

"What did he want?"

"What makes you think he wanted anything?"

"Just a hunch."

"He offered me a job."

"Doing what?"

"Working for you."

Shenan raised an eyebrow that resembled a particularly ill-groomed caterpillar.

"Guess he's in charge of recruitment in this town, huh?"

"His fingers are in everybody's pies."

"I bet."

"You take the job?"

"You think I'd be in here if I had?"

"You saying you been framed?"

He leaned in close enough for his forehead to press against the cold metal of the cell bars.

"Three possibilities Sheriff; either I did it, this Emily girl has mistaken me for someone else, or this is a set-up. I know I didn't do it. I don't see how she could mistake me for someone else, given we've never met, so that leaves a set-up – dunno how they got her to say my name, though. Some trick, huh?"

Shenan's brow creased, the uncertainty, unease and confusion poured out of him. Along with a name Amos didn't know, but one that clearly meant a lot to the Sheriff because it was lantern bright in his head.

"I'll go talk to the girl tomorrow; you're staying here for now. It's safer," Shenan nodded before turning and slowly walking away, touching his hat as he sauntered past Molly.

He looked across the intervening empty cell at Molly, who was standing in the corner staring at him. For some reason, she looked faintly pleased with herself. Which was worrying.

"Molly," he asked, once Shenan had closed the door at the top of the cells, "who is Donny Bildt?"

*

"This mattress is shit."

"If you've got a more comfortable one at home," he sighed, "you should have stayed there."

"Sheesh..." Molly sniffed, "...gratitude."

"Why did you come here?"

"To get you out?"

"It didn't work."

"A little lying might have helped with that."

"He wouldn't have believed it – and neither would a jury."

"Yeah, how silly, obviously, no one would believe a man might want to spend the night with me."

"That's not what I meant."

"It's the effect I have; men just go into a panic and make a dash for the door as soon as I flutter my eyelashes. Dunno what the Mayor's thinking. I won't make a fuckin' dime for him in the cat house."

"You're not going to let that go, are you?"

"Nope."

Silence followed. He laid stretched out on his back. After collecting their plates, Blane had turned down the lanterns at either end of the cell block. They still gave off a sickly orange glow that made the stale, damp-scented air even more oppressive.

"I didn't do it, in case you were wondering," he said after a while.

"Do what?"

"Hurt that girl."

"If I thought you did, I wouldn't be helping you."

She actually wasn't helping him at all, but it seemed unappreciative to point that out.

"I've done some bad things in my time, but never anything like that."

"It's too soon for confessions."

"They're not going to hang me."

"You think?"

"Pretty sure."

"Got a better alibi than me?"

"The Sheriff doesn't think I did it."

"You could tell that, huh? Mr Mysterio strikes again."

"Well, he has doubts at any rate. He's not like Blane or some of the other deputies."

"Hate to piddle on your parade, but it doesn't matter what the Sheriff thinks; it's what twelve good men think – and with a young girl telling 'em it was you who attacked her... they might be more easily persuaded."

"It won't go to a jury."

"What makes you think that?"

He stared at the ceiling, numerous cracks scored the plaster, and his eyes followed them, trying to make crude stick figures.

"Amos?"

"Trust me, I have... just trust me, Molly."

"And if that doesn't work?"

"It will."

"But if it doesn't?"

Molly, he realised, had a certain child-like quality about her at times, although not necessarily in the endearing way.

"Then I'll think of something else," he sighed.

"Have you escaped from jail before?"

"We should get some sleep."

"This mattress is shit."

"Yeah, you said, but there isn't much else to do."

He heard Molly's cot creek as she climbed to her feet, "There's something I'd like to show you..." she whispered through the cell bars.

He rolled onto his stomach; Molly was bent over by the bars of her cell, hitching up her skirt and petticoat to reveal her stockinged legs.

"Don't look so worried, you'll like it... Tom said it was a really good one," she winked.

His eyes widened as his heart sank; dear God, did the woman never let up!

"We're in jail, Molly! I know there's not much to pass the time, but really-" he stopped and peered once she'd straightened up, the hem of her skirts clutched in her hands and her legs splayed apart.

"What..." he demanded, "...*is that?*"

"Haven't you ever seen one before?"

"Of course I've seen one before!" he hissed, scrambling to his feet.

"It's a .45," Molly said proudly, "...not that I really know what that means..."

"Put your damn skirts down!"

"Nobody is going to see," she pouted and tossed her head to one side.

Gripping the cell bars, he stared at the revolver strapped to the inside of Molly's thigh. He also noticed, despite himself, the bare white flesh above her stockings and that she wore silk underwear. Probably silk anyway. He raised his eyes quickly.

"What do you expect me to do with that?"

"The gun or my-"

"The gun, Molly! What do you expect me to do with *the gun*? Shoot our way out!"

"Well, luckily, I've been thinking about that. I have a plan!"

"Really?"

"Yeah, I thought I could pretend to be ill; you could shout for help, and when one of the dickhounds come down, I'll drape myself over the bed – or maybe the floor, that might be best – holding my stomach and groaning. If they eat the same shit they gave us, they'll buy that, and when they start opening the cell, you produce the gun, get the keys and, hey presto, we're free!"

"Hey presto?"

"Yeah, it's something magicians say. Maybe your mother would have used it?"

"She wasn't a magician…"

"Anyway, what do you think?"

"It's a lousy plan."

"Really?" Molly looked surprised.

"How'd we get out of town, assuming we can even get out

of these cells?"

"We get some horses."

"You've got horses and provisions ready?"

"Well, no... I thought we'd steal some."

"How long will that take?"

"Not long... we'll tie the deputies up and gag them. We'll have plenty of time."

"No."

"Why not?"

"It's too dangerous."

"Not as dangerous as being hung, I would have thought."

"They're not going to hang me, though breaking out of here and stealing horses would be enough to get us both strung up."

Molly raised an unconvinced eyebrow.

"Now, please put your skirts down. It's... *distracting.*"

"Sure... just let me get this thing off. It's starting to chafe..."

She hoisted her skirt and petticoat up further to fumble with the strapping she'd used to bind the gun to her thigh.

"Just... leave it where it is..." he turned away and slumped back down on his cot.

"There. Done!" Molly waved the gun in his direction as she let her skirts fall back.

"Just make sure they don't see it when you're released... or shoot me with it in the meantime."

Molly slipped the gun under her pillow, "I'm not a complete idiot."

"Got any other bright ideas?"

"I only had the one bright idea; I knew the alibi thing

wasn't going to work. I just wanted Shenan to lock me up so I could give you the gun."

"And if he hadn't locked you up?"

"Well, I knew if I annoyed him enough, he'd put me in a cell for the night, luckily..." Molly explained in a matter-of-fact voice, "...I can be *real* annoying when I try."

He didn't say anything.

The Widow

The wafer-thin mattress, the gun stashed beneath the emaciated straw pillow, and Amos' snoring conspired to keep her awake.

Snoring, for fuck's sake!

Tom had snored, particularly if he'd been drinking; prodigious, rasping snorts of air. How many nights had she lain awake listening to that awful din? About as many nights as she'd dug her elbow into his side to try and wake him up, not that that had often worked, Tom had always been a ridiculously deep sleeper. It wouldn't work with Amos either, given he was out of elbow range.

Still, she did have a gun if things got really unbearable.

She wasn't sure what to make of Amos' refusal to entertain her plan for busting them out of jail. Admittedly, it was a little sketchy in parts, but the basic premise (it was preferable to being strung up) seemed solid to her. Instead, Amos was content to stretch out and sleep with little apparent care or concern for his current predicament.

He certainly wasn't behaving like a guilty man. An idiot maybe, but not a guilty one.

Molly rolled onto her side and stared at her shadow on the roughly plastered wall, as much for a change of view than in hope of stumbling upon a comfortable position.

Guilt was not really the issue, of course; this was all being done to stop Amos poking about into Tom's death. If the Mayor wanted him dead, he'd be swinging out on the town square gallows regardless of guilt. She was worried Amos hadn't quite grasped that simple fact.

Besides, the thought of taking her chances trying to escape jail (and Hawker's Drift itself) was far more appealing than the alternatives currently available to her. If the worse came to the worse, catching a stray bullet would be a quicker and less painful death than working upstairs in *Jack's* or marrying Guy Furnedge.

She rolled over onto her back again and listened to Amos' wet snores. Tom's had been louder and even more irritating.

Her husband had spent more than a few nights in jail, usually for brawling or some other consequence of over-drinking. Had he snored in jail too? Probably, the combination of booze and the pig-headed dumbfuckery that had gotten Tom tossed into a cell in the first place would have combined just as effectively to help him snore off his cares regardless.

She'd had to bail him out of a few jail cells in their time together, but she'd never shared the experience with him. Still, as Granma Hildy had always said, you should try everything in life once... apart from incest and naked dancing.

Granma Hildy had been, unsurprisingly, a brainless old loon well known for drinking herself into foul-mouthed tirades against anyone in earshot before passing out face down in her own puke.

Molly, however, had always had a soft spot for her; she'd learnt some of her best cussing at Granma Hildy's bony knee.

The ceiling was proving no more panoramic than the wall, while the slats beneath the thin mattress dug into her either way, so she rolled over again to face the cell bars, where the wan lamplight illuminated a black-suited figure watching her.

She sat up with a start.

"Why, Mrs McCrea," the Mayor said with a nod, "what a pleasant surprise to find you here!"

She hadn't heard the door above open, or the stairs creak. She hadn't been listening for anything, but she couldn't see how he'd gotten into the basement housing the cells without her hearing; then again, he was a sneaky one-eyed cattle-botherer.

"I was being a nuisance, apparently," the bed's metal frame squeaked as she swung her legs over and stood up in as dignified a manner as she could muster.

"Oh, there's no need to get up for my sake."

"I wasn't," she said quietly, coming to stand before the Mayor as much as she wanted to run away from him.

The Mayor glanced at Amos' still softly snoring figure, "Oh, I see. How sweet... I suppose he has had a rather tiring day."

"What do you want?"

"Just checking in on the prisoner, making sure no one has been too enthusiastic; entirely understandable considering the wretched nature of the crime, but I like things to be done right in my town."

"How conscientious of you."

"*Conscientious?* I'm impressed; that is not a word I would usually associate with you. Your language tends to be far earthier."

"*Fuckin'* conscientious, if you prefer."

"Much more in character."

They stood regarding each other in silence. The Mayor, with his eye constantly flitting from point to point as if he were facing a room packed to the brim with marvels rather than a featureless cell, Molly clutching her hands before her to stop them shaking and wondering just what she should say next. She'd never been good with small talk.

"Why did you have my husband killed?"

The Mayor's eye stopped, "What on Earth makes you think that?"

"Because you're too high and fuckin' mighty to do the job yourself."

"I had nothing to do with your husband's death."

She remembered the dead animals and burnt rifle Amos had found but didn't think it would help their cause much to mention them to the Mayor. In fact, she wasn't entirely sure why she'd even brought it up; the Mayor wasn't likely to confess and offer to lock himself into the remaining unoccupied cell.

"I can smell it on you," she tried to sound dark, mysterious, and threatening, though she suspected she just came across as ridiculous and possibly a little bit mad.

The Mayor chuckled, seemingly thinking the same.

"Tom's death was an unfortunate accident, nothing more."

His tone was so assured that it bordered on smug bastard. The way he smiled suggested they both knew it wasn't true but that he was doing her a favour by being polite enough to lie to her face.

"What exactly did my husband do for you?"

"You mean apart from drinking my whiskey and screwing my whores?"

His quietly spoken words slapped her face, and she immediately hated herself for letting him get to her. She tried hard not to show it.

"Fuck off, you lying maggot!"

"Tom was useful to me, his death saddened me greatly, but life, so they say, goes on. I'm sure you'll be very useful to me too."

"I'm not going to work in the whorehouse."

"Are you going to start swearing at me again? I wouldn't have thought there was a big enough audience for you here," he turned his head towards Amos as he spoke. The Mayor moved along the corridor to stand outside the gunslinger's cell.

One of the numerous things that upset her about the Mayor was his ability to appear entirely unruffled by her, no matter how inventive her cussing got. She thought about the gun hidden beneath the pillow. That would get his attention. Sadly, it would also get her hung.

"So peaceful," the Mayor said, "it's hard to believe he'd do such a terrible thing."

"That's because he didn't."

The Burden of Souls

The Mayor offered a twitch of the shoulders before ambling back to Molly's cell, hands stuffed into his pockets.

"Are you really so sure?"

"Yes."

"You wouldn't be the first woman who denied the wrongs of a man she loves."

Her head jerked up, "I don't love him!"

"Of course not; after all, you know your heart so well, don't you, Molly?"

His eye bore into her. She couldn't shake the feeling it saw a lot more than it should do. Still, she didn't love Amos; she knew that much.

"Yeah, I know my heart well enough."

The Mayor leaned towards the bars and whispered, "Then why did you marry a man you didn't love?"

She took a step back, "How... that's..."

"Tom and I were quite close; I was rather fond of him. We talked at length about... *things*..."

Tom never talked much about anything. Not with her, not with anyone. Not stuff that mattered anyway. The creep was just trying to get under her skin. Tom wouldn't have talked to him about that, fuck, Tom wouldn't even have known about the way she actually felt about him.

Would he?

"The human heart..." the Mayor tapped his chest, "...one of my little hobbies. Quite fascinating."

"You're so full of shit I don't know how you eat your biscuits."

The Mayor laughed, "I can see what men see in you, sometimes anyway."

"I'm a real prize."

"Well, everything is in order here; just... *tickety* in fact!" He grinned a slow, knowing little grin before moving off.

She narrowed her eyes, "What's that supposed to mean?"

"It means you need to decide which horse you're gonna ride... a man who loves you or a man who's gonna swing from the end of a rope. Sleep well, Mrs McCrea."

She watched him disappear up the stairs. Only when she laid back down on the bed did she realise Amos wasn't snoring anymore.

*

She'd little sense of time in the cell, other than it dripped by like molasses from a spoon on a frosty day. It was impossible to judge when morning broke with no skylight or window. She managed to catch a little sleep, but only the fitful, restless kind that left her more exhausted than staying awake. She might have slept for a few hours or ten minutes. It was hard to tell.

One of the deputies, a bespectacled clerkish one called Royce, eventually brought them a breakfast of bread and milk. She'd thought prison meals of dry bread were just something from storybooks, but if they were, then Royce appeared to have read them too.

She'd glanced dismissively at Royce as he slid the unappetising crust under the cell door on a battered metal tray and tried to think of something withering to go with it, but the previous night's work must have drained her cussing gland.

Instead, she showed her disdain by ignoring the tray and rolling derisively onto her side to stare at the wall. Only looking over after Royce had slid a second tray into Amos' cell and retreated upstairs in silence.

Amos was already chomping on the bread.

"You want that?" He nodded towards her sorry excuse for breakfast as he sat cross-legged on the floor.

"I'm waiting for the pickles."

"Huh?"

"You have it – I've lost my taste for stale bread."

"It's not that bad."

She stared at him before slumping back onto the bed. Her stomach was rumbling slightly, but she wasn't going to dignify matters by eating the pitiful crust on offer.

"Could you pass it over?" Amos asked a few minutes later.

She sighed for effect, pulled herself to her feet and pushed the bread and mug through the intervening bars; she resisted the urge to throw the tray at him too.

"Sure you don't want me to hide the gun in that?"

"I don't need to shoot our way out."

"I suppose you could always bludgeon your way out with that crust if you have to."

Amos found time for a quick smile between gulps of milk.

"You still haven't told me how you're going to get out of this – unless you actually want to get hung."

Amos chewed on a crust and refused to meet her eye.

"Oh, fuck!"

"No, of course, I don't," it wasn't a particularly assertive denial.

"Then?"

"Trust me."

"Why should I?"

"You're trusting me to get you out of this town, aren't you?"

"And that does kinda depend on you not getting strung up."

"Or filled with lead during a jailbreak."

She retreated and plonked herself back down on the bed.

"*Does* Furnedge love you?" Amos asked once he'd polished off the second crust.

"I suppose he must. Or at least thinks he does. He asked me to marry him..." she stretched her legs out into mid-air and wiggled her toes, "...kind of."

"Kind of?"

"The price for paying off my debts. Apparently, he'll be quite rich once he inherits his wife's money."

"It wasn't his before?"

She pursed her lips "Dunno, think she came from some fancy family. She never told me the details."

"What was she like?"

"A bitter, foul-mouthed drunk... we got on quite well, really.

"Surprising..."

Molly poked out her tongue.

"You send him away with a flea in his ear?" Amos asked after a long pause.

"Thought it better to keep my options open. You never know..."

"Safer than running away with me," Amos said in a small voice.

She looked up. He was running a finger along the edge of the tray that now only held two empty mugs and a scattering of stale breadcrumbs. A frown creased his brow, like a small boy concentrating on a made-up game in his head.

"I'll take my chances... if we can get you out of here."

"I'll get out of here soon enough – now put the gun back where it came from. The Sheriff will be down in a bit."

"You know that, huh?"

"He'll decide I've sweated enough soon."

She did as he asked; she wasn't sure whether to smile or roll her eyes when he looked pointedly in the opposite direction when she started to hitch up her skirts.

Once the gun was safely taped up and out of sight for all but the most inquisitive of eyes, she eased herself back down onto the bed.

"Well-"

They both looked up as the door to the basement opened, and booted feet made their way down towards them.

Sheriff Shenan came in, followed by Blane and another deputy called Cully, whose hard, distant eyes and scarred face unnerved her almost as much as Blane. The Sheriff cast her the most cursory of glances as he passed, his stride a rolling half-waddle. He came to a halt outside of Amos' cell; Blane and Cully stationed themselves against the back wall, neither man's right hand strayed far from their holstered revolvers.

"I've spoken to the Godbold girl," Shenan announced as he slipped his thumbs into his belt.

"She still saying I did it?"

"Oh yes," Shenan replied with a slow jowl twitching nod, "she was very clear about what you did to her. Fair made my stomach turn, I have to say," he glanced in Molly's direction, "but I'll spare us all the details for now."

"Tell me."

"Pardon?" Shenan's attention snapped back to Amos, who still sat cross-legged on the floor.

"Tell me exactly what was done to her," Amos repeated in a quiet but steady voice, "I need to know."

"What kind of sick fuck are you?" Shenan spat back, his face becoming flushed as his knuckles whitened.

She didn't need any Mr Mysterio type gifts to know the Sheriff was filthy mad,

"You get some kind of twisted kick from hearing what you done?"

"No," Amos said calmly, "I just need to know what was done to her."

When the Sheriff glanced at Molly, she said, "Don't mind me, hun, I'm not easily shocked."

"Tell me," Amos repeated.

"I'm here to *ask* the questions, son!"

"And I'll answer them all – after you explain what he did to her."

"He?"

"Whoever attacked the girl," Amos answered without hesitation.

"Well..." Shenan cleared his throat, his early anger evaporating into discomfort "...she was raped, vaginally and anally, she was forced to take... her attacker in the mouth... she..."

The Burden of Souls

At first, she thought Amos was meeting the Sheriff's accusing glare before it dawned he was actually looking at Blane, whose face was as expressive as a two-day-old corpse.

As Shenan recited the full litany of abuse suffered by Emily Godbold, she dropped her eyes, not wanting to look at any of them, not even Amos.

The poor girl must have been terrified and in so much pain. The only blessing was escaping with her life, though she would be carrying that kind of hurt inside for the rest of her days.

She thought about Bert-Bert and the things he'd done to her. She tried to stop listening.

Did she really think Amos was innocent, or did she just want him to be innocent so much she couldn't admit to any other possibility? She knew men; that was one thing she did know, even if she couldn't figure out why she'd so often ended up with the bad ones. She knew what they were capable of, beneath the charm, jokes, laughter, and flattery. She knew well enough.

So why was she so sure Amos wasn't like that? How did she *know* he didn't have some demon – the kind only men seemed to get – curled up inside him, goading him on to do monstrous things?

He'd treated her well, if oddly, and seemed eager to help her. Which was equally peculiar given he didn't seem attracted to her. However, he'd admitted he was a killer; once she was alone with him, out there on the grass, then what? As unappealing as the alternatives were, she would have some degree of protection from what passed for the law here, either as a whore or as Mrs Furnedge. But out on the grass, she'd be alone with Amos and have nothing but her instinct that he was a good man to protect her.

An instinct that had failed her time and again in the past.

What if he had attacked Emily? What would he do to her out there with no eyes to see and no souls to intervene?

She shook the thought away. If he was guilty, why didn't he take the gun? Although she supposed being an evil bastard didn't preclude the possibility that he was also a fool.

"I see..." Amos nodded once the Sheriff had finished, "Did you ask her how she knew me?"

Shenan looked like he wanted to wash out his mouth, "No, I didn't want to interrogate the poor girl. She's been through quite enough already."

"I didn't do it."

"If that's going to be all you can cough up in your defence, son, then the trial's gonna be a lot quicker than the hanging."

In silence, Amos stared at the floor, his lips drawn into a tight, hard line.

Molly wanted to shout at him to say something but stayed her tongue. It wasn't going to help. Particularly if he had done it...

Amos turned his head to look at her, offering a wan, sad little smile as if he'd heard the thought. Which, if his Mr Mysterio thing wasn't complete bullshit, was entirely possible.

She gave him a smile in return, which she hoped looked reassuring and encouraging rather than forced or slightly deranged.

The Burden of Souls

"Have you got *anything* you want to say?" the Sheriff demanded.

"Yeah," Amos nodded, rising to his feet, "but let her go first."

"You still making demands?"

"She's done nothing wrong."

"Apart from providing a false alibi."

"You really gonna bother with that? Haven't you got more important fish...?"

Shenan puckered his lips and stared at Molly as if he'd something to think about.

"You can't keep me in here forever," she chipped in.

"You're right; that really would drive me mad. Fine, fine, just go, but don't cross me again, young lady..." he waved a hand vaguely in Molly's direction as he added, "...Blane, show her out."

"No!" Amos snapped.

"Huh?"

"Not him; he doesn't put a finger on her!"

Blane regarded him impassively, still leaning lightly against the back wall.

"More demands?" Shenan's eyebrows inched up.

"If he touches her, I'll kill him."

Blane's lips twitched with what might have been the hint of a smile.

"You're really in no position to make threats."

"Not him," Amos repeated, stepping towards the bars.

"Oh, for heaven's sake... Cully, you get her out of here."

Cully snorted a little laugh and shook his head, jangling a key ring like a discordant tambourine as he crossed to Molly's cell.

"Amos?" she said as Cully yanked her out of the cell by her arm.

He half turned back to her, "I'll see you later, Molly." His voice was calm again, in control.

She kept looking over her shoulder as Cully led her towards the stairs; Amos was pressed up against the cell bars talking to Shenan in a low voice she couldn't catch.

Before Cully pushed her up the stairs, the last thing she saw was Sam Shenan's mouth drop open…

The Songbird

"Have you heard?"

She looked up from the mug she was cradling; it was supposed to be coffee, but she was yet to be entirely convinced. Sye was wide-eyed and breathless. She half expected him to drop a ball at her feet to throw for him.

"Heard what?" she asked, knowing full well what he meant.

"Amos!"

"Oh, that."

She was sitting in the saloon, which was deserted save for a couple of the girls chatting in the corner and a worried looking Monty. All his regulars had joined the crowd outside the Sheriff's Office. He'd had to resort to sending Sonny out onto Pioneer Square to hawk booze to the mob to avert a potentially calamitous drop in takings.

Sye pulled up a chair and slumped into it. He smelt of fresh sweat, which was an improvement upon the stale sweat most of the saloon's patrons reeked of. It was nice that he'd made the effort.

"I knew... I just knew!" he exclaimed when she remained silent.

"Is there anywhere I can get a decent coffee in this town," she wrinkled her nose after another tentative sip.

"They have the best coffee in town here," Sye said in a low voice, half glancing at Monty.

"Sheeesh..."

"Well, Rosa's is good too."

She tried not to pull a face; she'd been there already.

"Didn't you think he was dangerous too?"

"Monty?"

"No! Amos, of course."

"Not really, no."

Sye looked at her like she was some kind of deluded simpleton.

"He was fine with me."

"Well..." Sye crossed his arms and nodded, "...now we know."

"Know what?"

"That he's dangerous."

"No, we don't."

"He raped Emily Godbold!"

"We don't know that."

"Yes, we do!"

Was he pouting?

"He's been accused of something, which isn't the same thing. You have due process, even here."

Sye frowned, and she mentally booted her shin. It was difficult to remember where she was sometimes. She took another sip of coffee. And sometimes it was easy. She put the mug to one side.

"I mean, there has to be a trial and evidence... and stuff."

"Well, yes, of course..." he agreed, still frowning, "...and then we hang the bastard."

She stopped herself from trying to explain the concept of innocent until proven guilty.

"There's a big crowd outside."

"Certainly is."

"Sonny is selling them beer apparently; it could end up being quite the party."

"You don't seem to be taking this very seriously?"

"I'm sure Amos is."

A dark little look crossed Sye's features. It didn't suit him.

"You like him, don't you?"

"Is that a hanging offence?"

"He's a rapist!"

"We don't know that."

"You mean you don't *want* to know that."

I really should practice keeping my mouth shut more...

She was supposed to be unobtrusive, a little mouse scurrying around the periphery of the locals' attention. She wasn't making a particularly good job of it.

"I don't know..." she shrugged "...maybe I just like to think the best of people."

Sye's face softened, "I know, you're a good person, but the world... the world is full of bad people."

She smiled. She'd always found being talked to like she was a child extremely irritating, even when she'd been a child.

"If you say so," she managed to reply.

"But you are!" Sye enthused.

"You really don't know me very well."

"I'd like to put that right."

Oh, dear...

She managed a non-committal little smile and looked around for an excuse to get away, but Sye leaned over and took her hand before anything plausible came to mind. She'd quickly built a reputation in the saloon for slapping men who grabbed hold of her. He clearly hadn't heard.

"What's wrong?"

"Nothing." Cece resisted the urge.

"Why don't you think you're a good person?"

"I don't need a therapist."

"A what?"

Her shin got another imaginary kick.

"Someone you pay to help sort out your problems."

"Never heard of that."

"We have them where I come from... back east."

"Whereabouts did you come from, you never said."

"A little place, you'd never have heard of it."

"Where's it near?"

"New York, I guess," she said after a pause.

Sye squeezed her hand, "Is it as bad there as people say?"

She shifted in her chair; she really needed to make an excuse to get away.

"It's..." she flailed around for the words, "...you know."

"Yeah... you must have seen some things, huh?"

"One or two."

"I can imagine."

Bet you can't.

"Anyway, nice seeing you again," she said, springing to her feet.

"Yeah, real nice," Sye said, standing up too. He was still holding her hand.

"I've got to go."

"Oh, really?"

"Got to... get ready for tonight."

Sye looked around the empty saloon, "You think they'll be many people here?"

"Well, can't compete with a hanging, but that won't be happening tonight, so people will eventually get bored on the square and come back. Unless they're getting tired of my voice, of course."

"Oh, that'll never happen."

"We'll see..." she glanced down at her hand that Sye was still clutching like a small boy "...I'll see you around."

Sye let her hand slip away, "Sure... look, I was wondering if you'd like to go for another ride, down to Hayliss' Creek this time... maybe?"

She looked at his earnest, eager little face and felt a mixture of pity, irritation, and guilt. It wasn't fair to string him along, even if he did provide a convenient cover when she wanted to get out of town.

"I dunno...we'll see." She tried not to wince at Sye's expression, which was more shocked and hurt than any of the men she'd slapped in her time in *Jack's Saloon*.

"Oh... well... let me know," he stammered.

"Sye, you're really nice, but I don't think I'm looking for anything here. My life is kind of messy right now. It's better if I just keep things simple."

"I see..."

"Just friends, huh?"

"Sure... friends... great... I'd better go... cows need milking," he forced a pained smile, twisted away, and hurtled out of the saloon.

As the doors slammed behind Sye, Monty shouted from the bar, "For fuck's sake, will you stop chasing my customers off, not today of all days!"

She slumped back down, picked up the dregs of her coffee and tried not to feel like she'd just kicked a puppy in the face.

The Sheriff

Sam had known the Mayor for a long time, and for most of that time, he'd been reporting to him on a regular basis. He had seen him react with both broiling rage and serene indifference to his briefings on Hawker's Drift's law and order goings on. He'd thought he'd seen everything between those two extremes over the years. However, as the Mayor stood ruler-straight by the chair he'd just erupted from, Sam realised he'd never seen dumbfounded, slack-jawed shock on his boss' face before.

"*What do you mean he's got no fucking cock??!!*"

The Sheriff leaned back in his own chair; he'd assumed for a long time that the Mayor, somehow, knew everything. It was somehow reassuring it turned out he could be as utterly gobsmacked as any mere mortal after all.

He glanced through the glass pane in his office door; a couple of the deputies looked up briefly before hurriedly pretending they hadn't heard anything. Molly McCrea was still out front, refusing to go home even though last night's mob had dwindled to a rump of the town's hardened gossipmongers with nothing better to do with their time.

Whatever her relationship with the gunslinger was, she clearly wasn't the slut the town had painted her. He turned his attention back to the Mayor; it wasn't his concern, and he'd more pressing matters to deal with.

"Well?" the Mayor demanded. He was still standing but was trying hard not to look like a guy who'd just found out his seventy-year-old wife was pregnant.

"He lost it..."

"Lost it? How the hell do you lose a fucking cock?"

"Well, I don't mean he mislaid it."

The Mayor's expression melted from astonishment into infuriated bafflement, and Sam tried to suppress the feeling that he was rather enjoying this.

It wasn't, after all, a laughing matter.

The Mayor took a deep breath, seemed to realise he was standing and sat down again after running both hands down the lapels of his jacket.

"Please, Sheriff, explain this to me? In your own time."

"Well, according to Amos, and I got no reason to doubt him, a gang of renegades attacked his farmstead years ago; they raped and killed his wife in front of him. After the bastards finished with her, they beat him half senseless then... as a parting gift, I suppose, they cut off his..." he coughed and made a chopping motion with his hand "...damnedest thing I've seen in a while..."

"He showed you?"

"Well, I couldn't just take his word for it. Under the circumstances."

"The circumstances?"

"He was accused of rape – not having a cock is strong evidence he didn't do it."

"But the Godbold girl – *she identified him!*"

The Burden of Souls

"Yeah, strange that, huh?" he looked up at the ceiling, "Actually, she named him; she hasn't identified him. There's a difference."

"He could still have done it."

His attention snapped back to the Mayor, and he raised an eyebrow, "That would be quite a trick..."

"Perhaps he has a prosthetic."

"A prosthetic?"

"A false body part – such as a wooden leg."

"You're suggesting he raped Emily Godbold... with a *wooden cock*?"

"The girl is only sixteen, from a good home. Would she know the difference?"

He let out a long deep sigh and looked the Mayor in his twitching roaming eye – which was something he generally tried to avoid – and said, "The fucker, among other things, forced his cock down her throat and made her swallow his load. That's some helluva prosthetic!"

The Mayor didn't reply. Wheels were turning somewhere inside.

"He didn't do it," he said, just in case the Mayor hadn't yet grasped the point.

"And what do you propose to do, Sheriff?"

"Let him go and find the fucker who did."

The Mayor nodded.

"He's a dangerous man, this... *character*."

"Perhaps to you, but not to women... and even you will struggle to find twelve men prepared to hang a cockless man for rape."

The Mayor's eye grew terribly still; he tried to meet the stare again, but his courage, if even possessed such a thing anymore, vaporised in the heat of its attention. He looked away. He wasn't used to pressing back at the Mayor, and neither, it seemed, was the Mayor.

"I only have the best interests of this town at heart, Sam, the best interests of my constituents; you know that, don't you?"

"Of course, Mr Mayor," frankly, he didn't have a clue what the Mayor had at heart. Or even if he had one.

"So, we have a situation. We have a poor, brutalised girl saying this man raped her... and yet, it appears he couldn't possibly have done it. Definitely a situation."

"Mistaken identity. She was scared, terrified, it was dark... understandable."

"But we need to find someone for this, Sheriff. The town will get... twitchy otherwise."

"You think? They seem to live with all those kids who go missing."

"Kids run away. Always have, always will. Run away from abuse, from authority, for a better life over the horizon where they think there won't be chores or responsibility. Where life might be better. Kids are full of shit. There's no mystery, no threat, but a girl raped and beaten half to death. That's different. We need to give them answers."

"Like we did with Nancy Klass?"

"Nancy... Klass..." the Mayor turned the words over in his mouth "...yes, of course, like we did with Nancy Klass."

"She was beaten with a belt too, as I recall..."

The Mayor twitched his shoulders, "Just a coincidence. It was a long time ago. These things happen from time to time, even in peaceful little towns like ours... this time, we'll have to make sure the culprit doesn't get away."

"I suppose..."

Had Donny Bildt really gotten away? He'd often wondered.

"Well, I'm sure your enquiries will be thorough," the Mayor slowly pushed himself to his feet, "...and when you're done, bring me someone we can hang for this."

The Sheriff didn't stand, "I'll talk to the family again; something isn't right there."

"Right?"

"How do you sleep through an attack like that? Kate Godbold reckons she did, but it ain't a big house..."

"You think she's involved?"

"Seems unlikely, but you never know. She's lying about something."

The Mayor looked down at him as he replaced his hat, "Take my word for it, Sam, being something of an expert in these matters, I very much doubt Mrs Godbold has a cock either."

His boss paused by the door, "Have you released the gunslinger yet?"

"No, he'd be lynched. I'll have to speak to Ash Godbold and put the word about that he couldn't have done it before I let him out. I don't want a murder to deal with too."

"Yes, probably best. Be sure to let everybody know exactly why he couldn't have done it..." the Mayor said after a moment's thought, "...for his own sake."

"Not something most men would want to be public knowledge."

"Ridicule and sniggers are preferable to being hanged... and there's nothing to keep him here, is there? Once he's left Hawker's Drift far behind his... reduced circumstances will be his little secret once again," the Mayor chuckled, like a man who'd suddenly realised things were going to work out all right after all.

He breezed out of the office, passing Molly McCrea without a glance. Molly was sitting by the door, her hands folded in her lap, trying hard not to look worried.

"No," Sam muttered under his breath, "he's got nothing to keep him here at all..."

The Preacher

The tree was unremarkable in every respect apart from its existence.

The grass stretched away in every direction, swaying in soft green swells. Other than the tree and the grass, there was nothing else to see. Just why or how this lone tree had grown here, Preacher Stone couldn't imagine; he was just grateful for something to rest his aching back against.

He had left town before dawn and had ridden hard all day, his horse was exhausted, but she was free now, as he soon would be. He wanted to be as far away from the town and its inhabitants as possible, far away from their prying questions.

He just wanted to be left alone until he died.

His stomach was worse than ever; it felt like glowing embers were crackling deep inside him without the candy to take away the pain. Then there was the other pain. The one that came from craving that black poison, the one that made his flesh spasm and his heart race, made his eyes ache and his tongue throb.

He sipped from one his canteen; the water tasted warm and leathery. He wasn't quite sure why he'd brought food and water. He'd die quicker without them. Perhaps he just wanted to see if he could somehow cleanse his soul out here away from the rest of humanity, away from the candy, away from the Mayor.

Not a task he was likely to accomplish in the few days he had left, but he'd nothing else to offer. So, he would walk into the west, pray and read his Bible, and look for some kind of redemption on his pilgrimage to the grave.

His horse was grazing on the rich grass, he should slap her rump and send her back to town, but he couldn't face the prospect of climbing all the long way back up to his feet again. He'd stripped off the saddle and gear; she was free now like he would be again soon.

The sun was a molten ball on the western horizon. He sat with his back against the rough bark of the improbable tree, watching it slip away. Tomorrow he would walk with it at his back and not stop until it sunk into the west again. Would he live that long? He had food and water; it was hot, but not unbearably so; however, he was old and sick, so there were no more guarantees.

He felt no fear at the thought; he would go to God and await His judgement. He'd been a weak and foolish man, and he feared he might have done a terrible thing, but now he was doing all he possibly could. He was walking away from whatever he'd done and from whatever he might do. If he stayed and slipped further into the thrall of that sick black candy, nothing would eventually be left of him.

There was food in his bag, but he wasn't hungry, just tired. He'd a blanket roll, maybe he would lay it out and use the saddle as a pillow. He wouldn't take them further, so perhaps he should just curl up beneath the tree and listen to the grass, insects, and wind in the boughs above him. Maybe then his sleep would be dreamless and peaceful again, like it used to be.

He closed his eyes, just for a minute.

*

The stars greeted him when he awoke. Had he ever seen so many before? He supposed he must have, but he couldn't remember. His stomach rumbled with hunger and pain, his throat was dry, and his neck ached. His mouth tasted of corruption from whatever was rotting his insides. He ignored it all and stared at the stars instead, their cold light bathing him and heralding his ascent to heaven.

"The stars can make you feel quite humble..."

He gave out a strangled cry as he turned to see the Mayor sitting cross-legged next to him, looking up at the sky. He turned slowly to examine the Preacher.

"...so I've been told."

"How... how did you find me?"

"Oh, I keep a close eye on my little flock Billy; you can't get away from me that easily. Not once you've drunk my candy anyhow."

He looked around; it was full night now, the grass pale and eerie in the starlight. There was no sign of his horse or any other.

"You couldn't have followed me..."

"Trust me, you have absolutely no inkling as to what I can and cannot do," the Mayor leant in close enough for him to smell the faintly sickly-sweet scent of perfumed smoke he often carried.

He wanted to run away, but he'd been sitting a long time, and his body ached. If he tried to get up, he'd just fall flat on his face and have to crawl through the grass. Which wouldn't get him far. Instead, he sat and felt himself pinned against the tree, knowing there was nowhere he could go to escape the gaze of the Mayor's restless eye.

"I just want to go," he said finally, in a weak, faltering voice, "please…"

"Is Hawker's Drift so terrible? Frankly, I'm disappointed in you… I've worked so hard to hold this town together. To make it safe."

"Safe from what?"

The Mayor swept his hand airily towards the sky, "There are more things in heaven and… oh, you know how it goes, Billy. Not to mention the renegades and outlaws that infest the land, of course. It can get quite dangerous out here."

"You don't seem too concerned?"

"No need to worry about me, ol' son! I'm tougher than I look," he clicked his teeth together like a dog snapping at a bone and let out a little chuckle.

Preacher Stone rested his head back against the tree, his heart was thumping and he felt light-headed.

"I'm dying…" he whispered.

"Of course you are."

"Then leave me in peace."

"I'll be leaving soon enough, you know how it is, errands to run, chores to do, people to see. No rest for the wicked; you can be sure about that."

The Burden of Souls

He closed his eyes and prayed for the strength to resist the writhing urge inside him. The urge to beg the Mayor for a little black bottle.

"I have a small problem," the Mayor said, his voice bright and matter of fact, "you see, we were all set to hang that Amos chap for raping Emily Godbold and – would you believe it – it turns out he has the absolute best cast in fucking iron alibi you can imagine. Which is all rather inconvenient because he's a man badly in need of hanging."

Preacher Stone's head flopped to one side; he managed to half-open his eyes and ask, "Why?"

"Details, Billy! Details you need not worry your balding, liver-spotted little head about, just trust me, some men are trouble, just born trouble. And only two things you can do with men of trouble; you either keep em close or send em a long, long way away. Mr Amos is proving unresponsive to both options."

"So who did rape Emily?" His voice sounded like slush and a coldness was creeping through him, a coldness which had no place in a man's bones on a warm summer's night.

"Why..." the Mayor exclaimed with a smile of surprised enlightenment, "...it turns out it was you all along! Who would have thought it, eh?"

"I-"

"Ssssh now, Billy! Don't worry if you can't remember. That's just one of the side effects of my candy; it can make people forget what they've done and even remember things they haven't. It cakes your soul, Billy, and I can sniff out the scent of it seeping from your pores; it's quite the smell, I can tell you. It's very useful stuff..." he leant in again and whispered with more than a hint of pride "...I squeeze it from my own black teats, you know, it really is the Devil's brew..."

He felt a distant tide of panic. Had he really hurt that girl? It was a terrible thing, but he found after a few moments, the horror slipped away as he stared into the Mayor's eye that had grown still. It didn't matter. What was done was done; he was dying...

"You know what they call this place, don't you?"

He could manage only the tiniest shake of his head.

"They call it the Judas Tree. Don't ask me why; there are some things even I don't know, but it's quite the perfect place for a remorseful old rapist to hang himself. Don't you think?"

"I didn't..."

"Now, now... of course you did, Billy. You remember, don't you? Just look into my eyes, and you will..."

The Mayor reached up and pulled off his eye patch. He'd always assumed nothing but scar tissue or a dead milky white eye hid behind it.

But it turned out it wasn't that at all. There was something else entirely.

As he stared into it, transfixed, images of that poor girl, naked and bleeding beneath him as he fucked her, flooded into his mind. Wriggling and begging, thrashing and fighting, he saw his bony old hand clamped over her mouth to shut her up. He felt shame and excitement, disgust and arousal as the memories flooded his mind, a torrent of black water sweeping away everything in its path. Tears trickled down his cheeks, and his throat tightened.

"No... this never happened... this isn't real..."

"Oh, Billy... you were a very bad boy... that's what everyone is going to say..." the Mayor gently took his hand and squeezed it "...there's no need to worry though, old man. I'm going to make everything right. Luckily, I just so happen to have this nice length of rope with me..."

The Farmer

He sat perched over his coffee, chin cupped in one hand as he leaned on the table and stared out of the window at the people strolling around Pioneer Square.

The town appeared to have returned to normal now the prospect of an imminent hanging had receded. Cece enjoyed a comfortable familiarity with Amos that he didn't care for. The news the stranger had raped Emily Godbold, and would be soon dangling from the town gallows, had cheered him up immensely following the disappointment of his ride with Cece.

He'd known the gunslinger was trouble from the moment he'd seen him, but Cece had been oblivious. He knew some girls were drawn to rough, dangerous men, but he'd hoped Cece was different. The whole business of bumping into him at the Mayor's ranch. That had to be more than coincidence, didn't it?

Had she just been using him as a patsy? A cover to meet up with Amos? He didn't know and couldn't work it out, but then she was a girl and, therefore, her motives and behaviour were far beyond the knowing of a rational mind like his.

The Burden of Souls

Still, when he'd heard the news, his immediate reaction was relief; if she was interested in Amos, surely the scales would now fall from her eyes. Instead, she'd adamantly insisted he was innocent.

He sipped his coffee. It was cold. He blinked. Just how long had he been sitting here thinking about Cece? Too long, he realised, though that was how he frittered away most of his time these days. His chores were backing up on the farm too.

He glanced towards the counter and caught Rosa's eye, ordering another coffee with a nod at his empty mug.

His attention slipped back outside; he supposed he was hoping Cece would pop out for a stroll and he could accidentally bump into her. Now Amos wasn't going to hang she might be in a better mood (even if it hadn't helped his day). Still, on the bright side, if she had been interested in the gunslinger, that would be finished now. Even he couldn't manage to lose a girl to a man with no cock. Could he?

But then what did it matter? She only thought of him as a friend. Her life was too messy for anything else. Whatever that meant.

Another coffee appeared in front of him. He was about to thank Rosa when the nattily-dressed figure of the Mayor eased himself into the chair opposite.

"You have a day job now?" he eyed the coffee the Mayor slid across the table to him.

The Mayor smiled, placed his elbows on the table and spread his long fingers out in front of him, "So, young man, tell me how things are going?"

"Things? Going?"

The Mayor's smile didn't falter.

"With the lovely Miss Jones, our little songbird?"

"Oh... y'know."

"That doesn't sound... encouraging."

"I don't think she's really interested in me."

"Don't be so easily put off. Some women like to be pursued."

"They do?"

"Most definitely... though it can be tricky telling the difference between a girl playing hard to get and one that's genuinely not interested."

"Then how do you know what to do?"

"It's a life skill, young man."

"It's one I haven't got," he went back to staring into his coffee.

The Mayor looked thoughtful and cracked his knuckles. Sye tried not to wince at the popping noises.

"Perhaps there's something I could do to help matters along."

Sye looked up. "You'd put a good word in for me?"

"A word? I doubt anything an old codger like me could say would really change matters."

"Oh..."

"I can do something much more useful, though."

"You can?"

"Most definitely."

The Mayor stopped cracking his knuckles and opened his right hand. He hadn't known the Mayor could do conjuring tricks too. A small black bottle sat in his palm.

"What's that?"

"Well, we could call it many things, but, in this instance, let's call it a love potion."

"A love potion?" he repeated, his nose wrinkling and eyebrows rising at the same time.

"Don't look so sceptical. *Please*! A lesser man might take offence. I'm not talking about some county fair quackery here. This is, very much, the real deal."

"Does it work?"

The Mayor placed the little bottle on the table between them.

"Only one way to find out."

The bottle was strangely compelling. The glass appeared extraordinarily smooth, as if it weren't really made of glass at all but something far more exotic. He wanted to reach out and run his fingers over it to see how it felt upon his skin.

"What do I need to do?" He felt stupid. This had to be some kind of a joke on the Mayor's part. Didn't it?

"Just get her to drink some of this. Only a little mind, it's very potent; a few drops are quite enough."

"What should I tell her it is?" His hand was edging towards the bottle.

"You don't tell her anything. Just put a couple of drops into her drink when she isn't looking."

"And... that's it?"

The Mayor drummed his fingers on the table edge and smiled.

"And then what?"

"You ask a lot of questions, don't you?"

His hand had curled around the bottle. He'd expected the glass to be cold, but it was curiously warm. Perhaps it had been in the Mayor's pocket for a while.

As his voice dropped a notch, the Mayor leaned forward, "Just give it to her, young man, and she will swoon for you... just trust me. With that inside her, she will do anything you want her to. She'll be all yours, Sye. *All yours.*"

The Mayor's voice was compelling, even if he was talking nonsense. He might only be a farm boy, but he wasn't a simpleton; he knew damn well that giving a girl a few drops of any potion wouldn't make her fall in love with him. But even so...

"What *is* this stuff?" he heard himself ask again, his hand already moving towards his jacket pocket.

The Mayor smiled, his eye roamed, and his fingers continued to drum out a beat upon the table.

"My boy, this is, quite simply, the sweetest candy anyone ever did taste, and it'll show you a whole new world..."

The Gunslinger

He hadn't quite known what to say to Molly.

He'd never talked to a living soul about his injury, as he tended to think of it, since he'd been well enough to ride away from his brother's farmstead in search of Severn and his men thirteen years ago. To have to discuss it with two people in one day seemed, somehow, unfair.

After the Sheriff and Blane left, he'd lain in his cell and stared at the ceiling, his mind a complete blank. The Sheriff had returned in the afternoon to announce he was free to go, and he'd had to let people know exactly why he hadn't raped Emily Godbold.

Shenan's eyes had slipped to the floor at that point, "It's the only way to avoid a lynching, sorry…"

The Sheriff had returned his gun belt and boots and warned him to be careful; there would be a few hotheads in town the gossips had yet to corner.

He'd been surprised to find Molly waiting for him upstairs, ignoring the smirks and silent stares of the deputies, save for Blane, whose features didn't seem capable of stretching to such extremes. He'd stood before her and felt vaguely like a naughty child who'd been sent to the headmistress to explain just why he'd been such a deceitful little boy.

He'd started to say something, one of those mumbling, stumbling sentences you have no idea how you're going to finish, but Molly reached out and gently squeezed his wrist.

"I heard... It's ok..."

Of course, it wasn't ok. Nothing had been ok for so long he couldn't even remember how it felt when things had been ok.

But it was enough, all the same.

*

When he tried to go to his room in the saloon, Molly insisted on taking him home instead.

"Best you keep out of the way of all the cock-sucking assholes in this fucking town."

Pulling up short, she slapped a hand to her mouth, "Shit, shit, *shit*... sorry, that was dumb, even for me!"

He stared at her.

Then laughed.

*

They'd made it back to Molly's house without any of the erstwhile lynch mob who'd fallen out of the gossip loop taking a pot shot at them.

Molly had made coffee and cut some bread and cheese, as much for something to do as through hunger, he suspected. They'd eaten in silence at the kitchen table, and she'd cleared away the mugs and plates the moment they finished.

She was feeling awkward. He should go. She shouldn't have to deal with any of this.

"I knew you didn't do it," she said finally, not looking back at him from the sink.

Ah, that was it...

"I know."

She turned back to face him, leaning back against the sink, a cloth turning in her hands.

"Actually, that's bullshit; when Shenan was telling you what had happened to that poor girl... I thought... I-"

"It's only natural, under the circumstances."

"I feel shitty. You're the only one in this town... I hate the fact I could even consider that you... were... capable..."

"Molly, it doesn't matter. You stood by me; that's what counts. You even put a gun in your panties for me..."

She snorted a half-laugh and looked at her feet, blushing, "It wasn't in my panties; you clearly weren't paying proper attention."

"I... have no answer to that."

Molly looked up through the long unkempt hair falling about her face before stifling a yawn.

"Shit, I'm tired," she folded up the little cloth and hung it over the side of the sink, "I barely got any sleep last night. I'm going to go to bed."

He nodded and began to rise, "Sure, I'll just-"

"Come with me, please."

He stopped.

"I can't, you know..."

"Just sleep with me."

"I can't," he sank back down onto the chair.

"Is there something wrong with your arms?"

"No," he frowned.

"You can put them around me then, can't you?"

"Why would you even want me to? I can't-"

"Yes, I know you can't fuck me! I worked that out. That's not what I'm asking for."

"Then what?"

"Jesus, are you really this dim?"

He blinked at her.

"You make me feel safe, Amos. I've spent my life following men, violent idiots for the most part, because I thought they could make me safe and keep this shitty world away from me. I was so desperate to feel safe that I ended up with men who beat me, abused me, and treated me like crap. Even Tom, who was the best of a sorry lot, dragged me from one shit hole to the next, following his hair-brained schemes or running away from the mess they caused."

She stood looking down at him, her arms crossed, almost hugging herself as she added, "None of them made me safe. My whole life has been spent hiding the fact I'm so goddamned afraid, hiding behind a bottle and a fast mouth."

She took a half-step towards him, "But you make me feel safe, even amongst all this shit with the Mayor. You make me feel *safe*. I don't care about anything else."

He was supposed to stand up and hold her. He knew that much. He remembered that much. But that was different from being able to do it.

"Molly, I can't keep you safe... I couldn't keep Megan safe. I..."

"I *know* you can't keep me safe. I'm not stupid. Sometimes the shit this fucking world throws at you is too much for anyone. But you make me *feel* safe, and I can't ask for more than that."

"And what about me? What about what I want?"

The Burden of Souls

"I'm not holding a gun to your head, yet you keep helping me... I thought... shit, how the hell am I supposed to even know what you want?" She took another half-step forward, "What the fuck do you want?"

"I want my wife, my cock and my life back."

Molly pursed her lips as her head tilted to one side, "Nothing I can do about the first two, hun, but the last one... who knows."

She held a hand across the table, "Come sleep with me, Mr Mysterio..."

Her hand stayed there, hovering in mid-air, her eyes were wide and her lips slightly parted, her red hair falling in tangles about her face. Just like Megan's had. He reached out, seized her hand, and let her pull him up.

Till that moment, he hadn't even realised he'd been drowning.

*

He'd insisted he kept his pants on, which Molly had agreed to. When he'd also insisted she dressed appropriately, too, she'd raised a quizzical eyebrow.

"What the fuck is *appropriate*?"

"Something that isn't... well... revealing."

Her eyebrow cranked up another notch.

"I haven't been... close to a woman in thirteen years."

"You think you might get carried away?"

"I'm not entirely... dysfunctional."

"Oh."

Molly smiled.

He squirmed.

They were in her bedroom; Molly sat on the bed looking up at him; he was hovering by the door, wondering whether the Sheriff could be persuaded to lock him up again.

"I, well... it's-"

Molly crossed her legs and started to take off her shoes.

"I think I'd better wait outside."

"You have a problem with feet?"

He hurried back to the landing, where it was shadowy, cool, and devoid of women undressing.

"Fuck..." he whispered under his breath, closing his eyes and leaning back against the wall. He shoved his hands into his pockets; they were shaking.

This was ridiculous.

How many armed men had he faced down in the last few years? He honestly couldn't remember. He'd never once felt fear or anxiety or gut-wrenching uncertainty. The prospect of sharing a bed with a woman, on the other hand, made all three churn about inside him like rancid milk on the back of a wagon.

He hadn't touched a woman in thirteen years. The last time he'd kissed a woman had been the day Megan died. There hadn't seemed much point since, though it wasn't that he didn't want to. He sometimes thought it would have been kinder if Severn had castrated him properly; he'd sliced most of his cock off but had left his balls. Maybe he would have just grown fat, lazy and indifferent like a neutered tomcat if he'd taken them too. Instead, he'd been left with his desires but no means to fulfil them, save with a scarred lump of tissue that ached horribly if he became aroused.

"I'm decent!" Molly called.

Part of him wanted to sneak out; it would save them both a lot of trouble and heartache in the long run. He couldn't keep her safe, and he definitely couldn't make her happy, while she could only remind him of what he'd lost and what he could never have again.

He shook his head, cursed himself for a fool and went back into the bedroom.

All he could see of Molly were a few messy ginger curls and the fingers gripping the edge of the bedsheet that she'd pulled up over her head.

"You're not taking this seriously, are you?"

There was a muffled giggle from beneath the sheet.

Molly had pulled the curtains shut, but the sun was still up, and they were thin enough to allow soft diffused light into the room.

"Start with your boots," Molly suggested peeking over the sheet.

He tentatively sat on the corner of the bed and did what he was told; he heard Molly shuffling onto her side, her back turned to him.

"I'm sorry if I'm being an ass," he pulled off his left boot with a grimace, "this is... difficult for me..."

"Uh-huh."

"I know it shouldn't be; this should be such a simple thing, you kind of take it for granted, not sex, but just being close to another human being. It should be easy, but..." he pulled off his other boot and placed them together at the foot of the bed.

He stood up and tossed his jacket over the chair where Molly had draped her dress. He slowly unbuttoned his shirt. His fingers seemed to have become fat and rebellious. He fumbled the buttons a few times before he could take it off. After he'd slung it over his jacket, he took off his gun belt, placed it carefully on the floor and pushed it underneath the bed with his foot.

Molly still had her back turned.

He peeled back the sheets; she was wearing a long off-white nightgown. He was faintly surprised at the twinge of disappointment that brought. He should take his pants off, really, but there was no way he could.

Instead, he sat on the bed, slowly swung his legs up and laid down on his back next to Molly.

"Thank you for your kindness," he whispered, placing a tentative hand between her shoulder blades, "I do not understand it, but it means the world. Really."

Her only reply had been a soft and gentle snore.

*

The room was dark when he awoke, and, to his surprise, Molly's head was resting on his chest.

He wasn't entirely sure how it had happened. He had an urge to shoo her away like an overindulged cat from his lap; instead, he counted to ten and listened to his thumping heart.

This is what it feels like to be normal.

He remembered, vaguely, how it had felt to wake up with Megan curled next to him in the darkness. Warm, soft, and quiet, the smell of flesh, sweat, linen, the touch of her breath on his skin, downy hair spread over his chest. It felt safe, as if the darkness and a warm body could protect you from the world beyond; a sanctuary built of small intimacies.

His arm was going numb beneath her.

Wincing, he gently shrugged Molly off and rolled onto his side, his back to her. She mumbled something before settling herself against him, her arm looping over him, hand resting on his stomach.

Sleep muffled her words, so he couldn't be sure, but it sounded a little like, "*Mish'd ya Tom...*"

*

"Don't worry, you'll get used to the stares after a bit," Molly whispered, slipping her arm through his, "I did, kinda..."

"What about the sniggering?"

"That might take longer."

"Suppose so... I could just shoot at them. That might stop it."

"You've already avoided one lynching; best not push your luck."

"I did say *at* them. I'd only actually hit them if they start pointing too."

Molly thought about it for a minute before shrugging, "Fair enough."

He felt warmth and kindness coming from her in gentle ripples that made his arm tingle where her hand rested. There was pity too, inevitably, but only a trace, and it wasn't why she wanted to be with him. He looked away sharply and blinked a couple of times.

It was the first time they'd ventured out of Molly's house since the Sheriff had decided it was safe enough to release him. To ensure his safety Shenan had made sure the whole town heard, precisely and explicitly, why he couldn't have raped Emily Godbold.

It was evening and the sun was sinking towards the distant horizon by the time they reached Corner Park. A few people were out taking the air; a grey-haired couple glanced their way. Whispers were whispered. He ignored them.

"Why'd we come here?" he asked as they came to a halt on the scrubby-grassed slope and looked out to the west.

"Because it's beautiful."

He puckered his lips. He didn't see a lot of beauty in the world anymore, maybe something had happened to his brain after Severn and his men had left him for dead. Where others stopped and stared at the view, he just saw grass, trees, clouds, rocks in randomly configured patterns.

Sometimes he thought he was missing out.

"Yes... it is," he said eventually, trying to sound like he meant it.

Molly was beautiful, though he was only even sure of that because she looked so much like Megan, and he remembered how beautiful she'd been well enough.

They walked a little further in silence to where a teenage boy was pinning a handbill to a wooden signpost on top of older sun-faded flyers.

SUMMER CARNIVAL

It declared in bold red lettering. Once the boy was satisfied, he turned and headed back up the slope. He glanced at them, but nothing held his attention, and his pace quickly accelerated to a trot, a canvas satchel slapping against his thigh as he ran.

"They have one every year," Molly flicked hair from her eyes. The wind was starting to pick up.

"Good?"

"Dunno, never been."

"Sounds like one of the highlights of the town calendar?"

"Yeah, it's about as good as it gets here. Tom and I went to the saloon instead. It was easier to get a drink than normal; Monty was even pleased to see us given there weren't many people around for Tom to get in a brawl with."

They stood in silence. He let his eyes slide from the flyer to the view across the plains; grass, sky and gold-fringed clouds glowing from the sun's last light. No, he still couldn't see it.

"I hope you'll both be coming to the Carnival?" A voice announced from behind them. Molly gave a slight start, but he just looked back at the Mayor, whose white suit was radiant in the warm light of the setting sun.

"I'll put it in my diary," he replied.

The Mayor ambled over to stand beside them, taking off his derby and running a palm quickly over his greased back hair as he squinted at the sun. He could feel Molly tense, wanting to shy away from him but too stubborn to show her fear.

"You be sure to do that; it'll be a helluva day," the Mayor replied finally, replacing his hat, "they'll be clowns and jugglers, games and rides when the carney comes to town. There'll even be a freak show. You'll love it."

Molly tensed; he could sense the cussing brewing up inside her.

"Go sit down for a minute," he nodded towards one of the benches, "I want a quick word with the Mayor."

She started to protest, but the Mayor cut her short.

"Yes, run along for a bit while we have a quick chat, man to man you might say," he glanced at Amos, "well, *almost.*"

"You really are remarkably unpleasant," Molly hissed before hitching up the hems of her skirts and stomping off to plonk herself down on the nearest bench. He'd never seen her quite so restrained.

"What do you want?" he turned back to the Mayor.

"Oh, just making sure there are no hard feelings after all that unpleasantness."

"You mean when you wanted to hang me for something I didn't do?"

"Yes... but the girl said it was you, why wouldn't we believe her? We weren't to know she was under the spell of Preacher Stone, were we?"

"It seems unlikely..."

"Yes, it does rather, a man of the cloth and all, but William Stone was an extremely sick man, he tried not to show it, but he was dying, rotting from the inside. That can change a man."

"Perhaps."

"Anyway, we'll never know; he was found hanging from a tree out by the Kransy Ranch."

He stared at the man, trying to get some sense of him, but like before, nothing came bar a dark echoing cavern, inside which something was hiding and watching...

"I hadn't heard."

"Terrible business. The Judas Tree they call it, God alone knows why, but it seems clear why Preacher Stone rode out there to kill himself."

"It is?"

"He betrayed God; he used his position to abuse a girl and then persuaded her to implicate you for reasons best known to himself."

"And why would he do that? I didn't know him."

The Mayor smiled, "Maybe he didn't like your face. At times, people can be quite... unfathomable, don't you think?"

"Who are you?" he grabbed the Mayor's wrist, "Really?"

"I could ask the same question of you Mr... do you even have a second name?"

"Amos serves for both."

"Amos Amos? Your parents seem to have lacked a little imagination."

"Perhaps, they also told me to be careful who you give your name to because if the Devil gets to hear it, he can own your soul."

The Mayor placed his free hand on top of his, "Take it from me, *Mr* Amos, that's just so much bullshit."

There was no warmth in the Mayor's hand, his skin was like winter silk, and still nothing came out of him other than darkness and the echoes of distant screams.

"What happens about Molly?"

"Ah... the heart of the matter."

"Well?"

"It's very simple. She owes me money. She needs to pay me the money back."

"By working in the whorehouse?"

"Not necessarily... any means will do. I just want my money back."

"And if I give you the money?"

The Mayor raised an eyebrow, "My, my... you actually do like her, don't you? That must be quite challenging, given your predicament."

"It's none of your business."

"I suppose not... you have that kind of money?"

"If I got it for you, you'll let her go. Let her leave town?"

"Oh," the Mayor pulled a sullen face, "leave? But I'd miss her quite terribly. She's such a character. Between you and me, Mr Furnedge would miss her even more."

"The lawyer?"

"Quite smitten. I understand he is a... rival?"

"There's no rivalry."

"No? Well, he does have the money to pay off her debts. So he, therefore, has the means which you lack to make her happy in two respects."

"You should be careful, Mr Mayor... I've killed a lot of men."

"Perhaps, but never for merely insulting you, I think. No, that would be below you, wouldn't it?" The Mayor pulled himself free of Amos' grip.

"If you want to deal for Molly, come and see me. Perhaps we can do some business," he flicked out his hands to straighten his cuffs, "but don't take too long; the bigger that deadline looms, the more attractive Mr Furnedge's offer will become."

"She isn't going to marry him."

"Perhaps. Perhaps not. Either way, don't try and skip town," his eye momentarily drew still, "it won't work."

"The thought hadn't crossed my mind."

The Mayor took a step closer, "Let me tell you something, Mr Amos. This town, on this hill, is an island amidst a sea of grass a long, long ways from anywhere, and upon this distant shore, all manner of folk get washed up; smart ones, brave ones, poor ones, desperate ones, and a whole fucking goddamn wagon full of dumb ones.

Folk who have done all manner of things, have all manner of secrets and all manner of stories. They stay because they think they're free here, on this distant shore so far from everywhere. The thing is, none of them are. Not one, no sireee..." the Mayor's mouth twisted into a crooked little smile while his restless eye shone in the sun's dying rays, "...their souls all belong to me. And that can be a real burden, I can tell you; it's lucky I have such broad shoulders and an eye that sees all there is to see..."

The Mayor tipped his derby back slightly before spinning on his heels and heading up the slope back to Main Street.

As he ambled slowly back towards Molly, the Mayor turned around, walking backwards up the hill, he raised a hand and waggled his finger towards them, "And don't forget that date for your diary, Mr Amos..." he shouted back "...the 4th July... the year of our Lord 2035!"

The Widow

Scars covered his body, at least the parts she'd seen. She guessed the parts she hadn't were even worse. Twisted tissue and keloids crisscrossed his chest and abdomen while what looked suspiciously like a healed bullet wound knotted the meat below his left shoulder.

The history of violence in Amos' life was written clearly upon his flesh, and even by the standards of the men she'd known and the times they lived in, it must have been terrible.

She'd wondered if they were all the result of the attack that had led to his wife's death, but she shied away from asking; it was none of her business. Besides, she'd tied herself to him now; she'd find out soon enough how violent he was.

"Why did you say you'd kill Blane if he touched me?" she asked as they sat in the drawing-room one evening; she was sipping whiskey. Amos was drinking milk, which seemed kind of wrong.

It had been nagging at her for the last few days, most of which they'd spent cooped up in her home, first by her desire to keep Amos safe and then from the rain that had swept in across the plains as they'd walked back from Corner Park.

Within a few minutes of the first fat drops hitting the ground, the rain had come down with the force of a bottomless celestial bucket being emptied upon the town.

"He's dangerous," Amos replied.

"I knew that already. You kept staring at him while the Sheriff talked about what happened to that poor girl."

Amos nodded.

"You wanna tell me why?" She finished her whiskey and set the glass aside without refilling it. She guessed she was still trying to make a favourable impression.

He was silent for a while, doing that thinking stuff he seemed so fond of, before he sighed, "I think he had something to do with it."

"But Preacher Stone..."

"That seem likely to you?"

She hadn't really known the Preacher very well, no better than she knew most of the town anyway; he'd seemed a crotchety old goat, but still...

"I wouldn't have put any money on him."

"Me neither."

"So why'd he run away and hang himself?"

"He was found hanging from a tree, which isn't necessarily the same thing."

"So, you're saying someone – and when I say someone, we both know who we're talking about – strung up Preacher Stone out on the grass. Why?"

"cos he couldn't hang me for it, and he needed to hang *someone* for what happened to that girl. An apparent suicide is a lot easier to manage than a trial."

Fuck, now I seriously need another drink...

"But why Blane?" she poured herself another shot, "apart from the fact he's a creepy little fuckard, of course."

"Fuckard?"

"It's a cross between a fucker and a bastard," she explained before adding proudly, "I made it up myself."

"Congratulations."

"Thank you... Blane?"

"Oh... I don't know he'd anything to do with it for sure..."

"But?"

"But... he was... well... aroused."

"You had that effect on fuckards before?"

Amos let the little joke pass with only the faintest twitch of the corner of his mouth. It wasn't a joking matter. Whiskey drinking for you.

"It was the Sheriff's description of the girl's assault that was arousing him; he was... he was ablaze, glowing with lust like he was going to explode."

"I know what you mean."

"You noticed it too?"

"Erm... no."

"Oh," Amos frowned.

She'd seen it plenty of times in men and occasionally felt it herself, but it had nothing to do with Mysterio stuff.

"It just means he's a sick fuck; it doesn't necessarily follow."

"Perhaps."

They sat in silence; the rain was hammering on the window while the wind squalled intermittently.

"Fucking weather," she stood up and crossed to the window, pulling the curtain back to watch raindrops trickle down the pane. The rain seemed to be easing a little. For a moment, she thought she made out a figure across the road, but between the shadows and rain-smeared glass, she couldn't be sure. Maybe the dickhounds were back. Great weather for it.

"We should go," she said eventually, "as soon as possible. Forget about finding out what happened to Tom or what those stupid provisions were for."

Amos didn't reply.

"Next time they might do a better job of finding something they can hang you for."

"They?"

She looked back from the window and let the curtain fall back into place.

"He."

She noticed how low her voice had dropped as if afraid the Mayor might be summoned if she spoke his name too loudly.

She didn't repeat herself.

"Once the rainstorm has passed," Amos said, finally.

"We'll be able to make it out of town, you think?"

"Sure."

She wanted him to get up off his backside, hug her, and tell her that slipping out of town and disappearing into the grass would be as easy as pie. She wanted him to say the Mayor could hire an army of dickhounds to look for them and never have a flying fuck in a coal mine's chance of finding them. That they'd be safe and no one was going to get hung, and no one was going to spend the rest of their life working in a whorehouse.

That's what she wanted to hear, but Amos wasn't that kind of a man, so she had to make the best out of "sure" that she could.

In all fairness, Tom had never been any better. The best he could usually muster by way of reassurance had been a cock-eyed grin and a theatrical wink that became progressively more cock-eyed and theatrical depending on how much booze he'd downed. It had taken her about six months to work out that the grin and the wink, when used in tandem, usually meant they were in trouble.

The fact that it took her song long to work it out was another reason she suspected she was more gullible than was entirely healthy for a grown woman to be.

She crossed back to where Amos sat, crouched down before him and, as he watched her with the wariness of an abused kitten, took his hand in both of hers.

If the reassurance ain't gonna come to Molly...

"You don't sound entirely convinced?"

He squeezed her hand, which was about as much physical contact as he seemed able to stand.

"It'll be fine; I'm good at this sort of thing," he gave her a smile and, after a moment, another squeeze of the hand.

"When?"

"A few days."

"A few days?" she repeated, "Not sooner? Wouldn't the storm give us more cover?"

"It's been raining heavily for twenty-four hours. The ground is sodden; the heavy going will tire the horses quicker and make it easier to track us."

She nodded. It sounded like Amos knew what he was talking about. Which was reassurance of a kind.

"Then what?"

"Then?"

"Where do we go?"

"Does it matter?"

She looked pointedly at him, "Where do *we* go?"

"Oh... I-"

She smiled and let his hand slip away from hers as she straightened up.

"It's ok."

"Let's get out of this town first, huh?"

"Amen to that."

She flicked her hair back and headed for the door, "I'm going to bed, don't be long..."

"Molly."

"Huh?"

"Why?"

She turned back from the doorway, "Why what?"

"Why... me?"

"Why not?"

He snorted a little exclamation, "I'm not even a-"

"If you're going to finish that sentence with the word *man*, you really are a dumb assed fuck-noodle."

"Fuck-noodle?"

"I'm on a roll."

She stood in the doorway, uncertain what to say when he said nothing in return. She'd been trying to act as lightly around him as she could; Amos was damaged, not just the terrible physical wounds of his past but also inside. Who wouldn't be? He'd separated himself from humanity, and the smallest familiarity or act of physical tenderness seemed to terrify him.

She supposed she was damaged in her own way too. Damaged by her father and the men she'd followed who had been so like him, by their blows and abuse, and her own inability to love a half decent man when she'd finally found one who didn't express himself with the back of his hand across her face.

Amos wasn't like her father or the other men who'd used her; he wasn't like Tom either. She didn't love him, but she was drawn to him in a way she hadn't experienced before and couldn't quite explain. And she badly needed his help too.

"Come to bed... I sleep better," she said, finally.

Amos nodded and offered a smile before staring at the closed window, his lips slightly pursed.

"What's the matter?"

"Nothing... it's just stopped raining."

He shook his head as if shaking a thought away before following her out of the room.

The Little Girl

Her tummy felt sicky and her head was thumping louder than when Mommy was banging on her bedroom door, yelling her to come get breakfast.

Mostly though, she was just scared.

It was dark; there were houses she didn't recognise on a street climbing up a hill. It was a funny kind of street because the road was nothing but mud, and water ran down the middle of it in dirty little streams.

She looked down at her slippers, which were now brown instead of pink, and the muddy rivulets running around them. Mommy wouldn't be happy about that.

She jumped and gave out a strangled cry as the world was momentarily engulfed in light before the darkness returned and a loud crashing noise came rolling down the hill.

Thunder and lightning; she knew about them because Daddy had told her once. Thunder was the sound of God moving his furniture, and lightning was... she screwed up her face. She couldn't remember. She'd have to ask him again.

There was a thing about counting the time between the flash and the bang so you could work out how likely it was that God might drop his wardrobe on you. It was something like that anyway.

"Mommy!" she called out, but there was no reply. The street was empty, and the windows in all the houses were dark. It had been raining heavily a bit ago, but it had all but stopped now, save for a fine drizzle.

She was soaking wet, which meant she'd catch a chill. Mommy had warned her she'd catch a chill every time she'd been in the rain, and she couldn't remember ever being this rained on before.

She trudged up the hill; it seemed as good a way to go as any, maybe they'd be a policeman at the top, and he could take her home. She'd been warned about talking to Strange Men (Strange Men did *bad* things), but it was ok to talk to a policeman.

She was halfway or so up the hill when she came to a halt. Her head was funny, kind of light and swimmy. She felt hot, too, despite the cold drizzle dampening her face, which didn't seem right.

A figure appeared at the top of the hill. It was too dark to make him out clearly, but he walked kind of funny as he hurried down towards her. He looked too fat to be a policeman.

He didn't seem to have noticed her and was whistling to himself, though it wasn't any kind of tune she recognised. As he grew closer, she could see he was wearing an old-fashioned kind of hat and a baggy, ill-fitting suit.

He stopped like he'd walked into a glass wall and stared at her.

"My!" he exclaimed, taking off his hat to reveal a few tufts of long spiky hair sticking out from the sides of his otherwise bald head, "what are you doing out here on such a night, young lady?"

He took a few steps and bent forward to peer down at her. He smelt of eggs. She was pretty sure he wasn't a policeman.

"I can't find my Mommy," she replied, her voice wavering. She didn't want to cry; only babies cried.

The man straightened up and looked about, "Where did you last see her?"

She shrugged and shuffled back a couple of steps, Mommy was always telling her not to talk to Strange Men and given he was wearing a dirty black and yellow checked suit, had a wilting paper flower pinned to his lapel and oversized shoes, he was clearly a *very* Strange Man.

"Are you hungry?" he pulled a greasy paper bag from his pocket and thrust it at her, "Care for a pickled egg?"

Even worse than talking to Strange Men was accepting candy from Strange Men; the same advice would likely apply to pickled eggs.

She shook her head vigorously and took another step backwards.

"Are you ill?" she heard him ask, but suddenly the whole world spun around her. She was vaguely aware she was sitting down in the squelchy mud as the darkness rushed in from all sides.

*

"We've been worried about you, hun."

She peeled open her eyes. A woman she didn't recognise was sitting by the bed. She didn't recognise the bed either.

The woman was very pretty. She had large twinkling green eyes and long curly red hair. She immediately wanted to reach out and pull it straight to see if it would spring back into a curl when she let go. She didn't, though; it would be rude.

"Where am I?" she tried to sit up but managed to lift herself a few inches from the pillow before slumping back down, "I feel yucky..."

The woman smiled and placed a hand on her forehead; her touch was cool and soft.

"You got a fever, sweetheart, you gonna have to rest up here a bit – luckily, I got a real big bed, so there's plenty of room for a little un like you."

"How'd I get here?"

"Mr Wizzle found you in the street outside my house and brought you in out of the rain when you fainted."

"Mr Wizzle?"

"That's me!"

The Strange Man called out from the corner of the room where he was sitting on a chair eating a pickled egg.

"Why are you dressed like a clown?" she asked, straining to look at him.

"Because I ran away from the circus," Mr Wizzle chuckled.

She let her head slump back into the pillows and looked at the pretty lady, "And what's your name?"

"I'm Molly," she said with a smile, reaching over and giving her hand a little squeeze.

"That's a nice name; Kelly Johnson has a dog called Molly."

"Really?"

"Uh-huh. Though Molly's old now, she smells funny and pees on the carpet a lot."

There was a sound that could have been either a laugh or a cough. It had come from another man she hadn't noticed before, standing in the doorway. He was tall with short, cropped hair. He had a hard kind of face, like a scary teacher or maybe a policeman.

Molly half turned towards him though she didn't say anything, but when she turned back, she was smiling, and her eyes were sparkling. She guessed Molly liked him a lot.

"Well, there's no other similarities... that's Amos, by the way, he's... he's my friend."

She smiled at him, and Amos gave a little wave. His half undone shirt revealing a vivid scar running across his chest.

"So," Molly said, "what's your name, hun?"

"I'm Amelia... Amelia Prouloux."

They all looked around at Mr Wizzle, who'd just dropped his bag of eggs on the floor...

Hawker's Drift

Book Two

Dark Carnival

Available Now

Dark Carnival

The Carnival has come to town...

"After the sun goes down the pleasures here are darker. A man takes his wifey and kiddies to the Day Carnival an keeps em entertained, but he'll creep back here under the moon for his own pleasures... we got just about anything a heart might desire. A girl, a boy, a nip, a smoke, a sniff, a snort, a turned card, a rolled dice... However a man cares to burn his money, we got a fire stoked and ready for him..."

At the same time, on the same day, every year, the wagons of Thomas Rum's travelling carney roll into Hawker's Drift and the town celebrates the fourth of July.

But beyond the games and rides, the carousels and candy apple stalls, the bunco booths and fortune-tellers, the jugglers and clowns there is another show that only comes to life at night.

The sequel to *The Burden of Souls* takes the inhabitants of Hawker's Drift on a dark ride as the Mayor continues to manipulate their souls for his own mysterious purposes. And as Amos the Gunslinger is drawn into the heart of the Dark Carnival he'll glimpse the secrets behind the town of Hawker's Drift as well as his own terrible demons.

By Andy Monk

In the Absence of Light

The King of the Winter

A Bad Man's Song

Ghosts in the Blood

The Love of Monsters

In the Company of Shadows

Red Company

The Kindly Man

Execution Dock

The Convenient

Mister Grim

The Future is Promises

The World's Pain

Hawker's Drift

The Burden of Souls

Dark Carnival

The Paths of the World

A God of Many Tears

Hollow Places

Other Fiction

The House of Shells

Further information about Andy Monk's writing and future releases can be found at the following sites:

www.andymonkbooks.co.uk

www.facebook.com/andymonkbooks

Printed in Great Britain
by Amazon